Dungeon Grind

Edited by Kandrel and Rechan

Dungeon Grind

Copyright © 2015 by Kandrel and Rechan

Cover and interior artwork by Unciaa

Published by FurPlanet Productions
Dallas, Texas
www.furplanet.com

Print ISBN 978-1-61450-277-7
eBook ISBN 978-1-61450-278-4

Printed in the United States of America
First Edition Trade Paperback 2015

TABLE OF CONTENTS

BLACKHORN

Tarl "Voice" Hoch

"Beware the Gnoph-Keh. Totems of great Ithaqua—they walk the northern wastes. Sometimes on two legs, sometimes on four, sometimes on six. They are his messengers, his guardians, and are bound to him through ice and snow. Beware their horn, beware their talons, and beware their teeth. But most of all, beware the beast named Blackfang, for he has tasted the flesh of the ursines of Heim Fjall. And for that we will never forget."
—Båhl Fellhammer's *Book of Woe*

It was a night for celebration.

The halls of the ursine mountain hold rang with the cheers and drunken revelry of Hjördis' entire clan. Bjorn had slain the ice drake Morneye and the clan had come out to feast in his honor. It would be a good year with the materials the dragon's corpse would provide to the bears. They had enough meat to last them at least a week before having to go back to relying on the stores, as the harshness of winter had settled over the mountains only weeks before.

Hjördis watched the others, a grin plastered across her muzzle. Here and there she caught the glances of more than a few of the males present, and felt another glow spread that had nothing to do with the flowing alcohol. Hjördis knew she was one of the prettier bear maidens in the hall, and though she was the Jarl's daughter, she also knew that her golden braids and piercing eyes drew many a stare from the male ursines. Her form fitting armour wasn't hurting much either.

A passing servant bear refilled the flagon in her meaty paw and she took a long drink of mead. It burned pleasantly down her throat and she smacked her lips in satisfaction. Glancing up again, she caught the eye of Bjorn as he mimed the slaying of Morneye for the dozenth time. She watched the play of the bear's muscles under his thick fur and armour with each movement. Hjördis admitted he was a fine specimen of a male. Bjorn's eyes were the prized ice blue eyes of their tribe, and they looked at Hjördis often. The warrior's beard was lush, its thick braids full of gold beads, bits of bone and runic talismans. He raised his treasured maul above his head without effort and it shone with attention and devoted care.

Now there's a man who could take care of a woman.

"In more ways than one…"

"Excuse me, Princess?" The southerner across from Hjördis asked.

Hjördis' ears burned and flattened against her skull before she composed herself and coughed lightly into her paw. "Sorry, I was talking to myself." She smiled at her father's vulpine guests. Oh, how thin and frail they looked to the heavy, stocky build of her people. Their kurtas and salwars were rich and elegant, motifs of vines and flowers edging their hems. The garments of Hjördis' own people seemed coarse and almost barbaric next to them. What a sight the ursines must be to the foxes, decked out as they were in their rune covered, thick plated armour.

"Are your celebrations always so…enthusiastic?" A female fox asked, her small, delicate paw using a fork to chase the smoked salmon around her plate. Unlike her male companions, the female seemed to be unable to bring herself to eat the pungent meat.

Hjördis smiled. "Bjorn's slaying of Morneye is a joyous occasion. The drake has plagued the holds of the mountain ursines for as long as any of the elders can remember. Its entries in the *Book of Woe* are long and many. With it dead, new trade routes can be opened, especially to the south."

"Which benefits both of us," The leader of the vulpines cut in, smiling first at his wife, then at Hjördis. "We are most interested in the smithing techniques of your people. The sheer durability of your weapons and armours is fascinating."

"If crude." The female stated, her eyes rose from her salmon to meet the tiny eyes of Hjördis.

The princess' ears lowered. "Where you think armour is just for protection, to my people they are far more than that. They are legacies. You record your lives on scrolls of parchment and secret them away in buildings that any simple fire can destroy. We wear our histories—successes and failures—tooled into the very iron of our tools of war. This way we will never forget where we have come from, or who we are as a people. And neither will our enemies."

The male vulpine gasped, gaze darting between the princess and the vixen before he quickly interrupted, drawing Hjördis' attention back to him. "Of course, we will offer our very best textiles and artistry in return."

"Not to mention the star metal your people keep mentioning." Hjördis' father laughed. The foxes immediately nodded. Where Hjördis was prone to talking, her father waited and chose his words with the care of a hunting eagle.

"Of course, great Jarl." The fox's needle thin muzzle bobbed up and down, his ears partially flattened. "The *elen tinco* will of course be part of the trade."

Hjördis regarded her father and couldn't help but let the wave or pride she felt swell her chest. Where Bjorn was as strong as a young drake, the Jarl was like the very mountains themselves: his pelt the colour of slate and his beard flowing like snow down his chest almost to his feet. Wearing a simple crown of beaten gold and a suit of ornate metal scale, the Jarl commanded respect and obedience.

"Attention!" The Jarl's bellow caught everyone by surprise, and it was with a small smile that Hjördis noticed the female fox's ears pressed heavily against her hair. The elder ursine rose to his feet and, after taking a massive flagon from one of the servants, he thrust it outward. Hjördis knew from experience that his eyes would be meeting the gaze of everyone present. The room quieted.

"Bjorn Winterbourne, drake slayer," The Jarl's gaze fell on the warrior, as did everyone else's present. "You have brought great honor to our clan. Your bravery is as tall and wide as the very mountains we call home. It is because of you we can once again venture southwards without having to resort to the long ships."

At this a cheer rose, and the Jarl motioned for quiet after a few heartbeats. "You are a worthy warrior, Bjorn Winterbourne, and I will not have others saying I don't reward such heroism." Hjördis glanced at her father, her ears rising at her father's words.

"As a reward for your services to the clan, the best among our blacksmiths and metal shapers are constructing a suit of armour for you from the scales of the dragon Morneye."

Bjorn's jaw dropped and the hall erupted in shouts and cheers.

Those closest to the warrior bear clapped their paws on his shoulder-plates, and it was with no small annoyance that Hjördis saw a few of the maidens present stare with outright adoration.

The Jarl raised his flagon. "Now let us drink until the mountains themselves crumble to the earth!" A sea of flagons were raised and Hjördis' rose with them. Her father flung his head back and downed the mead in great draughts, some of it missing his muzzle and spilling over his beard and chest. The room followed suit and soon the conversation rose to sound like the rumble of a landslide.

Hjördis laughed and hammered her flagon down, startling the vulpines as they stared around them with peaked ears. This only caused the bear to laugh harder, a claw raising up to brush at the longer fur that ran down the bottom edge of her muzzle. Sure, it wasn't much of a beard, such being a show of virility; she was a woman and such was the toss of fates. It was then that she noticed the disgusted look the vulpine woman was giving her and she laughed even harder. Surely the petite beauty was jealous of Hjördis' chin fur.

"Oaths!" came a cry from the crowd. Hjördis glanced and saw Ol' Folkvarðr raising a refilled tankard towards the Jarl. The ancient bear always did have a knack for getting others riled up. It took him shouting it twice more before other throats took up the call. Soon the hall thundered with the chant.

"Oaths!"

"Oaths!"

"Oaths!"

Hjördis found herself joining in on the cry, hammering the palm of her paw against the table in time with the cries. One of the foxes, Hjördis thought it was the female's brother, leaned forward and muttered something.

"What?" Hjördis had to shout over the cry. The vulpine flinched.

"I said," he shouted this time, his voice squeaking. "What is this 'oath' thing that everyone is asking for?"

The princess grinned in return, taking a swig of mead to wet her tongue. Motioning to where the long table was being cleared away further down from where the group sat, she smiled. "Oaths are a way of proving bravery. Each warrior, should they choose, gets up onto the table and makes an oath. Usually the first oaths are small, but slowly they get bigger and more fantastic. The only rule is they have to be achievable."

A young, almost beardless ursine warrior that Hjördis didn't know, climbed up on the table and the fox glanced at him before turning back to Hjördis. "What if they fail or back out of their oath?"

A cheer went up as the youth looked around, apparently unsure of himself now that most of the eyes in the room were upon him.

"It's a matter of injured or damaged pride."

"So they lose standing?" The vulpine looked at his companions and nodded. They returned the nod before looking down the table as the youth raised an arming sword over his head. Hjördis remembered her father mentioning that the foxes placed a large amount of importance on standing. Around the room the shouting quieted and the youth swallowed visibly.

"I..." The bear glanced around. "I swear to slay five of the Red Muzzle clan!"

Hjördis cheered with the others who thrust tankards and weapons upwards. The youth, looking proud and relieved at the same time, stepped off the table. His friends and some of the older warriors ruffled his hair and patted his back. A flagon filled to the brim was thrust into the bear's paws and he slammed it back.

The foxes looked back at Hjördis and she turned her gaze back to them. "A noble—if small—oath. The Red Muzzles have been raiding our lands for months."

"Wolves?" The leader of the vulpines' ears flattened.

Hjördis nodded. "They are encroaching further and further into our lands with each winter." Further down from where the princess sat, one of the young warrior's friends, this one a couple winters older, climbed onto the table. The room fell near silent.

"They are plaguing our lands as well," the fox stated as the ursine pledged to bring down a dire serpent. Some of the others in his group climbed up and pledged to help in their friend's oath. Hjördis motioned to herself, where she had two small nicks in an ear interspersed between heavy golden hoops.

"This summer a large raiding party of lupines tried to take one of our larger towns at the base of the mountain. We drove them off, but only because I and some clansbears were in the area. Two other settlements were lost."

The group of friends stepped off the table, each of them offered a flagon filled to the brim. Hjördis hammered her fist against her breast plate and downed the last of her mead before thrusting it at a passing servant who refilled it for her. That flagon quickly followed the first and the woman let out a belch before slamming the drinking vessel down. "If those flea bitten lupines think they can—"

"I swear that I will take the head of Sakgu!" Tryggr, one of the clan's axe masters, shouted from the other end of the table and Hjördis rose to her feet and thrust her drink at the warrior.

"Yes!" Her voice roared with the others around her. Even her father bellowed his encouragement, as did a couple of the foxes. Apparently the shadow coated wolf plagued their lands as well.

The hall as a collective whole downed their tankards. Servants rushed to refill them, darting around the rush of warriors that pushed and shoved playfully at their peers as they tried to climb onto the table. The oaths came with the speed of arrows shot from a vulpine bow.

"I swear to find the tome of Haraldr the Bold!"

"I will find the place where Koli and his brother Sigmundr fell!"

"I will lead a raiding party to free Frost Moore!"

To Hjördis' surprise, the fox who asked about the oaths gracefully stepped up onto the table. The room's shouts and murmurs lowered to a dull roar as the fox turned in the center of the impromptu platform. With an elegant movement, he drew a thin rapier from his belt and thrust it upwards. "I swear by the oaths of my people that I will defeat the dread lich Deathpelt and retrieve the crown of Aelrindel!"

A pause stretched for a moment and it looked as if the fox would lower his ears out of shame. Then the cheer of the feasters crashed upon the vulpine like a clap of thunder. Two ursines rose and pledged their assistance to the fox and they clasped their arms in the pledge of warriors. Like the others, when the fox stepped off the table, a flagon of mead was handed to him, the flagon looking oversized next to his lithe body. Hjördis couldn't help but smile as the fox tried to quaff the mead like the ursines and ended up sputtering it over himself. Rather than ridicule, all he got were claps on his back and inquiries as to the exact nature of his oath.

A few more oaths came and went, each larger than the last. Laughter ripped through the room and Hjördis was starting to feel the effects of so much good cheer and mead. Her vision swayed, no matter how she tried to remain still, and her speech was slurred. The foxes were scattered about the room, chatting with some of the ursines and other members of their own entourage that had been invited to the feast.

Hjördis found herself looking more and more often at Bjorn and catching him more and more often staring back. Her body felt warm, and she was pretty sure it wasn't just the mead. She was also pleased to notice that he didn't linger long when one of the women of their clan spoke with him.

Twirling one of her waist long braids in her fingers, she finally decided to suck it up and rose to approach the warrior. She was old enough to claim a husband and she had known ever since she had lain her eyes on Bjorn who it would be. But as she tried to make her way to the dragon slayer, she found her way blocked again and again by the press of feasters.

Hjördis thought she caught Bjorn's eyes through the mess of ursines as she watched him step up onto the table. Her heart hammered in her chest when Bjorn raised his rune engraved weapon above his head. "Though I have brought low the drake Morneye, I must again swear an oath to earn my right to the woman I desire. For Hjördis…"

She had seen battle a dozen or more times, had slain many a wolf, bear and even tiger. She was known as Kraken-bane for slaying a young member of the species with just her claws and teeth when she was nothing but a child. But as Bjorn's gaze locked with Hjördis', her legs suddenly felt weak.

"…I will slay the Terror of Ravenspire!"

The princess' chest heaved. Bjorn had sworn to kill the roc that roosted on the highest peak of the mountain range Hjördis' clan called home. It was the bravest thing she could think of, and he was doing it for her. Things low in her body tightened and warmth crept up her ears. Behind her the Jarl let out a roar of approval and other voices joined him. If Bjorn survived, Hjördis knew she would have her husband, the unspoken words understood by everyone.

But was she not a warrior as well? Did not she have any gift to give him, to prove herself worthy? Hjördis clenched her jaw. She would not give him the usual courting gift of the females of her people: embroidered bridal sheets for their wedding night.

No.

Hjördis climbed up onto the table, relying on the haft of her war axe more than she perhaps should have. Bjorn watched her, his laughter fading along with the others of the clan.

Hjördis spoke, grinning at the dragon slayer. "A worthy present Bjorn Winterbourne, for your bride to be. But I am a warrior as well!" She thrust her axe upwards, the gold chased runes on its smile flashing in the torchlight. "As my gift to you, my future beloved, I will slay the gnoph-keh, Blackhorn!"

Instead of a cheer, the room went as silent as a grave. Even the servants paused in their bustle to stare open mouthed at Hjördis. Bjorn took a step back before catching himself and lowering himself to his knee. "You have shamed me, my lady. Here I wanted to swear an oath that would quicken your heart and stir your blood. Instead you have turned the tables on me and stilled my breath. Slaying such a beast will take great strength, cunning and will; noble traits for a future bride."

"Hjördis." The Jarl's voice cut through the pounding of her heart. She turned to face her father. "My daughter, your oath brings our bloodline honor and swells my chest with pride. I give my blessing to your oath."

"Thank you, Jarl." Hjördis stepped off the table. No flagon greeted her, only shocked, open muzzles. Then Bjorn was beside her, guiding her to one of the numerous side doors of the chamber, the crowd parting around them. With one last glance at the head of the long table, the maiden thought she saw a glint in her father's eye a moment before she was past the arch of the chamber. Once outside, it took a couple of heartbeats before someone new took the table and the celebration continued.

"You didn't have to." Bjorn clasped Hjördis' paws in his own. She marvelled at how rough and strong they were and forced herself to look up from where they touched to the warrior's eyes.

"It was the only thing I could think of."

Bjorn chuckled. "Slaying Blackhorn?" He shook his head, the beads in his beard clinking against each other. "You are either foolish or the bravest bear in this hold. I think you stopped every conversation cold with your oath."

The creeping burn returned to Hjördis' ears and she couldn't help but smile like a lass with a crush. Bjorn leaned over and his muzzle brushed alongside hers, tickling the longer hairs of her jawline. Her body reacted and she pulled her claws from his to run them along the iron hard muscles of his arms. Upwards they travelled until they cupped his face, fingers buried in the locks of his hair.

"If we are to die—" She started to whisper.

Bjorn smiled. "Then at least we have tonight."

His muzzle met hers and their lips parted. Tongues met and he pulled her against him. She made a noise in her throat and let go of his head to run her fingers down over the hump of his back until she pulled his hips against her. A growl escaped her muzzle as she broke the kiss.

"My chambers?" Bjorn asked, blinking his eyes for a moment.

Hjördis nodded, not trusting her voice. Bjorn kissed her again before grabbing her paw and pulling her through the halls with haste. Hjördis giggled like a child and let her gaze admire the dragon slayer's broad back as they wove through the labyrinthine passages. The fuzz of the mead had faded to be replaced with something far, far more exciting, and when they reached the door to Bjorn's chambers she practically shoved him against the wall.

"I'm going to have issues unlocking the door…" he grunted when her paws started to undo the clasps of his armour.

"Do you really think I care?" Hjördis boldly stated. Her paw moved lower and Bjorn let out a grunt as he rose onto this toes.

He laughed. "I suppose not."

Bjorn maneuvered enough to open the lock and the pair stumbled into his chambers. Hjördis couldn't help but look around while Bjorn moved to close the door behind them. She wasn't sure what she had expected from the warrior's room, but what she saw took her breath away. Her own room was adorned with armour and weapons as well as looms and embroidery. Bjorn's, despite having armour and weapons as well, contained a large number of mounted heads. Her gaze moved over them.

"Basilisk. Griffon. Kelpie." She turned to face Bjorn as he came up behind her. Her face broke into an amazed smile. "You even have a manticore!"

Bjorn raised his gaze to where the manticore stared down from the mantel above his fireplace. "That one was a bastard if there ever was one. The healers had to pray over me for days while they pulled quills from my flesh."

"I never knew." Hjördis moved to press herself against the warrior's

15

chest.

"It's not common news. Not something I am proud of. I let my pride get the best of me and it took advantage of that. It was a hard learned lesson."

"I can imagine." Hjördis whispered, her fingers already continuing to work on the half opened clasps and buckles she had started on outside. Bjorn looked down at her and met her gaze, a smile splitting his muzzle.

"I don't think you can imagine much more than one thing right now." He flicked his tongue against her ear and she let out a sigh, her fingers working faster. Bjorn's own claws went to work on her armour. "The one nice thing about each of us wearing armour is that we both know how to get out of it."

Her breastplate hit the floor the same time as his. From there they were a flurry of paws on buckles, each piece of armour dropping to the floor. When they both had been reduced to their underclothing, Bjorn pulled Hjördis to him and their muzzles met. What she had felt below his waist earlier was now a brand against her side. The princess pushed herself away from the warrior and smiled coyly while her paw slide down his stomach to where his length lay exposed to the air. Bjorn kept his gaze on hers as she slowly dug inside his undergarments and traced a paw pad along his member's underside, flicking the tip of her claw against his glans, earning a grunt from the dragon slayer.

"You have an impressive weapon." Hjördis couldn't help but giggle. Bjorn stood up straighter the moment she wrapped her paw around him. The warrior halted with a shuddered gasp. "But I wonder, do you wield it as well as you do your maul?"

Bjorn rumbled in his chest, raising his paws to stroke against Hjördis' muzzle and cheeks. "If my lady requires a demonstration, perhaps I can oblige."

Hjördis chuckled and batted her eyes at Bjorn. "What if I want to wield it first?"

Bjorn's muzzle opened in question but stopped as Hjördis knelt before him. Instead, he lowered his gaze to meet hers. She licked her lips while slowly sliding her paw up and down his shaft.

"How's the grip, my lord?" Hjördis didn't raise her eyes, but rather concentrated on the length of warmth in her paws. Bjorn made a noise and another shudder rippled through him. The princess smiled to herself before inching her nose closer to Bjorn's 'weapon'.

His scent washed over her with each of her breaths. Heady, musky, a hard day's work mixed with something heavier, more primal. With one last breath of his essence, she slid her tongue from her muzzle and slowly drew it along the underside of him, following the path her claw had taken earlier. Bjorn gasped, his paws coming to rest on Hjördis' head, his claws intertwining with her many braids.

"You," he grunted as she flicked her tongue against his glans. "Your grip is masterful my lady." She ran her long tongue in circles around his head, earning another grunt and the tightening of his fingers in her hair.

"Good." She whispered, then slowly slid his length into her mouth. It was hot against her lips, its underside gliding along her tongue, each throbbing vein plucked by the ripples of her flesh. She pushed him deeper and deeper into her muzzle before he bumped the back of her mouth. There she kept him, feeling him pulse against the tightness of her muzzle before slowly sliding him out.

"Hjördis," Bjorn moaned, swaying slightly as she let him out of her mouth. His eyes were wide and filled with a lust she had longed to see in them. "That was an amazing technique."

"My lord flatters me, so let me flatter him." She grinned before sliding him back into her muzzle. This time Bjorn was ready and he spread his legs. Hjördis took the invitation and ran the paw not stroking his length along his inner thigh. Back and forth she moved her head, pressing her tongue against his shaft, letting his glans bump against the ripples it found there. Bjorn gripped her hair to the point where sharp needles pricked her scalp, and still she moved him along her tongue.

"Hjördis, please." The warrior's voice sounded weak, and Hjördis hummed something, the vibrations echoing in the bounce of his shaft as she started to move her paw faster and faster. More than once she pushed him deep into her muzzle, her paw pressing hard against the base of his shaft while her other played gently with his balls.

"Please, my lady, I won't last much longer."

Hjördis leaned back, letting Bjorn's length slide from her muzzle. Long ropes of saliva connected them before she played her paw along them, using the moisture to run her paw up and down him. Bjorn swayed while she raised her gaze to him, his muzzle open as he drew in great breaths of air. His eyes were unfocused and his ears flitted from raised and attentive to lowered against his skull.

"What if I don't want you to? Surely the warrior who slew Morneye can go for multiple rounds."

She knew it was a barb, but Hjördis wanted Bjorn. Here and now. So before the bear could answer her, she plunged him back into her muzzle.

Her head rocked, guided by his grip, moving her into longer thrusts, his tip almost sliding out of her muzzle. She flicked her tongue against his head and sucked him in with each thrust. His balls were tight against his body, and she could taste the light salt of his pre as it brushed her taste buds. Bjorn's body shivered, the tremble before an avalanche. Hjördis' body reacted, her inner thighs now soaked with enough of her juices that she was sure Bjorn could scent it on the air.

Bjorn's roar shook the weapons on the wall as Hjördis moved her muzzle back. Thick spurt after thick spurt of heat splashed against her long tongue, coating its top with heavy salty flavor. She swallowed what she could before having to pull him from her muzzle, only to have a rope of it splash across its top.

The warrior looked down at her almost sheepishly, his ears half raised in embarrassment. For a moment they were children again and he had somehow bested her at swordplay. Hjördis made a noise in her throat and licked the spilled seed from her muzzle before taking Bjorn's offered paw and rising to her feet.

"What a strong heart you must have," she practically purred to him, nuzzling his neck, pressing her body against him so he could feel how wet she had become. Bjorn didn't answer. Instead his paws traced along her sides before hooking her undergarment and tearing them off with his claws.

"See anything you like?" She asked. The look he gave her sent tingles racing down her spine.

Bjorn grinned at Hjördis, his ears lowering. His member was already rising to the ready as they embraced. Their kiss was fierce, no mere dance this. Instead two warriors locked in a struggle. Any remaining shred of clothing fell while their paws slid over one another's bodies. Bjorn shoved her back onto his bed to land amongst the furs there. She moaned and spread herself, watching as his eyes were driven to the moisture soaked fur.

"Show me how you use that weapon of yours, Bjorn Winterbourne."

It wasn't a request.

Bjorn moved forward, his paws meeting hers as he grabbed her arms. Pinning her with his body weight, he slide against her. The balmy skin of his shaft glided along her slick valley to bump against her tiny button at its apex. Bjorn grunted and slowly moved his hips back, drawing his member again against her.

"Are you sure, my lady?" His member's head finally found and rested against her entrance. She could feel the tip already pushing her slightly apart. It was like a dagger of heat waiting to plunge into her flesh, and it was all she wanted in the world.

"I am yours, Winterbourne. Take me!"

The warrior needed no further encouragement.

Hjördis threw her head back with a cry as his flesh parted her lips, gliding against her wetness and thrusting her inner walls apart. Bjorn growled as he pushed deeper and deeper, his weight on her arms preventing her from gripping him with anything other than her legs. And grip him she did, heels digging into the back of his hips and pulling him farther into her until his pelvis met hers.

They lay there panting, his member twitching inside her with the pulse of her inner walls. Their gaze met for a lingering moment, muzzles open in lustful pants before joining in another passionate kiss. Bjorn's hips withdrew slightly, making Hjördis squeak before sliding back in, bringing forth a groan from them both.

"Oh ancestors, yes." She gasped as their muzzles broke. Bjorn grinned at the princess and thrust again against her, shunting her body upwards lightly along the bed. Hjördis gasped and her eyes screwed shut for a moment, until Bjorn followed his thrust with another, and another, and another. With each slap of his hips against hers, Hjördis felt a pressure deep inside her. Something she hadn't realized she was missing was suddenly found again and no amount of stolen moments of self-play could match it.

"Harder." She grunted as Bjorn thrust into her again, rocking her body on the bed, causing it to moan in its own way. She met his gaze. "Harder."

Bjorn grunted but obeyed her request, slamming himself into her with more and more force as his body started to find its primal rhythm. Each time his pelvis met hers, Hjördis felt her world rock with each thrust within. The pressure was building in her, it wanted release and she threw back her head with gasps and moans.

Their muzzles met again, then broke only to reunite a moment later. Hjördis nipped at the warrior's throat only to get a bite on hers in return. The pressure became unbearable and Hjördis was about to yell something to Bjorn, anything, just to get him to release the tightened coil within her.

It was then that Bjorn let go of her paws and grabbed her hips, driving himself deeper than he had gone before. Something touched off and Hjördis threw her head back to let out a roar that was quickly followed by the warrior's. Her body shook with the force of an earthquake as she felt her inner walls flutter around his member, and it pulse in return. Heat filled her as his seed found her inner most depths. The very feel of it brought her to climax again, claws free to rake along his arched back.

They stayed like that for long minutes, panting and sweating, staring into each other's eyes.

***

The wolf's cry of pain turned into one of agony as Hjördis' axe clove through his armour to slide into the lupine's flesh beneath. The raider fell back, clutching at its stomach, but Hjördis was already turning, the killing smile of her axe lashing out in a glittering arch.

"Stupid, stupid girl," Hjördis muttered to herself as she brought her shield up to deflect an overhead strike by a wolf with a rusting long sword. She returned the strike with one of her own, the runes flaring as the blade met the bandit's shield, cutting a heavy gash in the wood.

Two of the wolves took a step forward, their blades flashing out. Hjördis caught one on her shoulder plate while the other screeched across the chain mail she wore under the plate. Her axe struck out, clashing with one of the swords. The rusty metal shattering into deadly splinters as her blade took the wolf across the muzzle, cracking bone.

She had been distracted, lost in her thoughts and memories of the night with Bjorn. Laying there in the dark beside him, she had decided to leave that night. With the fugue of alcohol and lust clear from her head, the oath kept swimming to the surface of her thoughts and sleep would not find her. Leaving Bjorn asleep in his room, she had collected her things as quietly as she could and had fled his dwelling for her family's.

Her father had been awake when she had returned, sitting near a fire almost gone cold. Their gazes had met, and Hjördis felt her ears go warm when she realized he would be able to smell the mating on her fur. He had simply nodded. "Bjorn is a good man. He will make an excellent husband and father."

That was all the Jarl said on the matter. Instead, he rose from his chair and Hjördis had winced at the creak of his bones. Her father pulled forth a large cloth-wrapped object from behind his chair, motioning that she should take it. Hjördis took it from him with tentative paws, her fingers untying the simple twine that held the cloth in places. While it hissed to pool at the floor, her muzzle had opened and her embarrassment at her current appearance all but forgotten.

"I am sure Bjorn's armourer will not miss one scale." Her father smiled then. "The rune-smiths and armourers have been working hard through the night since your oath to have it finished for when you returned. It was no easy feat to pull them from their tankards, as you can imagine." He chuckled. Hjördis rushed into his arms then and saw the tears that rested behind the Jarl's stone façade.

Hjördis lashed out with that very shield, the drake scale singing as its edge hammered into the neck of one of the wolves, causing the man to drop his weapons, paws grasping his crushed throat. She took the moment to glance around, ears flat against her skull. Too lost in her memories, she had let the bandits sneak up on her, to surround her. Now they darted in with small jabs and strikes, trying to wear her down. Already she carried a half a dozen shallow cuts where they had gotten past her armour. The wounds felt cold in the chilled wind of the tundra.

"Come and face me, cur!" She roared, turning to lash out with her axe, the blade almost taking off a wolf's arm. "It will take more than a few mongrels to take down a child of Heim Fjall!"

One or two of the wolves chuckled before launching another hit and run, but this time Hjördis closed with them, her axe catching one in the shoulder, severing his arm in a welter of crimson. The other's blade struck the drake-scale shield before catching the return strike of Hjördis' axe in his side, where his armour's straps provided the mildest protection.

Even while she struck the wolves down, Hjördis felt the telltale kiss of steel across the back of her breastplate. Another cutting edge caught her across the thigh, opening a shallow cut that stung in the cold. She whirled to find the wolves already retreating. Ears swivelling, she swung her left arm wide, the edge of the shield catching an impatient wolf as he rushed forward, crushing his helm and face with the blow.

"Give up, bear!" One of the wolves snarled. He was larger than the others, the fur of his muzzle dyed crimson. Hjördis noted that his weapons were in far better condition than his companions and he had the look of someone who knew how to use them. Crooked teeth shone through his smile. "Surrender now and I promise we'll give you some fun before you meet the gods."

Hjördis couldn't help but laugh at the wolf, even as she turned and blocked an axe blow that came from her side, shoving him back with her shield. "Come taste my steel if you think I am such a prize! I grow tired of your lackeys."

The leader laughed, raising his broad sword to point it at her. "I want a bit of the fight taken out of you before I have my fun."

The ursine felt another blade open up a gash across her bicep. She cursed, rewarding the wolf with a deep gouge in his breastplate. The creature went sprawling into the snow still alive. Her blow hadn't had the power behind it to crack open his armour. Hjördis gave another curse and turned, her axe clearing the area around her, giving her a moment's rest.

The lupine leader was right, she realized. The longer they harried her, the quicker her strength would fade and then she would be at their mercy. All it would take would be one lucky strike. If she was going to come out of this, she would have to do something, and quickly.

They circled her, ears raised, watching for an opening. Once or twice one would mock charge, but Hjördis stood where she was, her ears turning with the sound of the pack's panting and the crunch of their feet in the snow. Her attention remained on their leader even as she carefully slid her arm from the enarmes of her shield.

One of the wolves had finally had enough and charged forward. Hjördis turned and caught him with the shield boss before turning, using her momentum to hurl the scale at the pack's leader. The larger wolf stumbled back as the shield caught him in the chest, and by then Hjördis had pulled a heavy gladius from its sheath at her side and, with an earth shattering roar, charged.

Metal clashed. The red muzzled wolf barely got his sword up in time to parry the brutal strike of Hjördis' gladius. He stumbled as her axe glanced off his helm. The ursine pressed her advantage, pushing the wolf back with a thrust of her sword, forcing the pack leader to parry each stab while avoiding the sweeping arcs of her axe. Behind her the cries of the pack sounded when they realized what was happening and rushed to the aid of their master.

It was too late.

Hjördis' axe cut a sweeping arch towards the wolf's head and he raised his sword to block. The gladius came in low, too quick for him to block while the heavier weight of the axe took his sword with it. The steel tip caught the red-muzzled wolf in the throat and severed muscle, tendons and bone until its tip finally passed through the back of his neck.

With a grunt, Hjördis wrenched her sword free and turned to the rest of the pack, a bellow of rage driving them back. Those too slow were chased back by the crimson stained edges of her weapons. She took a step forward, her lips pulling back from her teeth. The wolves eyed her and their fallen leader, their ears flicking up and down, their tails held close to their legs.

Barking, they fled, leaving their fallen where they lay either dead or dying. The ursine watched them run, too tired to give chase and knowing that it would be pointless. They'd be back as soon as she was far enough away from the site, likely looting their dead and fighting over who was going to be the next leader.

Wolves.

Hjördis hated to admit it, but she loathed the flea bitten mongrels. A plague on the cultured lands, they bred quickly and their raids were getting worse and worse. There had been talk of another great scourge like in the days of Hjördis' grand-father, but such a thing was impossible because the horse clans had retreated from the land and the constant threat of invasion by Lu-Kai and the tigers from the East.

Moving over to where her shield lay on the ground, she cleaned her gladius before sheathing it and pulling the dragon scale onto her arm. The chill of her wounds faded slightly as a couple of the runes shimmered with light. Those that now lit up helped against the cold, the same runes were also carved into stones worked into the multiple braids that cascaded down Hjördis' shoulders. Her father had been wise when he had told the rune-crafters what to put on the shield.

Where she was going, she would need them. Already the nights were getting significantly colder, the trees long left behind to be replaced with an endless plain of snow drifts and rock. Hjördis hoped her rations would last. She did not relish the thought of trying to hunt or forage for food in such a death-laden land.

She left the wolves' bodies alone, knowing they had nothing she would want. Instead, she took note of the sun's position above her and started north again, leaving the wolves behind her. The wounds ached with the dull pain that told her they were healing while she moved. More than once Hjördis paused to check on the deeper ones, using some of her carefully rationed poultice only when she thought she detected the hint of infection.

When the sun finally started to set, a light snow began to fall, adding to the thick blanket already on the ground. Hjördis took care to avoid the deepening drifts. More than once she slogged through the hip deep snow, breaking it up with blows from her axe haft. Idly Hjördis wondered if the foxes would have such a problem with the snow, with bodies smaller and lighter than the ursine frame.

Hjördis laughed to herself as she imagined the vulpines prancing around on the snow with their unusual movements. Always darting, always wary, a look of cunning in their slitted eyes. As a child, she had been told tales warning her not to enter any forest where she saw the spoor of the vulpines. It was said they would trick you with a cunning far surpassing any rune-smith and leave you either enchanted to do their bidding or naked and shamed.

Still, Hjördis had to admit a certain attraction to the red-coated folk. Sure, they were far too small, and she doubted they could please her as Bjorn had. Like the rest of the ursine maidens, she had heard the male vulpines had an unusual trait, something that would lock them to their women during mating. Hjördis chuckled to herself, blowing ice crystals from her muzzle and shaking her head so that the light dusting of snow fell from her fur. What would it feel like to have such a thing inside her?

Stopping near a large pile of boulders, she paced around it until she felt that it would make an adequate shelter. Taking a number of rune-inscribed stones from her pack, she set them up around her camp. If anything came within a certain distance she would know. Sweeping aside the snow the best she could with her shield, she placed a heavy blanket on the ground and, using some of the bush scrub she had collected, made a small fire.

The last of the sunlight faded around her and she admired the way the land felt without the warmth of the sun. The north fascinated her, as did the legends of the creatures that roamed it. A species of winter ursines once lived upon this white land, blood thirsty beasts that were kin-slayers and monsters. Where they were now, the ursines of the mountains no longer knew.

Chewing on a piece of salted fish, Hjördis placed a couple of rocks in her fire to use later for warmth. For now though, she was content to watch the shadows deepen on the landscape. Here and there she could hear the local wildlife waking from their slumbers, and wondered idly how they could survive in such a barren landscape. But, she supposed, many could say the same of Hjördis' people living in halls carved into stone.

The thought amused her, and she shovelled some dried berries and nuts into her muzzle, carefully keeping an eye on her supplies. She decided she would sleep in her armour that night, if only because she felt too weary to take it off. Her wounds were starting to pain her again and she cleaned the grime from around them with pawfulls of snow once she had packed her rations away.

Darkness finally settled over the maiden as she unrolled another heavy blanket and wrapped it around herself. Making sure her stones were not getting too hot, she pulled one close to her as the fire died. Facing away from the fire, Hjördis let the ache of her muscles and the pain of her wounds pull her into sleep.

Something moved in the dark.

Hjördis felt the hum of her warning stone between her breasts. She sat up, paws instantly grabbing her axe. Ears flicked back and forth as she tried to pierce the darkness around her camp. The fire had died long ago, and from the coolness of the stone she had pressed against her, it had been a number of hours since she had fallen asleep.

Her stone buzzed again, this time with more agitation, and Hjördis rose, her muscles protesting the movement. "Where are you?" she whispered to herself, the sound of her voice sounding far too loud to her ears. Out in the blackness, she caught the sound of snow crushed beneath something's feet.

Another hunter come to test themselves against me?

Hjördis turned her head, her ears flashing up at the voice as it brushed her mind like hoarfrost on steel.

Have they forgotten already the horror I brought to their very halls?

The ursine moved to the edge of her stone ring, the buzzing of the rune against her chest now quiet, but she could still feel it out there. It brushed her mind with its own. Instinctively, she knew what it was.

Blackhorn.

It knows me.

Hjördis' paws tightened painfully on the grips of her weapons, taking comfort in their mere presence. If it attacked her here and now, she wasn't sure she could defeat it. The circle of stones would only provide a meagre defence against something that had breached the heavily warded doors and halls of her people's home.

The hint of something enormous shifted at the farthest range of her vision, white on white, standing impossibly tall before falling to the ground like a felled tree. She could feel the impact through the soles of her boots. Hjördis wished the moon was closer to showing its full face but the clouds continued to hide it. The maiden desperately wanted to see the beast before it attacked.

We will meet soon enough, ursine. Do not rush into your death so carelessly.

It was gone—the feeling of frost in her mind vanishing like a morning thaw. Hjördis' weapons dropped lower and she shivered against the cold that surrounded her.

"Blackhorn." The word felt like ice on her lips. It had come close enough that it could have killed her in her sleep, yet left as swiftly as it came. She peered out into the darkness, fixing the location in her mind. When the sun rose, and no sooner, she would go inspect the location where she had seen the shape among the snow.

If Hjördis had learned anything that night, it was that she no longer had the upper paw.

***

For seven days Hjördis continued north and for seven nights she felt nothing brush her warding stones. Yet somehow the bear couldn't shake the feeling Blackhorn was following just beyond her sight. Playing with her like a tiger *bushi* swordsman before the kill, drawing it out so its victim appreciated the full horror of their situation before finally going to meet the gods.

Hjördis snarled for the dozenth time at the thought. She had indeed gone to where she had first seen the creature as soon as the sun had risen. There, she had found three sets of heavy paw prints among the snow, though of the tracks before and after it, there were none. The creature had somehow left only those six prints on purpose, so she would know what was stalking her.

She had held out her paw against one of the prints, claw-tipped fingers spread wide. The gnoph-keh's were easily twice the size of her own. Hjördis obliterated the prints with a few well-placed kicks. She knew it was pointless to stop and try to build a defence against something that had made it to the middle halls of her people undetected. No, she would forge further into its lands, forcing it into a confrontation instead of having it toy with her. Sooner or later they would meet, her and the beast.

So Hjördis continued northwards, her ears ever alert to the sounds of movement in the snow and ice. Yet nothing invaded her thoughts with a touch of frost, no clawed tracks were left near her camps. Still something tickled the fur at the back of her neck, a sense that she was being watched carefully. No matter how she deviated her path, double backed, used the odd ice covered streams to her advantage, it was always there.

The snow continued to fall, growing ever thicker and heavier the further she moved north. The drifts were larger and it took more work for her to break them up as she pushed through. Hjördis had taken to travelling with one of her blankets draped over her shoulders to block out most of the blowing snow and ice that got past her shield and the runes inscribed on it.

Hjördis kept glancing upwards to find the sun, wary that without it she would get lost quickly, all of her training on hunts worthless among the featureless landscape of snow and ice. The glare of the sun off the continual whiteness was becoming painful and she found herself squinting against it, sometimes hiding her eyes behind her shield so as not to lose herself to the glare.

On the eighth night, when she bedded down in a hollowed out pit in the snow, she was forced to build a wall of cut snow blocks to keep the wind back as it howled across the landscape. Her stones had been quickly buried where she had placed them, forcing her to use part of her remaining kindling to mark their locations among the snow.

Huddling with her back to the wall, she closed her eyes and for the first time cursed her oath through chattering teeth. Her paws felt numb and she flexed them in their gloves, keeping them moving. Her rations were getting painfully low as she was forced to eat more than she had planned to keep her energy level up, most of it burned through keeping warm and from the sheer effort of pushing against the thigh deep snow.

The darkness of night came far faster than it had before, swallowed up in the howling wind that swirled the snow around her in a wall of white. While there should have been light from the full moon the maiden knew hung in the sky above, she could see none of it past the blowing flurries. Hjördis rubbed her paws together and kept her shield close, the anti-cold runes on it casting a faint light into the night.

She weakens.

The amulet hummed against her fur and Hjördis snarled, her paws moving to her weapons. Rising slowly, she hissed at the sheer effort it took her despite having only just settled down. He was out there again, the frost on her mind stronger now, closer.

Still so defiant.

Hjördis' ears flattened against her skull and she snarled at the swirling snow around her. She could hear nothing, smell nothing and see nothing. Effectively blind, Hjördis was at the creature's mercy. A sound rose from her chest and she rolled her shoulders to loosen up the cold muscles. If she would die here, she would go down like a true child of the mountains.

Her amulet flared to angry life and something moved in the snow before Hjördis. The bear roared and charged, axe already moving. The swing met nothing but air, the shape a ghost moving in and out among the falling flakes. Hjördis let her rage take her, warming her with anger as she swung again and again, her blade tasting nothing but snow. It was toying with her and she knew it.

Hjördis surged forward, following the ghostly shape's movements in and out of the blowing snow. Then it turned, and the ursine got her shield up barely in time as something heavy smashed into the dragon scale. Hjördis stumbled back, her arm going numb at the impact. She roared and lashed out with her axe, feeling it hit something that felt like iron, the runes on its surface flashing like the sun.

This time something answered her roar from the blowing snow. The bawl was deep and rattled her bones, a wall of force as hard as any rock.

The warrior maiden struck again, her axe glancing off something just beyond the flakes and Hjördis felt the frost on her mind deepen. Raising her shield, another blow hammered against it, and she felt the runes flare to life along its surface like a swarm of angry bees.

Do you wish to die so quickly, female?

The words sounded more annoyed than angry, but Hjördis paid them no mind as she pushed after the massive shape. She was utterly lost in the swirling storm raging around her, her only focal point the hint of the beast before her. Again and again she swung at the fleeing shape. The creature turned and she caught it only to have a massive limb fling out of the snow to batter her to the side. One of the runes on her shield broke, and she let out a cry as the muscles in her arm pulled.

"You will not take me without a fight!" Hjördis swore at the beast, bringing her axe down on a furred limb that seemed impossibly thick. The axe bit deep and crimson so dark it could be black splashed her muzzle. The creature roared.

Enough!

The force of will slammed against Hjördis, driving her back in the snow, her boots cutting furrows through the packed whiteness. As if on command, the blizzard parted around her and she was left facing the creature she had sworn to kill.

Blackhorn.

The first thing Hjördis realized was that the beast was an ursine like her, only far, far larger. Shaggy fur as white as snow covered the beast. Hjördis raised her shield and readied her axe as the beast spread two pairs of arms wide, black claws longer than her fingers gleaming in the soft moonlight. The beast looked down at her, his bearlike head regarding her with eyes that shone like rubies in the darkness. Sprouting from the middle of his forehead rose a curved spiral horn of the blackest night.

So now you see what you face, tiny female. Blackhorn's voice rung in her head, the slither of steel on ice. *Do you still wish to find the feast halls of your ancestors on the end of my claws?*

Hjördis didn't respond, instead raising her shield so that her eyes peered over its edge. Whispered blessings fell from her lips and the runes along her armour flared to life, lighting up the night and the snow around her. She met Blackhorn's crimson gaze with her own.

"I am Hjördis Stoneshaker, daughter of the Jarl of Heim Fjall." Her voice was crisp and clear despite the tremble in her limbs. "I am oath-sworn to kill you."

The beast's laugh echoed in her head. He fell to his second set of paws, leaving his top limbs free and bringing him down closer to her height, though she still had to raise her eyes to meet his gaze.

Well Hjördis Stoneshaker, as beautiful as you are, you are to be disappointed.

Hjördis rushed forward even as Blackhorn brought the curved horn downward, lowering himself to all six paws. The killing smile clashed with the blackened spiral and their dance began.

Blackhorn rose up and lashed out with his claws, the air hissing around them as Hjördis ducked under the blow. She slashed upwards with her axe, scoring a line of crimson along the underside of the limb. The creature's other claw hammered into her body and it was only through sheer willpower that she remained standing, runes breaking to dissipate the force of the blow. Inside her head she heard the beast chuckle, and she clenched her teeth against the numbness that flooded the side of her body, managing to hold onto her axe.

Do you really think you can stop me?

Hjördis' roar cut through the ice covering her mind and Blackhorn lashed out to catch the first two of her blows. The ursine turned, hammering the edge of her shield into the beast's muzzle, forcing him to rise up. Hjördis darted forward, her axe cutting under the rising monster to chop into Blackhorn's stomach. It felt like trying to cut into an oak with a hatchet.

Blackhorn dropped to all of his paws with a bellow and Hjördis moved to the side, narrowly missing the descending bulk, even as she prepared her next blow. The gnoph-keh turned, jaws snapping around Hjördis' sword arm like a vice. The ursine cried out and battered the skull of the beast with her shield.

The gnoph-keh shook Hjördis like a child's toy. She snarled and brought her shield up to strike the creature's throat. Again and again she brought the edge of the scale against the hanging skin until Blackhorn finally let go, sending the maiden crashing to the ground in a clatter of armour.

Do you still wish death, little one?

Hjördis rose, her paw clutched to her chest, crimson dripping from a dozen rents in her armour, a rainfall of red on the snow below. She dropped the shield, most of its runes reduced to faded burns along the surface. Drawing her gladius, she bared her fangs.

"As long as I draw breath in my—"

Blackhorn charged her, the point of his namesake gleaming as it speared forward. Hjördis turned her body while she reversed the grip on her gladius. The horn caught her in the right shoulder, easily parting the rune inscribed steel and piercing the flesh underneath. Hjördis brought her sword down on the beast's neck with the last of her strength, the tip of the blade piercing the shaggy fur and cutting through the thick skin.

The gnoph-keh let out a snarl and pulled back, Hjördis feeling every lump of the spiral horn as it pulled free of her flesh. She fell to her knees and gasped for breath, her vision swimming before her eyes. Blackhorn moved back, shaking his head while dark crimson spilled from the gaping slash in his throat. Hjördis raised her gaze and grinned, her teeth smeared with her own life fluid.

"Not so confident now, are we?" She spat a wad of red on the snow. Painfully she rose to her feet, gladius raised. Her first step almost dropped the maiden back to the snow, but she managed it, and then a second. Blackhorn raised his eyes to her, wary now, head swaying back and forth like a serpent on edge.

You will not survive this.

"Neither will you."

Blackness that had nothing to do with the night edged Hjördis' vision. She was surprised that her final thoughts weren't of Bjorn or her family, but rather of the beast before her. There was something majestic about it, something eternal. It had been a fine opponent, and she felt nothing but pride for what she was about to do. What a tale she would have to tell her ancestors when she arrived at their table.

Blackhorn dipped his head in salute and in reply Hjördis raised her sword to her eyes and nodded back. They rushed each other, the clash of blows quick. Hjördis felt the gnoph-keh's teeth pierce her shoulder the same time her blade came down. Though she struck true, the point of her gladius slid off the heavy spine and missed its mark, cutting a swath through the tough flesh.

It was with a final roar that Hjördis went into the darkness, her oath unfulfilled.

***

Wake up.

Hjördis groaned.

Wake up.

The ursine maiden struggled to open her eyes, the effort harder than anything else she had done in her life. A slice of light cut through the darkness of her mind and she screwed her eyelids shut against it.

Try again.

It was then that Hjördis realized the voice in her head was not that of her ancestors, but the familiar tickle of hoar frost. Her eyes flashed open in an instant only to shut again, a whine of pain escaping her muzzle.

Good. Now try it slowly.

Cursing, Hjördis took her time, the bright sliver of light slowly broadening until the world came into focus before her. She was in a cave that seemed to glow with some kind of luminescent ice. A white shape came into view above her.

There you go.

She tried to speak, but only croaked instead, her throat hoarse. Something bumped the bottom of her muzzle and she tilted her head slightly to see that it was a bowl held delicately in one of Blackhorn's massive claws. The urge to turn her head faded when she smelled the water within and her tongue flicked out. It was warm, not at all the frozen snowmelt she expected. Soon her tongue touched a dry bottom and the bowl was pulled away.

Better?

Hjördis nodded, the aches of her body distracting, but not enough to keep her from what she wanted to know the most. "I'm supposed to be dead."

So am I. At least I should have been, if your blade hadn't missed.

The maiden saw it now, the gleaming scar tissue where Blackhorn's shaggy fur hadn't grown back. Her blows had been true and she couldn't help herself from smiling as she saw just how expertly she had struck. Blackhorn seemed to sense where her gaze travelled and nodded, turning crimson eyes upon her.

You fought well. No one has come that close to besting me in combat before. That's one reason you are here.

"Where is here?" She turned her gaze to the roof of the cave. Where she expected hanging icicles, there was only a smooth expanse of shimmering luminescent ice. A thick, masculine scent permeated the air, strong but not unpleasant.

This is my home.

Hjördis turned her head back to the beast.

"Why?"

Blackhorn lowered his head. Hjördis noticed that he stood on four of his six limbs, leaving two of them free to maneuver the bowl. It was also then she realized her wounds had been bound.

Never has someone come so close to ending my existence. You fought like a Valkyrie and your blows were true even when you were mortally wounded.

Hjördis' heart thudded in her chest. "I was dying."

The gnoph-keh nodded, his horn catching the light. *You were.*

"And you saved me."

Again the beast nodded.

"Why?"

I am bound by certain rules of this plane. Ithaqua the wind walker keeps me here as his voice, one of a few that are forced to exist in his land to bring him forth when he is needed. It is he who allows us to control the winds and the snow. It is through him that I was able to make it so far into your keep, using the wind to walk through your defences as if I were Ithaqua himself.

Hjördis blinked and tried to raise her body up. Blackhorn made a move to help her but paused when she glared at him, daring him to come closer. Instead the beast stepped back, letting the ursine maiden slowly move herself to a sitting position.

"You came to our hold and slaughtered many, terrorized hundreds more. You became the stuff of nightmares for my people." Hjördis levelled her eyes at the creature.

Your people were preparing to march northwards, to make war on the remaining tribes of the north. The northern people refused to give up their lands to your continual encroachment. They were a fierce people, but the ice bears were already weak in number, forced to flee further and further northwards with their white vulpine allies. The mountain ursines considered them unclean, nothing more than beasts.

Hjördis' brow furrowed. She remembered something about the clan preparing for war. But with the growing attacks by the lupines and with the daring attacks of the tigers growing in number, Hjördis had assumed that it was one of them that her people donned their armour to go to war against.

But against their distant cousins of the north?

You see it now, don't you? The bears pleaded with Ithaqua for help and in his wisdom he sent me to your hold to sow destruction and superstition. Ever since I have been left to guard the borderlands that separate the mountains from the tundra wastes, many have tried over the years to try and find your northern kin, and each time I have stopped them.

"But why, why save me? If what my people did was so horrid—"

Because there is still honor in this world, Hjördis Stoneshaker, daughter of the Jarl of Heim Fjall. Bravery such as yours should not be let to pass from this plane lightly...

Their gazes met and Hjördis accepted another bowl of water from the gnoph-keh, lapping it slower than her first. The creature watched her, his head cocked to the side. Hjördis set the bowl aside and winced as her wounds pulled tight. Blackhorn grunted.

Your wounds have still not healed. I can work some limited magic on them to speed the knitting of your flesh. After that, you may go, if you promise never to return to these lands.

"And if I don't?"

Blackhorn snarled, his lips pulling back from fangs that sent shivers down Hjördis' spine. She painfully raised her paw, palm facing the creature. "Point taken. But I have an oath—"

Is your oath worth your life?

"Among my people, it is."

I can give you proof then, of your prowess in battle. That should be enough to fulfill your oath. To prove your bravery.

Hjördis nodded, not knowing what else she could do. She tried to move her right arm to push herself to her feet, but the limb refused to move. Blackhorn regarded it with a motion of his massive head. *It has been damaged the most. I will have to spend extra time on it to heal it fully, though you may always feel pain when it gets cold. A reminder if you will.*

Now remove your armour. I will help.

The maiden, with some difficulty, unbuckled her breastplate with the beast's help, the twin pieces falling to the ground where she moved them to the side. Struggling, she managed to get her chain mail off next, finally sliding it down her unresponsive arm. What she saw made her vision swim for a moment. Her shoulder and arm were a mess, chain links driven into her flesh where the mail had been punctured. Already she could smell the stink of infection and wondered how long she had been out.

"What now?" She swayed slightly, despite still sitting on the floor of the cave. Without her armour and the heavy cloth, only bands of soft leather were left to cover her chest. She expected to be cold, only feeling a slight chill, barely felt past the heavy fur of her body. Blackhorn dropped to all six of his limbs to shift around her before moving his muzzle close to the wound on her shoulder where his horn had pierced the woman's flesh.

This is going to feel strange.

"What do you mean by stran—" Her voice caught as Blackhorn's tongue slid from his muzzle to pan across the wound, its broad, flat top catching every surface of the ragged edge. It felt cool, numbing, yet something tingled with its touch. Hjördis watched as Blackhorn licked the wound a second time. This time the tingling was stronger, coursing through her body. Her nipples hardened against the cloth that bound them, and Hjördis gasped. The familiar tingle made its way to her groin.

The tongue slide out a third time, then a fourth, and Hjördis bit her lip against the groan that threatened to escape her muzzle. If Blackhorn noticed, he didn't respond, too intent on tending to her injury. Through the tingling that raced through her body, Hjördis noticed the wound looked older with each lick, as if she were watching the days pass with each brush of the gnoph-keh's tongue.

When Blackhorn finally stopped licking, Hjördis' breath was racing and her ears felt hot. The beast blinked at her and she saw a twinkle in his eye even before his voice entered her thoughts.

I told you it would be strange. How does it feel?

"It feels like you're…" Hjördis realized he was asking about the shoulder rather than the sensuous feeling it brought. To cover her embarrassment she rolled her arm. "It feels good, though I can feel the twinge you were talking about. Like a shard of ice buried in the wound."

Sadly, there is nothing I can do about that. Still, it's preferable to permanent loss of the limb, is it not?"

Hjördis nodded in response. Reaching out with one of his enormous paws, Blackhorn took her arm and turned his attention to the bite wounds there. His first lick—from her elbow to finger tips—left Hjördis' lower body clenching. The sensation of his tongue travelling along her fur—the coolness of his magic at work—made things low in her flutter with each brush. She wasn't sure she could deal with this long enough for him to heal all of her wounds, and yet Hjördis found herself wishing she had more wounds for him to tend.

Are you well?

The bear nodded her head, not trusting her voice while Blackhorn continued to draw his tongue along her wounds. It took all of Hjördis' willpower to simply watch the wounds as they closed, the pieces of chainmail falling from the flesh, and not to succumb to the physical sensations each lick brought to her.

Long minutes passed before the wounds on her arm began to close and seal into pink scar tissue that—once her fur dried—would barely be noticeable. At least she would have something to show for her efforts against the beast. Looking over her arm, Hjördis realized she would have to figure out a way to explain how her wounds had healed so quickly.

Remove your britches.

Hjördis gaze rose sharply to Blackhorn who stood before her on all of his legs. He lowered his head so that his horn tapped the outside of her thigh, and the memory of it plunging through her shoulder made Hjördis flinch.

I need to tend to your legs. You have fine cracks in the bones there, I can smell the damage. Untended, they will grow to pain you as you get older, eventually leaving you a crippled woman.

The maiden lowered a paw to her legs and rubbed the muscles there. A lance of pain was her reward, and she gritted her teeth against it. With some effort she unclasped the rest of her armour and wiggled out of it before removing her pants. The cold tinted air felt good on her fur and she was surprised to realize she didn't feel self-conscious around the monster that had tried to kill her hours earlier. Or was it days.

I apologize for any discomfort this might cause you. Blackhorn moved forward and Hjördis instinctively leaned back as his massive head moved to the shin of her left leg. His tongue slide out and again she felt his magic at work, this time deep in the muscles. Where the feel of him licking her arm had been strong, the brush of his breath and the shiver of cold along her leg made her bite her lip.

Again and again his tongue travelled along her fur, his head moving higher and higher up the limb, each lick long and dragged out. Blackhorn had his eyes closed and Hjördis had to fight not to let the sounds that were boiling in her chest escape.

Higher and higher his tongue moved, each lap making more of her leg tingle, the line of ice travelling straight to that secret place in her body. Bjorn's tongue on her nipples had been nothing compared to the lightning that coursed through her, speeding up her breath and causing her blood to pound in her ears.

When his tongue reached her inner thigh, Hjördis couldn't handle anymore. Claws gripping the blanket under her, she let out a whimper as she felt the tip of Blackhorn's tongue travel to the edge of the cloth she had wrapped around her woman-hood, and then down to her knee. The gnoph-keh stopped and raised his gaze to her, cocking his bearlike head at her.

Do you want me to stop? Am I hurting you?

Hjördis' eyes widened with shock. "No, no, no. Please no. I don't think it's healed yet." She reached out, her paws grabbing either side of the beast's head. "Just don't stop, please. It feels…good."

Blackhorn held her gaze for a moment more before sliding away from her paws. Hjördis could have sworn he was smiling as he lowered his head and licked her again, this time the heavy tongue glided from the outside of her inner thigh to the bottom, travelling along the fabric that hid her. Hjördis wondered if Blackhorn could tell what he was doing to her when she threw her head back with a shuddering gasp. He had to know, she thought. The maiden could smell her arousal filling the cavern, waves of it brushing against her nose. And with his muzzle so close to her…

The tongue brushed along the dampness that had soaked into her undergarments, and something snapped in Hjördis' body. She let out a cry, her body starting to shake. Ice seemed to flow along her nerves, leaving behind traces of burning that made her want to reach out and pull the monster's muzzle against her sex.

She could feel how wet she was becoming, each lick causing her lower regions to spasm and quake. Fluid dripped out of her to soak the fabric that kept her dignity from the monster. Each brush of the tongue felt like ice flowing to fire, the dual sensation making her whimper and moan, her cries echoing off the walls.

Blackhorn rose up onto four of his legs. *I can stop. You seem to be having some kind of reaction to the healing.* The voice was cool and concerned against her mind and it took Hjördis a few moments of blinking to clear her vision. She looked down her quivering body as it begged for more, and saw something. Hjördis squeezed her eyes shut and then looked again.

Hjördis suddenly realized why Blackhorn seemed to be spending so much time in an area that she was pretty sure wasn't injured, even with her pleading. The damned beast was enjoying himself, his excitement quite evident from between the four paws that remained on the ground. The maiden laughed and pointed at the monster's excitement.

"Perhaps we should stop, as it seems to have affected you as well."

Blackhorn dropped to all of his legs and levelled his head with hers. Up close, she realized just how massive his skull was, his teeth gleaming in the luminescence of the ice. The gnoph-keh moved close enough that their noses almost touched, his breath warm against her muzzle.

I admit, there are certain things that I have found enjoyable so far.

Hjördis nodded slowly, still trying to catch her breath, wincing as her body tried to collect itself. This close, the beast's scent filled her nose, the musky scent rolling off of it. It was heavy, almost ursine but somehow different—more pungent, more powerful. Among the sharp scent of her own arousal, she could also detect the smell of his. Unlike the scent of his fur, this was heavier, thicker. Hjördis licked her lips and felt her ears grow warm as they flattened against her head.

Her paws reached out and stroked along the heavy ridges of Blackhorn's skull, feeling the thick bone that rested under the skin. The beast closed his eyes as she explored him. The maiden moved back, one paw moving to the creature's horn and gripping it. She guided his muzzle down her body to where she knew her scent would overpower every other scent in the room.

"Please." It came out more pleading than she had expected, but Blackhorn obliged and his tongue once again slide along her, rekindling her shivers. Hjördis growled low in her throat, continuing to hold onto the horn as she felt each brush of the gnoph-keh's warmth against her. The pause had only helped to further the need that was now coursing through her body, driving her to a cliff's edge of passion. Each lick, each probe of the fleshy appendage against her covering, made her whimper and moan for more.

And then it stopped. She couldn't remember if she had torn the fabric away or he had. Cold air chilled the moisture that soaked her fur. The next brush of his tongue against her made her cry out, back arching.

Hjördis tried to make sense of the feeling as the gnoph-keh's tongue slid along her, its heavy weight parting her folds and teasing the pink flesh within. She had once experimented with an icicle as a young girl still exploring the feelings that ran through her body. Blackhorn's tongue felt very much like the icicle when she had slid it into herself, parting her lips with the coldness of winter. Where it chilled, it burned like fire when the ice retreated, making her body writhe in want of something to fill her.

Blackhorn lowered his forequarters to shift his head to a better angle even as Hjördis leaned back, arching her hips to meet his tongue while it slid once more from between his lips. Hjördis gripped the blanket under her, claws tearing through the fabric when the chilled warmth of his tongue explored her dampness. The maiden could feel the tip of his tongue brushing her slit before flicking across the tiny bud at the apex of her sex. There it teased back and forth before Blackhorn dragged the entire length of his tongue against it, the sensation making the ursine woman buck and her thighs quake.

But it was when he pushed that dextrous appendage into her that Hjördis' full orgasm finally hit. Inner walls clenched around the fleshy invader that twisted inside her, filling the princess with a warmth she desired after being teased with the ice of his magic. She may have sworn to the gods or called his name or simply screamed nonsense words to the walls of his home; she did not know. When her orgasm passed, the princess' hips fell to the floor. She fought her body for control while Blackhorn watched her. It was hard not to miss his the engorged member bobbing between his hind-most legs.

Hjördis eyed it with a greedy need.

"Come here." She reached out to grab a fist-full of the beast's neck fur, and Blackhorn did not resist. "You have something I need."

Is that so?

The touch of ice on her mind was playful and Hjördis grinned while she pulled him higher on her body. As the throbbing member of flesh grew closer to her, the ursine woman realized just how large he was. Her eyes widened at the sheer girth and length of the organ before her, a drop of pre shining like a pearl at the tip of the spade-like head. Hjördis reached out a tentative paw and ran it along the shaft. Barely able to get her fingers around its girth, she felt the four lines of tiny hard knobs that ran from glans to the base of the organ.

Do you think—

"I have to try." Hjördis cut off the beast's thought. Blackhorn rose to his hind legs, suddenly towering over the ursine woman. His length seemed larger somehow, no longer hidden under the shaggy hide. Hjördis bit her lip and swallowed, suddenly doubting herself.

On your paws and knees.

The bear raised her gaze to where Blackhorn looked down at her. From that angle he seemed very much the monster she had fought in the blizzard. King of winter, master of the storms that blanketed the peaks of her homes and this northern wasteland.

Hjördis obeyed.

Turning over, the princess lowered herself to her elbows as she thrust her rear towards the towering beast, a dribble of moisture sliding out of her slit to run down her inner thigh. Blackhorn lowered himself over her, covering her with his enormous form. She could feel his weight above her, pressing along her back, his legs surrounding her like a cage.

His member prodded her ass. Its wedge-shaped head slid along the crack to bump against the base of her tail. Hjördis made a noise and Blackhorn moved above her, his tip retreating only to return, this time gliding along the top of her slit. One of the bumpy ridges slid along her clit and she gasped, closing her eyes as the sensation coursed through her body.

Blackhorn made a noise deep in his chest, the sound echoing around her, his member withdrawing. This time the tip pressed against Hjördis' entrance and she bit her lip hard, claws digging into the ice of the floor. The beast didn't ask if she was ready. He already knew she was.

Slowly Hjördis could feel the head parting her folds, pushing aside the fleshy entrance to make room for him. She panted at the slowness of it all, trying to relax her body as she felt him enter her, spread her, fill her. With a pop, his head finally passed her entrance and the flesh tightened around him.

Hjördis moaned, her tongue hanging out of her muzzle as her ears flew back and forth. Above her Blackhorn shuddered, the belly of his body pressing down to trap her while he started to push further inside. Hjördis made a mewing noise as she felt his shaft spread her again and the head move deeper into her body.

"Oh my ancestors," she was barely able to breath out. "You're so big."

That's only because you are so small. Blackhorn shuddered again, pausing for a moment before starting to slide more of himself into her. *And tight. By Ithaqua you are tight.*

It was with a gasp of pain that Hjördis felt the wedge head hit her deepest point. Above her Blackhorn froze before shifting his feet, the movement causing his length to throb and bob inside her. The bear's body shuddered and she realized she was completely at the beast's mercy.

Slowly the beast's length pulled out of her, each of the four lines of bumps plucking at her inner walls, popping out of her entrance until the wider end of the head stopped just before the chill outside. Hjördis moved her hips, feeling the unusual head tease against the spongy spot just inside her that she had often run her own paw pads over when alone at night.

Hjördis expected the beast to go slow, but his next thrust was harder. Faster. The head of his member slid along inside her. The bumps passed through her entrance in a rapid hammer of sensation. The tip hit her deep again and her eyes widened as the pleasure made her vision swim. Again and again he almost pulled out of her before shoving back in, each time the gliding of his member against her inner walls teased warmth and cold along her core.

The warrior lost herself to the thrill of her body. Everything was forgotten, her oaths, her father, her clan, even Bjorn. All that remained was the feeling of Blackhorn filling her, moving along her skin with his own, the weight of his massive body above her and the danger that he could kill her at any moment.

Hjördis didn't care. The sensations flooding her body were headier than the best mead to ever touch her tongue. Blackhorn twisted his body, driving his member in and out of her at different angles, the head of his sex twisting inside her to touch every part. The bumps along his length were lightning to her body, making her shiver and squirm as he shunted her along the blanket.

The maiden's body spasmed around the member, her cries peaking with each thrust. She sounded like a lass with her first male, discovering her first orgasm. She clawed at the ice of the floor, shredding the blanket under her. Each thrust hit something primal in her and Hjördis could feel the build-up approaching with all the fury of a spring's first thunderstorm.

Blackhorn grunted with each thrust, the black claws of each paw digging deep in the ice of the floor. Hjördis caught the sight of snow as it fell around them before squeezing her eyes shut. The monster's thrusts grew harder, faster, his body shivering more. More than once he paused, leaving her to quake around him before starting again. Hjördis could feel her inner walls clenching and releasing around him. His grunts and pants were growing closer, faster.

He was going to cum.

The very thought of the beast above her releasing himself inside her brought her over the edge. Hjördis opened her muzzle in a scream of pure animalistic pleasure as her thighs shuddered like an avalanche. Her inner walls clenched around Blackhorn's length, squeezing against the spade head and the lines of ridges. Tears flowed down her cheeks as she screwed her eyes shut and lost control of herself utterly and completely.

Blackhorn answered her cry with a roar of his own, shaking flecks of ice from the ceiling. He thrust as deep as it could inside her before Hjördis felt the first torrent of heat splash deeper than any male she had ever felt. Another jet hit her and her body climaxed again, and again, each of the monster's bursts of cum sending her through another body-shaking release. Hjördis could feel it spilling out of her womb, the pressure forcing it between the seal of his member and her entrance to drip onto the floor.

When it was finally over, Blackhorn was forced to place his forepaws on her shoulders to hold her in place while he slid out. Hjördis let him, her body refusing to respond to any commands her mind issued.

She let out a gasp as his splayed head finally came free in a welter of fluid, both hers and his.

Hjördis curled against the gnoph-keh while he bent his body around her, covering her with his legs, his head coming to rest in her lap while she rested hers on his side. Sleep claimed her quickly, lulled by Blackhorn's steadily beating heart.

***

When she awoke, Blackhorn was no longer in the cave. Hjördis stood on shaky legs, her inner thighs caked with their love making. Self-conscious, Hjördis used the ruined blanket to clean herself, her ears burning the entire time.

"If only father could see me now." She whispered, her gaze moving around the cave while she tidied herself the best she could. The ice had lost its luminous glow and now seemed to be just normal frozen water. Beyond the grooves carved into the floor by both her and Blackhorn, she would have almost been able to convince herself that the entire encounter had been nothing more than a hallucination brought on by the blowing snow.

That was until she saw her neatly folded clothing and armour.

Resting on the top of the pile was Blackhorn's namesake, hewed off at the base. Beside it Hjördis' axe rested, many of its runes burned out to accomplish the feat, she was sure of it. Carefully, she moved over to the pile and picked up the curved spiral horn.

Turning it, she marvelled at the mixture of greys and blacks that marbled its surface. It was colder than the air around it. Bending down, she carefully wrapped it in one of her bedrolls. She had her evidence, her oath was fulfilled as far as anyone would know.

Hjördis dressed, amazed at how good her body felt, even with the pleasant ache between her legs. Her wounds, from both the wolves and Blackhorn, were now nothing but old scars hidden by her fur. She could feel the ice slivers like Blackhorn said, but she felt invigorated, younger. Hjördis stepped out into the sunlight, the sky clear of any sort of cloud. The ursine glanced at her paws. The fur shone like it had when she was a girl. Not only had the gnoph-keh healed her wounds, but had renewed her somehow.

Looking at the sky, she took a long draught of the chilled tundra air and exhaled a puff of fog before closing her eyes.

"Thank you. I will not forget."

The wind ruffling her fur was Hjördis' only answer as she started south.

FIFTY SCALES OF GREY

Sarina Dorie

My nerves tingled with anticipation as the knight penetrated the inner depths of my cave. His sword was drawn and visor down, obscuring what I hoped was a pretty-boy visage. He stumbled twice over heaps of gold, arms stretched out, groping in the darkness since he hadn't thought to bring his own light. He probably hadn't thought to bring any bondage gear either.

"Here, let me set a little mood lighting," I said, blowing fire on the sconces lining the limestone walls.

His eyes widened as he took in two tons of curvy, green dragon beauty. That's right, I was a big girl; larger that a peasant's hut and stronger than a battalion of warriors. And he wanted me. He didn't even ogle the mountain of jewels and gold where I perched. All that last knight had cared about was my treasure. He'd run away when he'd seen me. This one stared in awe at me, mouth agape.

"You are Dragonacia the Wicked?" The knight struck a sexy defensive stance, legs spread apart, sword raised. A tremor of what I suspected was arousal laced his youthful tone. "I am here to rescue the kidnapped princess. Release her or I shall slay ye!"

My lips curled into a smile. "Oh yes, talk dirty to me. Tell me what else you're going to do to me, you naughty knight."

Silver armor glistened in the golden glow of candlelight as he charged toward me. Elaborate patterns of flowers and vines decorated his fashionable armor. He struck at me with his sword, the metal raking over my scales. In truth, he was a little too gentle for my liking, but then, we were just beginning. He thrust at me again. I rolled over onto my back to allow him more access.

I winked at him. "Ahem, there happens to be a satin cord in the corner. You know, in case you want to tie me up." Just the idea of being bound made my eyes roll back in my head.

"Do you jest?" he asked. "You're going to willingly allow me to restrain you? Surely this is a trick."

I giggled. The sound rumbled from my throat like thunder. "I would never jest about bondage. By the way, our safe word is 'red.'"

He retreated, fumbling through the treasure chests for the cord. I waited as patiently as I could despite being deep in the throes of foreplay. But he was so slow. I actually had to tell him how to tie me up properly.

My ears detected the distant echo of footsteps. What was this? Another knight coming to join the fun? Princess Katherine exited from a tunnel, her delicate features obscured by the hefty book her nose was poked into. She turned another page, stumbling on a satin cord stretched from the wall. She was about to ruin everything.

"Ahem," I said, trying not to attract the knight's attention. I didn't want him to spot her and get distracted.

The knight was busy tying up my legs. He didn't look up.

Katherine halted, glanced from the knight to me and back at the knight. She shook her head, sparkles of magic drifting from her golden hair. From the way her brow crinkled and her mouth opened as if she might object, I suspected she intended to broadcast her disapproval. To my relief, she slipped back into the cave without a word.

I sighed.

"Tighter. Harder," I said to my knight. "Hit me with that sword like you mean it. Show me you want me." Just because the knight wasn't an experienced lover didn't mean we couldn't have a worthwhile and meaningful relationship.

He picked up a bronze axe left behind by a previous knight. Perspiration dotted my scales. I loved it when they wanted to try something new.

"Oh my!" I said. My tail thrashed about in excitement.

Unfortunately, the knight came a little too close to the razor sharp spikes on my tail. With one fatal swipe, his head flew off his body and rolled out of the decorated helmet. I wailed in frustration. His large brown eyes stared up at the ceiling in frozen horror. He'd had such a smooth, pretty face too. My heart sank with disappointment. I decided the only thing that would make me feel better was to gorge myself on his remains and then roll around in my treasure.

How I loathed my clumsiness. I just wanted a hot knight to love me. And to tie me up and dominate me. Was that so much to ask?

***

By the time the next knight arrived, the excitement over my previous encounter had dwindled away. My desire was kindled anew once I saw this knight wasn't like the others. His armor was inlaid with jewels. Though he wore a helmet, the visor was up, showing off his dignified visage. I'd never gazed upon such a handsome young man. His chin was strong and square, a few days worth of stubble giving him a rugged appearance.

Not only did he bring his own torch for the sconces, but chains swung from his belt. He carried a small trunk under one arm. I could only fantasize about what it might contain. Imagining what he might do to me made me squirm with delight.

He paced, managing to stare down at me with his icy blue eyes, though I was elevated on my hoard of gold. He didn't act the least bit intimidated. "You're that female dragon with the knight fetish, are you not? I am Sir Grey the Great. Prepare to be conquered."

Oh my! What an arrogant son-of-a-human! I liked him already.

"Get down here where I can reach you," he commanded.

This was new. They didn't usually take charge like this. That was so... hot. I happily obeyed.

Sir Grey hammered spikes into the walls and attached the chains. I allowed him to cuff my arms and legs. He was experienced enough to know to chain down my tail as well. I eagerly waited to see what he would do next.

He prodded me with his sword, slowly, teasingly inching his way down my belly.

My breath came out in a rush of warmth. "That feels so good."

"Silence. I'm looking for your weakness. Should you be missing any scales, I'll find the spot and when I do, I'm going to hurt you like no knight has ever done before."

I bit my lip. "Is that a promise?"

He sounded so earnest. I relaxed into the heap of gold, allowing him to rake his sword over my naked scales. A few times he thrust out unexpectedly, making me shiver with delight. No knight had ever made me feel this way before.

"You should bow down to me in thanks for this. I'm taking time out of my busy schedule to figure out how to slay you," Sir Grey said. "Really, you're unworthy of my attention. A female dragon with such a small trove of gold. I doubt you even have a princess worth rescuing."

"Yes! Yes! Trample my self-esteem. Tell me I don't deserve you. Make me want you." Sparks flew out of my nose. Desire boiled in my core, pulsing through my veins.

He unlatched the trunk he'd set aside. My muscles clenched with anticipation. I craned my neck to see what he was doing, but he lifted his chin, barking out a stern command. "Get back down or I'm not going to finish."

My fiery breath came out in pants. The chains rattled against the mounds of gold as my muscles quivered with excitement. This waiting, this wanting, it was torture. I had to have this knight.

He slowly approached, locking eyes with me and holding me there with his commanding gaze. He held up the queerest looking sex toy I'd ever seen: a tubular glass case filled with liquid with a long metal needle attached. He pressed the bottom of the vessel and a spurt of gold fluid erupted from the top.

That pushed me over the edge. I gave such a strong involuntary shudder I tore the chains from the wall. The metal arced up into the air toward my lover, battering him with the spikes that had been hammered into the stone. In my state of heightened arousal, a geyser of fire erupted from my throat. Within seconds the knight lay at my feet in a smoldering lump. He was in several pieces. I supposed my tail must have sliced him up a little.

I had been so close this time! It wasn't fair. I screamed in frustration, then having nothing better around to sink my teeth into, I nibbled at his crisped remains. Barbequed human was as close to comfort food as I was about to get at the moment.

Moments later, Princess Katherine found me moaning on my belly. She smelled of earthen tunnels and herbs. Her long, golden hair flowed over her shoulders, sparkling with magic as it often did after she'd been testing out spells all day.

She kicked the chains out of her path and set down a steaming bucket of liquid next to my head. "Heartburn?"

"And heartache," I said.

She stroked my horns. "I made ginger tea. It should help with one of those, anyway."

I sipped the spicy concoction, feeling lower than ever. My tears soaked her dress as she knelt beside me. If I didn't stop gushing over that last knight, she was going to look like one of those princesses who entered wet tunic contests.

"It isn't fair. The problem is, I keep roasting them," I admitted.

"Sweetie, that's only part of the problem. You can't have your cake and eat him too. Katherine stroked my nose. "You really would be better off without those good-for-nothing knights. Half of them would kill you and carry me off given the opportunity. The other half are such cowards they aren't worthy of you."

I lifted my head, staring into her pitying blue eyes. "Just because you came here to hide from strong, dominant men doesn't mean I have to do the same thing. There isn't anything wrong with wanting to be submissive. I don't get on your case for being such a knight-hater."

She nudged the broken glass vial at her feet, watching it roll to the bottom of my mound of gold. "I didn't say anything's wrong with you. I'm saying you're going about it the wrong way. Those princes don't deserve you. You need to establish a relationship with someone first, so you can trust him not to kill you." She bent to pick up shards of glass, depositing them in a leather pouch attached to her girdle. She sniffed at a piece of it. "You do know what was in that vial, don't you? It was dragonsbane. He would have killed you, stolen your treasure and then kidnapped me."

I sunk down, not meeting her eyes. My knight fetish had endangered both our lives.

Katherine stroked my head. "Not only do you need a partner you can trust, you need someone strong enough to ensure you don't hurt him… or her. I've stood by and watched you torture yourself with failure for months. I can no longer watch you be sexually frustrated." She stood, raising her chin with the dignity and command royalty possessed. "I am making you my love slave."

I smiled at her and blinked away my tears. "You are so sweet, princess. I appreciate what you're trying to do, but I would accidentally roast you alive and eat you. If an armor clad, muscular knight can't survive pleasuring me, I have a hard time seeing how you could."

She looked down at her brown dress. "It's the lack of armor, isn't it? Metal turns you on? I'll be right back." She lifted the hem of her dress and scampered over mounds of gold toward one of the tunnels she'd carved with magic.

As a natural extrovert, there weren't many humans I was willing to shut myself up in a cave guarding, but that dear girl was one of them. After I'd heard her tale of forced marriage to a tyrant who wouldn't allow her to express herself by practicing magic, I'd offered to let her stay with me. Attracting knights who came to rescue her was an added bonus.

Though, that hadn't exactly turned out the way I had hoped.

Katherine returned, clad in polished armor that hugged her slender frame so tightly it left little to the imagination. Was it a trick of the candlelight or was that armor... gold? Oh my! My stomach fluttered at the sight. She waved a sword in the air that was far too heavy for her diminutive stature. She stumbled forward in a most endearing manner.

"Princess, I value our friendship far too much to endanger you by getting excited in your presence. By the way, you look adorable in that armor."

"Thank you. I made it myself. You don't mind if I get rid of those chains, do you? I have something more comfortable in mind." She lifted a hand and waved it in the air, the chains breaking and clanking as she pushed them into the corners with an invisible wind. She muttered an incantation, making symbols in the air with her hands as she was wont to do when casting a spell.

The whispering scuttle of a million miniature legs swept toward us. Streams of black spiders flooded into my treasure room. I watched in fascination as they wove about each other, braiding thick white cords from the walls. I gasped in delight once I saw they meant to bind my arms, legs and tail.

"It's magically reinforced spider silk. I tested it already." Katherine trailed the tip of her sword over my neck.

I loved the give of the spider silk, the way I could still move—but not too much. I thrashed out experimentally, but the cord held me in place, making me feel weak and vulnerable and feminine. The yearning to be dominated pulsed through my veins. No, I would not allow myself to become excited. I would not ruin our friendship by eating her.

"You're forgetting about the fire," I reminded the princess.

"Give me your best shot." The arrogance in Katherine's tone surprised me—delighted me. "Let's see if you can burn me."

I hated the idea of endangering Katherine, but I did need to show her the harm that might come to her should I lose control. I inhaled and puffed a mild wave of heat at her. Smoke and sparks shot out my mouth, but parted around her body as if an invisible shield surrounded her. Seeing it had little effect on her magical barrier, I drew up the fire churning in my belly, showering her with actual flame. It billowed around her, not even touching a hair on her head.

"How'd you do that?" I asked.

"Ahem. Magic." She winked at me. "Who says only princes can be dominating, demanding lovers? I am a princess. I do know something about bossing people about."

For the first time since I'd discovered my knight fetish, I realized I might have a chance of success. Tears of joy filled my eyes.

"By the way, our safe word is 'dragonsbane,'" she said. "Now, let's have a little fun, shall we?"

FORBIDDEN GNOLLEDGE

Marderschaden

Pain.

The first thing that entered Brennain's head as he regained consciousness was pain. Dull, throbbing pain. The ferret struggled to remember what he must have done to get into this state, but the stabbing agony made it almost impossible.

What did I do?

The question echoed through Bren's mind as he wrestled with the cotton wool and clamour that fouled his thoughts. He tried focusing on what he could feel—beyond the pain, at least. Excruciating, head-splitting pain. The roguish adventurer tried to reach up to touch his forehead, but his hands were misbehaving. They just refused to move. His legs were also ignoring his feeble commands, and the hot itchiness in his scalp, at his shoulder, and along the fur on his face was maddening.

Where are the others? Where am I? Focus, Bren. Focus.

Next, he listened. He heard nothing over the sound of his own panicked, erratic breathing.

Finally, he tried to look around, he couldn't open his eyes—they were gummed up with something that caked them shut.

Whatever it was, he thought, *it was either very, very good, or absolutely terrible.*

Brennain strained to move his arms to wipe at his face again, before realising that they were trapped behind him. Not merely trapped either, they were tied securely.

Yeah, terrible.

He wriggled, testing the bonds for any give, and quickly realised that his ankles were similarly restrained. Holding back panic, he forced himself to lay still and think, trying to remember how in the nine hells he ended up in this mess—he was no stranger to waking up in dire situations, at any rate.

We were on the road, Brennain decided, fighting the urge to fidget, groan and vomit. *On a job, yes. We left Silverdale. Tansy, Ren and I. We were taking something somewhere, looking for something. Oh, Gods, were we with the twins? Didn't they want to go hunting for something?*

The jittery movements of his eyes behind his eyelids bore acciden-tal fruit—one opened a crack, and the bright light of day cut through Bren's retina like the razor edge of a well-honed stiletto. He sank back into the welcoming dark of unconsciousness with a pitiful, strangled whimper.

"This way," Ren said, standing from where he had been crouched for the last few moments. "The patrol's tracks are at least two days old, no Gnoll has been this way for a while."

Brennain shrugged, and broke down the last of the traps he had set around the camp overnight. Once the parts were stowed, the fer-ret shouldered his pack again. He trusted the old fox's tracking skills, they'd kept the party safe all the way to the savannah after all, and Ren's skill with the bow and rod made sure they all ate well.

The ferret's mind caught on 'rod', and he quashed a strong urge to make some salacious comment about the fox's familiarity with rod-handling. He was supposed to be a professional trapper today. *Anyway, that one's too easy. No point going for the low-hanging fruits.* And then the thought of Ren's low-hanging fruits completely derailed any sense of professionalism entirely.

"Bren," came an authoritative female voice. "Hang back, watch the rear. If Ren's blazing the trail, I want you to make sure we're not followed."

"Sure thing, Tansy," Bren answered, clearing his throat. "You can count on me if there's a rear involved." He grinned broadly at the wild-cat, who returned the gesture with a grunt and a glower. "It's not just rears, though. You know I'd be more than happy to help you explore the softer side of your personality."

Tansy's grunt quickly became an exasperated gasp. "Bren, I cut you a lot of slack on the job, and much as I enjoy our little verbal sparring matches," she said, a little sharply, "There's a time and a place."

"Hey, hey, no need to cut out a little fun between friends, Tansy. If we start acting too seriously, I'll lose my edge," Bren protested.

"Stop that, Bren. Eyes on the trail. We've made it this far without any trouble, and honestly, I'd like to keep it that way." The feline's hand strayed to the haft of her mace, and her ears flattened back briefly as she turned her head sharply, nostrils flaring. Her eyes stayed on the ferret, with a stern look of disapproval before she shook her head, and turned her attention in the direction Ren had indicated. She maintained her alertness for a few seconds before she caught sight of the twins. The pair of diminutive weasels ambled along after Ren, seeming lost in their own oracular robes. "I swear, those two are more trouble than they're worth. I just knew that they'd call in a favour after they'd been running with the three of us for a while."

Brennain shrugged, glancing after the twins before turning his attention back to Tansy. "They're young, they're capable, and they love pretending to kiss when I'm watching out for them." A toothy smile from the ferret was met with stone-cold glaring from the wildcat.

"We discussed this moments ago," was her irritated response. "Besides, they're older than you think. They've been emissaries for the Moon's temple as long as I've been at the convent."

"Ahem. Sorry. You're a different person in the wilds, Tansy." Brennain glanced away, and coughed pointedly before continuing. "You've seen what they can do when the wind's blowing right for them. I don't have a problem with helping them out after they've been so useful," he said with another smile. "They're solid. Cute. Reliable. Almost as reliable as my... contraptions, and not the ones I employ in the bed—" he paused, then changed the course of his words as he caught scent of Tansy's rising irritation. "I think they're going to pull their weight, even if they don't quite act like responsible adults all the time. They're like me, that way."

Tansy scowled, but the steady growl she almost started died in her throat as quickly as it began, as she changed the subject. "Your traps gave us plenty of warning last time we were out, yeah. They're the only reason I have the time of day for you, when you're usually more interested in fiddling with other tools, and the less said about those, the better." Despite the sting of her words, the wildcat's expression was softening, at least a little.

"Yeah, well, that's one in my favor," Bren admitted, turning to look over his shoulder. "But the slingshot machine jammed right after I almost put a rock through Ren's head. That's probably down to the rough handling it had on the trip, but that instability is fixed, now." He kicked at a stone, then gave the surrounding area another keen look before continuing. "The spring-loaded lock-pick is perfect, totally ironed out that release glitch. Sorry about the mishap back in Silverdale, but you're pretty good left handed, so no harm done. Best let me deal with the complex machinery in future, you're far better than me at crushing skulls anyhow."

A finger pressed to the ferret's lips silenced Bren instantly. "Shut it," Tansy advised. "You're a clever slinky, Bren, and your inventions help far more often than they hurt. Just… keep your head in the now."

"Not a problem," Bren replied, tactfully refraining from licking the wildcat's fingertip. Instead, he just exhaled lightly, letting his warm, moist breath tickle past her paw-pads. "You were saying the twins were how old, now?"

"Older than you," Tansy grunted, recoiling with a mock grimace. "And before you try making a comment on how you prefer a bedmate with experience, remember what you said about me and skulls, okay?" she chided, just in time to spot Ren waiting patiently for an opportune moment.

"Now that you're done," the fox said, his expression carefully composed. "Something's not right. The tracks are wrong, they're muddled in ways that make no sense, old prints mixed with new. Trails that stop with no explanation, or that seem to start out of nowhere." The hint of a knowing smile at the corner of Ren's lips faded, replaced with a mildly worried frown. "I don't like it, and I can't explain it. They haven't been disguised, they just simply don't make sense. The weasels haven't said anything though, and they claimed to have thrown their crystals, or whatever it is they do."

Brennain looked from the fox to Tansy, and waited for her response. The news was enough to distract the lecherous ferret from any even slightly sordid thoughts.

Tansy pursed her lips, and her frown deepened. "Ren, move further ahead. You're woodsy enough to hide yourself if anything should happen. Bren, you watch the rear, and throw up a screamer if anything gets the drop on you. I need to watch the twins, and see if they've… heard anything." The woman made a vague gesture in the general direction of the sky, then shrugged.

"Sure thing," Brennain replied as the wildcat turned to jog after the giggling mustelid pair ahead of the group. "Sure thing."

Ren met Brennain's gaze for a moment, then pulled his hood up over his tall, pointed ears. "Walk softly, and may your blade be keen," the fox offered, before angling away from cat and weasels, aiming towards the heavier brush on the road ahead.

The ferret found his eyes following Ren's tail as the fox lost himself in the undergrowth, before he shook his head and rubbed at his eyes. *Too old,* the ferret figured. *Though… he looks after himself well.* Brennain grinned to himself, then shifted his attention back to the task on hand, his thoughts straying to a taut, red-furred rear and what must sway beneath it. *Low hanging fruit,* he thought with a low chuckle.

Ahead of him, Tansy caught up with the weasel twins, who turned to greet her with their customary, chirpy conversation. Brennain turned his attention to the path behind the group while reaching into one of his many pockets to seek out one of his simpler inventions, a streamlined hollow cone with cunningly carved holes in the surface. He toyed with the flint mechanism at the flattened base while carrying out his assigned role—that of watching the rear.

Nothing. Just the lazy sway of the branches in that lone copse of trees, and the rustle of bushes in the wind. A reddening leaf fell from a branch, and fluttered towards the ground, at which point Brennain found his attention wandering back to thoughts of a red-furred foxbrush flicking back and forth in the breeze. He grinned, sheepishly, and started to turn back towards Tansy and the twins, before something snapped him out of his sure to be sordid reverie.

A rock, surrounded by thick undergrowth. The ferret was sure that it wasn't something the group had passed. In fact, he was certain it was not there before. The leering, razor-toothed face between the bushes most definitely was a new addition. Bren jammed his index finger into his conical device, and threw it straight up into the air as the flint within struck fire-powder, propelling it further upward with an absolutely horrific shriek.

"Ambush!" Bren yelled, alerting the others, "Behind us!"

The Gnolls were not just behind the group. Somehow, Bren and his friends were completely surrounded. One moment, the group were walking alone across the savannah, and the next the air was filled with snarling cries of challenge, high-pitched yips that sounded like mocking laughter, and the rising wail of the ferret engineer's screamer. It made no sense, and yet there were Gnolls everywhere. Their thrown spears were also everywhere, and as he stepped on one that skittered across the ground after falling short, a net was dropped on one of the weasel acolytes by a Gnoll in a tree that must have been hidden by some unnatural spell. Cara, the very slightly shorter of the two weasels, gestured towards her attacker, who fell from his branch with a strangled gasp and a distinct smell of burning fur. Jor snapped his fingers and shrugged off the net, which had been reduced to ash in an instant.

Brennain heard—rather than saw—the two arrows Ren almost instantly fired past him, into the newly appeared rock and bushes the ferret noticed. One jammed solidly in the leering Gnoll's eye-socket, while the other disappeared into the foliage with a satisfying, meaty thunk. The shrill yelp of pain that followed moments later confirmed that the hunter's second arrow had been perfectly on target.

The ferret raised his crossbow, and fired it directly at the closest charging assailant. The spear-wielding Gnoll tripped and fell clutching at his knee. Bren aimed for the thing's head, and pulled the trigger. No response. He cursed under his breath, keeping an eye out for danger as he went down on one knee to clear the jam. A glance over his shoulder noted three more Gnolls slinking out of hiding, and advancing on his exposed position. He stood and sprinted towards Tansy and the weasels, looking past them in time to see Ren turn smoothly, loosing shaft after shaft into the bulky, intimidating shapes of their assailants.

"Bren!" Tansy yelled, from where she stood over the twins. The weasels huddled together, speaking rapidly to each other before nodding. They moved back to back, eyes half-closed and showing only the whites as they began to drone and gesture in the weird tongue they used when invoking their deity. They seemed completely blind to the spears and primitive hatchets whistling through the air around them.

"Something's weird," Brennain called, his lips curling in a grin as he felt the familiar give in the loading mechanism, and another bolt slid smoothly into place. He immediately turned to fire, striking a Gnoll charging him from the side. The beast's snarl only intensified when the projectile sank into its side, and when the second bolt pinged out of position and fell to the ground rather than smoothly sliding into a primed firing position, the ferret's breath caught in his throat. He thumbed the mechanism, and this time it worked perfectly. Brennain's second shot caught the Gnoll squarely in the gut, downing it, at least for the moment. "They came out of nowhere! And my crossbow is proving problematic."

"Tell me something I don't know," Tansy grunted as the ferret closed the distance. Her heavy, wickedly flanged mace was in her hand now, as was her battered shield. It looked like she'd had an ill-informed encounter with a netter, if the remnants snagged in the joints of her armour were anything to go by. The wildcat's expression was one of anger as she raised her shield to deflect a thrown spear. Confusion was the most apparent thing in her eyes, though. "I thought you'd fixed that thing? Anyhow, protect them," she told Bren, pointing to the twins. "Ren's too far ahead."

Bren nodded, drawing his short-sword in his off-hand while casting his eyes around the area for a likely target. Tansy was much more direct in her action. She charged into one Gnoll, a swift shield-bash to the head removing one from her path, while a savage kick to the crotch doubled another over. She wasted no time in caving in the prone Gnoll's skull with fierce blow that slammed into the back of its head with a sickening, wet crunch. The monster did not even have time to scream.

A snarling scream drew the ferret's attention back to his own, more immediate dilemma. He turned just in time to jab his sword awkwardly at a charging Gnoll's midsection. The blade skittered off the barbarian's piecemeal armour, and gouged a shallow but painful slice across its ribs. Bren dropped, throwing himself at his attacker's ankles, and found himself regarding the Gnoll's digitigrade footpaws detachedly. *They look strange up close,* he noted, as the Gnoll crashed to the ground. He aimed his hand-crossbow, and fired three bolts in quick succession into its unprotected back, pride welling in his chest as the mechanism reloaded perfectly each time. The Gnoll did not get up.

"These modifications are totally worth the bolt-cartridge reload bother," he mentioned to the chanting weasel twins, who ignored his pride, locked in their communion with the God-goddess of Trickery, Illusion and the Moon. He grinned smugly at the two further Gnolls approaching him and the weasels with a lot more caution now. After all, they did not know that the weapon only held two more bolts.

Meanwhile, Ren was holding his own against the Gnolls in front of the party. He fired on the run, backing towards the rapidly approaching Tansy while loosing his arrows more as cover than to actually strike home. One rose from behind a rock with a blood-curdling scream, and the old fox turned smoothly, releasing a shaft to take the Gnoll high in the throat without missing a step. At such close range, only the very tips of the fletching were visible in the hollow of the hyena-thing's throat, and even then only for a moment before the feathers were completely hidden by a river of blood and gore.

Ren's bowstring was still humming with release when he was blindsided by a thrown bola that pinned his arms to his sides. He already had his long dagger out of the hidden sheath at his wrist and was sawing at the entangling cords, standing over his bow protectively, when the first hyena-like monster crashed bodily into his side and sent the fox flying. A second tackled him into the ground, pinning him in place while a third followed on top with a crude dagger. Bren watched its arc, overhead in the filthy spotted hands and down towards Ren's body, and his eyes widened as the blade disappeared into the hunter's gut.

"Ren!" Tansy screamed, as she crashed into the knot of wrestling bodies bearing the fox to the ground. Another solid, boot-enhanced kick lifted the dagger-wielder from the pile, dumping him unceremoniously to the ground a few feet from the wildcat with a strangled exhalation. She wrapped the fingers of her shield-arm in the mane of a second, and pulled it to its knees allowing her to swing her mace in an underhanded arc that lifted the Gnoll from the ground, obliterating its jaw with the force of the blow. The third rolled onto its back just in time for Tansy to raise her booted foot and stomp down on its throat, crushing its larynx beneath her heel. The hyena-creature clawed fruitlessly at the wildcat's armoured boot, lacking the strength to reach higher to the unprotected spots at the back of the cat-warrior's knee and thigh. Tansy twisted her foot, causing the Gnoll to make a sound that might have been a yelp, if it could get any air past its lips. Meanwhile, her gore-stained mace lifted, then fell with all the finality of a battering ram as she buried it square in the centre of the creature's face with a primal scream of rage and anguish. Tansy then stood panting over the wheezing fox, and wrenched her mace from the ruins of the Gnoll's face, shaking off fragments of skull and brain while keeping as many of her enemies in view as possible.

Bren's breath caught in his throat. Ren was down, possibly dying, and he still had two Gnolls facing him down. The ferret shot one of the attackers in the biceps as they moved closer, making him drop his cudgel. It barked something in its own filthy tongue, and Bren recognised the term as something less than flattering.

"I was aiming for your throat," he said by way of insincere apology, as the shot Gnoll's accomplice surged forward, tongue lolling from its jaws and trailing spittle behind it as it screamed a challenge at the shorter ferret.

That's a long tongue, Bren caught himself thinking, before he almost lost his sword in the charging Gnoll's guts. He twisted the blade, spilling a steaming pile of entrails at his feet as the dying hyena-thing landed a solid, ringing blow on the side of his head. Bren saw stars, staggered backwards, then fell, a whimpering mass of muscle and spilled guts bearing him to the ground. Another yell heralded the approach of the other Gnoll, and Bren levelled his crossbow over the struggling, screaming Gnoll's shoulder, before pulling the trigger on his final shot. The bolt struck home solidly just below the dark flesh of the filthy creature's exposed nipple, the white fletching quivering there among the dirty, tawny fur. Behind him, the area around the twins seemed to sparkle and warp as their chanting rose in pitch.

Bren struggled from under the cooling body pinning him in place, even as the Gnoll he shot fell to one knee. He rolled to his feet, then unceremoniously drew his sword's edge across the dying beast's mottled throat, narrowly escaping the weakly snapping jaws. Both of the Gnoll's hands were wrapped around the bolt in its chest, all of which turned dark with gore as it bled from the wound in its neck.

The ferret turned just in time to see Tansy slam her mace into the ground, throwing up a protective circle of divine force around her and the wounded Ren. He could not make out the words she spoke, but recognised it as an older tongue she used in her prayers each morning and evening. Bren stepped around the twins, their own chant rising in pitch and volume as the weird sparkling and unnatural distortion grew in turn. The engineer dropped his bloodied sword, and cast a handful of caltrops between himself and the Gnolls surrounding Tansy and Ren as they turned towards him and the twins instead. As the glow around wildcat and fallen fox seemed to solidify around them, there was a low boom as the weasel's workings came to a head, and the ferret was flung face-first to the floor, as his world went dark.

Dirty water hit his face, dragging him back to the present. He hacked and coughed, pushing the invading fluid out of his nose and mouth, and found himself strangely grateful at how the water was helping clear the blood caked over his eyelids. His nose was less grateful, as it caught the rank, bitter scent of the stagnant water. *Please*, the ferret hoped, *let it be water*. The guttural voices and near hysterical laughter that followed his pathetic coughing set his teeth on edge and raised his hackles instantly.

Gnolls.

Realisation spurred Brennain on to get his eyes open, and after a strained attempt to rub his face on his shoulder, enough of the stuff gumming his eyes shut gave way and he got one eye open. He was on a pile of something uncomfortable—backpacks he thought—and he was definitely tied up. His tail was tucked into his boot, and strapped to his leg with a couple of leather strips. The ferret bristled his whiskers, and tried not to gag on the filthy water and the pungent scent of a Gnoll warband.

"The Korrok... it is awakes!" declared one of the larger, dirtier males. The brute lifted one leg and planted a heavy kick on Bren's ass. The force of the blow lifted the scrawny ferret from the ground, and he twisted in mid air on instinct, taking the brunt of the fall on his hip and shoulder. He rolled onto his side, and looked up at his assailant, with an expression that he truly hoped was defiant.

Brennain's mind raced, as he tried to make sense of the situation. The broken common tongue, the black cord tied around each Gnoll's left ankle, and the smell. Then he noticed the grey bandage binding the monster's right biceps, and the stinking poultice smeared on its chest. *Oh, I shot that one. The one kicking me and yelling 'weasel' in Gnollish.* Then, *Where are the twins?*

"You little dart gun not good to kill Dagra, Korrok!" the big, brutish Gnoll sang, the emphasis on every other syllable, stepping in to throw another solid kick at the ferret's ribcage. The Gnoll repeated his refrain, lashing out with another kick every time he stressed his rhythm. Bren took the blows with grunts and whimpers, and rolled to one side to put some space between them, before locking eyes with the swaggering bully.

"Really? It sure seemed to make you squeal like a stuck pig when I shot you, Bogra" Bren countered, throwing in a little of his knowledge of their tongue, a word he believed translated as 'One who cleans the latrines'. "I mean, you dropped your weapon and rolled around like I'd kicked you in the balls, and the noises you—"

This time, the kick caught Bren full in the face, snapping his head back against the packs he was lying on, and making his eyes water and his head swim unpleasantly.

"Shut up!" Dagra yelled, "Shut up shut up shut up!" All attempts to mock the ferret with out of tune cadence were thrown aside as the Gnoll placed a leather-wrapped foot on Bren's stomach. Dagra leaned forward, letting his weight rest on the smaller ferret relentlessly. "You coward! Coward use little cog bow," the enraged monster spat, along with a rapid-fire barrage of his own native tongue that Brennain had no hope of following. "Strong warrior use spear, club, axe. Own strength, not city magic and book secrets."

Brennain felt that he should retort with a snappy come-back, but right now, the stars circling his eyes and the foot on his stomach made it really hard to focus. Instead, he coughed, spat, and thought he saw a tooth in the blood-laced phlegm on the front of his tunic. A chorus of insane giggles erupted on all sides of the ferret, sounding like an army of Hyena-things around him. But he had only seen six, maybe seven before everything had slid out of focus.

A vice-like grip took his muzzle, lifting his face to stare blearily into a pair of mad, bloodshot eyes, as the technophobic Gnoll raged inches away from him.

"You taste as good if I kick you all way to camp as you do if carried, Korrok!" Dagra screamed, before Bren lost the ability to concentrate on what was being shouted at him. He rocked back, groggily, then managed to roll onto his side and vomit. The Gnoll stood, his expression one of disgust as he pointed to the smallest of their number. He then sneered, addressing the smaller Gnoll too quickly to Brennain to translate. He caught more uses of 'Korrok', the Gnollish word for 'weasel', as well as a few words for the moon, 'stench' and what appeared to be a name, 'Ankil'. After throwing one last kick at the curled up ferret, Dagra growled, and stalked off towards the camp-fires, head held high.

'Ankil' heaved his shoulders in a sigh, and stepped forward as the group dispersed, leaning heavily on his spear. He ignored Bren's coughs and splutters, and let his eyes and ears sweep over the darkened plains, away from the main Gnoll camp.

Gnolls, thought Bren, fighting to ignore the pain of his beating. *What do I know about Gnolls... What did I read before?*

I remember looking up some anthropology book for burial practices in desert tribes... There was that section on Gnoll society and practices and I got all hung up on their courtship rituals, their harem culture, dominant females that mate with the best warriors, but only when they were in heat. Glad we don't have that problem in the cities any more. Heh, the public induction rituals must have been something. Not to mention how they're still packing the wild animal sheathed arrangement.

Wait, he thought, as his thoughts drifted towards the more erotic. *Male Gnolls bully the smaller ones, when the females aren't in heat, they bugger each other stupid any chance they get. The smaller ones, though, they never get to...*

A plan began to form in Bren's head. A sordid, filthy, stupid plan. But it was just stupid enough to work. Or was that just his dick doing the thinking? The growing tightness in his breeches suggested the latter, but his options seemed pretty limited at the moment. It was time to put his shaky command of Gnollish to test.

"Salutations," Brennain coughed, propping himself up awkwardly on one elbow. "Ankil?" The overly formal word was the only one he could remember.

The young Gnoll's ear flicked, but his head did not turn. Ankil continued to stare out over the plains, watchful and attentive.

"Ankil," Bren insisted, tenaciously. "Salutations Ankil. How many—" he paused, groping for the words that would at least get his point across. "How much they fuck you?" the ferret taunted, before another series of coughs silenced him for a while.

That got a reaction. Ankil started to snarl, even as the fur on the back of his neck and shoulders stood on end. "Shut fuck up," he growled, trying to make his higher-pitched, almost boyish voice sound more threatening. His grasp of Common was not as strong as the bigger hyena's.

"How many dicks they make you suck, Ankil?" Bren asked, once he caught his breath again. He threw in a weak mime, a crude gesture to reinforce his shaky Gnollish. "You sick of being clan Matriarch? You want get your own fuck? Wait few summers before you get chance to, Ankil. You too small." The ferret paused, sure he had tripped over his grammar at some point.

The young Gnoll thumped the butt of his spear on the ground. "You're smaller," he snarled. "What is stopping Ankil from making you his woman?" A threat, it seemed, if Brennain was understanding Ankil's accent correctly. One he was counting on.

"Not this one," he countered, wriggling around to get his hindquarters in the picture. "All tied. Any man that want can just breed, and wipe dick on tail when done." The ferret deliberately flicked his tail upwards as he spoke, as much as he could against the binding. *Come on, take the bait.*

Ankil paused, his eyes drawn down to the wriggling weasel's ass. His lips parted slightly, and the tip of his tongue flicked out for just a moment. "You stink," the Gnoll stated after a few moments, in the common tongue. "Stink like fear and sweat and… and hraaka," he spat, using an unfamiliar Gnollish word.

Brennain looked over his shoulder, and fixed Ankil with a stare. "Ankil. Buddy. I've been on the trail for almost a week, in a fight with however many of you guys jumped us, bled on, probably pissed on while unconscious, and probably pissed myself when you beat the tar out of me, so." He shrugged. "I'm sincerely sorry I do not smell at my best right now."

The young Gnoll just looked dumbly at the ferret, obviously not comprehending that little speech. He snorted, planted the haft of his spear on the ground again firmly, and looked out into the plains, dutifully. From where Bren was lying, he could catch the subtle tilt of the Gnoll's head towards him, and the flared nostrils. *Huh, he probably likes the way I stink right now,* he mused.

All this wriggling had purpose, though. Bren had managed to get a thumb hooked into the back of his breeches while he spoke, and with a grunt and a tug, he managed to pull them down after some struggling, exposing the fur of his rather shapely rump. Another wriggle undid the strap for his tail, and allowed the short appendage to twitch aside, still caught by the straps on his thigh. "You're really not interested in this?" he goaded, rolling onto his side as he attempted to kneel, to raise his hindquarters enticingly. His attempt in Gnollish was far less eloquent, however. "Harem butt," were the words Brennain chose, cursing himself for being unable to come up with anything classier.

Ankil just stared straight ahead, his nose twitching fitfully, until a quick glance down at the ferret's raised ass gave Brennain what he needed.

"You know, in the cities, we're a little more civilised," the tech-tinkering thief admitted. "Men do, occasionally, put it to other men, if you know what I mean." He licked his lips, then propped himself up on his forehead and shoulder, while struggling to his knees. Ankil's confused glower suggested a complete lack of understanding. Again, Bren tried to elaborate in Gnollish. "Big cities, more polite." He spread his thighs, and glanced up at the young Gnoll from his compromising position. "No shame when man is harem butt. I like laying with men." He switched back to Common, grimacing a little. "Just use some spit to make it easier."

The younger Gnoll was looking down now, nostrils flared, while his spear was starting to droop. *His other spear, though, looks quite lively,* Bren noted. He couldn't help it; his eyes naturally gravitated that way. *And, to be fair, Ankil's one hell of a lot more attractive than the other, older Gnolls I've had the pleasure of knowing recently. But once he's close enough...* The ferret's fingers strayed over the belt around his waist, reassuring himself that it, and the his ticket out of here, were still in place.

More wriggling—a movement with which ferrets have much skill—and Bren had his breeches down to mid thigh. He started to pull one knee free, while flagging the base of his tail towards his captor. "Come on," he urged. "I don't offer this up very often."

Ankil replied by stepping forward, and pulling his loincloth to one side. What Bren saw, obscured by his own hindquarters in part, was a sheathed, mostly animalistic member quite unlike those he was used to. *Huh, the diagrams were pretty close after all. This is going to be edu-cational.* The dark red flesh was slick with arousal, more of that fluid dripping from the tip. The ferret tinkerer licked his lips in anticipation, before sternly reminding himself that his aim was to escape, not to end up trapped on that monster for the night. He rolled onto his back, now that his breeches were mostly off, and edged towards the Gnoll, coinci-dentally managing to grip his belt in one tied hand. With his own half-hard prick flopping around lewdly on his stomach, his downy-furred nuts jostling beneath it, the ferret pushed up his hips, and addressed the Gnoll once more. "You might need to lift up my legs, or at least one of them," he suggested, "But you'd need to undo the bonds." Again, he switched to Gnollish. "Cut ropes?"

Strong, rough fingers wrapped around that ankle, yanking it up sharply, along with the one it was tied to. Bren yelped, caught off-balance, and slipped. Ankil sliced the leather thong binding Bren's ankles with his knife, then dropped it on the ground beside him. He spat into his free palm, and slathered the saliva along the length of his dick, now fully rigid and exposed. Bren's claws scrabbled on the ground as the Gnoll knelt, pulling him further towards him. Ankil brought one knee down across the ferret's thigh, pinning it in place, as he roughly grabbed the bound weasel's hip. All the while, his eyes never left Bren's own. The sentiment there was obviously one of distrust and vigilance than anything romantic, however. After a brief movement, Bren felt firm, moist heat slide between the cleft of his cheeks. Contorting his back while reaching as far as he could managed to bring his belt into tantalizing contact with his fingertips, until Ankil's slickened tip caught at his pucker, giving him no warning at all before a rough push penetrated him and the belt danced out of reach.

"Ow, nnggh. Go easier, you'll—" Bren's protests were cut off by a hand wrapping around his muzzle.

"Shut up, this Ankil's time," the Gnoll insisted, but thankfully, he heeded the ferret's advice. At least to some degree. After some grunting and shoving, Bren found himself with his ankle caught between Ankil's chin and shoulder, with one Gnollish hand on his hip, pulling him onto his captor, with the other still wrapped around his muzzle. Luckily, his breeches were still caught around his free ankle. Freedom was still within reach. After giving a sigh of contentment, Ankil released his grip on Bren's snout, and ground firmly into the ferret's ass, sending waves of shuddering pleasure through the speared mustelid, despite the now mild discomfort that entry caused.

"Much better this way, huh?" Bren asked, panting. The regular motion swung his breeches back and forth, and after a few attempts, he managed to snag his belt again. He pulled it free, and started to search for his last-ditch means of defence. He didn't need to put too much of an act on to show the Gnoll his enjoyment, either. It actually did feel pretty good. "When there's no fighting?"

Ankil answered with a shrug, a grunt, and a smooth motion of his hips, that drew back a few inches, before burying himself back to the hilt with a snarl. Bren's eyes widened, and he held back a whimper by biting his lip as he forced himself to relax. Just as he was getting comfortable again, Ankil gave the ferret's rump another bucking thrust, and another, quickly gathering speed.

What the Gnoll lacked in skill and talent, he made up for with his eagerness. The angle made things that much more pleasurable for the ferret too, feeling rough, insistent pressure on that hidden spot a few inches in that made his toes curl, and his tongue loll. Through the panting and whining, the mustelid managed to hold onto his aim—his claws finally found the hidden seam in his belt, and deftly drew forth a short bodkin with a curved, needle-like blade. He gave the yielding hilt a squeeze, and then turned the hooked tip away from his body. The ferret pushed his way closer to the Gnoll enjoying the hospitality of his body, and prepared to strike. Noticing that the Gnoll's head was tilted back, and his eyes were rolling back into his head, Bren turned his wrist, and pressed the tip of his needle-dagger into the soft flesh of Ankil's inner thigh.

The sound that came from Ankil's throat was no word Bren recognised, but the rage in his eyes was easily recognisable. "What you—" Ankil started to say, before his body sagged. "What..." but before the Gnoll could repeat his question, he fell across Bren's body, and started to snore loudly.

"Thank the Gods," Bren muttered, shrugging the Gnoll's sleeping form from him, and rolling to a sitting position across his hips. He could not help a small moan of pleasure as the Gnoll's still hard prick nudged at sensitive areas inside him again. After bending down to snag Ankil's obsidian dagger with his teeth, Bren tossed it behind him, dexterously catching the grip in one hand, before setting to work at his bonds. Seconds later, he was free. He rubbed his wrists to get the blood flowing again, while rocking his hips back and forth almost without thinking about it. He blinked, glanced down, and slowly wrapped his fingers around his own arousal, pulling back gently to tease the dark skin away from his plump, slippery cockhead.

This won't take a minute, Bren assured himself, before quickly making use of Ankil's still hard dick within him, aiming to leave the poor Gnoll with a sticky souvenir across his chest and stomach for his troubles. He steadied himself with one hand, while the other stroked himself faster, and his hips rocked back and forth to urge the firmness within him to nudge all the right places. *Won't take a minute,* Bren insisted, as his tongue lolled from his muzzle and his panting quickened.

Despite Brennain's special talents being in other, more esoteric areas, his short time travelling with Ren had taught him a thing or two about tracking. Thankfully, tracking a huge group of Gnolls with no regard for their own stealthiness was far from hard. It did not take him long to pick up their path through the savannah, and track it back to what appeared to be their village. That is, if you could call a loose collection of tents pitched around a mostly ruined sandstone villa in the scrubland a village. Sneaking, on the other hand, was one of Bren's greatest gifts. Picking his way through the shabby tent town was well within his abilities, and he reached the central stone structure quickly and without incident. The Gnolls in the settlement were few and far between, he observed, and not especially vigilant. As he pressed himself up to the shady side of the villa, Brennain noticed a number of shapes and sigils carved into the soft stone. The roughened edges and lack of evenness suggested that they had been cut into the walls with primitive tools and a lack of civilised skill, but the symbols themselves were no language the ferret recognised. After a few moments perusal, he shrugged to himself, shouldered his retrieved pack, as if to reassure himself that it was there, and quickly slinked up the stairs on the outer wall to the building's flat roof.

From here, Bren peered over the low ridge around the edge of the roof, and surveyed his surroundings once more. There were a few more of the hyena-creatures in the camp, drinking, gambling, fighting. He turned his attention back to the roof. It had a large square hole that, on further investigation, revealed a surprisingly well-kept garden complete with an ornamental fish pond and even an alabaster statue of a nude human female. The pristine white shape had been crudely splashed with paint—at least Bren hoped it was paint—around the crotch and breasts to leave dark red stains. A wide, clown-like idiot grin was painted across the ornament's sober expression, and the eyes were two sooty black splotches, one larger and noticeably higher than the other.

Brennain cased the rest of the garden. After deeming it safe, lowered himself over the edge. He dropped to the ground without a sound, and quickly ducked behind the nearest convenient chunk of foliage. His eyes lingered on the defaced statue for a moment, then he occupied himself with finding a way into the building. Almost immediately, something caught his attention. A beaded curtain shifting back and forth in the still air, there was no wind to move them. A whisper of tattered silks brushing against the beads warned him of something's approach. Then, the silken ribbons parted to reveal her, the broad, physically impressive figure of the warband's leader—a Gnoll Matriarch, easily recognisable as such despite her lack of the expected arms and armour.

At over seven feet tall, the hyena-like creature dwarfed Brennain's five and a half feet. He crouched involuntarily, making himself harder to notice in the shadows of the garden as his ears plastered themselves back against his skull in fear. A few seconds later, the scents hit him. Clashing perfumes and fragrances, clumsily over-applied in a mockery of the high-society women of the city states. Sandalwood and vanilla. Bren had met a woman sporting that mix of scents over a year ago, and he still had some of the jewellery he had stolen to fence after that memorable night. Then he caught patchouli and rose, and recalled the week he spent in an older woman's parlour, and the speedy retreat he had beaten wrapped in her scented silks, his pockets heavy with gold and silver. The overpowering smells infiltrated his nostrils, and with a dawning sense of horror, the ferret realised that he was about to sneeze. He quickly covered his nose with one palm, bit his lip, and tried to hold the incriminating noise-to-be in check as if his life depended on it.

He tasted blood, and bit down harder, concentrating on the pain. The sneeze passed. The towering Gnoll female strode towards the pool, adjusting her silks and finery around her, then turned her head slowly, one dark eye looking straight at the ferret's hiding place.

"Will you stay there all day?" she suddenly asked, her head turning to show the sneer on that blunt, powerful muzzle. "Or are you of a mind to gaze longingly at my haunch for awhile longer, thief?" The hyena-thing's short tail swished, disturbing the silks enough to expose a curve of rump, a hint of thigh, and the Matriarch stepped back slowly, turning towards the hiding ferret.

Taken aback by the knowledge that he was spotted, Brennain hesitated.

"Come, come," she said, impatiently. A faint hint of annoyance crept into her tone.

Brennain stepped clear of the obscuring plants, covering his shock with a low, courtly bow. *Think, think, think,* he urged himself, fighting to keep his ears from flattening to his skull timidly. *Flattery. Try flattery. Keep her talking. She's a barbarian trying to look like a noblewoman. Use that.*

"My lady," he said, his smooth, almost smarmy tones belying his fear. "If I were able to drink in your beauty for time eternal, I would skulk in the shadows at each and every opportunity." Inwardly, he shuddered. *Please tell me this is what she wants to hear.*

The Gnolless responded by spreading her arms, causing the silks to fall from one shoulder to expose a large, rounded breast. The ferret couldn't help but stare at the dark-skinned nipple peeking from the tawny, spotted fur. "Behold my majesty," she invited, barking a laugh that stretched into a titter, then a giggle, before it finally stopped. In those long moments, Bren forced a smile, and let his eyes wander, looking for anything that could be considered a weapon on her person. A dagger. A heavy sceptre or chain. Anything that could cause him hurt. He was momentarily distracted by the series of gentle curves swelling against the silk draping her torso. *She's got more than two teats, should have expected that after Ankil,* he found himself thinking. The Matriarch's voice caught his attention quickly, though. "It smells like you have enjoyed one of the men of our tribe already. And you have the gall to call *us* the barbarians," she finished with an amused snort.

Bren froze, and straightened up. His smile grew forced and stiff as his mind raced for a reply.

"Though if you managed to get here without being seen, evade the marauding warbands in the savannah, and almost escape my notice, there must be something to you, weasel. Come here," she ordered, pointing to a spot in front of her. "Kneel. Let me see you. Perhaps I could gain something from your intrusion, and you too, should I see something of worth."

"Your command of the common tongue is impressive," Bren waffled, dipping his head in another small bow. He did not, however, move toward the indicated spot. "Were you tutored, or are you one of those naturally skilled with such things?" He raised his head once more as he spoke, and was greeted with sharp words, and a growl.

"Be quiet, any questions shall be from me," the Matriarch insisted, gesturing towards the ground before her "Do as you are told, kneel, and wash my feet," she suggested, splaying her toes as she did so. An offhanded gesture with one hand lifted an orb of water from the nearby pond, and floated the bubble towards Bren. He watched the globe's approach with confusion, before the Gnolless snagged his attention by snapping the fingers of her other hand. A splash of water from the floating glob caught him full in the face.. "Take off your shirt, and use that, while I think."

"My shirt?" Bren asked, still refusing to approach. "My lady, surely you are too forward. We should share tea and sweetmeats, talk about ourselves, get to know one another before I even think about touching your feet." Her strength of will, and the way she expected to be obeyed reminded him faintly of Tansy. Bren straightened his back, and stood taller, raising his chin in defiance.

The Matriarch's tone changed suddenly, as if two voices spoke, interwoven and overlaid. One was hers, though harsher, lacking the more refined notes. The other was impossibly low-pitched, and yet shrill. Grating, while somehow ingratiating. "Remove it, kneel, and wash my feet. Come on, rat. They won't clean themselves."

Forced against his will to comply, Brennain removed his protective shoulder-piece, shrugged out of his jerkin and under-shirt. He folded the garment into a pad, and touched it to the magically floating water. It shrank some as the fabric soaked up a portion of the liquid, then the ferret dabbed delicately at the hyena's toes. *What in the world?* Bren asked himself, though he could not help but carry out her command. He bared his teeth in a grimace, and even managed a low growl of defiance before a steely glare silenced him.

"The pads, you stupid city-dweller," the Matriarch scolded absently, only a hint of the second voice weaving its way between her words, now. Brennain had the strength of will to look up, seeing another gesture, which dragged an ancient wood and metal bench from against a stone wall to stop behind his captor. She sat upon it, crossed her legs, and proffered dusty paws to the engineer with an encouraging sound. "Come, now. I am told this is one of the ways you civilised sorts initiate courtship."

"Only about a hundred years ago," Brennain replied, unable to stop himself. *So her control isn't absolute, I suppose. What is she? Some kind of wizard?* "And generally, a man would court a lady's favour because he wanted to, not because she used witchcraft to compel him." He did, however, start to rub the dust and grime from those feet while his mind raced for an escape plan. After a moment, he added, "My lady," to his statement.

The Matriarch responded with a lazy wave. "Not witchcraft. My patron may be somewhat behind the times, I admit," she said, breezily. "But it has told me quite a lot about you and yours. Especially about those twins we captured. Mmm, yes. It was especially interested in the twins."

"They're here?" the ferret asked, ears canted forward in sudden, rapt interest. His question was rewarded with a scowl from the Gnolless, and she raised her foot. Taken by surprise, Bren caught a face-full, the recently washed pads smearing across his muzzle.

"Do try to concentrate. The fate of the twins is no concern of yours. In your position, in fact," the hyena growled, with a toothy smile that didn't seem to reach all the way to her eyes, "I would be worrying more about your own pretty hide. Grey and black, quite striking. Handsome and resourceful, hmm." She lifted her other foot, and pushed it into the ferret's hands for cleaning. "And a quick tongue. One wonders how well it can be put to other uses, hmm? All characteristics I could benefit from using. Yes. I believe we can come to an arrangement."

Recoiling from the foot in his face, Brennain leaned back, and tentatively started to clean the second paw. "An arrangement," he replied, his tone dubious. "You tell me where the twins are, we leave without taking what we came for, and we speak no more of this?"

"Oh, stars, no," the hyena replied, her braying giggles threatening to turn into crazy, grating laughter. "Not even. You leave me the gift of your seed, I nurture and grow it within me, and add your traits to my tribe's bloodline. No twins or deals for you, merely freedom to return home with your short, pretty tail between your legs. How does that sound?"

Brennain was, for one of those rare moments in his life, at a loss for words. His mouth tried to form them, but all that came out was confused, stuttering sounds. Eventually he managed, "...what? You want a *cub*?"

The Matriarch fixed his gaze with her own. "Do you really think that would work? No, of course not, just your seed. Your essence. Your talents and ability. You gift me your seed, I take what I need from it with the power of my patron, strengthen my tribe, and you go on your way."

Again, Brennain just stared. "Your patron," he said, finally. "From what I knew, you Gnolls worshipped the Gods within the desert sun."

"A fool," the hyena-thing replied, with a snarl. "A limiting, backwards fool. The stars know all, do all. Their gifts are myriad like the points of light in the heavens. The face of their subject, the moon, sees and knows all. The cold between them is at my command, the enormity of their dwelling space, their knowledge and their power is mine. They allow me to do as I state," she insisted, her mood shifting from smug to wrathful in an instant. The faint gleam in her eyes, as well as the fixed snarl and the smattering of foam at the corner of her mouth was suddenly obvious.

"The stars can do all that?" Bren asked, choosing his words carefully as he wrapped one of the woman's paws in his damp shirt, slowly rubbing at the pads. He licked his lips, feeling himself start to react to her sheer force of presence. *She's crazy,* Bren thought. *Moon-addled, star-struck, crazy. But she's kinda hot,* he found himself deciding. *In that 'older woman' sorta way. Wait, is she making me think that?*

"All that and more," she replied, her breathing slowing again as any perceived slight or conflict were abruptly forgiven or forgotten. "So. Do we have a deal, weasel?" The Gnoll shifted her foot abruptly, splaying her toes to catch Bren's throat between them. There was no strength in that grip, but the sharp claws digging into his skin were adequate threat on their own. "Or do I kill you now, feast on your corpse, and offer up your brain and balls to the stars above?"

Don't. Stick your dick. In crazy, Bren. Don't. Though if the alternate is being eaten, maybe just this once? I need to get close to her.

The ferret held still, swallowed, then nodded slowly, resting his hand upon the foot at his throat. "My lady," he replied, eyes flicking between the Gnoll's toes, and her own insane glare. "Is that any way for a lady to speak to her ardent suitor?" He dipped his head, and pressed his lips to the Matriarch's clean, damp pads. A moment later, his tongue snaked between them, teasing at the tender, ticklish flesh hidden by moistened fur. *Less of the killing, lady. More of the seduction. I can get behind that,* he mused. "How would we go about such an arrangement, amicably?" He kissed one pad, then another, then took the largest of her taloned toes into his mouth to suck gently.

"Oh, there is but one way," the Matriarch replied, curling her toes to push just a little further into the ferret's muzzle. She shrugged her shoulders to let more of her faded silks fall from her body. "You treat me like a woman of the city, seduce me, wear down my defenses with clever words and the tongue that speaks them, and eventually mate with me." She then spread her thighs lewdly, a glimpse of her dark-skinned sex visible for a moment as the silks settled.

This is crazy, Bren thought, stunned into inactivity and silence once more. *So totally crazy,* but the feeling of tightness at his crotch was becoming uncomfortable. *She could break me so easily, but...* He removed her toes from his mouth, and bestowed a long, slow lick from her dewclaw-pad to the ball of her foot, a low groan accompanying the motion. *Why can't more women in the city know exactly what they want from a guy?* "Forgive me, but how can I trust a woman so powerful, with the power of the stars at her beck and call?"

"We do not eat our mates, like the insects of the desert," the Gnoll insisted, chuckling quietly at the ferret. "You have nothing to fear, as long as a deal is made. Bring me wine from the stand, and fruit. Tempt me, pamper me, make me feel like a fine woman of the city." As she spoke, her chuckling grew and rose between her words, until at the end, those insane giggles were bubbling from her lips near-constantly. One hand fluttered towards the corner of the garden, and Bren spotted the mentioned stand with food and drink upon it. He bowed his head, hands by his sides, and retrieved the carafé and glass.

"Should I pour for m'lady?" he asked, as he presented the glass towards the Matriarch, while swirling the deep red liquid around the insides of the flask. "Or would you prefer to drink directly, perhaps?"

"Pour," she commanded, taking the glass in a clawed hand. "Then fetch me a pomegranate and cut it for me. Treat me to a taste of your civilisation, the regard you have for your painted, silk-draped lady-folk." Her smile grew wider, with more teeth becoming visible. A lewd movement of her hips towards the ferret snagged his attention, drawing his eyes downwards again. "Concentrate, weasel. Concentrate!" the Gnolless chided, with another warbling titter.

Bren tilted the carafé carefully, filling the woman's glass with wine, then bowed low before retreating back to the table. He trotted back quickly with a pomegranate and a small knife, which he used to peel back the thick, orangey rind. "How would you like me to serve you the fruit, my beauty?" he asked, adopting an easy, inviting smile. He slipped into the role of adoring, eager to please lover quite easily, though a nagging doubt still remained at the back of his mind. How much of this was his choice, and how much of it her magic?

"One ruby red seed at a time," replied his maddened captor, her tongue sliding over her lips suggestively. "Careful with your fingers, though. I have been known to bite. Chew. And swallow," she continued, before cutting off with a whooping laugh, which she silenced with a hand. "Mmm-hmm. Ahah. Fruit, now." She opened her mouth, and waggled her tongue at the ferret without a hint of shame or any attempt to disguise it. The ferret found his focus on 'playing along' waver again, and reached down as tactfully as he could to adjust the way his growing arousal strained at his garments.

The engineer dug one single seed from the cut fruit with his fingertips, and gently laid it upon that proffered tongue. His fingers were slurped, and briefly suckled upon before the Gnolless drew back, smacking her lips in appreciation. She washed the tiny morsel down with another swig of wine.

"More," she demanded.

Brennain obliged, one seed at a time, suffering the indignity of having his fingers teased and held between those fearsome, bone-cracking jaws. A stirring in his breeches caused his ears to flatten, as the Matriarch dragged her tongue slowly from the base of his outstretched finger, all the way to the tip, which she then wrapped her lips around and proceeded to suckle with loud, shameless lip-smacking.

"Perhaps the lady hungers for more than fruit seeds," Brennain suggested, testing the waters with a faint smile that his head did not quite echo. The growing stiffness at his crotch was another matter though. *Damn you*, he thought to himself, fighting the urge to shake his head. *And damn me, and my staff, and my sex drive. This isn't the prize, they're... somewhere else.*

The Gnolless replied by grabbing at his gently twitching breeches, and squeezing the thickening shaft they did not quite hide. Bren squeaked, and pulled away briefly, before leaning into the grope with a roll of his hips.

"You could say that," she admitted, taking another swig of her wine, draining the glass. "More wine," she insisted, gesturing towards a pile of pillows by the pond, dragging a few of them to pile on the bench behind her with that arcane power she demonstrated.

Brennain's sharp eyes noted a brief gleam at her throat, hidden by the rich silks and scarves the Matriarch wore. He bowed, and retreated to the wine table, undoing the fastenings on his breeches on the way. Once there, he dumped the half-finished pomegranate in the fruit bowl while picking up the wine carafé, and a second glass. "May I?" he asked upon his return, while tilting the wine-flask to the hyena's proffered glass. "My throat is a little dry."

The Gnolless' eyes dropped to the undone breeches, brushing them aside to reveal the ferret's turgid member, moisture darkening the skin at the tip while making the slightly exposed glans glisten. "Your cock isn't," she stated, plainly, before trailing off in yet another fit of crazed giggles. "By all means, wet your whistle then dip your wick, my pretty-pretty weasel." She drained her glass in one gulp, tossed it behind her to shatter on the ground, and settled back in the pillows, spreading her thighs while brushing her silks aside, to reveal the dark lips of her sex amidst the bush of thicker fur there. Another gesture at her neck pushed aside more silks, revealing the first, and largest of the breasts on her right side, with a thick, proud nipple that matched the ebon skin of her netherlips. She cupped said breast with one hand, and rubbed the nipple delicately between her fingerpads, leering at Brennain as a thoroughly unladylike thread of drool dangled from her lips.

Oh Gods, she really wants this, the ferret thought to himself, while looking his soon-to-be lover over. In other situations, this could be quite pleasant, but now... *I kinda do, too. Not just for the twins, either.* He became very aware of the heat at his cheeks and ears, and wondered just how obvious the flush of colour was to the woman. Bren steeled himself by draining his glass and mirroring her throw, letting it shatter on the ground with a high, clear crash. He pushed aside the front of his breeches before joining the Gnolless on her bench, crouching between her thighs. He lowered his face to her crotch, making a show of inhaling deeply. Her earthy scent replaced the sweet wine and fresh pomegranate in his nostrils. "The first course," he quipped, before dragging his tongue across those lips, skilfully searching out the hooded nub they hid, the place he'd learned to pay particular attention to when with a woman.

"Oh, civilisation," she moaned, hooking both ankles behind Bren's thighs, pulling him closer to her. "How I love your little customs." The

Matriarch's words gave out to a low, contented buzz punctuated with reflexive yelps and chortles here and there, while the rocking of her hips pushed an engorged clitoris against Brennain's tongue—one that surprised him with its size. Undeterred, the ferret wrapped his lips around it, suckling at the hot flesh firmly, while bringing up a hand to stroke his thumb across those moist pussy-lips, before gently easing it inside. He pulled down there, even as he tugged up at the erect nub between his lips, coaxing a groan and growl from the Gnolless beneath him. He continued to tease and play with lips, tongue and fingers for a few minutes longer, before a frustrated grunt from the Matriarch followed by a set of clawed fingers fastening itself in his scruff made his head snap upwards. She pulled him forward, settling his hips against her inner thighs, then tugged his head up against her largest exposed breast. "Do come in," she urged, her voice low with veiled threat and animal lust. Another gesture called a breath of wind to blow across the back of his neck and fluttering ears.

A deft movement of his hips dragged his straining shaft through the hot, moist valley of the Gnoll's sex, painting his own flesh with a mix of his spittle, and her own eager juices. "Oh, I shall," he murmured into her breast as, with a slight change of angle, he guided his arousal into the wet, needy heat between her thighs. *This isn't so bad,* Bren's dick told him as he hilted smoothly—one of the advantages of being with a woman over a man, he thought—and he held himself there with a shudder, enjoying the sensation of pressure and slick warmth pressed all around him from root to throbbing cockhead. When the Hyena wrapped her fingers around the base of his tail, and pulled, he yelped in surprise, and the follow-up grind against his hips with hers deepened that shock, as she all but started to push and pull him back and forth like a wooden toy to achieve her own pleasure. Such was her strength, that each time she pulled him into her, she scooted back slightly in the pillows, tittering excitedly when she realised what her antics were causing.

In reply, he matched her growl with a feebler version of his own, and dragged his teeth cross the flesh of one dark-skinned nipple as he was forcibly moved within her. *They've never done this,* he thought, finding it hard to concentrate as the 'civilised' art of lovemaking became a growling, bucking mess of limbs and animal lust. Just as he neared his climax, another gleam of light at the Matriarch's throat caught Brennain's attention, and he saw it more clearly—an irregular, spiked crystal, a curious shape with no symmetry and odd angles tied around her neck with a slim leather thong. His fingers dug into the pillows they rutted in tightly, and old silk ripped beneath his claws. He stared at the bauble, and how it was worn. *That's important*, he assured himself. An instant later, it fled his mind as she ground and wriggled against him, a yip-yip-bark of exultation sounding from her throat that pushed him over the edge too, causing his vision to blur, and his ability to concentrate on anything but the sensations to leave him completely.

The two of them laid there, limbs entwined, as Brennain absently stroked the fur of the Matriarch's cheek and neck, forgetting where he was for a moment. He rested his head upon her heaving chest with a sigh. The Gnolless just laid there, rocking her hips up against his, panting heavily. She let her arms rest by her sides, and Bren seemed to cuddle closer, bringing his hands down over her biceps and wrists as they lay, recovering from the exertion.

"Your gift will strengthen the tribe," the Matriarch gasped, her wind still not yet recovered. "For that, we thank you. It seems a pity that you must remain as a slave," she muttered.

Brennain answered with a grunt, seeming spent and exhausted. He was in no real state to argue in a typical post-coital male fashion.

"The disciples of the false-faced moon will strengthen our patron," she went on, "once it has drained their strength in the temple below, and our tribe shall glow in its adoration, strong enough to take our rightful place in the thrones and cities of the green lands." Her eyes were blank, shining as she ranted.

"You're monologuing," Brennain finally pointed out, slowly wriggling down the woman's form, to start massaging at her freshly-washed feet. He paused a moment to suckle again on a toe as he slid from the bench with a grunt, his wet, spent cock slapping lewdly on his sweat-and-sex soaked thigh. His strong thumbs dug in between the pads, and the Matriarch arched her back with an indulgent groan.

"So? You are in no position to change things," she stated, with a shrug of her shoulders. "The temple is impregnable without the key, which I hold—" she stopped, and looked up, yanking at her wrist which was now bound to the iron frame of the bench with strong cord. The other was similarly tied where it lay by her side. The Hyena's eyes flared with rage as she struggled to kick at Brennain, only to find her ankles restrained similarly.

Brennain smiled, and continued to massage the hyena's bound feet with one hand, while the other dangled the rough, irregular crystal in front of his now-captive. "I can only assume you mean this?" he teased, bending his head to kiss at the sole of one foot before standing. He produced his curved bodkin from his belt, and touched it to the Matriarch's throat. "How do I get in? Tell me, and you live. Don't, and you die, and I probably figure it out anyway. I'm a very clever thief-weasel when I want to be," he gloated, showing his own teeth in a smug, self-satisfied grin.

Seeing the star-shaped crystal, the Gnoll's whole attitude changed instantly. All fight and fury just drained from her, and she struggled weakly against her bonds. "No no no no, not the shard," she whimpered, tears forming in her eyes. Brennain seemed taken aback, if she hadn't been bound, she could easily have overpowered him hand to hand, the ferret thought. Gnolls, especially females, were far stronger and tougher than a man his size. "Please, please do not harm the patron. You cannot, even if you were to find it. It is powerful, all powerful, and… and…!" She stopped, then smiled, the insanity obvious in her glazed look and crazy grin. "I was right to choose you to strengthen the brood," the Matriarch said with a giggle. "You will find the way if you follow the shard. But you will never unlock its power!" The giggle became a laugh, then a wave of irrepressible barking, yelping sounds that might, if one were generous, call laughter.

"And how do I do that?" Bren asked, shaking the crystal in front of the laughing hyena, "Answer me, damn you!" His fingers curled around her muzzle, and he dangled the charm in her face. "How does it work?"

The laughter did not cease, even muffled by his grip. That is, until the crystal shone with an unhealthy, sickly light that was mirrored for a moment in the Matriarch's eyes, before they rolled up to show the whites. She sighed, shivered, and then lay still. Even as the ferret felt at her neck for a pulse, loud, lazy snores started to resound in the woman's chest as it rose and fell. With a roll of his own eyes, Brennain rearranged her silks to cover her modesties, then wiped himself mostly clean with a scarf before tucking himself back into place. Once he was done fastening his breeches, the stone still glowed, weakly. Bren lifted the stone, examining the chain it hung on. The soft glow at the stone's heart pulsed, and at the brightest point, swayed very slightly away from the vertical, before settling back as the light faded. Armed with this knowledge, he swung it around the room, finding that the glow brightened and the stone tugged almost imperceptibly as it passed by the pool. After another couple of swings, he shrugged back into his jerkin, shouldered his pack, then followed the glow like he would a lodestone, stepping towards the water.

With a backwards glance towards the snoring hyena, Brennain held the crystal out over the pool, watching the glow grow brighter the further out he held it. The thief circled the pool, watching the stone's reaction, and as he turned back towards the centre of the garden, the crystal's light dimmed again. Bren lifted it to eye level, peered at it owlishly, then slowly turned around to face the garden's corner. Again, the stone's glow returned, and was answered by a similar glow from an otherwise unremarkable tile set into the stone. At the tile's centre was a curious sigil—some kind of asymmetric five-pointed star with a weird, curling mark at the centre. Bren traced the mark's outline with one fingertip, and yelped as a spark flew from the carving to his hand. Instead, he brought the glowing crystal closer, shielding his eyes with his smarting hand as the light grew brighter and brighter.

Until he was somewhere else.

Bren could not see a thing. He squeezed his eyes shut, stars dancing behind his eyelids from what felt like a flare of bright light, then opened them. He was still blind. The quality of the air had changed, he noted, and after a few exploratory sniffs he determined that all he could really smell was stone, damp, and moss. The acoustics in this new place suggested that he was in a high-ceilinged, enclosed area. He could hear drops of water hitting the stone floor around him, and faint echoes afterwards. Underground. *A cave?* the ferret thought, as he squeezed the irregular crystal star in his hand, feeling the roughened edges bite into his pads. He still had it, which was reassuring. After passing his free hand in front of his eyes a few times, Bren found he could just about see it, as his eyes slowly adjusted to what he realised was almost absolute darkness. The only sounds of life he could hear were his own.

"Hello?" the engineer called, quietly.

Nothing.

Then he heard his words repeated, though that had to be an echo.

He cleared his throat, and moments later, a cough came in reply. The ferret reached into his pack for his hooded lantern, closed his eyes, and quickly pulled the quick-lighting cord causing it to flicker into life. Another invention of his, and one he was quite proud of. Opening his eyes just a fraction, he let them adjust without blinding himself, and took in his surroundings. He was in what appeared to be a large, enclosed chamber of some dark, green-veined rock. No exits were immediately apparent, but there was a rather solid wall nearby which he quickly sidled up to. Putting his back against something solid made him feel secure.

Now that he had a little more confidence behind him, not to mention the wall, Brennain started to survey his situation more closely. He adjusted the lantern to throw a tighter beam directly ahead, and inched his way along the room slowly.

"Bren?"

The ferret jumped, startled by the sound, and whipped his hand around to cast some light in the direction it came from. It illuminated a sorry figure indeed, but a familiar face. A bruised, battered, and scared looking wildcat.

"Tansy?" Bren could barely keep the surprise and relief from his voice as he spoke.

Tansy covered her eyes with one hand, and lowered her head. "Bren, quit it with the light, you're blinding me!"

Brennain quickly covered the distance to his friend, and put a hand on her shoulder, guiding her back towards the wall. "What happened? Where is this place? What's going on?" he asked, the questions coming in a barrage. He checked the woman for wounds too, noting her lack of armour and weapons, but found only minor cuts and bruises.

"We... we fought. They won. They killed Ren, I didn't see what happened to the twins, or to you. Oh, Bren, by the Gods of the Sun, I'm so glad you found me." Tansy, still with her eyes completely closed to the light, wrapped her arms around Bren's waist, and squeezed tightly.

"I think the twins are alive, they wanted to use them for something," Brennain replied. "I also think it's their fault we were caught, but... I have the key to free them though, that's how I got here. I just don't see a way out. Yet." He did his best to keep the frustration from his voice and sound confident, remembering all the times Tansy had done the same for him. This was a total role reversal, he'd never seen her this scared, or this flustered before. She was the strong one, the rock they could all lean on. "I'll figure it out, though. I always do."

Tansy squeezed Brennain tighter, and pulled herself up to rest her cheek on his shoulder. "You always do, Bren," she agreed, cuddling in close. "I know I can count on you for… everything."

The ferret paused, trying to focus with the distraction. Now that she was so close, he could smell her strongly. His hand stroked down to her hip, and pulled her a little closer. "Aye," he agreed, continuing to look around the room again. Still no obvious exits, he was going to have to start tapping along the walls, or figure out if the crystal could get him out again. His attention was suddenly brought back to other, suddenly more pressing issues, as Tansy's hand snuck between his thighs to squeeze his recovering masculinity. "Uh, what?" he asked, looking down at his friend.

The wildcat's expression was somewhat embarrassed, her eyes wide and innocent as she wore a faint smile. "I couldn't help it," she replied, as her fingers groped for the buttons on the flap of his breeches. "I can smell it, it's driving me wild, Bren."

"This isn't like you," the ferret replied, sounding vaguely unsure of himself. He'd tried seducing Tansy, several times. *She always refused and rebuked me. Something about a vow,* he recalled. *Celibacy? Something like that.* "This isn't you at all, stop."

"Oh, I've wanted this a long, long time, Bren," Tansy assured him. "And given how we're trapped in here, we might as well make things a little more comfortable, right?" One button was now open. "It's not like we'll find the twins, or get out of here, is it?"

"Stop," Bren insisted, gently taking the wildcat's wrists, and pulling them away from his crotch. "You're not yourself, it's gotten into your head, twisted things up." the ferret stated. "Besides, I have a headache. I don't want this. I don't what you this way." *Why does my head hurt so much? He asked himself. It's getting worse.*

The girl's face shifted, giving an annoyed pout, before she vanished utterly. Brennain stared dumbly at the space she previously occupied, then wildly cast his light around the room.

"Perhaps you'd prefer something a little more… manly," came another voice, this time from Bren's left. He turned his torch towards the sound, then widened the beam to reveal the speaker. Ren sat on what appeared to be some sort of throne. Naked. One leg hung over the arm of the seat, while the other was spread wide, draped over the seat itself. One arm hung over the throne's arm, holding a goblet of wine. Bren found his gaze drawn down over that strong, grey-dappled chest, the firm stomach, and to the half-hard, dark-skinned member that jutted lewdly from the older fox's crotch looking like something that would be more at home on a stallion.

"Ren's dead," Brennain replied, ignoring that lazily twitching dick, moisture at the tip glinting in the torch's light. "You're not Ren, I don't want this, and I'm pretty sure that's not what he was packing."

"So?" 'Ren' replied, sipping at his wine while the other hand wrapped around his prick, jerking back and forth casually. "Doesn't change the fact that it'd feel pretty good getting bent over by it, does it?"

"Oh, shut up," Bren stated, raising his voice. "Get out." He lifted the hand holding his torch towards whatever the fox was, and let the crystal dangle from his hand. It gleamed.

"I see," Not-Ren said, before vanishing.

"Hey, hey Bren," another voice said, this time from behind him.

"Yeah, Bren, hey!" said a second, this time slightly higher. The twins?

Bren turned, and the light proved his suspicion. The two young weasels, robes open from throat to stomach, stood where Tansy previously lay.

"This isn't funny," the ferret yelled, stalking towards the twins, light and star-crystal raised threateningly.

"It's not?" "It could be!" The twin simulcra tittered, before one punched the other in the arm.

"Where are the REAL Cara and Jor?" Brennain growled, swinging the torch between them. "Where's Tansy? Where is this place?"

Jor slipped a hand into Cara's robe, cupping his sister's small breast while lolling his tongue at Bren. "Does it matter? We're here now." Cara, meanwhile, was hitching Jor's robe up towards mid-thigh.

The crystal caught Bren's eye again as it started to glow, the closer he got to the twins. He reached out, and touched it to Jor's forehead. The weasel vanished, as did his sister, and air rushed in to fill the gap with a soft pop.

Voluptuous barmaids, strapping barbarian warriors, heaving piles of sweat-soaked bodies. All this and more paraded before Bren's eyes, before the ferret lost his temper. After all, that stimulus was getting him incredibly wound up.

"What in the hells is going on?" Bren demanded, turning in place. All his light touched was walls. Smooth, featureless walls of green-veined stone. He gripped the roughened shard of crystal in his palm, and squeezed in frustration, gasping as one of the irregularly shaped spines stabbed into his flesh, tasting blood.

Answers. You want?

The question did not exactly form in his head, but it wasn't a voice. Some low, insistent buzzing that could be felt in his teeth, or in his brain, rather than heard by his ears. And somehow, he could understand the intent.

"Yes," he called, into the empty air. "Yes, I want answers."

Answers shall then come, was the silent reply. A dull pain made itself known at the back of his mind. *Though perhaps not in the way you would want them.*

Understanding the words started to become distinctly uncomfortable, and Brennain was surprised to find that he was bleeding from one nostril. He pressed the back of his hand to his snout, and nodded his head. "A threat? If that's what it takes." The ferret panned the light of his lantern around the room, slowly.

What is that?

Bren felt a pull on his lantern, then a sharper tug yanked it entirely out of his hands. The beam of light danced crazily around the cavern, illuminating the ground, but nothing else. Brennain suddenly felt that much smaller, that much more alone.

How does this shine a single point so strongly? The presence inquired. *Tell us.*

Anger grew within Bren, and he felt his temper fraying. He retrieved his lantern, and cast the light around the cave again after briefly adjusting the shuttering. "Answers, okay. Well, the interior of the chamber is reflective, and—" Blood streamed from his nose as the dull pain in his head flared to an intense point. Images of the time he spent making and designing the lantern skittered across his mind's eye, and each felt like a fragment of his self was tugged free. He pressed one hand to his nostrils, and searched his pockets for a rag. "You could let me speak, rather than pull my mind apart," he shouted, screwing his eyes shut against the hurt.

Too slow, was the response. *This is better. What else can we find?*

Brennain fell to his knees as an explosion of white hot sensation blossomed behind his eyes. Thoughts of his inventions came unbidden to his attention. His spring-loaded dart trap. His gas-powered repeating crossbow. His failure of a quick-release dagger sheath.

A learned man, the voices mused. Bren was sure there were more than one in that cacophony of silent speech. *Civilised. From the cities? Interesting.* A cold needle jabbed into another set of memories, and this time views of Pendlehaven, the largest city in Silverdale flicked through his head in rapid succession.

"Stop," Brennain gasped. "I... need those." He dropped the lantern, and curled into a foetal position, gritting his teeth to stop himself from screaming. He failed. The pain was intense. He felt warmth run across his cheek and brow. Now his ears were bleeding.

The pain suddenly stopped, or at least abated to a point where it wasn't the only thing Bren could focus on. The image in his head was one of a dandy fop of a nobleman, frozen in time as he bowed to a fennec woman in a ridiculous wig, and a dress that looked more like an overdecorated cake than something someone could comfortably wear.

Oh, Bren thought. *That man's coin-pouch kept me in wine and women for a month.* He marvelled at his ability to recall the encounter, given the circumstances.

What, his invaders asked, *is that?*

Before he could answer, the pain returned, though more manageable now, as more images and memories were rifled through by the unknown intelligence.

Why? This makes no sense. That, what is that.

This time, the memory was of a pair of dogs in stiff-starched uniforms that forced them to look straight forwards, and up slightly. The palace guard, and their ridiculous attire that the Viscount insisted they wear.

"That's civilisation," Brennain replied wearily. "Isn't that what you wanted to know more about?" *I can use this,* he told himself, before conjuring up an image of the Viscount's daughter attending her suitors. He was still in pain, but he was sure it was receding now. "They have to wear that if they have a hope at being granted an audience, you know," he said with a grimace, his lips pressed against the blood-slick stone floor.

This makes little sense. The tone had changed. Now, it seemed unsure and confused, baffled by the choices made by the gentry.

Bren now threw in something ridiculous. A table, set for dinner, with a myriad of different utensils, plates, small bowls, and glasses arranged around the place-mat. *Good luck making sense of that,* he thought. "Each piece is there for a reason," he said aloud, wiping his nose and mouth clear of blood with a handkerchief. "And if you don't know exactly which piece to use for each course of the meal, well. It won't go down well."

But each piece seems interchangeable, the presence noted. *Slight differences in size and position, but nothing that would impede or improve performance for different consistencies of sustenance.*

"Oh, it's nothing to do with anything so sensible," Brennain answered, settling on one knee as he once more picked up his lantern. "Instead it's everything to do with some complex set of rules that no-one remembers making. But like I said, if you get things wrong, your reputation is ruined." *A little embellishment can only help things,* he noted privately. *Wait, what if it can listen in on my thoughts? If it can flip through my memories so easily...* The ferret set his jaw, and straightened his back. "High society has many pitfalls. If you think the table settings are complex, well." He envisioned an envelope on the plate. Ink enhanced with the lustre of gold dust, the usual gaudy and expensive touches that the nobility seemed to think were stylish. "Just wait until you have to reply to an invitation. Or engage in courting. The rules there are even worse."

In his mind's eye, the envelope was opened, the paper inside removed and unfolded. Bren felt little pricks and tugs at his mind as whatever was in his head pulled the words from some barely remembered dinner party.

It seems simple enough. Accept, or reject. The entity's words felt smug, confident and superior.

"And the trap is sprung," Brennain retorted, still scanning the chamber for anything other than darkness, or featureless walls. "You can't just reject the invitation, even if you wanted to. You have to make up a previous engagement, or some other excuse. Telling them flat out that you won't be there is a grave, grave insult. Sign your death warrant amongst your peers, that would."

Noted. Civilised politics seem simple enough. Lie to prevent insult. Truth and flattery to establish trust and connection.

"You wouldn't last a minute while courting a real lady," the ferret went on to say, rubbing at one ear. His hand came away sticky with drying blood. "It's never as simple as that. Similar premise, but very, very different. You can't apply learning or science, it's an art form. Lie to establish trust, or not. Flattery that's sincere to catch, and an outright fabrication to hold. Or the other way around, depending on the situation. It's always different, and you can't predict it."

There was no response, only a slowly spreading warmth from the engineer's temples to the back of his skull. A warmth that was slowly becoming a burn. Brennain fastened his attention on the shifting rules of polite, high society courting, while burying the source of his knowledge—gossip, pillow-talk and the catty annoyance of both serving staff and lesser nobles—as deep as he could manage. He instead concentrated on a pretty young Contessa asking a question, waiting for a response with a smile.

Affirmation is asked for, affirmation given. The thing's tone was slower, more deliberate.

"Maybe. Maybe not. She could be leading you to condemn whatever it is she's asked for an opinion on. You can't know. And if you go delving in her head for an answer, and she ends up with blood on her collar, you're out," Bren insisted. "Blacklisted. You wouldn't be invited to any of the dances or dinner parties after giving a headache to the flower of the city."

What. The word wasn't a question. Bren could feel the pain growing, so he pushed back with more nonsense.

"Do you think this gown makes one's rear look overly large?" asked the nobleman's daughter with a giggle. *"The designer is new, recommended by a friend. Very expensive."*

"You just don't know," the ferret said, his voice now almost raising to a shout. "She might want you to tell her no, of course not, she's beautiful. She may want you to condemn the tailor as untalented and overrated. She may even be expecting you to agree with her that the person that made it deliberately made it that way to embarrass her." Bren sucked in a breath, his volume now a full-on yell. "She might even want you to tell her that her arse is too big, and encourage her to eat less blasted cake, and you'll never, ever know which because you lack the ability to understand us at the most basic level!"

No response at all was forthcoming. The voice was stilled. The warmth in Bren's head gathered to a point, then sudden blinding pain exploded behind his eyes, sending him to the ground once more, hugging his arms to his chest as he whimpered. He cried blood.

Then nothing.

The ferret uncurled from his foetal knot, and wiped blood from his eyes. A scent of ozone and something vaguely floral wafted across his nostrils, something he associated with two young, old friends and their magics. Directly in front of him, he could see the twins. They were sat facing each other, eyes closed, cross-legged. He reached out towards them, only to encounter cold, unyielding crystal. He grunted, smearing blood across the transparent stone, and lurched towards it, suddenly aware of a low buzzing in his ears. Was it coming back? Already?

The Matriarch's pendant swung, and touched the imprisoning block. It instantly faded away to nothing, and the twins stood.

"Grab the shard," Jor said to his sister, as he quickly traced a complex sigil in the air with one finger, empowering it with a divine word. The symbol expanded, and the insistent buzz in Brennain's head intensified in a shriek, before receding to almost nothing.

Cara took the rough crystal from Bren's weakly gripping hand, touched it to her forehead and lips, then tossed it towards the glowing sigil hanging in the air. It hung suspended in the centre of that light, changed from an eerie white to a threatening dark red, then cracked with a high, clear note. The oppressive presence was gone.

Jor snatched the crystal from the air, pocketed the thing, then nodded towards Brennain. Both weasel mage-priests helped the ferret to his feet, and Jor dabbed at the blood streaming from his nose while Cara recited a prayer of recovery, hastening his healing.

"High Society nonsense, good plan. Really scrambled their assumptions. Shorted their thoughts for a while. Well done. But... something you want to tell us, Bren?" Jor said, supporting the weakened engineer as their magic did its work. "You came all that way for us, very telling."

"Do you like us, Bren?" Cara asked, with a giggle. "In *that* way? We're older than we look, you know."

"...wha?" Bren managed. "What happened? What'd you do? It's your fault we're... Where's Tansy?" he gasped, leaning on the twins heavily. "What was that thing? Is it gone? What'd you do," the ferret stammered, squeezing his eyes tightly shut as another wave of nausea overtook him.

"She's upstairs," one twin answered, tilting his head back and flaring his nostrils. "She's fighting her way in. Ren isn't with her."

"You don't want to know what that thing was," said the other. "But it's gone."

"And we did our thing," Jor finished. "Don't worry, we know what's up. That was a rogue shard of the crazy moon god-goddess we worship, and we got what we came for," he said, nodding towards Cara.

The other weasel held up the now-cracked crystal, and grinned. "Let's get out of here," she said, raising it above her head as she began to speak in some strange, garbled tongue that made Brennain's head hurt.

"So... this was all part of the plan," Bren asked, grimacing. "You wanted to get here, get this... nngh."

Everything went dark, at least for Brennain.

Four figures passed through the town's gate, dragging a small wagon behind them laden with sacks and one small strongbox.

"Bren, help pull the gods-damned loot," Tansy ordered, her voice more than a little annoyed.

"No, no, I believe I helped save your life, their life, and our lives in general, and besides, you're far stronger than me," Brennain chided. "Also, you teased me with your delicious breasts in my moment of darkest need then disappeared on me."

"That wasn't me," Tansy grumbled, dropping the wagon's handle as she arched her back, working out all the kinks. "And you know it. And I believe that I saved *your* lives, fighting my way into that sad collection of hovels to get you out, though I couldn't save Ren."

One twin nudged the other, who then stood on Tansy's right, taking hold of the handle. "Actually, it was you, sort of," Cara said, waiting patiently for the wildcat warrior to take up the load again. "Or, at least, how Bren wishes you were."

"But I wouldn't take it personally," Jor interjected, taking a position at the back of the wagon to help push. "He imagined us taking our clothes off and playing with each other right there in front of him. He's a filthy, filthy ferret pervert. A monster!"

Tansy narrowed her eyes at Brennain, and helped pull the wagon towards the inn again, this time with two other sets of hands. "You're lucky that the Gnolls had so much stuff in their shanty town, and that the twins managed to set the ones left chasing an illusion so we could recoup our losses," the wildcat muttered. "And they're right. You're a vile, filthy creature, Bren. There's more to life than getting your dick wet."

"Oh, I agree. I quite like getting my nipples sucked, my toes massaged, and getting something substantial under my tail," Brennain admitted, without any hint of shame. "And you don't because your God thinks it's wrong or something."

"No, it's because I don't want to end up with cubs," Tansy grunted, snapping her jaws at the engineer while the weasel twins laughed behind her. "And because if that happens, I have to leave the temple, so…" She let that trail off, then pulled the wagon into the safe house they maintained in this village. "You can fence that stuff tomorrow, and we'll split the cash. Shame about Ren, we'll have to look for another scout. He was a good man. We can hold a service at the temple, then split whatever money's left between us."

Bren's face fell, as he followed Tansy into the house. "You want us to all pay for his funeral? We don't even have a body," he said, grimacing. "The Gnolls probably ate him."

Tansy fixed Bren with a glare, then stomped up the stairwell. "I burned him after they took you three, once my bastion of sanctuary released us. He is at rest. Goodnight, Bren."

"Tansy."

"What?" She sounded intensely annoyed now.

"Thanks, for saving us, for getting us out of that place, and being so strong, stable and positively smoking hot. Thanks for coming back."

"It's my job, Bren. I had to get them back to get paid. Go to sleep," she called over her shoulder, before disappearing into her room. She slammed the door. But… was she smiling as she went? Bren couldn't be sure.

The twins then fell in on either side of the ferret, as they pulled him towards the stairs.

"Bren," Jor asked.

Cara added, "Bren," with a giggle.

"…Yes?"

"We're scared. Will you protect us tonight?" Jor asked, his face alive with mock-fear and laughter.

93

"You've got such a big sword," Cara added, reaching across to squeeze at his breeches. "Nothing would dare attack us while you swung that around."

The ferret paused. *This was all their fault,* he thought to himself. *And they're going to get away with it, Ren's death, the Gnoll ambush, entirely on their shoulders. I should lay this at their doorstep and walk away. Smug, sarcastic weasels. Chaotic, enigmatic, flirtatious... damned hot weasels. I need to just turn around, close the door, and let them stew in their own mess. They deserve it. But... maybe I can beat them at their own game here. And get some quality time in the sack with them. Yeah. Let's go with that.* He draped his arms over the twin's shoulders, guiding them towards their bedroom, ignoring his own. "You'll both have to help me clean it first," He said with a low chuckle, as they walked through the door, and let it swing closed behind them. This was proving to be an interesting night.

"So how is he?" Jor asked, as he picked up Bren's discarded small-clothes. He sniffed at them, then tossed them over his shoulder to land on the ferret's shoulder.

"Sated. Clueless. Content," Cara replied. She tugged the underwear to rest across Brennain's muzzle, hiding his beatific smile from view as he dozed.

"And the passenger?"

Cara rested the heel of her hand on Bren's forehead. "Similarly clueless, dormant, and probably quite vexed," was the answer, after a moment's concentration. "They're not aware of each other, it knows it's trapped, just..."

Jor finished his sister's sentence. "Just not what it is trapped in. Good. Bren can handle it, for a while at least. He's resilient."

Cara crawled over Bren's chest, and tugged on Jor's clerical choker. "Tired?" She inquired, her voice now a whisper.

"Not in the slightest," the weasel replied, snuggling in against Bren's side as he pressed his lips to hers in a kiss. "Let's see if we can wake him up with a show, hmm?"

The giddy giggle Cara gave in response was enough agreement, as the pair embraced around the sleeping ferret. Bren slept on, reflexively cupping one mustelid's rear in his palm as it brushed against his fingers. His lips curled further in a smile, as the unfelt presence in his head coiled around itself, its rage and insanity smothered in a warm blanket of ferrety satisfaction.

EYES IN THE BLACK

Kandrel

My evening began with a lie. It was both a big lie and a little lie, all rolled into one appealing package. Clasped at my throat was a white pearl, enchanted and beglamored by a witch far from our kingdom's borders. For one night, it would provide me with safety, here in the king's court. Just for tonight, it would make me look like everyone else.

They floated around me, the king's courtiers, in every stage of celebration of Winterdown. The Marble Hall was resplendent in dazzling white. Even though the hall was roofed, a little of the king's own enchantment had brought a light snow that obscured the ceiling. Above, all that was visible were brilliant fae-lights that danced and glimmered off of the flakes of snow. Of course, none of those flakes ever touched the floor—that would be far too slick. Instead, they disappeared just inches before, leaving the broad expanse of the hall's marble floor unblemished in white. Of course. What other color would it be? We all served under the Alabaster King, in his white Marble Court, in the White Kingdom. Everything is snowy. Everything is bright. Everything is milky and pearl and sunny and *white*. Everything. The king was a white elk. His people were rabbits and polar bears and cows and minks and each and every one of them white. Everything, in the king's unimaginably long reign had been white, except for me. Me, the little throwback. Me, the unlucky. Me, the marked, the raven, the *black*.

I am beautiful

How many times must I tell myself that before I believe it? Mother had been a gorgeous oryx, with pelt of snow and horns the color of pearls. Why could I not have inherited that? How many times must I look at those around me and realize just how different they are—no, how different I am? I looked out among the king's court, dressed in white straight to their birthday suits, and here am I, the storm in among the fluffy clouds skidding across the king's sunny sky. But if different isn't beautiful, then being different has made me strong. All the white clouds that surround me might have a silver lining, but me? My lining is solid steel.

Well, at least tonight I'd be one of them. The enchanted pearl at my neck painted my coat a gorgeous white. Tonight, I'd blend in, and tonight I'd meet the king.

The music was playing. It was nothing like the music I'd grown up with. That had been forthright and brash. This was light and airy. Of course I detested it, but who doesn't prefer the music of their youth? I hated the way it lilted and soared, apparently unable to pick a note and stick with it. Still, like it or not, I had to act like I liked it. I had to be another courtier. I had to be inconspicuous. I had to blend in—to get close enough.

So I used all the experience my favors had bought me. How to dance—that had cost me a bit of larceny and a night with a minor noble's son. How to talk like a courtier—that had cost information about whose wife was spending evenings with whose husband. How to move and carry myself like I mattered—that had cost me a lifetime of lying and half of what remained of my precious confidence. I fit in. Or, at least, I didn't stick out so much that people seemed to notice.

The court itself was a dance. All around me, the king's courtiers were going through their paces. Here were a hare and muntjac and sheep, all doing exactly what they should have been doing, in exactly the way they should. Even when their feet weren't prancing in time to the music, they were talking in appropriate circles, and drinking the approved amount of fizzling champagne.

I caught their dismissive stares. I moved like one of them. I danced with a hare, and he made no complaints, but I felt the scorn. I was unknown. I was new. No one knew the little lady with the horns and the hooves. And since no one knew her—me—I was of no importance. I smiled into their gazes. None of that mattered. They had already taken the bait. They didn't know me, but still they assumed that I *belonged*.

Light little dainties were served on trays by mice. Everything I did had to be right, or else I'd stand out. The way you moved, the way you talked and flirted, the way you danced and even the way you ate and drank was circumspect. It was all a part of the dance.

And dance I did. From partner to partner, I approached. Their perfume almost covered their scents. Closer and closer I drew to the center of it all: the impassive king sitting motionless on his throne. He was the eye of this particularly orderly hurricane. The snow glittered around me and the champagne danced on my tongue, and the insipid music wormed itself into my ears until I almost liked it. It was all enthralling. I almost forgot why I was there.

Then there was a presence. It wasn't anything physical, but when I felt it, my current partner—he was a short little ermine with the smell of jasmine following him around like a cloud—stopped mid-sentence and mid-step, turned, and left. Around me, the swirl of the dance evaporated, and I was left in the storm's center. I turned to look, and I found looking back at me the starry eyes of the Alabaster King.

He had moved—that alone was a surprise. When I had been learning, the minor nobles who had deigned to give the poorly gutter-girl lessons on acting like a lady had mentioned that he'd gone entire seasons without ever seeing the king even twitch. I'd thought I'd get close, unobserved and unnoticed, but here I was caught in the direct gaze of the king like a moth in the lantern's glare.

Worship me.

It wasn't so much heard as felt. No one had spoken, and the king's head hadn't moved while I watched. We were more than twenty paces distant, but there was a circle around us that no one's feet dared to cross. No one even seemed to notice. The courtiers acted as if no one had seen the king shift on his throne, and even the servants seemed to take the long way around our inviolate circle. It was the king's magic. It must have been, along with the wheedling little voice whispering in my ear.

Worship me.

"No." I mouthed the words, and immediately I saw the king's mouth tug upwards. He was smiling.

"I do not know you. How could this be so?"

His voice was deep, and rumbled in my ears in a way that made my knees turn a little soft. Even though we were at distance, his words were clear as if he were standing close enough to touch. Then I realized his mouth hadn't moved. He was speaking to me without wasting time on sending the words through the air between us.

"Your majesty, I—"

"Do not trouble me with words. It is not necessary." He shifted again in his throne. I hadn't realized when I first saw him just how much elk there was to the frame that sat at such a distance from the hall's entrance. This close, though, I could watch muscles move over sinew and over bone, all immaculately sculpted and perfectly formed. He was exquisite. It was as if his body had been created to fit perfect proportions and musculature for his regal size—and had never been used since its inception. If the rumors I'd heard were true, perhaps that's exactly what had happened. He was supposedly an elemental spirit given form, rather than some mortal who had become the regal being he was now through succession. That would also explain the faerie magic the king commanded. How else could he have cleared the hall without having said or done anything, or even kept anyone else from noticing it? How else could he be talking directly into my head?

"Or, it would not normally be necessary. How is it that I cannot see into your mind?" He leaned forward. Previously, I had seen the way the king almost melted into the background when he took no interest in the doings of his courtiers. Now I bore the weight of the king's full attention, and it almost forced me to my knees. His intent gaze was so intense it seemed to tunnel straight through me. "Where all my courtiers are open books—albeit shallow, childish ones—you are a closed tome to me. This is intriguing. In the many years of my rule, I have not met one like you. How interesting."

There was a sprig of *aeonium* tied around one of my horns. Its leaves were thick and waxy, and pitch black. It was hidden under my fur. It was a charm of color. How had I known to seek it out and harvest it? It was a little whisper at the back of my mind. I don't know how I knew, but I knew. Just like now I knew it was the armor that was preventing the king from seeing into my thoughts. I returned his smile. He was so much more than I had imagined he'd be. He wasn't just a malicious spirit. He was a god of the hearth. He was a force of nature, given flesh. But with all his majesty, he still had his weakness.

"Fine, my precious child. I give you permission to speak to me. I do not know how you've achieved this wonder, but now you have my attention."

I hadn't intended to have his attention. I hadn't intended to have anyone's. I had only thought to get in, do my work, and then leave under the cover of chaos. But my life had never exactly gone to plan. I was a past expert at rolling with the punches—sometimes quite as literally as figuratively. So I had his attention. I could work with that. I smiled back at him.

"I don't know, your majesty. Surely I am not so different than the rest of your court."

"I know my court. Each and every one of them. They have grown about me like mushrooms around the base of an oak. I have seen their minds as they grew from children to the adults they now pretend to be—and for most of them that was not so far a journey. You are new. You are intriguing. So tell me, my enigma, from where do you hail?"

"I grew up in a little hamlet far from the capital, sire. You probably would not have heard of it: a little village by the name of Stenner's Ford."

"Five miles east of Mill Hollow. Yes, I know of it. I gave Arthur Stenner permission to build that ford over two hundred years ago. Do not mistake me, girl. Just because your mind cannot contain the details of our vast kingdom does not then mean that mine is also incapable of such a feat. How fares the town, then? And how does a little farm-girl come to my side, cutting her way through my minnow pond of a court like a carp?"

The blood froze in my veins. If he knew so much, did he also know about me? Had word traveled so far? But his gaze held nothing but interest. I saw no sign of apprehension or doubt on his now fully-animated features.

"I am sorry, majesty. While I was born there, I have lived in the capital for most of my life."

"Really? So gorgeous a girl as you in my very own city, and I have not heard of you? That must mean my dear, that either you are very good at hiding, or you are not the noble you are pretending to be. I very much doubt the first, so it must be the second. Is this true, my child?" He held up a warning hand to me. "Before you feel the need to lie, realize that I care equally for all of my subjects. These creatures around me are only noble by their own claim. I will think no less of you if you began with much less than they were handed at birth—in truth, I might think more. So, with that in mind, from what humble beginnings came my mystery girl?"

I hung my head, but it was false modesty. He frowned, and I knew that he saw through it. So I threw out all the lessons in courtly manner I'd been taught and talked plainly. "I'm a gutter-girl, your majesty.

I have lived my life in your city since I was very young, but in all that time, at no point have I ever even owned the roof over my head." The king smiled. Then he stood.

He was glorious. Curled on his throne he was an apathetic, indolent form, but standing I realized just how perfect a body he had. More, I saw all of it. The king did not bother wearing such troublesome things as clothes. If he truly was some powerful spirit, then simply wearing this body may have been clothes enough. He was the most gorgeous buck I had ever seen. His pelt was pristinely white. Not even shadows dared fall across his pelt. He had a lanky musculature that both fit and enhanced his form. And that white pelt went all the way down, and by the spirits was he anatomically correct. I felt myself growing weak at the knees again, and this time it was for entirely different reasons.

Desire me.

The voice was soft and insidious, and it sounded nothing like his. What impulse was it that was drawing me to him? Was it some subconscious control? As soon as I thought it, I knew it was true. Intentionally or not, the king was attempting to control me. And when I realized it, the spell was broken. I tore my attention away from the sheath that hung slightly away from his belly and impressive balls dangling between his legs, and instead looked squarely at his face. He smiled again. He knew I had resisted his charm, and it only intrigued him further.

"Dance with me, my mysterious gutter-girl, and tell me of your life."

We swung out into the dance floor. Courtiers parted for us like commoners before a runaway coach. There were cries of shock and wonder from either side. The king had risen from his throne, and he was dancing! Entire generations of nobles had gone their entire lives never seeing even a blink from the Alabaster King, but now not only had he woken from his stupor, but he had stood, and he was dancing! Stories would be told of this day, no doubt. I must admit to some pride. Even though the entire show was a sham, meant to hide my true identity, I drank in the shocked wonder and jealousy from the amazed courtiers. By the end of the day, I would be that 'nameless woman'. Maybe they'd think I was just as much a fae spirit as the king. Legends would be written about the mysterious girl who danced with the king.

I am beautiful! And for the first time, everyone around me seemed to agree.

But then, with a sobering thought, I remembered that I'd planned to give them much more to remember than just a dance.

"Why are you all alone, my beauty? Where are your father and mother—who must have doted on such a precious child."

The king's words brought vivid images. My mother, framed in the doorway as a mob threw stones through the window. She was lit in silhouette from the lantern and torchlight, protecting me and my siblings. In my memory, she was beautiful too, though sable-white instead of black like me. I alone in my family had been born different. Her greatest strength was that even in the face of the angry mob, she had never given me up. She held Da's sword, too big for her small frame. The tip was dragging on the reed floor of our hut as she stumbled out to meet our friendly neighbors. Her head turned, and she whispered, "Run" before she closed the door behind her.

"Dead, your majesty." It took every ounce of self-control to keep the smile on my face. The king must have caught something in my expression, because his face softened.

"Ah. I am sorry. I conjure sadness within you. Siblings then. A brother? Sister? Are there more hidden jewels scraping for scraps in the gutter of my glittering city?"

More images. My brother Sam, held aloft by a towering bear of a guardsman. 'Thief' they'd called him. And so he was. So was I. Both of us had nicked food and clothes for ourselves and our little sister, Bess. Thieves don't have to wait long for the king's justice. Two days later he'd been hanged.

"My brother was caught with a loaf of bread." I couldn't hide my flinch. The king swung me out on one arm in the dance, and when he pulled me close again his face was contrite. "And my sister—"

I had only seen Bess a few weeks ago. I'd sneaked into the priory where I'd left her after Sam died. She had looked beautiful—just like mother. I had been so eager to see her again. I was sure she'd recognize me, even though it'd been nearly fifteen years since I'd left her there. I can still remember the look of shock on her face, right before she raised her finger, pointing at me. "Demon! Defiler! Beast of darkness!" Her screams had chased me from the convent, along with the white paladins.

"—we are not speaking."

"Again, I bring you pain. I am sorry."

"It was not your intent, your majesty. Let us speak of more pleasant times." I tried to free a hand. I had hid my secret in a pouch in my sleeve, but I couldn't quite reach it.

"Let's. For example, I intend that you never return to those gutters that have so wronged you."

I smiled plainly at him. "That, your majesty, is already fact. You have danced with me. I could live the rest of my days in the gentle keeping of your nobles, if only as a curiosity."

He twirled me around. "Could. Was that your goal, my mystery girl? To dance with me? If so, you have won."

I fingered at the button that held the hidden pouch in my sleeve closed. I felt within my little surprise. Now was my only opportunity to turn back. I could smile, finish the dance, and live the rest of my life—

—live the rest of my life hoping the enchantment that hid my colored pelt never faded. No. That was no life. And I was owed blood.

"No, your majesty. That was not my goal."

He leaned close. I felt rather unclean as his naked pelt pressed against my front. Even though he was gorgeous, something about him repulsed me. He was chiseled and fit, the true pinnacle of form that under any other circumstances would set my blood on fire. Pressed so close, I could feel every one of his muscles shift as he danced with me. I even felt something against my front. He was getting hard. He wanted me. He wanted me to want him. I felt nauseous.

And all the while, the voice whispered in my head. *Desire me!*

"Will you join my court, my mystery girl? Sit for a while at my side?"

I swallowed back disgust. "No."

"I thought not." Then he pushed me back. His hand clasped at my neck as I stumbled. In his hand he clutched the enchanted pearl. I was kept from falling by the fragile chain around my neck that kept the glamour anchored to me. "Did you not think I could recognize sorcery when it paraded itself in front of me? Foolish girl. Shall we show these nobles the crone that tried to fool their king?"

He thought me a crone? I laughed in his face. For all his fae magic, he still could not see beneath the shroud. I held my head up haughtily, and I put a hand on his that held the pearl. Then I gave it a tug, and the cord snapped.

The Alabaster King stumbled back, holding the remains of my enchantment. I felt the tingle of magic slither down my body as the illusion faded. It had done nothing for my features. I was still the same beautiful girl. I *am* beautiful! But instead of the pearly white, now the king's astonished face tried to comprehend the sight of the jet-black oryx that now stood before him.

Around us, the hushed murmuring of his courtiers turned to panic. There were screams and the sound of stampede as they trampled each other to reach the exits. I ignored it all. "Do you see now, your majesty? Do you see why my whole family suffered and died, just because I lived?"

His astonishment turned to anger, but I met his mercurial emotions with my own present. I had freed it from the pouch, and it lay heavy in my palm, hidden. It was smooth and spherical, no larger around than the first knuckle of my thumb. It was a piece of basalt, mercilessly black, and polished to mirror sheen. I drew my arm back and threw.

The marble impacted the king's muzzle, and instead of bouncing away, it splashed as if it were made of tar. Rubbery tendrils splattered across his face, leaving a broad shadow in his snowy complexion. He held a hand up to his face, but underneath I could still see the shadow growing.

"What have you done?"

He blinked, and his hand began to glow. Some fae enchantment stopped the shadow's encroachment, though it did not shrink.

"What have you done? Witch! Demon!"

"I've heard those words before, *your majesty*. Shouted, usually, by *your* people bearing stones and torches."

His hand shot out. "Then clearly you require a more formidable weapon."

I felt myself lift off the floor. His fae magic gripped me. I writhed, but my hooves found no purchase. I had thought—it was a vain thought—that once stained his magic might desert him. It hadn't done so. The king was no less potent, and now he was angry.

"I cannot hurt you, being of blackness, but I can send you elsewhere. Go join *him* in his prison. May you dark-spawn keep each other company!" He flicked his fingers, and I felt myself being thrown backwards. There was the sensation of falling without end, and the screams of the king's courtiers drifted into ringing silence. The snow-scattered marble hall and its winterdown finery faded, and I was consumed by shadow.

**

I breathed in.

The first emotion to hit me was surprise. *I'm alive!* That alone was worth a celebration. Everything hurt. My shoulders were sore—bruised maybe. I had a headache, and my horns felt like someone had been tugging on them for hours and just let go. But bodily aches could be damned, I was alive! Look at me—tussle with the Alabaster King, and here I was still pulling in air.

But the second emotion that quickly chased surprise was fear. Sure, I was alive. But, where? Stone was beneath me and above me. No more than ten steps in any direction and I could find more dark, cold, rough stone. A dungeon. No, even worse—an oubliette. A dungeon was where you put people until you knew what to do with them. An oubliette was where you put people when you knew exactly what to do with them—and that was put them away. Forever. This was no work of the king's. The rock was dark. No marble or sandstone, this. So he hadn't wrought it, but used it to dispose of his unwanted. I had no reason to be afraid. I was out of his reach now. I was no longer in the white. I was free.

Fear came unbidden, anyway. Of course I had reason to be afraid. I didn't have water. I didn't have food. My ball gown was little protection from the leeching chill of the stone, and my pelt was thin. Cold it was. Not icy. Not chill. Instead, it was the dull, bone-deep cold of apathy. It was the gradual cold that stole life from fingers until the hand was useless. I had reason to fear, because even though I was alive, that could easily change.

Why was that such a surprise? Hadn't I gone into the night expecting to die? Surely, no one could do to the king what I'd done and survive. I could have faced his guards and died with dignity. A swiftly thrust polearm, or a long walk to the gallows. I'd have held my head high, and I'd have marred their white flagstones red with blood.

But I'd survived. Through all probability, I was alive, and now that my life was mine again to do with what I chose, I found myself quite firmly clasping it. I wanted to live. Yes. Look at what I'd done—not just done, but I'd lived through it! I would survive to see the day when my gift finally brought the king low, and now that the thought had wormed its way into my head, it took up residence and changed the curtains. Fear is what I felt.

I stood. My knees were shaky, so I leaned against the wall for support. I hobbled along the wall while feeling returned to my limbs. Stone bricks, roughly hewn and uneven. I was in a room, but a corridor led away. Left. Right. Straight ahead. My hands traced the walls, and the cold bit at my fingertips.

Within five minutes, I was turned about and convinced I was going in circles. By the time it occurred to me that my prison might be less dungeon and more labyrinth, I had already lost my bearings. Not that I'd had them to begin with, really. The place I'd been deposited hadn't seemed to be significant in any way, and I found a hundred such corners in my turnings, seemingly identical to the place where I'd appeared. To a certain extent, this was gratifying. If the place I'd been deposited wasn't special, then at least I'd done myself no harm in losing it. I was completely lost, I told myself, but I'd started that way. If I kept moving, then I'd eventually find something—and then I wouldn't be so lost anymore.

I must have been walking for hours by the time my stamina started to fade. I was thirsty, and I'd found nothing that even hinted at water as I walked. My heart sank. I was willing to wander the labyrinth for as long as it took, but I couldn't do so without the necessaries of survival. I sat to rest, and optimism slowly faded into despair. Despair was then edged out by exhaustion, and exhaustion descended into uneasy sleep.

My dreams were full of dark thoughts, but the content of those auguries fled when I was woken suddenly by a bark. I jumped in shock at the surprise, and my eyes took half a minute to readjust themselves to the darkness. I could see, if only just. There seemed to be a pervading glimmer to everything that fed my eyes the bare minimum they required to make out shapes and walls, and on occasion, details. When my eyes adjusted from whatever I'd been dreaming I saw, I was able to make out a creature. It was dog-shaped, and would have come up to my waist had I been standing. After a few seconds of staring, my brain registered something that—until today—was simply so far outside my experience that it took a few more seconds for me to accept it. The dog was black.

Fear me.

The fear that had been riding me like a demon took control. I ran. Left, right, straight ahead. My knees buckled and I scraped my thigh. I grasped the wall and pulled myself upright. It was black. It was a demon. It was the devil. It was here to devour my soul.

Yes, I see the dichotomy now. But a lifetime of propaganda drilled into your skull isn't so easy to displace. I felt it every time I saw myself in a puddle. There's that instinctive jump as I see myself in a mirror. *I am beautiful.* But I am also exactly what I've been taught to fear. If only it were so easy to banish from the mind. Instead, it drove me. It whipped at my flanks when I stumbled, and it stung my eyes when I fell.

I could see it chasing me. Every time I looked back, there was that shadow pacing behind me.

Fear me.

It was a voice—a sibling to the whisper I'd heard in my own mind when faced with the Alabaster King. *Fear me*, it said. And I did.

I ran until I couldn't any more. Then I curled up in a corner and cried. Breath came in desperate gulps. I didn't want to die now. I'd just been gifted my life back, and now that it was mine again, it was precious to me.

Fear me. It repeated. I couldn't run any more. The shadow slowed in its pace. It hung just far enough away that I couldn't see its details. Now that my footsteps weren't thundering in my head (though my heart was still doing its best to ruin my hearing) I actually listened. That voice. It was so familiar, and now that I heard it, I recognized it. I wasn't afraid—not really. I was being ordered to be afraid. And as soon as I realized it, the spell abated.

The creature's pelt was colored just like mine. Of course I shouldn't fear it. Look at me—I'm just as much demon as it is, and I don't feel particularly demonic. It was just more of the alabaster propaganda. No, it wasn't evil. It was my brother.

I called out to it, and its ears perked towards me. It was twenty feet away, at the junction of two more featureless hallways. When I stood, though, it turned and fled. I could barely hear the scraping of claws across stone as it disappeared into the distance. I was ready to dismiss it as strange circumstance, but when my eyes further adjusted, I realized it had left something behind. I approached cautiously, in case there were more of them, but nothing made itself apparent as I walked to the small pile the dog had left at the junction.

It was something wrapped in cloth. When I lifted it, it felt heavy in my hands. When I unwrapped it, I found myself holding a metal bottle that was cold to the touch, and capped with a cork. I popped the top and sniffed. There was liquid inside, but it had no scent other than the tang of the metal container itself. I poured a little onto my tongue. Water! Cold, crisp, delicious water. When I had been in training to act like a noble, I had tasted fine wines and cordials, but nothing had tasted so good as the water I now held. I drank until my sides ached.

Finally able to ignore the pressing needs of my body, its lesser complaints started to surface. The gown I'd worn to the Winterdown festival hadn't been designed for running, and it had already torn half-way to shreds. It was now more hindrance than garment, so I removed it. After my little sprint, the cold seemed to have abated. It was warm enough that even without the gown, I felt no need to shiver. I sat for a moment, letting the water settle in my stomach, then answered my bodies other necessaries in a featureless corner. Finally, I felt ready to continue, hopes rejuvenated by the mysterious black labyrinth denizen. So remembering the direction it had fled, I stuck a foot forward and started to wander again.

Left, right, straight ahead—I felt heartened as I walked. Maybe I was never getting out of here, but at least my remaining days would be spent somewhere that fit me. I was a misfit little gutter-girl, never meant for the bright streets and marble halls. I imagined myself as a monster of the dungeon, prowling around the labyrinth as if I owned the place. Left, right, straight ahead. I had no idea if I was going in circles, but I didn't care. I wasn't a flighty oryx; I was a cat! I was the thing in the darkness. Even the other dungeon creatures brought tithe to their dungeon queen.

I was woken from my waking reverie by another bark. The scampering black beast was at the end of an adjoining hallway. Full of vim and vigor now, I turned and chased after. It bounced in place, then when I closed to within a few paces, flicked its tail and fled. It turned, and I followed. Was it leading me deeper into the labyrinth, or towards the exit? Was there even an exit, or was it some magical construct without one? I didn't know. I had no way of knowing, and no feasible way of finding out, short of being led to the exit anyway. I had never been one for worrying or wallowing in despair. Instead, the beast fled, and

I chased.

I don't know how long I followed, but by the time we reached what appeared to be an open room—the first of its kind that I'd seen—I was out of breath. The creature was only about four or five paces ahead of me. It occurred that it had been about that distance away the whole time. It must have been pacing itself so I could keep up. I didn't flatter myself so much that I thought I could outrun or out-think a native in their own maze. It sat on its haunches, and I picked a nearby wall to collapse against. When my butt reached the cold floor, the beast stood and walked to me. I squashed the immediate impulse to pull away. If it'd wanted to hurt me, it wouldn't have been helping me along like it had been. I held my hand out, and it pushed its nose up against my palm. Then, with a very cat-like show of affection, its head thumped against my chest, and it curled against my side.

"What have I done to deserve your love and attention, hmm?" It ignored my question, though its ears flicked to acknowledge that it'd heard something. I rubbed its neck, and it rumbled contentedly against my side. As I caught my breath, I thought. Something told me this was wrong. I'm in a magical labyrinth, and the local guard dog had taken a liking to me instead of hounding me like the demon it was probably meant to be? But in another twisted way it made sense. Hadn't I spent my whole life being told what a monster I was? Hah. Well, if I'm a monster, at least I'll get the perks in addition to the prejudice.

I stroked behind its ears. "Well, whatever your reasons, thank you. What should I call you? I can't just keep calling you it." I considered for a moment, then ducked my head to the side and forward. 'He', not it. The black pelted head lifted and looked at me, and I smiled at him. "Jet. I'm going to call you Jet." The black tail smacked against the dungeon floor in a rather dog-like fashion.

"So, Jet, where next? Shall we just roam the labyrinth and—"

Jet's head swung around and stared at the entrance opposite us, and I saw eyes detach themselves from the uncertain shadows around the doorway. Another creature, similar yet different to Jet, prowled into the room. It was slightly larger, and had tufts of fur sprouting from each of its joints that gave it an almost spiky silhouette. I stayed still as it approached. Somehow, I felt that if I were in danger, Jet would let me know. The newcomer and the beast curled against my side touched noses, then the newcomer rubbed its head against my arm. I felt awkwardly honored. I didn't know what I'd done to befriend the local population, but I was immensely relieved that they'd decided to treat me as a friend rather than an enemy.

The newcomer—an unmistakable bulge in its shadow against the far wall made it clear it was also a 'he'—opened his mouth. My relief that I wasn't considered dinner panged acutely when I glimpsed those sharp canines dripping with saliva. Then it closed over my hand. I jerked my arm reflexively, but the sharp teeth held over my wrist. I felt a cold chill run down my spine, but the newcomer didn't bite. Instead, he just tugged. I felt the fangs pulling little furrows through my thin pelt and prickling at my skin. Jet stood, and looked at me expectantly. When I followed, the second beast let go of my hand. Then leading me at a much more sedate pace than earlier, they led me back into the labyrinth.

Left, right, straight ahead. I still felt hopelessly lost, but my two guides seemed to know where they were going. In my mind, I had named the second one Obsidian, for his jagged edges and rough personality. At all times, one walked pressed to my leg, while the other led the way. As time passed, I started to notice differences in the labyrinth's layout and design. The dark stone it was hewn from changed, going from shiny and smooth to rough and lumpy, to crude brick and mortar. We passed hallways of rooms, and curving spiral stairs, and an open gallery through which I could see another four stories upwards of the labyrinth extending on, as far as I was concerned, forever.

We rounded another turn, and we were on an arched bridge overlooking a chasm with no visible bottom. Halfway across the bridge was another beast, curled at its apex. It stood, and it—she—loped towards us. The bridge was smooth and shiny, so I named her Onyx. She was smoother and softer to the touch than Jet or Obsidian had been, though she didn't plaster herself to my side like they did when she wasn't leading.

Another turn, another long corridor, and then we met Jasper. I have to admit, by this time I'd about run out of names based on gems. It's as if a childhood spent stealing scraps and living in the gutter hadn't prepared me for eclectic uses of mineralogical vocabulary. He was larger and more rambunctious than the rest. When we turned the corner and found him waiting for us at a crossroad, he jumped up on me. His paws caught my front, and claws snagged on the fabric of the few under-things I was still wearing. I tripped and fell back. When I came back to my senses with a lump on the back of my head, Jasper had the decency to look properly miserable. When I stood, I was naked. I considered being embarrassed, but they were just beasts. They never wore clothes, so, I reasoned, neither should I. I left my coverings behind when we walked on.

Left, right, straight ahead. My pack led, and I followed. Along the way, we acquired Beryl, Pearl, and Garnet. It was about this point that I stopped trying to name them. It was difficult enough keeping track of them, let alone trying to remember the details that differentiated one from another. By the time we'd been walking another hour, not only had I run out of names but I'd also lost count. They preceded me around corners, and disappeared back to the last intersection. I was carried on an inevitable tide, carrying me towards uncertain future. Around me, the beasts yammered and bickered. It echoed strangely off of the stone corridors.

Through the whole journey, Jet stayed at my side. He was never gone long enough for me to wonder whether the wiry fur rubbing against my thigh was him. I buried my fingers in his pelt, and he leaned into me. For the first time in—well, maybe for the first time at all—I felt like I was part of something. They may have been beasts, but they accepted me more than the haughty people back in the capital ever had. Hell, I'd only been here in the labyrinth for less than a day, and already these scampering things were more 'people' than any I'd met back home.

How long had we been traveling? Hours? Days? No, I couldn't walk for a day without getting fatigued, but I'd so totally lost track of time that I couldn't tell if it was night or day. Maybe that didn't even matter. Was there such a thing as night or day here in the labyrinth? If it was some special magical place, created by the king to keep his prisoners, then maybe there wasn't even a sun here to give day and night definition.

I was thirsty, so I decided to stop and drink. Jet folded himself at my side. When I poured water from the flask onto my tongue, he licked at my lips. I poured water out for him, too. He took a few laps at that, then ignored it and licked my lips again.

"Pthbt!" I exclaimed, rubbing my muzzle. "Aren't you going to buy me dinner first?" I joked. His ears fell. I pulled him into a hug and kissed his forehead. This is when another of the beasts stuck their nose in, and I kissed that too. I couldn't immediately identify who they were. I felt more of the creatures crowd in around me, and the feeling of intense belonging climaxed, and I was crying. Jet licked my face again, and this time I didn't pull away. I just hugged his neck and buried my face in his black pelt.

When I felt ready to move again, the river of creatures carried me onward. Left, right, and then straight ahead.

By this time, I was used to seeing slits in the black shadows. They were all around me, reflecting strange pseudo-light that didn't seem to come from anywhere, but still made their eyes glow. When we turned the corner, I saw another pair in the distance, before whatever head owned them turned away. My guides led me inside, and the ground began to slope down. They fanned out ahead and behind me, slowly filling the room for as far as I could see. Visibility wasn't perfect. I could only really see maybe twenty or thirty feet ahead in the gloom, so I didn't realize until I'd lost sight of the tunnel behind me just how massive this room was. And then, with a slight chill, I remembered the eyes. They had appeared to be no larger than the creatures around me, but if they'd been that far away, the creature that owned them must be massive.

The head at the center of the chamber turned towards me again, and I quailed under eyes that looked down at me. It must have been the size of a bear—or even larger. Then a massive paw stepped into range of my vision, followed by the rest of Him.

I think all the creatures I'd seen so far had been copies of this majestic template, though inferior ones. He was a panther, mixed with a lion, mixed with a wolf, mixed with a mastiff. When he moved, the shadows gathered around his legs, as if they didn't define a creature that was there, but instead a hole in the world where a creature could fit. He wasn't black. He wasn't any color at all. Defining him by giving him a color would have been a disservice to him. Instead, he was the absence of color. He was void given form.

Really, my dear. I am not so dire as that. I have form. If you touch me, you will feel me.

Just like it had with the Alabaster King, the words seemed to skip the space between us without actually traveling. Instead, they arrived in my mind as fully-formed concepts, without being so unkind as to trouble my ears. I shrank back from him. At my side, I could feel Jet's tail behind my knees. He leaned into me, and my fingers tightened on his scruff.

I am not him, and he is not me.

He spoke to my panic. In moments, it was clear. Of course he wasn't the Alabaster King. If anything, he was the absolute antithesis of the king. He approached me, and I steeled myself. I put my hand forward, and he pushed his massive head against my palm.

See? I am real.

I did see. His pelt was soft, and he was warm. Running my fingers over the fur on his muzzle was a pleasure. "So you are. I assume, then, that you are 'Him'?" I thought back to what the king had said when he'd banished me.

The prisoner. Yes. The beast. The creature. The dethroned king. I welcome you, my child. You may call me Shadow.

That's what the king had called me. I bristled. "Am not! Don't call me—"

And if not mine, who are you a child of? You think black pelts just randomly appear in the usurper's domain?

"Why not? Children aren't always like their parents. We kept sheep, and every once in a while a lamb was born that wasn't quite right."

But always white. Am I wrong?

I didn't respond. They had always been white. Purely, pristinely white.

You are right in more ways than you know, my child. Yes, children are born different, but color—that's an entirely different arena when you are born in the Kingdom. It is the bastard's magic that keeps everything white. Everything is tidy and bright. Stagnant, stiflingly white. If not for some outside magic, you would have been a normal little girl.

The thought brought tears to my eyes. "So it's your fault—"

Did I raise the stone? Did I throw the torch? Did I swing the blade?

The massive black head pushed itself against my front. I stumbled and fell over Jet, who was still leaning into me from behind. He yelped and managed to disentangle himself from me, leaving me propped up on my arms on the cold stone.

My fault. It is my fault you were born like this.

"Black."

Yes.

"Flawed."

Perfect.

I hid my face behind my arms. "Hideous."

Beautiful.

He pushed his nose against my arms, and I hugged myself against his snout. He was massive—as large as a horse. I shivered over his loving sympathy, and forgave him.

You are beautiful. Never forget that. My child. My princess. My queen.

The creatures gathered in around me, and the belonging I'd felt earlier rose in my head like a warm, bubbling sensation. When I'd been in the king's court, I'd tried champagne. It had fizzed and tickled all the way down my throat, and then up my spine and between my ears. This was just like that, but with a warmth and glow that the fizzy drink could never match. His tongue flicked out and licked my whole front. Immediately, I regretted being naked. I'd left behind my clothes because they didn't seem to make sense in the labyrinth, but now when the shadow beast's tongue flicked over my bare pelt, I felt significantly more exposed than I'd intended.

Don't. You are beautiful. You should never cover that gorgeous pelt. You wear shadow like a gown. The darkness is the only clothes you should ever need.

I shivered, then released his head. "You said I'm your child. How—"

I met your mother when she was searching for your father. He was lost and injured, and would not survive without her. Shadow pushed with his head again and pinned me against the stone. I felt another shiver slowly work its way up my spine. When he touched me, it was almost electric. I felt a hot flush that burned in my stomach. *I made her an offer, just like I'm about to make you an offer.*

His tongue slid against my front again, and the warmth in my stomach blossomed. My whole body felt like it was on fire. It felt... It felt glorious.

"You will find your man, and he will live." I offered her. You were my price. She agreed, and I took her right there on the rocky ridge where she'd found me. She braced herself against an oak tree, and I took her, then again when she lay down in the brambles.

His voice was husky. Something hot and wet tapped my leg. I jerked in shock, then felt my breath catching in my throat. I found my knees spreading of their own accord.

So I'm going to make you an offer, too. I offer you this: Vengeance. I will show you how to end the Alabaster King and all those who have brought you pain.

I felt myself slipping away, but years of self-taught control allowed me enough presence of mind to ask. "And the price?" My own voice was as husky as his.

You. I want you. I want everything you are. I want to own you. I want to be on you, and inside you. I want you to want me, and need me, and fear me. I want you to be my queen. I want you to be at my side as we watch the kingdom of the White King burn.

I didn't even need to consider. When I'd walked into the Alabaster King's festival with regicide on my mind, I'd been sure I was going to die. I'd already paid my price. Everything from now until I died, these were stolen days. And I couldn't imagine a better way to spend them than at Shadow's side. I let my knees slide to the side, and Shadow took me.

At some point, I will look back and wonder how I survived without the darkness that filled me in that moment. It was as if I'd been an empty vessel, just waiting for the day when my purpose could be fulfilled. Well, that's exactly what I was, no? I'd been created for this. I was destined to be by his side.

But at the moment, I was much more concerned with being beneath him. He wasn't gentle. He put one forepaw on my chest as I felt him slide slickly up into me. I was no novice to bedroom games, but I quickly realized that I'd never had a lover quite so majestic as Shadow. His tip was slim and slippery, but as his powerful hind legs bunched around me, I felt myself stretched wider and wider. I hugged the limb that pinned me down, and raised my legs to fold over his massive haunches. His head bent down to me, and I lost myself in his eyes. They were black, but in them I could see stars. Or maybe that was just the way my vision went dark when his hips finally impacted mine. He held himself deep. His balls rested on my up-turned rump, and twitched every few seconds. It was all deliciously lewd. I loved every second of it.

When he started to growl, I was surprised. When he'd spoken to me, it had all arrived directly in my mind. Now his rumbling was giving my ears an unexpected workout. It was so deep—so bone-rattling—

that I felt my whole body vibrating with the intensity of it. I hugged myself around the paw on my chest. It was almost as wide across as my waist. Shadow looked into my eyes, and his hips pulled back.

For a moment, I saw stars even when I wasn't looking at him. It wasn't painful so much as so intense that I momentarily lost track of… Well, everything. I was welcomed back to consciousness by the smooth friction of him stuffing himself back in until his anatomy bounced off my legs. The second time wasn't nearly so intense, and I could actually feel the tugging and gripping of his length against my inner walls. When he pulled back, I was filled with a warm rush, and when he shoved forward, I felt liquid dripping down my thighs and under my tail. My horns clattered against the floor as he pushed me bodily across the stone.

I don't know how long we were like this. Maybe minutes. Maybe hours. All I remember is feeling empty when he stepped away from me, yet still feeling more full—no, fulfilled—than I ever had.

My child. My princess. My queen.

Yes. I was. There was no doubt or hesitation now. I was his queen. I looked around us, and I saw the ungainly shadow beasts that had led me here. They were my minions. I knew them, now, and I could hear them chattering in my head. I found Jet, still close to my side. When he looked at me, I could finally understand him. It wasn't words, so much as emotions and convictions. I was his queen, and he was mine. I'd been born to rule them, just as they'd been created to serve Shadow and me. Jet stood and walked over to me. I couldn't tell what name he'd had before I'd met him. Whatever he'd been before had been wiped out—overwritten the moment he met his queen. Now he was the one by my side, my staunchest protector. I pushed myself from the floor, still shaky and wet from Shadow's indoctrination, and put my hand on Jet's head. I cupped his ear fondly, then pulled his muzzle towards mine and kissed him.

They are yours now, my queen, just as you are mine. You will bridge the worlds for us, and we will all walk into our new kingdom, together.

Shadow stood above us, gazing down at us with eyes full of stars. Slowly, the rest of the beasts crowded in around us. I pulled Jet to me, and he and his fellow beasts welcomed their new queen as only they could. All the while, Shadow looked down at us, and I felt his presence in my mind, drinking my joy and living each carnal, liquid moment vicariously through my eyes. And when we were done, and I was sated, I lay across Shadow's broad front, with my hands between his legs, and pleasured him one last time. Just as he had with me, I felt his sensations and bliss in my mind, and when he came, my thighs clenched and I sprinkled my release down into his ebony pelt, just as he painted his own across my back. We lay like that for some time before the world drifted, and I fell asleep.

When I woke, the labyrinth was gone. I didn't doubt what I'd seen even for a moment, though, because I could still feel Shadow in my mind where before there had only been my own thoughts. I could even still feel him inside me in a more literal sense, too. There was a slick sensation when I moved, though I guess that could have been any one of the shadow beasts, rather than our dark king.

I recognized where I'd woken. I was in the center of the capital, in the center of the alabaster statue of the usurper king. The marble felt cold under my back, and a fountain stretched out a good ten feet in every direction from the plinth where I lay between the king's feet. Even though the daily traffic of the city spun around us, no one deemed to notice the black oryx girl that shakily stood to her feet, then steadied herself by grabbing the statue of their king's by an unfortunate piece of its anatomy. I waited until the world around me no longer spun, and I was feeling ready to move. Ready to do more than move, in fact. I was ready to walk. Ready to run. Ready to conquer the whole kingdom.

Go, my beautiful child. Go, and we will be with you.

I hopped down from the plinth into the knee-deep water. It splashed up at me, and I realized I was still wearing no clothes. When I'd left the capital, that would have sent me running for shelter in embarrassment. Now it was the only outfit I felt was worthy of gracing my frame. In fact, I wasn't just nude—I was stained with the love of my king and our subjects. It was a mark of pride. As I walked to the edge of the fountain and crested its walls, it was as if I passed through an invisible wall, and I was noticed.

There were shouts. I ignored them. People ran screaming. I opened my hands and felt my fingers dragging through the air as if it were a dense liquid. Behind me, long rifts opened and disgorged my shadowy minions. They crowded against my side, and I buried my hand in the pelt of the closest ones. I felt Jet at my side, and he sang out his love for me in an ululating bark. In front of us, the city watch appeared. They had truncheons pulled, but they quickly dissolved back into the crowd when they decided that they just weren't enough to stop us. With my beasts at my heel, we marched on the palace.

At the gates, the fiercest of the guard had drawn pikes. The shadow beasts were on them before they could swing. I never broke step. By the time I reached the grand marble doors, the guards had been dispatched and pulled away. I put my hand on the door, and a black shadow crept across its otherwise pristine white surface. The shadow spread from my hand like oil dropped onto milk. The marble still shone bright, and when its shadow reached the edges of the door, it swung open without complaint. Behind it, another cadre of guards had formed. They fell like the first as I walked forward. Where I stepped on the white tiles, small black circles formed under my bare hooves, like lily pads on the water. The king had no shortage of loyal minions, but his were well-fed and indolent. Mine were hungry and angry, and had been waiting for this day for generations. I never needed to even pause my casual pace towards the throne room.

When I reached the marble hall, the king was on his throne. He was scowling, though the expression was marred by the splash of color I'd given him before he'd exiled me. The black on his face had spread across his stony features until it'd devoured half of his snout. It'd even started to crawl up one of his impressive antlers. My beasts spread out across the hall, but the Alabaster King ignored them.

He stared at me. I knew he was trying to get into my head, but he no longer even had the ability to plant words in my mind. He was forced to open his mouth and push air past his tongue, and I could tell that angered him. "Have you come back to finish the job, *witch*?" I could feel his emphasis on the last word. It was a foul word coming from his lips.

I smiled sweetly into his frown. "Is that what you think I am, *king*?" I gave it the same emphasis he had. "When I was first here, I was a scared little girl looking for revenge. Now, though, I am so much more. I have to thank you. If you had not sent me away as you did, then I wouldn't be complete. I wouldn't have met my true master, and he would not be with me, right now, watching you foul the air with your speech."

The king scowled and spat as he rose from his throne. He was not moving well. My parting gift must not have been agreeing with him. He staggered when he stood, and his eye under the black stain remained shut. "You were a foolish girl, and you remain one. I care not what you found in that void between worlds. You will go back to the abyss where I sent you, or—"

"Or what?" I approached him at a walk, then a run. Then a sprint, and then a leap. He moved not an inch, and I carried him back down into the seat of his throne, with my feet perched on its armrests. The whole heavy throne rocked back, then found its legs again with a heavy crack. "Or you'll banish me again, *brother*?" This time, it was Shadow, speaking through me. He was there, riding my mind like he'd ridden my body.

The Alabaster King's eyes opened wide, and I saw their kinship. His eyes were the same black, and I watched stars in their depths. He recoiled in shock, and shrank back down onto his throne.

"Brother? Shadow? I thought you—"

"You could never finish the job, could you? You sent me there and just expected me to die. Have you really been lying to yourself all these years? Did you really think that I'd curl up and give up? Pathetic." I closed my hand over the Alabaster King's throat, though with my fingers spread I barely spanned even the front half of it. It didn't matter. He coughed and squirmed like I was choking him. "Well, brother, your era is at an end. We ruled together, you and I. There was balance, and everything was full of color. Do you remember it? No. I expect you've chased even that from your mind. Well, I've spent the last hundred generations in exile, watching from a distance as you ruined it all."

The Alabaster King scowled, and in a petulant voice like a spoiled brat, said, "Fine. Take it. I'll leave peacefully."

He tried to rise, but I pushed him back down. It must have been a pitiful sight. The grand Alabaster king, tall and majestic, pinned down to his throne by barely a handful of a girl. "No. You won't. I don't trust you where I can't see you." Shadow whispered to me, and I obeyed. I ground myself down against the king, trapped against his throne. On his face was a look of panic, but he reacted just like he had when I'd danced with him. When my hips met his, I found him hard and wanting. I slid myself up to find his tip, then dropped myself back down when the slim length jumped up against my slit. He shuddered against the throne. He made no other noises as I started to ride him, up and down and pressing my hips flush to his kingship's. He was slim, and I could feel it twitching hard and eagerly within me, but it left me disappointed. After having Shadow, this king just didn't measure up.

When I lifted myself from him, I saw that another black mark was creeping across his pelt. His shaft gave another jump inside me, then I felt it go rigid. He clawed at the throne in panic, but the shadow quickly engulfed his chest, then his shoulders, and then his head. And when it had covered all of him, I felt him subtly change. He wasn't simply stony or stone-like anymore. He was actual, rigid stone. He was smooth black marble, unmoving and unliving. I stood and felt his—its—stone penis pull from my depths. He would make a remarkable statue to replace the one in the town center. He still had royal, majestic presence, but instead he was hard. Even a few dribbles of his spunk had solidified with him, beading at the tip of his member. And best of all, he was no longer white.

I left him laid back rigid against the throne. Behind it, I carved the air with my hands. A massive hole formed where before there had been the smooth marble of the hall. From it emerged Shadow. He flowed against me, curling like a tiger and pressing himself to me in the most intimate of ways. Our beasts joined us from where they'd been guarding the hall. It was done. The usurper was dethroned.

Into the hall came a chamberlain. He was dragged by one of the beasts—I believe it was the one I named Onyx. The chamberlain was a lanky white hare, though he wore an air of intense shame and embarrassment, and he sported a patch of black over his muzzle. Onyx looked satisfied and pleased with herself.

"Bring that to the square, and have it installed in a place of honor. Then spread word that the White Kingdom is no more." The chamberlain shook and bowed in acquiescence. "Today begins the reign of Shadow, and I, his queen."

Velvet

Rechan

The single shout snapped Willem's head up. His ears turned and strained into the silent moments that followed. An urgent, muffled thumping confirmed someone needed him in the worst way.

Hurling his bulk from the chair, the horse stomped across the parlor, accellerating to a sprint by the time he reached the stairs. Each quick step echoed through the house, the deafening rumble a signal he was coming. He reached the door, twisted the knob and found it locked. With one lunge Willem put his hoof to it, splintering the door with a crack as loud as his kick. It swung open to display the scene in full.

Petra knelt on the bed, still weakly pounding a fist on the wall as the wolf strangling her from behind with a scarf or a stocking. Their commotion stopped only long enough for the two to glance Willem's way—the sheep with her watery brown eyes bulging, the wolf's ears flattening in surprise—before Willem was beside the bed and lifting the wolf up by an arm.

"But I paid—" the wolf barked and let go of the scarf.

Willem's throw sent him through the door, into the hall and smacking against the wall. Before the wolf could shake the stupor off his face Willem stood over him and glared. "Go," the stallion grated.

"Do you know who... I-I will have you know that I..." The wolf tried to stand and pull his pants up, and shaking fingers failed at both. It's likely no one had ever shoved him around even once in his life.

Willem itched to hurt him, but wasn't allowed unless the customer didn't leave or stop when told. Rich men didn't take punches like real men, leaving with their ears down to never come back; no, they made problems well after leaving.

Finally the bastard got himself together and when Willem took another step closer, he bolted down the stairs. After the front door slammed, Petra came out of the room, rubbing her throat. "Thank you," she said with a voice raw and scratchy.

Willem enjoyed throwing customers out, but even more he took pleasure in hurting them. Though he didn't like it for the same reason men like the wolf liked hurting girls like Petra. No, the way the sheep now looked up at him turned Willem's chest into a lantern. It wasn't the look of pity, or the discomfort of the other girls, or the superiority of everyone else in the world. Instead, in those moments of brutality he showed them his true worth. He was more than manual labor. He could see in their face they remembered it and were thankful for it. Sad, how their appreciation could only come after abuse.

Lorelei stormed around the corner and came to a stop at seeing them, her sharp green eyes taking it all in. "Are you well?" she asked Petra.

The sheep coughed and swallowed. "No pretty talk for me, but I can work fine."

"Good." As Petra returned downstairs Lorelei gave Willem one of her rare genuine smiles. "Good work. Now fix the door."

Willem pointed at the door. "Why do we... l... l-lo..." He frowned.

"Lock?"

He nodded.

The snow leopard considered a moment. "Sometimes the ladies and the gentlemen are not noisy, so we need some way to signal the room is in use. Also, a guest who feels he can break the rules of decorum may try to peek in to watch, and the interrupted customer could rightly demand his money back. Especially our guests who have things they wish to hide and the wealth to make it an issue."

With a nod he knocked his knuckles against the broken door jam, turned and kept his clopping to a minimum on the way down the stairs. The same effort went into keeping his face plain all the way into the basement storeroom. Once alone in the quiet darkness he stomped and snorted, punching the air.

Why did he bother asking? Why risk saying a stupid word he hadn't said in years?

He hated tripping over his words—which he always did—even in front of Lorelei, who hadn't reacted the tiniest bit to this since Willem was a boy and his mother ran the house. Even when it was a word he knew well, it would come out slowly. Often he mumbled through them or they fell apart near the end. While Willem thought as fast as anyone else, to others speaking slow meant thinking slow, and the horse hated being seen as dim, or worse treated like it. Since the age of ten he adopted the oath of "Never Speak", but curiosity or the situation often ruined his best efforts.

At least he could put his anger to work, take out his frustrations with a hammer. Lighting the lantern, Willem gathered spare wood and his tools before returning upstairs with the added light.

***

Before any of the night's customers arrived, Lorelei took Willem's arm. "I have an important job for you. Follow me."

At the bottom of the stairs Lorelei passed the storeroom to stop at an always-locked door. "Olaf is sick with the shakes, and I need someone to take care of this." Removing a key from about her neck, she slid it home and opened the door. At first he thought she revealed a closet. Inside, a door sat on the tiny room's opposite wall next to a lever. "Fetch the lantern."

Willem pondered the discovery while he complied. Having lived in the big house all his life, the horse knew about the door, but his mother wouldn't tell him what was inside, and he never bothered to ask Lorelei. Sometimes clients and someone else—usually Olaf, the male whore who otherwise served drinks—disappeared down into the basement, only to emerge an hour or so later, on occasion the guest needing to be helped or carried out.

When he returned with the light he paused, gawking at what it revealed—the door in the little alcove had a window made of glass. Actual glass!

"See this bar here?" she said, tapping the lever. "Any time you step into this room, make sure it's up like it is now." To drive the point home she stared into his eyes. He nodded, but she kept on looking for a moment more before opening the door with the window. "Good."

Stale air with a hint of something odd sifted out to meet them. Lantern light exposed walls barren except for the occasional candle in a holder, a naked stone floor, and something in the middle. It called to mind the plug at the bottom of the claw-foot tub upstairs, only much bigger. The broad iron thing could have filled half of a wagon, sat as tall as his knee, and was round, set flush with the floor. Cut into it, facing the door, was a seat. No doubt about it—a cushion sat in the niche, and in front of it stood an upholstered footstool.

The snow leopard walked around it, the long fluff of her tail twitching, a sign that always put Willem on guard. "See this hatch here?" He brought the lantern over. Atop the metal plug he found a little door, no bigger than a slice of bread. "Every day you will fetch a bucket of water, open this hatch, and pour it in. Once you do, close it immediately." Well, that explained what Olaf did with that bucket every day. "Understand?"

He nodded, and spared a glance down at the iron plug in the floor. Up close he could see long, thin slots in the metal, folded to look like shutters on a window. "Why?" Was there a plant inside?

"You don't want to know." With that she padded to the doorway and he dutifully followed. Once she closed the door with the window, Lorelei turned back to him. "When a special guest requests the most secret and costly of pleasures, you'll bring them down here, light the candles in the room, and close the door. Only when the door is closed will you pull this stick down. I'll give you an hourglass, and when the sands run out, you come back and check on the guest, help them up the stairs. You may need to clean up, too. Think you can do this?"

When Willem nodded she passed him the key. The sound of the front door opening upstairs and voices drew their ears. "Good. Lock the door once you've watered it," she said and prowled up the stairs.

It? He glanced back at the dark window for several moments before following behind.

Nothing interesting happened when he opened the hatch. Just a little iron grate inside. Willem poured the bucket in, closed up, locked the room, and in a week it became so routine he stopped thinking about the whole matter. He shared the duties with Olaf, which meant he was free of the chore only when Olaf couldn't scrape up the sliver of an excuse.

A few nights later, a squirrel in a gold waistcoat arrived. He stood straight backed, his tail high and proud. It always impressed Willem how even short fellows like this one could manage to look down their muzzle at things, or merely stand like they owned the place. Like Lorelei, but without having earned the right.

"Welcome to Velvet." Elke rose from a couch in the parlor. "What is it you're—"

"I'm looking for the lady of the house." He replied more to the air around them, not acknowledging her at all.

Elke's smile didn't falter. "Of course." Lorelei described the ermine once as greatly poised regardless of the customer. Her black tail-tip disappeared up the stairs in a wink.

Willem hid his smirk as he anticipated the squirrel's disappointment—Lorelei didn't loosen her corset but for the fattest of purses or other ladies. When she appeared and the conversation started anew, the squirrel's voice dropped to a conspirator's whisper the horse still caught. "I was told you had a very special service, one I couldn't find anywhere else."

"Ah. *That*. Of course." She only needed to make eye contact with Willem to get him moving. After a moment to remember the instructions, he went about lighting the candles, casting a sultry glow to the drab chamber, and walked out just in time to catch the guest on the stairs. Willem waved him into the chamber and closed the door.

He lingered there in the little room, watching through the window as the squirrel sat, fussing with a wrinkle on his coat. The horse tugged the lever down and watched, curious to see some change. Those narrow slots running along the plug's top flared open, leaving dark grooves along the metal. The squirrel's eyes caught his, and Willem panicked, stepping back from the window.

Inside the storeroom he found the hourglass Lorelei gave him and turned it over.

"Willem!" Petra called. "We need water for a bath—fetch some, please?"

When he returned half the sand had gone. Willem peeked in the window again to find the squirrel sprawled out in the seat, his breeches about his ankles, looking most excited and either waiting for a woman or about to attend to it himself. Yet he sat still with his eyes closed, his features twitching in a delighted smile, and as Willem watched the man's hips shivered.

Very odd.

Carrying the hourglass up to the parlor with him, he resumed his typical post while keeping an eye on the sand. When he returned downstairs, he found the squirrel having stained his chest in his excitement and otherwise looking quite content with himself. The stallion flipped the lever and opened the door. Languidly the squirrel rose and adjusted his breeches, ignoring the stain on his waistcoat.

The squirrel returned after two weeks, and again a week later. It surprised Willem to see his clothes disheveled, as if he'd slept in them and spent only a moment straightening them. "Here, take this, let's go now." The man turned to Willem, thrusting a stack of coin at him.

Even if he didn't normally go quiet, the horse was at a loss for a response.

The squirrel prompted him with, "Well?" Gone was the earlier tone of collected superiority, replaced by real impatience.

With a snort and a shake of his head, the horse stuffed the coins in a pocket and led the way. Along with the clop of his hooves he picked up the jangle of the money, more than he'd ever held by… well, more numbers than his mother chose to teach him. Only enough to aid his carpentry, as "Broad shoulders need know no letters and sums," she had once said.

Once he unlocked the outer door, the slender squirrel slipped past him, opened the windowed door, and pounced the seat. Willem could feel the man's demanding eyes on him as he went around the room lighting the candles, and heard a sigh when he stepped out and shut the squirrel in. Flipping the lever, he grabbed the hourglass and carried it with him up the stairs on his way to confer with Lorelei he'd received the accurate amount of money.

When he returned and stopped at the interior door, Willem's hand halted half way to the lever. The squirrel lay face down in the floor, at an angle like he had tipped over forwards.

He ignored the lever, throwing open the door—slamming the man's arm in the process—and hurried over to sit the squirrel upright. The customer still breathed, but his eyes rolled about in his head, and he moved sluggish and boneless like a drunk or an opium eater. With a grunt and a deep breath, the stallion lifted him in both arms like a child and stood.

As he stepped through the door, a faint voice tugged at the edge of his hearing. Pausing in the threshold, Willem strained his ears.

"Wait… Don't go…"

It came from behind him. The horse looked back over his shoulder to find the chamber empty.

A chill raced up his back. Willem kicked the door closed and charged up the stairs.

After a few minutes on one of the couches, the ladies fawning over him and Olaf stuffing a stiff drink in his hand, the squirrel found his strength. Willem watched him leave before the horse disappeared back down stairs, yanking the lever up and peering at the chamber through the window. The candles still burned. Lorelei's tail would certainly be in a knot if he let the wicks melt down. Still…

He opened the door. Nothing happened. Moving like the room was on fire, Willem threw himself inside, blew out the candles, and rushed out of the room. He couldn't help but slam the door behind him.

Before the house settled to sleep as the sun rose, Willem tried to chase away the unease the chamber put into him by sharing his bed with Elke. He didn't use the girls often, even if they had no issues when he did; many times the girls remarked he was the rare man who gave them any sense of respect or tenderness. While he enjoyed laying with her—the way her whole body clung to his, how she only muffled her genuine noises by pressing her face into his chest, the wildness she brought to the sheets—he had another need.

She must have sensed it. As her breathing evened, she propped an elbow on his sweat-dampened chest and peered down at him. "Now that you're feeling better, can you tell me what's wrong?"

Willem snorted in dismissal and ruffled the fur of her cheek, leaving it comically askew.

The normally well-groomed Elke didn't even rub her fur back into place. "Come come, Dumpling," she cooed, using the name he'd acquired after stuffing himself with the apple treats every holiday. Her nose nudged at his shoulder. "Something has you acting off tonight. Your smile barely comes out of hiding, your attention has been miles away."

The real concern filling her eyes nearly brought wetness to his own. He blinked it away and looked down, unable to look at her. Instead he played with her tail's dark tip, and bless her, she didn't flick it out of his grasp.

"You may keep your secrets, then." In her voice he could hear the disappointment as well as the warning; she would not pry, but the others wouldn't when they noticed.

Elke wiggled along the crook of his arm and nuzzled his throat, drawing a contented nicker from him. He wished he could have found the strength to say it all, let alone the words. The horse did not want to be alone, and Elke responded the best to being held in the quiet of the morning hours, the ermine like a delicate doll nestled against his bulk.

Normally the horse had no trouble sleeping in his tiny room by the kitchen, tucked out of earshot for his snoring. That day though he lay for hours listening to her rhythmic breathing, and eventually his mind found its way into the basement. In all his years he'd never heard of a ghost, or someone dying in the building—it couldn't be that. Was someone trapped beneath the metal plug?

Through the next two nights Willem struggled to keep the room out of his mind. It worked until Olaf forced the matter.

The horse sat next to a bed flipped on its side, mending a broken board, when Olaf called his name. He looked up to find the rabbit passing him the hourglass. "I took a new customer down into the basement while you were working, but now I've got a regular. You make sure to get the new man, yes?"

With a wary glance at the hourglass, Willem sighed and nodded. Another so soon? The squirrel must have told his friends.

Once the sands ran out the stallion took his time clopping down the stairs to linger at the basement door. Finally he trudged out and peered through the window.

The stag inside was clothed but still staring off into nothingness. Willem yanked the lever and when he waved to the customer, then knocked on the wall, the stag didn't seem to register it. Opening the door and clearing his throat did it, the man turning his head.

"Is it time?" He blinked blearily and reached into his waistcoat, withdrawing a gold pocket watch. With a disappointed snort he stood.

The stag paused mid-way through the door. "Are you Willem?"

Willem nodded.

"She said you should come see her."

He cocked his head. "Who?"

"Her," the customer said, gesturing back into the empty room. "She emphasized how much she wants to see you."

The customer passed up the stairs, leaving Willem gawking in his wake.

***

Well into midmorning, Willem wrapped his hooves in cloth. He crept into the parlor and down the stairs with but a soft rustle across the wood, pausing on each step to listen. Not a creak. Still in the dark of the basement he shuffled about until he found the lantern before unlocking the door. The scrape of its hinges made him wince.

Only after he'd entered the small chamber and closed the outer door, preventing any light from spilling into the corridor, did Willem light the lantern.

The small room remained as barren and dull as before. He circled the plug in the floor. After several moments he said, "Hello?"

Nothing.

Willem turned to leave and paused, noticing the lever. Of course. He clunked it down. Turning back he found the room the same, except for the slats in the plug were now open. He peered inside, brought the lantern up, but even the glow could not pierce the darkness beyond.

"Willem."

Even the soft voice startled him enough to jerk up, and he nearly dropped the lantern. Lorelei stood in the doorway.

"Curious, are you?" she asked, stepping closer.

At first he wanted to apologize, to explain, but something made him hold. He stared at her. Lorelei did not look at him with the keenness she often did, nor did she stand quite the same, like she owned not only the building but the whole world and you should listen to anything she said. He then caught sight of the door over her shoulder. The closed door that had not made a whine when she came in.

He backed away.

"You're clever. More observant than anyone gives you credit for."

"Who are you?" At the sound of his voice the stallion gasped. His words came out with no halts or shakes, as smooth as any other. He looked in confusion, then fear at the snow leopard.

"I'm sorry to startle you," the not-Lorelei said. "I should not have tried to fool you. My name is Velvet, and by lowering the lever there you have allowed me the freedom to speak with you."

"How?"

"In your mind." She gestured to the open vents. "You've let my scent into the air, and as you breathe it in, you let me into you. I can make anything possible, and I know how much you wish you could talk. You can do so with no limitations, I've freed you. Go on, try."

He licked his lips. "My name is Willem and I am a horse." It came clear as well water! "I can talk!" The horse beamed and almost danced in the spot. "Wheelbarrow! Cobblestones! Three greasy geese go to give the greedy grocer's green garden a gander!" Mastering the child's word game brought a warmth bubbled up inside him and he couldn't stop his laugh, Velvet joining him.

Eventually his attention returned to her. "So you're beneath that?" He pointed at the big iron plug.

The amusement in Velvet's features withered, her eyes souring. "Yes."

Why she had been confined was clear—he had seen the men come and sit, the coin they had paid, and now he saw what Velvet could give them. "How long have you been here?"

"Before your mother was born." Velvet shook her head. "I've waited so long for someone like you, another who might listen to my truth. But I can't keep you long—I'm not able to grasp how time moves within a man's thoughts. A breath can seem like a night and a night can seem like a breath."

"I'll bring the hourglass with me next time," Willem said. "We can watch it move and know."

"Good. But please." She crossed to him and touched his chest, her gaze an ache in his heart. "Please come back, so that we can talk freely."

Willem said, "I swear."

Like a candle snuffed out, she was gone.

Was that a dream? He tested his speech and once more it was a broken instrument. He went to bed to find himself haunted by unanswered questions and restless sleep.

***

Willem nearly put a patron through a wall after mistaking a particularly noisy romp of Olaf's as a struggle. Most of the day went like that, the horse's mind clogged with thoughts of Velvet, leaving him stumbling through his chores.

When the squirrel strode through the door, Willem nearly missed him. Not until he passed through the horse's line of sight, focused as it was on the basement stairs. Willem came up and caught the squirrel by the collar as he descended the first step.

He bucked in Willem's grasp. "Let me go!"

It wasn't until they were half way across the parlor that Willem recognized him as the same squirrel who had visited Velvet so often. Where he had been dressed clean and sharp, now his fine clothes were rumpled and dusty, like he'd been sleeping in a crawlspace or beneath a porch. His fur lacked the luster of proper diet and health, unkempt and knotted in places. But his eyes, his eyes flicked about like dropped coins.

Willem dropped the man, who dropped to the floor with a start. "Is this what you want?" he howled, up again and throwing coins. "Here, take double! Give me twice the time." A jittering shake ran through him as he spoke. Squirrels were naturally twitchy but this reminded Willem of an old woman who fell in the market, thrashing and jabbering with a fit.

"Sir, you look ill. Perhaps you should wait a while before visiting."

Willem glanced up to see Lorelei on the stair landing. Thump! Something sturdier than a coin thudded his chest. Glancing down, he found the squirrel actually hitting him. "No! No I'll see her, you can't stop me!"

While the scrappy little fellow had enough fight in him, it just didn't do much to the sturdy horse. Once more Willem snagged him by the collar and dragged him towards the door.

The squirrel's gasp startled him. The crazy bugger leveled a dangerous glare on him "You've been with her, haven't you?"

The accusation, both so venomous and accurate, stunned Willem enough he let the squirrel go.

"You want her all to yourself, don't you? Well you can't have her, she's mine." It would not have surprised Willem had the man been foaming at the mouth. He wasn't, but still hit with both tiny fists.

"We'll collect your coins for you, and keep them for your next visit, sir," Lorelei said, unmoved. "Willem, see him out please."

That was all he needed. The squirrel had left the door open, so Willem merely shoved him through it. On the porch he actually picked the man up and dropped him the short distance over the railing into a bush, rather than fling him onto his tail. "Go," he said with finality, and slammed the door.

The stallion held the knob closed and, sure enough, a few frantic tugs came before the man gave up. With a snorting whuffle, Willem let the knob go and stepped back.

"They get like that, sometimes."

Lorelei's words gave him a jump. He turned to find her a pace behind him, her eyes on his. "Starved for it, like opium eaters."

"What…?" He pointed downwards and gave her an imploring look.

She shook her head, tail snapping. "I don't know. It was here before the woman who managed your mother bought the place. Before then this house was some scholar's lodge or something."

That bit was tucked away in the crusty cubby of his mind. "Why keep?"

Lorelei lifted some of the loose coins the mad squirrel had spilled about. "Keep an eye out. Someone else came by for the basement room, yes? Some deer? Next time, delay him a few days. The temptation only lingers so long."

The horse nodded and helped her gather the scattered money, but the whole time he kept watch on her. Did she know he had visited Velvet? Was he acting off already? More nagging though was the concern of going back to the basement so soon.

***

By the time the last set of bedsprings settled into birthing the occasional sleeping squeak, Willem could take it no longer. It didn't matter whether it was the mysteries that drew him or a hook, like the squirrel, Willem needed to go.

"No, I can't freely give you that," Velvet said once he'd opened the slats and stepped inside.

"Why not? You can see me. I want to see you."

Not-Lorelei's head shook. "You wouldn't … no."

She could have shown him anything and said it was her. Since Velvet didn't try it, he supposed she couldn't read his thoughts. "I know what it's like to have people look at you like you're nothing. You let me be me. Let me let you be you." Even with his words working, that sounded silly to his own ears.

"No," she pleaded.

"Then let me touch you."

For a moment Velvet didn't react. Maybe she had to make herself do things in his head. Finally she tilted her muzzle and coiled her tail in an un-Lorelei way. "Only if you do something for me."

It was his turn for hesitance. "What do you want?"

"No one ever asks me that," she said with a sigh. "I'll make my request another time. If you want to touch me freely, then listen." She not only told him what to do, but he could see the instructions unspool before his eyes, like he could see into the future.

Willem went in search of the right tool. The pick to clean the grit from his hooves curved too severely. Ah! Inspiration struck when he saw the chisel he used to lever up nailed-in boards. Taking it and his hammer, the horse returned to the chamber, making sure to close both doors, lest he wake someone with the racket.

He opened the square hatch he poured water into daily. Setting the chisel's point against one of the tiny metal bars, he cracked the chisel's butt with the hammer. Two more whacks and the metal gave a snick as the chisel broke through. When the grate hung by only a few thin bars, he bent the mesh back and folded it flat against the roof of Velvet's prison, out of the way.

When he pulled his wrist back, the base of a broken bar bit into his fur. It took him several moments of careful wiggling to free himself without being cut. Willem fetched a pair of pliers, bending each jagged tooth down and to the side.

Once satisfied with the work, Willem leaned forward to peer into the hole. It was the darkness that lurked at the bottom of a well. Even fetching a candle he could not pierce the pit, and a lantern would likely fare no better.

With his nose so close to the hole, he could taste Velvet's scent now, like rich flowers sealed in a crypt. What was he dealing with? What was it that lived in the dark corner of their home?

Those thoughts were cut short when a white cloth bumped his nose. Willem jerked his head back and goggled. No, not a white cloth, he could now make out the silky white branch emerging from the hole. Branch was the wrong word, but it was the closest thing: a slender stalk covered in light fuzz, capped with a thin white fin, flat as a leaf.

The longer he stared, the more it reminded him of a feather. Yes, a feather, but one with a long naked base. He reached out and caressed it, the fluff smooth but velvety. Heh. So that's where she got the name. After a few strokes the branch trembled against his palm, and Velvet sighed behind him. Not quite a sexual sound, but definitely pleased.

"Come back tomorrow night. There are things we should be free to discuss."

Willem shifted to gaze sidelong as his digits ran through the big feather's fluff. "Why can't we talk now?" It shifted in his grasp and he glanced down to catch sight of it disappearing into the hole.

Velvet shook her head. "You need your sleep, otherwise Lorelei will get suspicious."

"But—" Before he could get much more out, she was gone.

He closed the hatch, retrieved his tools, and sealed the chamber. When he returned his tools, Willem picked up the hourglass. He'd turned it before stepping into Velvet's chamber and now all the sand was at the bottom. It hadn't felt like an hour—hell, it hadn't felt like half of one.

**

Something swatted his nose, snapping Willem awake.

"Welcome back." Lorelei leaned over him, her eyes ever critical. "Pleasant dreams?"

He'd done it again, dozed off in the front room chair. The horse dipped his chin and looked away.

"Lately you haven't looked rested. Are you well?" While she sounded concerned, he knew her suspicion something was amiss.

What could he say? What would she believe? He glanced up, then away, and an idea bubbled up. "Scared." The stallion pointed at the basement stairs and flashed the whites of his eyes.

"Ah." She claimed a stool and sat before him, her paw on his knee. "Don't think about it. I often forget it's there until a customer reminds me. Picture it as a leaky roof or a drafty room. You only think of those when they leak or the wind blows cold."

"But... monster?" Willem had held that thought locked away, unwilling to even dwell on it, but it still lurked back there.

Lorelei laughed. "Maybe, but it can't get out. If you follow the rules, it can't touch you. Whatever's down there belongs there, not out in the world. We inherited it, we follow the rules, no need to worry."

No need unless the rules are broken. That, and discovery, was what worried him.

***

When he returned to her the next morning, Velvet regarded him with curious eyes. "You truly want to know what I want. I can see it in you."

The horse shrugged. "You deserve for me to at least try." While those words sounded true to him, something else he couldn't put his nose to nagged at him. Without thought he opened the hatch and waited for her feather to emerge.

"I want to please you."

That turned him around. He glanced at her, still as Not-Lorelei, and shook his head.

"I know you don't want me like this," she said, and brushed her fingers along his muzzle. It felt as though she really was touching him, too. "Not like this. Not in your mind. That I have to do for so many, and it's been a long time since I've been free to satisfy someone as a proper lover. I want to please your body. Will you give me that freedom?"

The stallion looked from her to the giant iron plug. "How?"

A faint scrape emanated from the plug, a light clicking that escaped the open hatch. "You said you wanted to see me. I'll show you a small, delicate part of myself, and you might recoil."

"I won't turn away," he said, steeling himself. No matter what, he would accept it. He needed to give her that. The one person who understood him deserved that.

Braced as he was, he didn't expect what emerged from the open hatch. At first he took it as a closed fist or perhaps a rolled up bit of cloth, grey colored with white along the crinkled rim. When he touched it, the fist unfurled like a long, tubular flower. Inside blushed a pale pink and he saw the wetness there, smelled Velvet's scent, intense like the exotic incense tent in the market. It was a cunt. Or perhaps some sort of mouth... part. Below it stretched another stalk, grey and curved.

The outside of it was soft but dry, while caressing the inside he found it as natural as any woman's interior. Beneath his touch the flower trembled, and Velvet sighed in pleasure and promise.

The flower conjured images of something vast and many limbed, like a fish. His thoughts then slid to something like a mermaid: foreign and abnormal but none the less beautiful. Velvet was no simple woman. Not to mention the strange fact that her scent could open his desires to her, could give him the gift of unbroken speech.

"What are you?" His voice came out more marveled than repulsed.

"Something from a fairytale," she cooed. "A granter of wishes. I have my own wishes I desire to come true, Willem. The first of which is to free your seed from you. Will you let me?"

The stallion traced the edges of her flower, intrigued. "Yes."

Her chuckle was rich with lust and promise, a sound he'd often heard in the brothel. "You need to be free of your trousers."

As soon as his pants hit the stone floor, the flower angled downward, its stem stretching until it bumped across his length. The opening bloomed wide and slid itself over him, swallowing him like a hungry snake. Even a stallion such as he fit inside with only the mildest of stretching when the fleshy sleeve sealed around him.

Warm, though not as damp as a woman would have been.

She conformed to his length, squeezing every cranny. The skin rippled and pulled him, a tugging suckle that slid along each nook. A nicker parted his teeth and he leaned his knees against the metal plug, only to have the flower jerk him, forcing him on all fours.

The women he had known, talented in their craft, had usually begun slow and teasing before raising a man fast to finishing. Here the horse found no hesitation, his length nursed with instant insistence. A hungry rhythm set in, each suckling pull ending with a squeeze that touched every lick of skin.

Velvet groaned in his ear, phantom fingers slithering through his mane and over tensed shoulders like she lay beneath him, taken as a normal woman. "It has been so long for me. Never so large a man either. This pleasure is freeing all on its own."

Another great pull dragged Willem lower, reeling him until he sprawled across the metal, his tool threaded through the hatch. Even though a pleasured neigh flew out of him, a panicked thought beat against his skull. What had he done? Would the next yank geld him?

"Do not fear," she cooed in his ear with Lorelei's purr. "I'll free you once you flow."

Willem clung to the metal, gasping as the flower clamped down. The tension turned the milking into a maddening fire. So intense, so perfect a pleasure, he could not last long. Unseen legs clutched his hips, claws prickled his back, and Velvet's moan echoed inside of him.

Sweat lathered his pelt and great gasps blasted past flared nostrils.

He was aware of his edge only as Velvet threw him over it.

The horse crashed through his climax with a thunderous whinny. It was as though his insides gushed out of him, leaving him hollow. Each surge of his seed was a full body throb, and Willem shook, barely able to draw breath until she wrung the last of him. And wrung she did, those pulls a steady draining that he imagined dragged up his stones.

Finally the pressure eased and she released him, leaving him gasping, his shaft sore with the sudden prickle of naked air. An ache set in, a boneless weakness like the rest after a hard day's labor. Never before had the horse experienced so furious an orgasm.

While he recovered, Velvet stroked his ears and mane, soothing him like a loved pet.

"Are you well?" she asked.

He was, as if her very words revitalized him, or she knew the moment he regained his strength. "Very."

"Good," she purred. "I need something of you, Willem."

Slowly the stallion rose, carefully removing his spent shaft from the hatch and rocking back. "What is it?"

"Free me."

A cascade of pressure and emotion crashed through him. For a moment he was aware of every time she had said "free", each utterance like a nail in a board. For that moment alone he saw she had built a cage in his mind, and her command the final hammer blow.

The cage and the knowledge of it were then gone, replaced by a single thought that held him: Velvet should be free. This cruel place had used her, worse than the women upstairs—they earned, they could leave, they were free. She worked only to survive, earned nothing but her meal, and had been pinned down there before this place was a brothel. Lorelei had gone along with it, earning coin off of her prisoner. Freedom was the only right thing to do, how had he not seen it before?

Picking himself up, he surveyed the room in a new light. How could he unmake it, take it apart to unshackle Velvet from her prison?

Willem circled the great plug, inspecting every inch. There were latches which unclasped after some pulling. When finished, he oiled the plug's hinges while he thought. Were it made of wood he could wedge a crowbar between the seams, but there wasn't a chance with it being unyielding iron and so heavy.

The crafters didn't build the whole thing inside the room; it was brought there and installed. How'd they get it into place?

He looked up. A thick iron loop hung above him, drilled into the ceiling long ago.

When he was a boy, Willem's mother wanted a bathing tub in her private quarters. Getting a tub up the narrow stairs would have both wrecked backs and stairwell, so they used another method. He remembered watching three strong men set a pulley and winch in his mother's room and pull it up towards the window.

Whoever brought the hatch in had used the same idea to get it into position and lower it carefully. He could reverse it.

Building a winch wouldn't work. He'd need to see one up close and toy with it before getting a good grasp of it, but more importantly he couldn't do it in secret.

Closing the outer door to muffle the noise, Willem broke the inner door's glass window. He sawed a narrow wedge free from the inner door's window and smoothed the new notch's splinters down with sandpaper.

He found a long coil of rope in the basement—for what, he didn't know. The great iron door to Velvet's prison had a bar to secure a rope to, so he tied one end there, then began tying knot after knot into the length. When done, Willem threaded the rope through the ring in the chamber's ceiling. Finally he tossed the rope through the inner door's broken window, stepped outside of the chamber, and closed the door.

Willem was no stranger to hard labor. Lorelei had occasionally loaned his back out to neighboring shops, before he was big enough to serve as doorman. Taking up the knotted rope, he bent at the knees, squared his shoulders, and stepped forward like the men had done all those years ago.

Like trying to lift a house, it nearly pulled him back with his efforts rather than move on its own. He grunted, pulled with back, shoulder and leg, and something shuddered in the room behind him. Even oiled the metal protested after being left at rest so long. It budged, not much but enough. The horse pulled downwards until he felt a knot slip through the door's slot he'd sawed, and relaxed for just a moment. As soon as he eased, the door took the weight for him with a groan.

It went like this for several minutes, the stallion struggling to earn every knot of the rope, soon panting and dripping sweat. After what felt like an hour, he turned to gaze into the room. The hatch was open at a severe angle. Still it was open, and he could push it backwards now.

He scrambled over to the open hatch, squatted, and pushed up and forward. It took every muscle he had but the weighty lid rocked from near shut to near open, the rope catching at the same angle on the other side. Willem nearly fell in, his knees catching on the lip, but he managed to roll over onto the stone floor.

Rising, the horse gazed into the hole. Darkness, so deep it could swallow him. He backpedaled to the door and, seizing the rope, released the knot from the slot. Immediately the weight dragged his hooves across the stone, but he caught a leg against the lip of the plug and, almost lifted off the floor, he fought it before the weight clanged on the other side. With care he eased it down, and once it settled he dropped to the floor to pant.

A soft cloth-on-cloth rustle drew his eyes to the open hatch. Something big and white emerged, too fast for him to settle on what he was seeing. Not until she was free of the hole. Even then she could not spread her wings, as the room was still too small. She arched before him, allowing the horse to soak her form in.

Velvet was beautiful.

Her head turned to regard him, the great antenna with their feathery fronds bobbing and brushing him. Even though the moth's dark, bowl-like eyes lacked pupils, he knew she stared at him. Six legs brought her over and her body's velvety white fluff brushed along his as she climbed atop him. At even her size—twice as much as he, not even counting her wings—very little weight settled over him.

"You're free."

"Not yet. Open the door. Set me free." She had no mouth to speak, just a curled up tube which she must have used to sip water. Yet he still heard the words as clearly as any she'd spoken.

"I will…" The powers that let him speak must not need his voice to do it, because the words came freely even as his breath hitched in his throat, fat with emotion. She would leave him behind.

One frond antenna stroked his muzzle. "My drone. It is day, and I will fly blind and in pain. You must help me find a place to hide 'til the night, and protect me then. Just as you will protect our offspring."

"Offspring?"

Velvet said, "There are no males of my kind. I need you, the offspring will need you, Willem."

His eyes flicked down the moth's underside. All he found amid the fluff was the flowered tube that had nursed his arousal, perched low between her back legs. It could extend? If she bred with men, it would make it easier. Even now with her body atop him, it was awkward and would not do well for mating.

They needed him. Just like the girls here, he would have purpose. Velvet though would give him a voice, see him as more than any had. Could she love him?

"Yes," she said, without him having voiced the question. Something inside of him was tickled by this voice, rubbed over with a feather, and after that touch he believed her.

Willem slid from beneath her and went to the door.

SIGHS FOR THE LABYRINTH

Slip-Wolf

The heart is a maze one must never get lost in. I now understand this.

A soldier knows duty and discipline and the elements that batter against them. A soldier knows bravery, cunning and the fear that would undermine them. But there is no martial remedy or countering defense for a heart swollen with yearning, a flutter of the soul for another's caress. Love sneaks up with a blade in its teeth, smothering with sentiment, stealing reason away. I was lost because of it.

I was raised to fight, and the world desired nothing more from me. So I came to believe that love was another land to be conquered, a war needing only the right words as weapons. It was for this reason I came to stand before a pyre on which my heart burned down to nothing.

Attica fell. That's what the Spartans would write and no more. The defeated would do little reading anyway.

Lukan, third standing General of Sparta, strode amongst his troops and saw the red-robed wounded proudly awaiting inspection. Victorious smells of men hot with sweat from battle tickled the young General's nose and he burned with pride as he passed them. Tired ashen bodies leaned on their spears, languidly beautiful in the sun. Their chests heaved with the swell of victory. Among the battle-slaked Spartans, Lukan could see a few of the aliens who had fallen into their fold. Greek helots, second class warriors, were outfitted with the traditional hoplite weapons of shield and spears and relegated to manning the flanks. Even fewer were creatures of the mists. A dark-furred sileni cleaned his cleaver, appearing like a centaur cut in half and packed into a small biped body, tail lashing furiously as he grumbled. The creature kept his naturally piercing eyes averted as the General passed. Lukan next caught a brief sight of the other half of his army's hooved menagerie far in the distance. The horns of the minotaur glinted and its huffing bull's nostrils twirled the dusty air. Broad muscles rippled under a glossy pelt the brown of an olive pit.

Lukan mounted a hillock, standing with endless acres of dead Athenians behind him. He gathered his torn cloak. "We have won." Soldier's eyes hungrily met his as he spoke. "We are but steps from the marble walls of Athens, where Pericles' chattel shudder in terror. We will make corpses or slaves of every man when we storm their Acropolis and they will know to their dying breaths what folly it was to defy Sparta!"

The answering roar rumbled up to the gods. Lukan's gaze traveled across his ecstatic brothers, basking for the briefest moment in the glory that he would share with his King when he arrived. Rumor had that the King had not come alone.

"Attention!" The command all but startled him.

Impulses forged since training in the childhood Agoge school brought shields to shins and warriors to stance. There was no preamble, honor guard or escort. Such things did not befit a Spartan King here. A sallow-faced Ephor, whose function was to observe the King's activities on behalf of the Spartan assembly of elders, hung far back as King Archidamus the second strode forward. At his side, sparely dressed in wrappings designed for athletics, was his only daughter, Kerata. While the King himself was of unremarkable stature, solid in muscle but grey and haggard with war against advancing years, his daughter was truly striking. She had eyes the green of a lush grove and the dark hair swept into a pony's tail exposed a slender, sinuous neck. High cheekbones and a narrow chin gave her the imperious countenance of the Helen of legend. Trojan women were known well for being independent of mind and active of will, but Kerata's hungry gaze spoke plainly of a relentless nature. Lukan, a man of some prospects, suddenly knew his moment to shine for her attentions had come.

The king was speaking to him. "You have done well. Sparta could walk to Athen's gates on the carpet of their dead. You will wear your scars with pride."

Lukan blinked, reminded of the gash in his cheek from a close arrow not an hour ago. The ache had been shrugged away. He had few scars upon him, still looking markedly youthful despite his many battles. He shrugged, as was proper. "I will subdue Eleusis within the week. The Athenians smuggle spies in through the port—" The young General's gaze drifted from the Spartan King to his daughter's hard glare. Her eyes crossed him as though he were foreign terrain. His voice caught. Why was the air so dry? "We can strangle any resistance in Attica by completing our conquest there."

"Better they surrender to us and send a message to other Greek states that the Athenians are a simple ally to abandon," Kerata said abruptly. Lukan felt his heart stop as she added, "but preferably not before you kill a few to remind them Sparta is a dangerous enemy to have."

The King nodded. "Port cities flee fast to their waves. What befalls them will spread far and quick. You see that my daughter, though lacking the martial instruction of her brothers, has a fighter's mind."

Lukan was speechless. The King's daughter was of course right, and Lukan was as impressed by her candor as her fit beauty. What words could appreciatively convey this? He had only met his King in council where Lukan was just one of many supplicants. He had long aimed to meet the King's daughter and gain her favor.

And now his mouth was wordless. A creeping feeling descended over him, quivering his thighs and freezing his vitals. The first cold bead of sweat came down his brow.

It was fear.

Lukan buried it under the same stoic reserve that carried him through fogs of war. The sounds that finally came from his mouth were as clipped as a blade glancing off a grindstone. "That is of course wise. I do hope you grant us more of your council in future, princess."

So formal and dismissive sounding!

She opened her mouth to speak but he cut her off. "I do not mean to say that a woman should not speak of war. Quite the opposite, though you cannot fight, you have assets that a man would be proud to—" He realized where he was going and feinted fast.

"I respect you." He bowed stiffly.

Kerata blinked, looking away. It burned a brand of shame in Lukan's heart when he heard her exasperated sigh. "We have other fronts to visit father?" She asked pointedly.

The King looked from General Lukan to his daughter, his expression laconic. "In a few days, after we oversee the next phase."

The next front was to the north, where Sparta's ally state of Potidaea was under assault. The General assigned to secure that field did not face the same dangers that Lukan did, but knew better than to complain about potential glories lost. Brassul was handsome, much loved within the Senate and seen as employing a silver wit. Jealousy welled up within Lukan when he imagined Brassul's tongue at work on the King's daughter. He felt himself blush, a burning sensation in his cheeks to which he was unaccustomed. The realization that it had happened and could be seen made him blush all the more.

"I see your duties have you preoccupied," The King said with uncertainty. "I leave you and your men to regroup for the march east. We will follow the camp for another few days."

Lukan felt hollow, only wishing for the encounter with his King and the woman whose attentions he desired to conclude. "My King," he grunted.

The King moved on, his daughter with him. She did not meet Lukan's gaze and he was secretly thankful, even though he would rather gut himself than turn away.

And so Lukan suffered his first defeat, fear and regret stinking on him as he dismissed his men to prepare for their victory meal.

Cyrantus could see much of the camp with his immense height and wide-spaced eyes. The Spartan's tents were indistinguishable from one another, their caps fluttering like sails on a coastal wind.

Another night far from home, dawn to come without broad arms around him. He had all but forgotten the scents of fig and olive trees waiting across the roiling seas. As was his learned habit, Cyrantus was alone on the outskirts. His great head hung low as shadows passed him in the dark, men who studiously moved to avoid him. The hoplites, both Spartan and otherwise, were afraid of him. On many nights that would be wise.

A voice from the dark spoke, weary but firm. "Why does my greatest alien complain? He's eaten far more than any six fighters within my mess. Have we shorted you in some way, Cretan?"

Cyrantus jerked his head around in surprise. Men's words directed at him were typically commands or calming sounds meant not to raise his ire. What surprised him further was the identity of he who addressed him so directly. The General, Lukan was his name, had blond hair, locks flowing long. Tightly packed muscles flexed under his blood-hued cloak as the Spartan stepped from the darkness and studied Cyrantus from head to toe.

Cyrantus snuffled. "Men of Crete would disparage your label for me. They do not revere my stock. Rather they place value in the dumb creatures that share features with us. They are... easier to control."

The Spartan General blinked in surprise. "It is indeed a strange world in which a bull can rise from eating and rutting and carry an ax into battle."

The minotaur blinked and cleared his throat. He folded his arms across a broad furred chest that bore only the leather strap binding his ax to his back. "When I long past saw men quit hurling their shit to master spears instead, I thought much the same."

Silence could not fall on the flank of a camp filled with thousands, but a pocket of quiet chill found them for a moment. The General dismissed the tension with a grunt. "What do they call you?"

"I am Cyrantus, General."

"What places you amongst us?" General Lukan asked.

"You don't know?"

Lukan shrugged. "Exotic though you are, I inherited this army from General Pelaertes, who fell in combat, a man whose sandals I could not fill in ten lifetimes. I know each of my brothers as I know myself, but many curiosities gather to an army over time."

"And I am one." The minotaur scuffed a heavy hoof. "I came to your predecessor's command by boat."

Lukan blinked in the following silence. "That's it? You came—"

"Crete is far south across the waters. It's a tough walk."

"What I meant—" Lukan grunted. "Never mind. I saw you cleave through Athenians like... well, I have to say I was impressed, despite what I see now."

The minotaur's bovine ears flicked in question, but resisted a sigh. "What do you see?"

Lukan continued. "You sit here as though near weeping. Your features aren't so strange to my eyes that I can't see your sorrow for something. Have you none like yourself to confide in? What of the sileni?"

"He is disposed only to drink and brawling and would not care for my troubles." Cyrantus looked away. "I find myself disturbed because I miss my mate, from whom I was separated many years ago." He left it at that, hoping the Spartan would not press for details.

Lukan snorted. "Most of us have left loved ones behind. It's a pitiful weakness to dwell on absent company when the brother at your flank depends on you to stay sharp."

Cyrantus leaned against a rocky outcropping. The ax pressed to his back was cold in a familiar, comforting way. It was the tool he most depended on to keep him alive. But not the only one.

"I stay sharp enough when the arrows and spears rain down. What you see as weakness is rather my strength. One needs something to return to when Athens burns, something that drives more strongly than food, wine or spoils." The minotaur lowered his horns to bring his bovine muzzle in line with his General's chin. "Have you no desires beyond this war? Even a Spartan has un-bloodied dreams." Cyrantus had watched carefully at the presentation of the troops to King Archidamus. He had seen all that followed. Would his new General deny it?

"What draws me is this war. I have bred for it, trained for it. My father was denied satisfaction with the onset of the thirty-years peace with those damn Athenian merchants and philosophers. Now they plunder the treasuries of the rest of Greece to feed their larceny—"

"With respect, my General, I know your thirst for war and am well-disposed in filling your cup." Cyrantus gauged the General's reaction before continuing. "Is there not something you seek for when the war is won and Athens is toppled? Is there not someone who draws you to her?"

The sounds of merriment carried over, ghostly remnants of Spartan song and helot drunkenness crossed one another like competing wakes. General Lukan's expression was hard with guarded thought. Ready soldiers were never far. Had Cyrantus spoken too far out of turn, it would take but one shouted word.

Assuming the General would not attempt to slay him personally. His bare arms under the red cloak were glistening with the sweat of a hot summer night, his sword hung ready.

Cyrantus filled the gap. "You seek the hand of the King's daughter in marriage. A clear match as you are both fit for one another, not to mention attractive in what standards pass for your kind."

"What business does a creature such as yourself have in the affairs of Kings and Generals?" Lukan rumbled. A flick of fire in his eyes was the only betrayal of emotion he surrendered.

Cyrantus stood and straightened his loose loincloth, his brown-tufted tail swinging behind him. He kept his voice neutral, feeling blood start to boil in response to the threat he skirted with and forced calm on himself with learned effort. "I meant no offense, General Lukan. Quite the contrary, I see the challenge before you and I would offer my assistance."

The General blinked as though taken for a fool. "What did you say? You would assist me with… what?"

The minotaur expected this reaction. He picked his words as carefully as he would select a blade for skirmishing. "I know that a Spartan's way in the world is with deeds rather than words, but it is your mind, not your martial prowess, which is unknown to she whom you would court. Spoken wits are no less important to a female than martial prowess. This I have observed in my travels."

Lukan looked about himself and Cyrantus watched the disbelief play on the man's face. It were as though a Dionysian chorus of drunken revelers would leap from the bushes and laugh at a joke being told at his expense. Cyrantus realized his bovine features were still all the man could see. A demonstration was in order. "Why do you care for her? Tell me in your words. Is it merely because she is the daughter of your king? Is it for her power or wealth?"

Lukan nearly spat upon the ground. "You mistake me for a plucker of gold. I appreciated her pedigree, but desire her because she is a pure woman, stronger than all other Spartan women who are strong by their very nature."

Cyrantus nodded his great bull's head. "Strong in what way?"

Lukan opened his mouth to answer, but nothing was ready on his lips. "She is… very strong."

"Bodily strong?"

"For a woman, yes."

"So you yearn for her because she is physically stronger than other women?"

"No. That is the merest of her strengths—I cannot grasp the words." Lukan furrowed his brow like a youth battling a scholastic problem.

"Is she strong of heart?"

Lukan just looked at him.

"Is she strong of will? Does she still your breath because her every word thickens the air with their power? Is she strong of mind in that her wisdom shines through as fire cutting the dark? Is she strong of heart with love for her family and country, a love no less firm and solid than the ground upon which Spartan children warm their feet?"

"Yes!" Lukan's stern façade broke and he brightened with realization. "That is her precisely! That is Kerata!" The General looked left and right, but found that he and the minotaur were still alone. "How does it come that a talking beast should be so stocked with words?"

Cyrantus folded his arms, anger building within despite himself. It took a moment to regain control, as he always did in the face of men whom he wasn't set to kill. "I cannot fight my way out of everything, Spartan. My head would be a courtyard ornament if I were not amply supplied by a ready mind."

"I had heard that most beasts of the mists were dumb and brutish," Lukan muttered with wonder.

Cyrantus found himself torn between fury at the casual insult and wonder at the utter lack of guile the Spartan displayed. He bit back a growl. "There are minotaurs stupid enough to eat their own feces, General, but if men are so intelligent and dignified by comparison then I ask you to explain the ball-scratching lewdness of Messenian sailors."

Lukan coughed. "Point taken."

Cyrantus realized that he had opened himself back up to the question of what brought him here. Fortunately, the General's mind was singularly focused. "I do seek to gain Kerata's favor, but there are many generals and nobles who vie for her. I know not what would sway her. My feelings have no voice, and have never required one."

Cyrantus could see realization burgeon within the Spartan that he was opening up to an alien, a creature from distant lands under his command. Were the minotaur a red-cloaked man of the Polis like Lukan himself, how different would this engagement be?

It then came to Cyrantus with startling clarity. Lukan was alone. Despite the dozens of men who shared his laden mess tables, clapped his back and paid him honors, the Spartan General could bring nothing of his concerns or fears to the men who depended on his stern character, steady spear and sound mind.

Cyrantus was, in this moment, the safest of confidants. He didn't share the General's table, nor his extended company. There was no circle within which the bullish creature would spill his secrets.

He chuffed aloud. "I will keep your concerns in confidence. And if you wish, I may help you in expressing your desires to the princess who lurks among these tents for a few days more."

"You would help me in this way?" Lukan met his gaze with reluctance.

Cyrantus could tell Lukan was still juggling disbelief with worry. Courtship was as slow a war among these Greeks as it was with his own kind—a commonality across species. "In return for my help, I ask for but one thing once Athens has fallen."

"Name it. It is a city of wealth to be taken by fighters who crave none."

"Dead Athenians need no ships. I want one, with a strong sail and provisions. With so many spoils laying about, this will be within your power."

Lukan gazed back at the tops of the tents of his army. Wind fluttered canvas sheets like mirrors of a stormy sky. Under one of those concealing layers the King's daughter brooded on the merits of endless suitors. "That is within my power, minotaur," the Spartan said. "Help me compose the workings of my heart."

A skirmish found the Spartan camp the next morning. Scouts caught an insurgency prowling the Attican foothills and Lukan directed his men in a fierce, pitched skirmish. Very few Spartans suffered injury with their numerical superiority and Lukan personally killed two Athenian infantry. His own thrown spear pierced one fighter's pale throat and his sword dragged through another soldier's bowels. The screams of felled Athenians roared in his ears long after he removed his tall helmet, scraped off their blood and took stock of the dead.

King Archidamus was disappointed that he was late to join the fighting himself. The Spartans and their helot auxiliaries fought well, as did the creatures of the mists. The sileni took an arrow and hissed threateningly at the medics who offered attention. Cyrantus, out on the flanks, was scarred lightly by spear tips that nearly pierced his hide, but killed many with broad sweeps of his ax.

Lukan gathered his men together and had the Athenian dead collected. He then had the tents dismantled and the whole camp moved closer to their next objective. The hills the Athenians used for their sneak attacks were now behind the Spartans, separated by open plains.

"Thanks to Athenian foolishness we are now closer to our objective. The unconquered portions of Attica are fading," Lukan told his King.

Archidamus nodded. "You have done admirably. I must soon direct my attentions to the state of Potidaea, where the Athenians are trying to put down a revolt. I have faith in the gods that choosing you as our General for this front of the war was a wise choice."

Lukan swelled with pride as Kerata stood by, speaking commandingly to a helot attendant. The King's daughter sent her slave from the King's tent with a smack on the rump before joining her father. "When do we leave?" she said crisply.

"In a day, once all instructions are relayed to the troops," The king answered absently.

There was a brief space following this answer and Lukan stepped in swiftly, remembering the words prepared. "I would hope that the Princess does not leave us bereft of her company too soon. Such swift mind for tactics brings encouragement and insight we find invigorating."

Nobody said anything, not Archidamus, Kerata or the two Ephors in their midst.

"Few would realize that beauty is merely one of many assets you carry. I would ask you to stay and watch us lay the Athenians low, but I dare not ask your father to separate himself from your council," Lukan said directly to Kerata.

As his coach in words had explained, the complementary offer was bold but not forceful, allowing refusal that would cost no one face. Suggesting the King benefited from his daughter's council would have been an insult among most Greeks, but a Spartan woman was comparatively free, able to pursue her own agency. Complimenting her wisdom complimented her parentage, her father and mother equally.

The King remained stoic as his daughter's eyes narrowed like a suspicious bird. "You have such thoughtful words. I would wonder if your tongue is honeyed on this occasion or was it soured on the last."

Lukan cleared his throat, unsure of how to handle the question. "Well, my Princess, I had concerns upon me that night." That didn't sound sufficient. "After the latest victory, I am more confident of

Athen's imminent fall." Lukan resisted a frown. Proud proclamations of victory were so simple when he stood tall before hundreds of war-lusting Spartan hoplites. Why was it so difficult to declare in the glare of one woman? Her hard green eyes flickered in the light of the tent's mounted braziers, testing for flaws, hammering Lukan like plated bronze. Lukan reached into his memory for his next weapon. "It is your approval that carries me between victories. I care very much for the grace of your good fortune." What was that next part? "Your happiness, my princess, is my victory made manifest." Now to bring it home. "That is why you find my words increased. Each battle brings your dynasty closer to glory."

Lukan fell silent, hoping that the earnestness of Cyrantus' prepared words were enough to impress. Kerata's eyes stayed narrowed while she looked at her father, who remained as implacable as the votive statue in Apollo's temple.

Archidamus looked to Lukan. "We will speak more on my daughter's travel affairs later. Now I wish to tour the camp and see how the troops fare." The king turned to his daughter and asked evenly, "Shall we ask the General to escort us?"

Lukan felt his heart thump faster, as it did when enemy spears rose over a horizon and the march of opposing sandals thundered the earth. Fear prickled him anew.

"Yes," Kerata replied. "I will dress more appropriately." She wore the same athletic-freeing garb that she wore the other night. She marched to the King's tent flap and let herself out past the Ephor who bowed stiffly, remaining silent.

The King immediately faced his General. "Tell me your intentions."

Man to man, no honeyed words were necessary. Still Lukan balked at stating his mind. "I seek to offer myself as a candidate for marriage to your daughter."

The King frowned, turning to the table where a map spread in the low light of the tent's braziers. "My daughter has many powerful men who vie for her affections. Her desires..." He studied Greece's craggy contours on the map. "Her will is stronger than most and would break bonds forged without care. You do have position enough to merit attention."

Lukan stood tall, gazing at the cloaked back of his King. He was searching for the right words to make his case when the King spoke again. "She is beautiful and smart. But know that you must come to love her, not her attributes, if you are to gain her favor. Without that, a King's endorsement isn't worth a piss in a cold lake." Archidamus abruptly turned and slapped Lukan's shoulder. "Come. I would know the disposition of my army."

Kerata rejoined them, dressed for the cool evening in a plain but trim stola. Her short hair bobbed about her small ears and she strode on her father's left as Lukan guided from the right. The Ephor observer fell in behind.

They came across Spartan warriors in calisthenics, armored, lightly attired or naked as Olympiads. Helots, some servile, many elevated to fill military roles in the advance upon Athens, darted about to maintain the camp. At its perimeter, Spartan sentries fixed eagle-eyes east under their peaked helmets. The tour of the outskirts passed pits of refuse that attacked their noses, and then they came across the small lake where the men had seen to elementary hygiene.

And where one odd last soldier now splashed itself in the river. The creature was thick with the loam of countless departed bodies. The King regarded the minotaur calmly as the creature stood from a crouch, facing away, digging at film in his eyes. "What remarkable spectacles the gods upturned in this world," Archidamus mused. "Where my own ancestors would have cursed the very idea of other Greeks within our ranks, now we find ourselves hosting beasts along-side us as though arming the very horses we ride on."

Lukan said nothing. Out in the sinking sunlight, Cyrantus was an imposing figure. His horns curved like deadly spear-tips into the sky and his massive shoulders glistened wetly, casting light off the upward curve of each bristling muscle. A broad back trailed down to where a thin tail beat its tuft below curvaceous buttocks. The bend of its bullish legs and hooves were concealed beneath the water, but as it turned, they saw a rolling, hardened abdomen taper down to a thick waist and Lukan blinked at what the water did not conceal. The thick, dark shaft of its ample penis drooped to the water's face, narrowly covering a lightly-furred sack beneath. The lengthy member quivered bronze in the reflected light as the minotaur shifted its stance on the mud beneath the waters.

Lukan fought to avoid openly marveling at the impressive proportions that nature gave the half-bull. Was this the creature that had fed wit to his ears the very night before? Had that been some dream? As he gazed upon the minotaur's physical magnificence, finding sensations stir in him unfelt since his trysts back in the Agoge, he heard Kerata mutter disdainfully, "It has many impressive aspects for a raging beast. I should wonder how it performs." There was a sardonic tone in her voice.

Her father nodded, though he missed or ignored his daughter's jest. "This creature was brought into the army by General Lukan's predecessor, Peleartes, though we don't know the means by which this pet was tamed. I assume that relief from its war lust was reward enough. I know not what flesh it eats, that of Greek or otherwise."

"It is fully tame," Lukan rushed to say. "And it is a valuable...tool of this army of course, far more than the war elephants the Persians use."

Cyrantus appeared to hear the muttering at the lake's flanks and turned to see the King, Lukan and the King's daughter staring at him. His shoulders slumped, but he made no attempt to cover any part of himself. Dark eyes found Lukan's and the General realized that this beast knew precisely how he was expected to act in front of a King. There was a strange flutter in Lukan's heart when he spoke the next words loud enough for the minotaur to hear. "This beast is a violent brute. But it has an agreeable disposition when properly cared for. It knows whom to gore, and I will happily employ it in my army till we take Athens."

"What use for it after that?" Kerata asked.

Lukan swallowed as his gaze drifted back down to the minotaur's vitality. He felt himself quavering at the tone in Kerata's voice, but he was unable to sort out what in her words made him feel that sensation. He tried to find the right words to answer, but remained silent. His monstrous muse remained mute, dripping wetly and staring back with dark and disdainful eyes.

Lukan kept to his war council, laying out strategy. He put off thoughts of the princess and all the issues that surrounded her. The squad leaders thrilled to his every urgent command, eagerly preparing for victory.

The next few days saw further success as they pressed south, pinching the Athenians at the coast and raiding the port town of Eleusis. Without the long walls that protected Athens and its port companion of Phraneus, the Greeks had no choice but to face them on the field. The orderly arrangement of hoplite formations turned into a rout when both Spartan and Elusian phalanxes fractured.

"Hold formation!" Lukan shouted as his shield bore the brunt of the front-line barrage. Calamity to both sides confirmed that order had broken. Missiles flew and swords were drawn. Lukan's spear tip passed a shield and found the eye-slit of an Eleusian helmet. There was a scream of agony as the shaft sunk in and Lukan was forced to release his spear. He switched to his xiphos, the Spartan's traditional short sword, hacking at the Athenian soldiers in his path.

Out here, wearing the very same peaked helmet as his brethren, Lukan gave ecstatically to his craft. He killed one with a jugular stab and crippled the thigh of another. For precious moments, he was no General, merely another hacking arm of the greater Spartan nation, dealing death in spades. Lukan turned to shout encouragement to one of his Agoge mates, Skeptus, who had trained under the General and spilled blood with him on countless campaigns, but his Captain was lost among the enemy throng.

Then Lukan heard the roar.

An Elusian soldier screamed as he was hurled and a streaming red gout painted the corner of Lukan's vision. Thrusting spears were cut to kindling by a massive war ax, born by dark-furred arms that blurred in the meager sunlight as the minotaur Cyrantus heaved and cleaved. Lukan found himself isolated in a momentary pocket of calm amongst the throng, and watched the muscular half-animal demi-god flex his great arms before they came together on the ax which thundered into the helmet of an Elusian commander. It parted the metal and all within it as though it were black broth on a mess table. Blood painted the minotaur's chest and shoulders as he roared. The Elusians in his midst fled in terror.

To think that the city fathers would decry the inclusion of Cyrantus into the ranks as an affront to Spartan purity. Lukan observed the minotaur's flanks twist when he found a new target and his thighs pumped as Cyrantus charged into the routed throng.

The sight of Cyrantus' barely-clothed buttocks tightened Lukan's breeches as the creature leaped like an element of nature towards life or death. The General's blood lust returned almost immediately, his carnal reaction forcefully pushed back and he regained his discipline.

The next wave swarmed in and Lukan was drawn back to killing his enemies joyously, as his pedigree demanded.

Hundreds of Greek soldiers in Athen's league were consigned to the afterlife. Lukan celebrated the victory with a rousing speech and the Spartan force, diminished by a mere handful, roared in triumph.

Lukan's words were backed by sober realization. More noble deaths to celebrate and the hardest work still lay ahead of them. Pericles and the Athenians lay behind a long wall that would repel conventional invasion, leaving the sea as a field of battle that did not favor them. They needed another way.

As Lukan broke his men to messes and returned to his tent, the Spartans poured their nourishing broth and echoed the plains with song.

Cyrantus suffered mere scratches on this sortie, but he held on to little pride. He was still furious from his experiences prior to the battle he'd thrown himself into with wild abandon. Excellent work for a loyal, doting beast. He scouted far, hunted and brooded, collecting a lame deer with far less martial effort than he'd used to expend Elusian men. He brought back his contribution to the Messenian hoplites under Spartan command and ate quickly in silence, apart from the others. The sileni, who was his counterpart, favored the minotaur with a curt nod. Cyrantus then found himself out past the camp's new perimeter, staying clear of the port for the calamity his mere presence would bring to the wailing wives of the Elusian dead. The stench of the battlefield faded but he felt as though its miasma followed him. He was thinking long on the circumstances that contributed to his isolation and misery when he caught sight of a figure skulking the secluded foothills that had concealed the Elusian's earlier sneak attack. By his troubled posture and proud gait, he knew the silhouette to be General Lukan.

Cyrantus stamped down ragged breaths of indignant fury and muttered a short prayer to Zeus for self-control before intercepting the helmetless General. "I would speak with you." It was no question.

"As I would with you." Lukan said. "I have nary the chance to leave my tent much less the camp with our final offensive so near."

"Of course, you are an important man. We grateful tools too must bow to your every nod."

To his surprise, Lukan appeared stung. "I have sought moments to slip away for the past two days. My responsibilities multiply as we near Athens, and I can shirk none of them. Surely you understand."

"Burdens of command, of course," Cyrantus nearly spat.

"That alone is not all that concerns me," Lukan replied.

Cyrantus wondered how much anger he could allow himself. They were hidden beyond the town and camp among the foothills, nobody knowing where to look for them. Cyrantus came and went because he could take care of himself and few dared challenge him. Lukan had either pulled rank, or simply slipped away stealthily as Spartan youths had trained to do for centuries. There were never any Spartan deserters of course, such was a shame worse than death. "What beyond a war could concern you? Oh, I almost forgot. The princess whose affections you seek. You need your violent brute with a slave's disposition to weave more magical words for her."

"No. That is, not now." Lukan cleared his throat. "Though battle gave me brief respite, I have been in a crisis of conscience."

Cyrantus blinked as he read the Spartan's expression. Greeks had plain faces that were easy to read when one knew how. Spartans merely disconnected themselves from joy or grief until it suited them to do otherwise. Lukan couldn't bury the worry in his eyes.

Unconcerned with the Spartan regard for propriety in that moment and still biting back on his anger, Cyrantus lowered himself to a rock and sat upon it, adjusting his loincloth. The night was warm as the Spartan regarded him. With extreme reluctance, the General lowered himself to a stone and relaxed the same.

Cyrantus sniffed through his broad bovine nose and flicked his ears. "I will listen."

Lukan took awhile to find the words. Like most Greeks, he was too complicated to sort himself out, a maze of a man whose largest twists were invisible. "I don't know what I want," he said at last. "The princess Kerata has everything a Spartan man should yearn for. Beauty of a goddess, dynastic influence and startling intelligence. But I feel… wrong about her."

"She does not smell right to you," Cyrantus said.

Lukan looked confused. "She keeps clean with lye and scraper—"

"I talk not of her lack of dirt! I give a plain explanation. The princess Kerata does not smell *right* to you. This suggestion merits a yes or a no."

"Then I say no."

"Why?"

Lukan gazed at the thin tendrils of smoke in the failing light that rose from distant Athens. "She remains as distant and cold as the mountains."

"So you do have some command of words."

Lukan grunted. "I have sought to know her heart, to understand her wants, but she remains closed to me. I don't think she has any feelings for me. Or any man."

Cyrantus nodded. "I have heard suggestions within some poetry of the isle of Lesbos. Perhaps she is of the persuasion to seek the gate rather than the key."

"What does that mean?"

Cyrantus grunted. "It doesn't matter. Have you yet talked to any of your brothers about this?"

"They bleed for me as I would for them, but we tolerate no weaknesses that interfere with the highest of duties. I can bring them none of my problems. I would diminish my stature with them for doing so."

Cyrantus couldn't resist. "But taking the advice of a talking wartool constitutes the ultimate weakness, doesn't it?"

No answer. Cyrantus would have been freshly enraged if he hadn't been expecting this disregard precisely. All the same, he wanted to stamp the earth. "So tell me what you want. I gave you words to sway the princess, and now this. Why come to me with fresh problems?"

The still air carried less noise than the last time they met in seclusion. The General took a deep breath, reached out and roughly slapped a palm against Cyrantus shoulder, which he held for a moment, testing the strength of the minotaur's muscles.Fingers combing through the minotaur's fur slipped away slowly. In Cyrantus' disgruntled state, the surprise from the contact was brief compared to what lingered. The unexpected warmth of the casual touch was a startling, almost forgotten sensation. Years old memories crept to the fore that were both saddening and yet invigorating.

Cyrantus did not immediately sort out what the Spartan's disposition was, and he found the man's eyes. "Find words," Cyrantus said, his chest heaving. "Find something. Now."

"I wanted something from the King's daughter that she could not give." Lukan grunted as though through a debilitating wound. "And now that I am of the age to put such things aside and obey my responsibilities…I still desire it."

"Desire what?"

The minotaur's ears fluttered, blushing with heat as though his senses already knew the answer. Without a further word, Lukan's other hand reached out and found Cyrantus' singular, modesty-claiming cloth and dipped underneath. The Spartan purposefully took Cyrantus' formidable maleness in his hand, wrapped firmly around it and the minotaur felt himself stiffen in response.

The shock made the words difficult to form. "You desire…me," Cyrantus breathed through his wide lips.

Lukan seemed as though he were fighting to remain expressionless. "I desire to be desired. Such is a weakness that knocks the knees and conquers reason, so I have disdained to admit it. But the curves and recesses of a woman have never drawn me, not even when I choose the most superior specimen in Greece as a hopeful repository for my affections. I sought her, I lied to myself about her."

He continued, his hand warm on Cyrantus' cock. "Playing with Agoge-mates is the casual game of younger souls. My duty, as with all Sparta's eligible males, is to bear children. But I enjoy the scent of men. I savor the firm touch of strong hands. It was while appraising your aspects that I suddenly realized how strong that desire is. There is something about the purity of you that draws me out in a way other men do not." Lukan's eyes met his. "I cannot escape it."

Cyrantus' thighs parted like a waning sea as he sat straight, his tail beating the dusty stone under his buttocks. "Surrounded by men, by their vitality and vigor, such has been a hard battle for you, hasn't it? The hardest of wars won in silence," he rumbled.

"It was not so difficult." The sun found Lukan's back through a break in the hills and lit his red cloak in a brilliant flame. Sweat gathered on the bare shoulders underneath. "Until now."

Cyrantus' anger subsided and the acceptance of Lukan's truth began to warm him as much as the General's touch. "You haven't fought it alone."

Silence passed for a moment as they both tested their senses to discover if they were alone under the lengthening shadows. The minotaur studied the Spartan man, the proud badges of scar and muscle built from a life of discipline and restraint and desire. But Lukan's eyes, twin orbs of cobalt blue, held a pain that buried their truth deep. They told tales of a heart caged within a labyrinth of obligation where it would not escape from duty and all its dull agonies. Lukan's hand caressed the minotaur's growing maleness and its mate found the minotaur's ample scrotum. The touch brought a deep sigh as Cyrantus found the slip of his cloth and released his fabric bonds. They fell to the dirt and the minotaur's thick hands reached out, questing for the joins in Lukan's breast plate, untying them two-by-two until it fell from his broad, sweat-slicked chest and its counterpart slipped from his back. Soon, only the red cloak covered the Spartan's back. Lukan's own hands released Cyrantus to struggle at the ties on his breaches, tugging them away with deliberation, the leather stretched with his erection as he rose to his knees and slipped the covering away. A moment later, the Spartan allowed his cloak to fall and Lukan and Cyrantus were both naked as the reliefs of Theseus and the cursed, mindless minotaur that dotted temples and gardens of Greek cities all across the Aegean Sea's flanks. It was an ironic representation to recall in this moment. The ideal man struggling with the ideal monster, battling for control. The only enemies that man and minotaur fought here were of the ensnaring world around them.

Lukan thought briefly on Cyrantus' words of solidarity. "You feel as I do?"

"I did. I do. My silence is of a shame unique to my breed," Cyrantus said. "I have never spoken on it and wish not to do so."

Lukan's voice caught in his throat when the minotaur's vast, rough hands found the Spartan's maleness and fondled it to full hardness. Both staffs stood stiff and ready as an evening breeze slipped by and ruffled the Spartan's fiery golden hair and the minotaur's glistening dark fur.

"Will you turn and take me in?" The minotaur asked.

Lukan's eyes hardened immediately. "No."

For a moment, tension seemed to find the air in the same manner as the first night when the minotaur dared answer his General's barbs, but the minotaur's large eyes softened in compromise, spent of any ire. "If you will awaken me other ways, I ask for an invigorating touch. Then I will submit to you as you wish."

Cyrantus could read the thrill that rushed to the Spartan's countenance as possibilities multiplied. "Other ways?"

"I would desire a kiss upon my hardened flesh, but I don't know what acts you consider sensual or shameful.

Lukan's gaze met the minotaur's, silent with warmth and gratitude. He wore an expression of wonder as he regarded Cyrantus' fully engorged member, great in girth as a sapling tree. Its dark skin shone with a sheen of moisture. Curiosity brightened the Spartan's eyes. His reply needed no words.

Lukan leaned forward and his short whiskers brushed the minotaur's flaring heat. His lips touched it softly, warm with a caressing pulse. The man's tongue crept forth.

Cyrantus could remember what that tasted like, what Lukan was experiencing—salt of earth, the potent spice of raw flesh. Lukan's lips parted, tracing the member's head as his golden locks tickled the minotaur's inner thighs. Hot wet moisture enrobed the Minotaur's cock once Lukan's mouth opened as though to sing, and took the minotaur within his cheeks.

The sound that escaped Cyrantus lingered between growl and sigh as Lukan drew on the minotaur's vitality. Lukan's tongue slipped about while his questing hands traced under the minotaur's sac and around the soft down of his legs. Cyrantus rumbled deeply, gripping the scraggly earth behind him in steely hands. He was carried once more to memory, to a black-speckled pelt and youthful features, white horns coming together like a cliff diver's. Touch that alternated from forceful to supple haunted his senses wistfully, amplifying the pleasure this General of men bestowed upon him. Cyrantus found control, stealing his most beloved memories to the recesses of his heart when the Spartan disengaged, leaving moisture cooling on the Minotaur's member in the still air.

"I'll taste no more of you. Turn." Lukan commanded.

Cyrantus panted like a stallion off a charge. "Were I a woman, you would find better words to urge my participation." He didn't add wryly that the General would need Cyrantus to compose them, but smirked privately at his wit. His tail switched behind him as the Spartan's caress left his member and travelled to his flank. Cyrantus could not know Lukan's thoughts, but kept presence of mind himself to sniff for unwelcome scents that would invade their fragile seclusion.

They remained alone.

Cyrantus rolled onto his hands and knees and spread his legs, realizing as he did that the General had so much more to lose if watchful eyes befell them here. In pursing what he wanted, in risking death day upon day, Lukan was a risk-taker in all things. So be it. Lukan's own member, large for a man's but meager for Cyrantus' own kind, drifted across the minotaur's buttocks, teased by the tuft on his swinging tail. Cyrantus heard the General spit and then the slide of moisture on skin. As Lukan eased within Cyrantus, a budding flower of discomfort came and passed quickly. The Spartan was large, but not enough, the minotaur thought with a giddy pant, to press at the hot gates astride him.

Lukan began to thrust, keeping his breaths quiet with each windy slide in, then out. The discomfort in Cyrantus' rear turned to flutters of heat, blissful hot silk of skin within skin, tight enough to gaily tease his nerves. Lukan's hands slipped round the minotaur's flanks to his abdomen as though mounting a riding beast. His right hand slid low and found the Minotaur's member dripping stiff.

"Guide me like a spear, firm and resolute," Cyrantus said.

Lukan coughed. "Your gift for words isn't necessary here. I understand what to do." Cyrantus sighed as the Spartan's strong fingers worked his shaft again, his rump growing pleasingly hot from the General's invasion.

"I cannot help it, even in thought. The terms suit the act so well." He grimaced, a fresh spasm of pleasure passing through him. He was close now.

So was the General, riding hard, maintaining a warrior's discipline of near silence through the grandest of ecstasies, wary of a sentry's discovery. With a singular sharp grunt, Lukan shivered and the heat within Cyrantus pressed deeper as seed was sown. The minotaur, nearly at the point of roaring with the height of his bliss, went over the boiling falls to completion. He bucked in the General's hand and a few scant slip of the fingers later, tossed his vitality upon the ground, spreading ropes of ivory far enough to reach his grimacing chin. He quivered under Lukan's relaxed weight, his tail trapped between their hips, and hauled himself sideways to fall to the earth, the Spartan's arms wrapped round him as a cloud of dust coated the perspiration on them both. Cyrantus gazed at his spread seed under the glint of the moon as though it was the mythical start of a new ocean.

Cicadas marked time.

"What was his name?" Lukan asked his back, his voice an eerie, unencumbered calm.

Cyrantus sighed expansively. "Fiovas. I suppose I am practiced enough at receiving another male that it is obvious."

"Why did you leave him?"

"The elders who discovered us would not have it for the same reason as yours would not abide it now. There are too few of us, and our service to the herd is to assert supremacy and mate. One of us had to leave, a period of separation. He was younger, afraid of the world. I could not allow that to be him."

"And you came to my predecessor."

"Not immediately. The Persians found me first. From their court I observed the value of carefully chosen words, though they wanted only to teach me the lessons of the whip for the benefit of guests. They came to regret that when I managed to leave them. Much later, travelling the West, General Pelaertes was of a more practical mind. He knew what I was good for. Or most of it."

Lukan seemed to hold back a snicker. Cyrantus studied him. "And where did the General find his first affection?"

Lukan looked away. "Here and there, sporadically. A Spartan finds his own way and sex is another avenue for supremacy. We learn nothing from our fathers, who are off to war against helot uprisings too often."

"Your mother?"

Lukan shook his head, staring at a point in the darkness. "I was parted from her at age five for schooling in the Agoge and do not remember much about her. She died when I was nine. I only remember that like all Spartan women, in ways I cannot describe, she was… strong."

Lukan fell silent and Cyrantus breathed calmly, finished brooding about the past, no longer yearning for the future. There was a whole new world, brought to life as though by the Gods themselves in that moment. "I have never had a General before." He realized.

"You have never been had by a General. Such is distinctively different from a Greek perspective," Lukan muttered.

"Shared enjoyment is shared enjoyment. Spartans have male lovers like any man round the Agean, some proudly so. I do not see the difference."

"Because you are not one of us. I have no doubt that things are different among the Persians, but a Greek man in full adulthood would be shamed as the passive partner, as the lesser taking entry in a coupling. Such is the position typically taken by meek artists and weaklings and slaves." There was a beat or two before Lukan added. "Among my kind."

"And you believe I could not have you were I to press the issue?" Cyrantus rolled on his back.

Lukan's grimace bore neither malice nor mirth as he raised his jaw and looked Cyrantus square in the eyes. "That kiss was as close at it comes. Try to make a submissive of me and see what happens."

Cyrantus considered this for a moment. Spartans were wily wrestlers and Lukan would no doubt bear his girth without a shaming cry, but to pace before his men and fight with them after taking the minotaur inside, he would not walk or run without a trot for days. For countless reasons, Cyrantus knew it was wise to demure.

"Though the men allow me brief solitudes my walk has gone long. I am expected." The dip in Lukan's voice marked his reluctance to go. He picked himself up and began dressing.

Cyrantus sat up and gathered his loin-cloth. The glint of his seed had already dried out. "Someday," he said absently, "I should like to join you at your mess table and meet your brethren in blood."

Lukan was ready to go, and he fixed Cyrantus with a stare that could hide little of its regret. "Cyrantus. Please accept that you are close to me in ways that cannot be marked by men or Gods. But regardless, such a world would never be this one. Our secret must remain such. For that I am truly sorry."

Cyrantus said nothing as the General left. Insects and animals spoke into the rocks and trees as Cyrantus paced, seeking a place to take his rest, a cold pit forming inside him at the General's parting words. Halfway round to where the helots had their sub-camp and he had his, he was met by a messenger who coaxed him to follow.

The helot turned and Cyrantus heeded the request, knowing that something too heavy for a man to lift merely needed a beast to move it somewhere. Such was how things were.

Night had fallen and dry winds slipped through the Spartan camp. Lukan carried a sickening elation on the stride back to his war tent. He could still feel the hairy tassel of the minotaur's tail dancing against his chest as Lukan's cock thrust and heaved inside him. He felt light as a bird with relief, yet was caught with a snarling thread of doubt.

What had he done? To have been caught in the act would have been to risk more than his command. A simple tryst with one of his own soldiers would have been a serious risk, though humored in lesser circles. They were men at war, dancing daily about the cold throat of the underworld. Comradely pleasure could be seen as any man's due when he could cease to be at the Gods' merest whim. A General would not be easily forgiven, but given time...

Not however with a beast of the mists, a hoofed, horned half-animal of raw lust and musk whom the lesser travelled believed were myths. Lukan smoothed at the bulge that lifted within his leather breeches at the memory of those brown buttocks, rippling in the dying light, marked by the singular scar of a long-healed bullwhip strike. Like the scars upon Spartan muscles, the mark had been eerily beautiful, a mark of experience, a component of his indomitable character.

What had he done? Lukan felt filthy as a man back from war, and no less elated at the cause. The tougher question to answer surfaced quickly without regret.

When could he do it again?

His Captain, Skepteus, awaited him, perspiring from his nightly exercises. The slight stirring of arousal that all fit men made Lukan feel was abated in that moment, and the first words from the Captain's mouth teased unknowingly at the cause. "You smell like you wrestled a horse, General."

Lukan forced a shrug and a lie came easily. "I passed the equestrian pit at some point. A panicky stallion brushed against me."

Skeptus nodded. "No less danger in solitude I suppose. General, I was explaining to our King the progress we have made in seeing weaknesses in Athen's sea walls."

"And what did honorable Archidamus say to our progress?"

"You would not wish to simply ask me yourself?" Out of the corner of Lukan's vision, his King strode round a lit brazier and came nearly toe to toe with him.

Lukan was taken aback. "My King, I had thought you left hours ago."

"My sons and other Generals will benefit from my attentions, but not yet. Business commanded my attention right here while you were out seeing to your rounds, and I tarried in my departure. The

Athenians sent an envoy."

The whole of Lukan's personal internal turmoil popped like a bubble. "What? Pericles sent an embassy here? I was not informed?" Anger swelled within him. Archidamus raised a calming hand. "I have every confidence in your handling of diplomatic affairs, General, but while the next words will boil your blood, you will find amusement in the whole tale. The envoy demanded immediate audience with me and disdained to speak to the General who led the slaughter on his people."

"As would be a coward's wont. Little shits wouldn't face down the men who ended their sons." Lukan's spit sizzled into one of the brazier fires.

Archidamus nodded. "I am disappointed you did not see what followed. The envoy came forth, and who came out to meet him, but the royalty on hand."

Skeptus laughed despite propriety. He had evidently been present and Lukan felt a surge of fury. Had this happened while he was seeing to the town, or helping secure the captives?

Or visiting his new lover?

The King smiled like a great cat. "I sent the sputtering fool to bring terms to the Spartan Princess. Kerata received him on my behalf."

Skeptus grinned ear to ear. "I wish you had seen it General. The Athenian upstart, disdaining of women's free agency as they all do, was forced to put terms to her as an equal. The man was shamed and furious. Kerata handled his petty disdain with grace and guile. It was all I could do to keep from bawling with laughter. The dishonor he paid you was paid back a hundred-fold."

Archidamus proudly folded his arms. "My daughter told that idiot where he could shove his demands for peace and threatened to make him less a man than she was if he talked down to her any further. The arrogant bastard left looking like he would be sick. It will be a glorious story for those back home, let me tell you."

Lukan stood stock-still as his King and Captain roared with laughter, joining in reluctantly. The awkward moment passed, Lukan battling a fog of emotions as the trio turned to business, talking of weaknesses in the Athenian wall pinpointed by scouts. The Captain and the ever-present Ephor were summarily dismissed a few hours from dawn, and the King was alone with Lukan. Silence crept in as the fires sunk low and the King's muscles glinted in the dimming light.

The King's final words to Lukan came abruptly.

"I no longer need consider any further," Archidamus said. "I feel you would be a good match for my daughter, provided she accepts."

Lukan was taken aback, meeting his King's earnest gaze with a blank stare. He searched vainly for words but even with Kerata absent, he was bereft of reply as he was bereft of sense. To be truly married into the royal family, to secure a place for his descendants on the eve of their nation's greatest martial triumph, it was all too much to contemplate. He thought of the princess, so imperious and willful and… strong, the exemplar of all Spartan women.

But his imagination returned immediately to Cyrantus, broad furred shoulders glistening in the sun, the slow draw of breath through his broad fluttering nostrils. The minotaur's eyes were hard with intelligence, yet something in them fixed warmly in Lukan's mind.

The General was lost in a maze of emotions and his desires wound beyond sight, refusing to settle and provide any certainty. He didn't know if he truly loved Kerata, or could find it in himself to do so. What could the word ever even mean for one such as him?

His stoic walls restored themselves as the turmoil was buried. Lukan stiffly accepted the King's blessing before bidding him safe journey.

Lukan woke and ate with his brothers before the camp moved once more, marching east while a garrison stayed with Elusia. The Princess remained behind as the King promised she would while he went to the other war fronts, promising return when Athens was breached. Lukan drilled his troops and gazed at the marble limbs of the Parthenon, mere slivers in the distance. He wondered what it would be like to stare up at the giant representation of Athena within. Would the smoke of the burning city about her offend the God or bring her pride? He couldn't be sure. He bolstered the men's pride, saw to combat drills and spotted Cyrantus only a few occasions, practicing with his ax in the distance. The agreement they honored was a silent one, and Lukan could spare little time to ponder buried desires.

Reports came to him by way of the last lingering Ephor that the Princess had requested her tent be moved to the very back of the lines and that access be restricted by an honor guard who remained between her and the camp. "She has fallen ill," The Ephor confided when Lukan pressed for details.

"Send her a doctor."

"She has already refused," The Ephor replied sulkily.

"Then what the hell are you even doing here?" For agents assigned to watch the activities of the Royal family, some Ephors were downright useless.

Lukan convened in his tent to collect scouting reports. Confirmation finally came three days into planning that the Athenians had a weakness. "Here." Skeptus pointed to a spot on the collected tablets, a relief of Athens drawn upon them. "A sewage chute too small to enter, but topped by a large stone on which hundreds of stones collect. If we can dislodge it…"

"Could a force ram it?" Lukan asked.

Skeptus tapped the spot. "They would see us coming on the open terrain. I don't know if a log could be hurried in fast enough before spindles rain down on the carriers."

"Perhaps if a force were to sneak in and dig it free," Lukan wondered.

The scout, a fleet-footed youth not two years out of the Agoge, stepped forward. "It is heavily mortared and would take some time, perhaps a whole night."

"The noise would alert patrols," Skeptus noted glumly.

The tent was silent for a time before a voice broke in with a rasp. "The tool you require is in this camp. I have seen it."

Lukan was startled to hear the princess speak over his shoulder. Were all members of the royal family so stealthy? "Princess Kerata, you honor us with your presence. Are you well?"

Kerata coughed, her eyes squinting in the dull light. "I took a flutter but will press through it in private. Mind your plans, General." She gazed at the map. "I said that you already have the tool with which to breach this wall."

"To what do you refer?" Lukan forgot his propriety for a moment as he ran through every siege design he had ever seen or heard of. "We have no tools to complete such a task."

"It wanders this camp's outskirts. That bull creature of Crete would be strong enough to remove that stone."

Skeptus looked up. "Yes. Yes, General! I have seen the Minotaur toss Athenians like driftwood. It would surely have the strength to draw that stone."

Lukan looked at the map, then back at the assembled with him. "I don't know if Cy—if the minotaur could complete this alone. There would need to be support. Our best spear throwers would have to hold the wall clear."

"You don't want to waste resources. If it can get the stone out then its work is done. Such is the very reason why your predecessor allowed the vagabond to serve in our army, isn't it?" Kerata asked dismissively.

Lukan spoke with care, realizing that open concern for Cyrantus would be noted. He wondered if he would be forced to challenge the woman with whom he sought to match destinies. "If it falls short of the task, we have no other. Minotaurs are legend through most of Greece, much less ones that serve in armies. I would have this mission succeed." He looked to his helmet and spear in one corner. "I will lead the raid myself."

Kerata looked at the General cryptically before breaking into coughs. "Of course if the wall falls, you will immediately lead the charge into the city."

"Most definitely." Plain words, spoken with pride. That was something Cyrantus couldn't give him, Lukan thought with cold certainty. Kerata's eyes were like daggers. "Everything depends upon you, General. Spare nothing to ensure that."

He answered his princess with a shallow expressionless nod.

By nightfall, they were ready. Three squads of Spartans ran night exercises within charging distance as a small party of spear throwers stole through the night, Lukan and the minotaur among them. No archers accompanied them. Arrows were shameful weapons referred to by Spartan's as spindles, even if such weapons could make things easier. The force hugged shadows and carefully watched for silhouettes on the wall to gain proximity. Soon enough, the wall of Athens was rough at their backs and Athenian sewage assailed their nostrils. "We must be ready for the patrols. They will hear and feel the digging under their feet."

Lukan looked over to Cyrantus, who wore twin wrapped cloths to hide the shine of his ivory horns. "Are your tools ready?" He spoke with the formality of a stranger and the minotaur answered the same, brandishing two immense hooks that were thickly roped to a harness across his broad torso. "They are, General."

The still night had no moon to see by, so they counted heartbeats until a distant signal fire was briefly exposed, indicating the passage of the sentry. "Now," Lukan hissed.

Cyrantus faced the keystone, placing his hooves astride the channel of filth that dribbled out upon the ground. He began using the two rope-tied hooks to dig at the mortar holding the stone in place. The scraping was quiet at first, then louder with urgency as the second fire signal warned of the next sentry's approach. Cyrantus turned to place his back against the wall again, but a shout from above put a cold feeling in Lukan's guts. They had been spotted.

"Move faster!"

Cyrantus turned back and began frantically digging at the mortar, dust obscuring his form. More shouting rose from above and the alarm was called. A moment later, torches dropped to the ground, illuminating the invaders.

The first arrow whizzed down, narrowly missing Cyrantus.

Lukan rushed outward from cover, drawing fire and beckoning others with him. Away from the wall, arrows frantically trying to pin him, he lunged several steps and hurled his spear at a silhouette. The Athenian shrieked as he tumbled. There was a wet sound as Lukan's spear was drawn from the corpse by a soldier next to Cyrantus, who then tossed the spear back to Lukan. On the second running throw, another Athenian was struck, but fell back instead of forward.

There was a cracking sound at the wall's top and Cyrantus drew back both arms as a group of Athenians collected overhead. Lukan saw the torches lit above illuminate something large trundling forward.

A gout of flame, as though a brazier had been lit, brightened the faces of Athenian soldiers above. Lukan wondered for a moment what could possess the fools to reveal themselves in the dark as they did, but then it became apparent what they had brought fire to. His heart stopped cold.

He raced to Cyrantus and slapped his great shoulder. "You need to pull the stone now. Clear away from the wall!"

Cyrantus didn't look up, but turned from the hooks he had dug into the exposed sides of the de-mortared stone and threw his weight against the harness that joined the roped hooks to it. The stone slid forth an inch, but was deeply set, held in place by immense pressure. There was a wrenching sound far above as the heavy bronze cauldron was slowly tipped with urgent grunts and a line of black pitch hissed as it trailed against the wall. It would pour down its full contents in seconds. Cyrantus dug his hooves and pulled again. Lukan marveled at the quivering of Cyrantus' great muscles and felt a thrill, realizing the Athenian mistake. The added weight of the bronze cauldron on that wall would bring it down immediately once the key pulled free. His forces would be through the gates in minutes.

"Come, pull!" he shouted right in Cyrantus' face.

The minotaur looked at him, shine from the hellish burning light above glinting in fast tiring eyes. Another tug would do it, and Lukan could now see what he did not allow himself to notice before. With the cauldron's added weight, the massive stone's removal would immediately take the wall down, right on top of Cyrantus, rock and burning pitch and all. Lukan knew this, knew with the cold certainty of a war General that a sacrificial victim was trussed before him. He could hear the marching of his troops in the distance as the signal was given and they double-timed towards the breach position. The throwers fell back, their ammunition spent, and Cyrantus bellowed when the first drips of pitch popped off the wall and struck sizzling on his back. His hooves frantically sought purchase in the muck.

The stone shifted. It would come out. Given another minute, one, maybe two more pulls and Lukan would battle toward the heart of Athens for his glory. Another tug, and an anguished unworldly scream. Burning hair and flesh. The flaming pot upended above. Cyrantus bellowed. Lukan's heart immediately clenched as though dammed shut with anguish.

His Xiphos flashed out, the lines to the hooks were cut and a smoking Cyrantus tumbled down the hillock as stinking fumes and flame consumed the wall and ditch behind him. "Back!" Lukan shouted, and took the minotaur's arm under his, groaning under the weight as the raiding party fell back. The assault force was lit in a ghostly line that halted to the sight of their retreat.

Skeptus stood at their lead. "What happened?" Lukan, leaning under Cyrantus' weight, gave answer with his hollow gaze.

Their departure was orderly and quick, countless heads held low. Behind them, Athenians on the long walls cheered.

Lukan asked after the princess and discovered once news spread that she did not wish to see him. The hollow feeling within had no name. He decided to let her be, not knowing what he would say to her when they met.

When a helot doctor could not be found with skill or will to attend to Cyrantus, an animal herder was found instead. By the time Lukan was able to see to his brothers and reassure them of their eventual success, the minotaur had been released, eaten very little and gone to his usual seclusion. Nobody knew where to find him and Lukan kept his inquiries minimal. Those he spoke with no doubt assumed he wanted the creature to try again.

He could tell no one that he hoped no such thing and regret, far exceeding the sting of defeat, pursued him as he wandered for hours through the maze of tents in the dark. So many seasons had the minotaur been serving this Spartan army, his prior history told only by shame and whip scars. Lukan was only now coming to fully realize that Cyrantus had no comrades here and never would, not a soul beside himself to share his practiced wit and brutal honesty.

Loneliness was the least of complaints to a Spartan, a whine allowed to mere children. Despite this, few men Lukan ever knew had tasted the isolation that his creature of the mist had, born of godly influence to walk along the paths of mortal men. Like the fish in the sea or the wolves of the steppes, the rare abnormalities wandering Greece's fringes simply *were* either abject curses or useful blessings depending upon perspective. Among the Greeks, Cyrantus never had a friend beyond his General, the man who led him to near slaughter a night after using him for private pleasures. Much less a lover, did Cyrantus truly have a friend at all?

A cough at his shoulder pulled Lukan from thought. Skeptus was grave. "The Athenians have seen to the key-stone with a vast pouring of mortar. Cowardly shits didn't even come out from behind their wall."

"It's of no consequence," Lukan answered honestly, looking east to the walls and the hot lid of the rising sun. He met Skeptus' dismayed gaze. "We shall find another way."

"We must convene—"

"Leave me for now. Morning has come and I must tell the princess."

"She is still ill and requests isolation according to the Ephor, who wants to guard her from dire news."

"Guard her from what? The fool! Had we won she would desire to know immediately. Even if she will never rule, she needs to learn to face the truths before us. I am at—"

There was a whistle of air and an arrow shaft erupted from Skeptus's shoulder. Even wounded, he drew his sword as fast as Lukan. Both Spartans turned to the nearby clearing, heading low, charging with shouts. "Assassins!" Lukan called out. "Fall in!"

In the dark, they saw a form rise from the concealment of distant scrub and hurry for cover. A sentry hurled his spear after the fleeing Athenian and took him in the thigh. Lukan fell back as the sentry and Skeptus, disregarding his wound, hurried out to capture him. "Keep him alive," Lukan called. He turned to another young warrior who had heard the commotion and arrived first. "Muster your brothers to alert and fan out," Lukan ordered. "There must be others out there."

The soldier nodded and hurried to the Spartan tents. Skeptus and the sentry had the Athenian and Lukan heard the man scream. He immediately sorted through his priorities.

The Princess. Her tent was on the outskirts of the camp as per her decree. He could see it, unguarded, its attendant sentries missing in the low light of morning. Lukan turned on a sandal and raced, red cloak flowing.

The Ephor was at the tent's entrance and stood in his path. "General, what brings you here at such early—"

"There has been a sneak attack by assassins and I do not see Kerata's honor guard."

The Ephor swallowed as he took in Lukan's alarm. "The guard were dismissed at the princess' insistence. She said their walks disturbed her."

"How does that make any sense?" Lukan shook his head as he hissed, "I must see to her immediately." Just then, he heard a cry, high pitched and breathless within her tent. The Ephor startled. "My General, you must go and attend to your camp. I will see to the princess' needs."

Lukan shoved the Ephor out of his way and drew his sword as he heard another gasp, racing for the royal tent's flap. He hurled himself through the gap and crouched in a fighting stance, Xiphos drawn at the ready. The sight that greeted his eyes filled him with confusion and horror in equal measures.

Cyrantus was in the tent, bare but for filthy bandages about his shoulder and back, his wet member weeping in the light of a fiery brazier as he drew it out. Beneath the kneeling, panting minotaur lay the Princess Kerata, solitary daughter of the King of Sparta. Light pooled off the sweat that shimmered off her naked body and heaving breasts. Kerata's delicate fingers massaged her glinting sex, her wild eyes filled with the glow of interrupted ecstasy, her mouth curled in glee. The tent smelled of lust and musk, packed in to the point of stifling.

Kerata's eyes met Lukan's and her expression curdled. "General."

Lukan felt the world shrink around him, his vision tightening itself to a tunnel. His eyes sought Cyrantus, who refused to look back. "What is this?" Lukan hissed. "What is this?"

"This is not what it appears," Cyrantus said, his bovine face tight and expressionless. "The act is, but not the intention." The minotaur offered no more.

Lukan's gaze lowered to the Princess below, who was already recovering from the shock of discovery and her blissful expression giving way to what seemed to be annoyance. Her hand reached up and stroked the Minotaur's erect member, collecting moisture that she brought down to wet herself with. "He is typically more skilled with words, isn't he General?" She gazed at the minotaur's cock, sitting up on her blankets so that it quivered before her bare breasts. "But that is not the talent that serves my needs best." She stroked Cyrantus languidly. The massive creature stayed silent and still as a body-slave. "Nor yours, isn't that right, General?"

Lukan's knuckles whitened around his sword. Tears stung his eyes as fury ignited in him.

"I had her promise," Cyrantus bleated. "She summoned me, shortly after... her Ephor saw us. She demanded I come to her."

The Princess tipped back her head and slapped the minotaur's member open handed like she was scolding a pet. "You were seen, yes. The General who would court me to gain title and position and the creature who would assist in the transaction. Oh yes, I was well-informed." She spoke in mockery of Cyrantus' deep brass tones. "I know the truth."

Cyrantus' ears wound back in a flinch and he continued to pant. "I did as she bade, and in return I demanded that she accept your offer of marriage if I acquiesced. I would accept no other terms."

Kerata grabbed Cyrantus' testicles and squeezed. "Be silent. You enjoyed this game just like you enjoyed all the others you have played, didn't you, animal? Helping the man who claimed to love me deceive me with your honeyed tongue wasn't all you planned, was it?"

"I wanted no other terms," Cyrantus nearly cried. "I merely want passage back home. It is all I ever desired!"

"Oh, you want to go home," Kerata taunted from between his legs, growing angry. "You are at home right here, both of you, in the shadow of Athens! You think just like them, scheme just like them. I am just a pliable tool of transaction to you, chattel to be tricked into one man's bed or another's with the sweetest of lies!"

Kerata bit back furious tears as she hissed through her teeth and turned back to the General, his sword shaking in his hand. "Well I have my own desires, Lukan. And they require no man for fulfillment! Sex is no weapon for *you* to use against *me*. I have now completed a transaction of my own. How does it feel to know that I have taken my satisfaction elsewhere, General?"

Cyrantus stood, his member bouncing up against his abdomen, horns pressing the skin of the tent to the point of tearing. "You don't know my heart or mind. Nor his!"

"Silence," Lukan hissed, his back arched low and his blood singing in his veins. He could not hear the words spoken anymore, couldn't sort them out. Both objects of his affection had betrayed him, played him for a fool when all he ever sought was to understand the desires of his own heart. His sympathies and affections for Cyrantus, his hopes for approval and love from the princess, both were mere shades that melted away in a maelstrom of fury.

He didn't want to love or be loved. He didn't want to lead or be led. In the moment, the blade in his hand as the only certainty in the world, he wanted blood.

"I will send you down to a proper home in Hades." His sword swinging, Lukan lunged at Cyrantus.

The minotaur bellowed and leaped out of the way, Lukan's blade drawing blood from his flank. The Princess shouted angrily as the blade nearly caught her on the return arc. Lukan was mindless to his surroundings, screaming with rage. He swiped again, cutting a swath in the wall of the Princess' tent. Cyrantus knocked his arm aside, nearly bowling the General over with his strength and lunged at the gap.

He tore a mouth open to the night as he leapt through the ruined tent's skin and bound across the plain, his bent legs pumping and tail tucked low.

Lukan tore after the minotaur, breathing fire in his lungs, leaving the camp and the Princess and the distant Athenian wall far behind him. They were inconsequential abstracts in the dawn's gleam. Kerata's voice drifted after him. "Suffer me for a fool and see what it brings you!"

Lukan ignored her, charging into the rough. The wet on his face came not from rain.

Cyrantus wheezed, bereft of lust or pain, his legs on fire as he ran through the dark, all semblance of civility and sentience left behind him on a tent's royal carpets. He had obeyed the whims of the princess, and given her what she demanded just as he had served the whims of the man whom he had tried to love and would soon be cleft by. Gods damn these stupid Greeks.

His erection was fast fading and his balls ached where they banged between his thighs. The princess' sweat dried upon his chest, smelling of the perfumed deceptions in which he had taken part all to grant his Spartan lover what he wanted.

And to get what Cyrantus desired in return. Never had the possibility of a long love crossed either of their minds, Cyrantus was sure of it. If Zeus were looking down on him now, he'd spare the conniving minotaur no pity. Nor would Fioves, if time allowed him to remain the handsome bull Cyrantus recalled. They would never again rumble one another's bones with knocked horns, never caress with their loins cooled by the first spring's dew. Never sing to the gods for finding one another again. Their love would forever be denied.

An incoherent scream echoed after him as the Spartan gained ground, still unable to collect words into sense. Such simple creatures were men, despite their pretentions and gilded ambitions. It would have disgusted those who banished Cyrantus to no end to know he had sunk to loving one. He may very well be the first minotaur harlot.

Time to reconcile.

Over a hillock, Cyrantus tucked his legs and leaped, spinning and scrabbling for purchase with his hooves as he took a grappler's stance. Lukan crested the hill and lunged short sword swinging for the kill.

Cyrantus ducked under it, colliding with his breastplate in a strike that would have gored the Spartan had his armor not been still affixed. Lukan grunted and the sword's pommel came down on Cyrantus' skull, knocking him into seeing celestial lights. As the man backed away to reverse his sword and deliver the death blow, the minotaur's strong hands grabbed him and they grappled for the blade between them.

Lukan had tears in his eyes, and his pale face was alive with rage and sorrow. At the cusp of death, Cyrantus found it eerily beautiful. "I loved you," Lukan whispered through chattering teeth. "How could I love you, you animal?"

"You loved what I could give you." Cyrantus blew hot air in the Spartan's face, giving his golden curls a Medusaen shiver. "You would never bring me to your tent. You would never see me among your brethren. Which of us do you lie to, Spartan?"

Lukan brought up a sandal and nearly kicked Cyrantus' maleness, putting sole to abdomen and forcing them apart. He retained possession of his sword. "I opened my heart to you and you betrayed me. You could never be any brother of mine." He wound to swing again. "I should never have cut that line and let you burn. I may have lost a war for that."

"Your crude words at least find some honesty at last in viciousness. You and the princess truly belong to one another in that damned city. I should have known I would never find warmth in your company." Cyrantus felt his blood boiling over, his control slipping away. "You lie to each other as you lie to yourselves." Cyrantus lowered his head for the charge. "As you lied to me!" He leaped.

Lukan swung his sword, not even bothering to feint. He missed his mark on the minotaur's brow, his blade glancing off the bull-head's horns. Cyrantus felt the steel sing through his skeleton in a crude pulse as his sharpened tips found the join in Lukan's armor and bit flesh.

The Spartan went down under him, coming to the ground. A sickening crunch came with the sinking of Cyrantus' horn into his shoulder. The wine of life spurted into Cyrantus' eye and he drew back, drawing muscle and bone apart beneath Lukan's red cloak.

Blood forced tears to his eyes as General Lukan dropped the sword. He did not scream, did not convulse. Anger fled like a wraith from his blue eyes. He lay upon the earth and soaked it with life as the warlike aspect faded and his empty hand swept the air above him. It came to touch the chin of the monster that lay him down. Cyrantus' tunneled vision fell away. The tide and his blood cooled quickly. He searched the eyes of the man whom he'd loved and fought and killed. In the distance, Spartans mustered and shouted and skirmished with other Greeks. That was another world.

Lukan searched Cyrantus' mournful visage intensely, running a hand along the lips that leant him his deceptions, seeking a path through painful twists in his dangling soul to a vital item concealed from himself, found at last when he stroked Cyrantus' chin. There was no man or god left to hide from.

"This is the love I wanted," he said and died. Cyrantus kept still as the sun rose to warm them both. General Lukan, third standing General of Sparta, was not yet cold when the minotaur finally saw through his bloody tears to lift him.

The camp was in disarray, the men furious. The Athenians had killed many with their cowardly ambush and the prisoners remained mute. The princess gathered herself, swore the Ephor to secrecy one last time and bid for privacy while she awaited the General's return. Her father would be proud of the trophy he'd collected, something to offer in the Parthenon to Athena when Athens fell, but his smile would fade when she rejected him publicly as her suitor.

But the shadow that fell over her was of no man. A hairy hand over her mouth stilled her shout when she turned. The minotaur was still as naked as he'd left her, his chest, arms and endowment speckled with dirt and gore.

"He chased the Athenians from the camp who threatened you. His body will not be returned, but he died saving you." The minotaur spat the words as he released her.

Kerata glared up at him. "Of course. One last lie to crown them all," she muttered. "What becomes of you?"

"Cyrantus of Crete was killed alongside him," Cyrantus answered. "But I suspect you'll forget my name."

Kerata was rooted to the spot long after the creature that served the Spartan third army slipped away forever.

It is a footnote in history that Lukan's replacement had no job to do. Plague swept behind the walls, killing Pericles and gutting Athens. Sparta won the war with a bad taste in its mouth and in a hundred years nobody would even care.

That night, I lit Lukan's pyre and spoke what rites I'd gleaned from countless spied funerals. The gods didn't care if I had the words right. They were the only witnesses. My pain burned away with the man who was my lover for a time as bright as it was short and I lingered until cold winds took his ashes away.

I now have my ship, and as waves lap the shore, I prepare to set out and seek someone I once loved. We are scarce, our scents and markings distinctive. If Fioves still lives, I will find him. Only his memory stirs anything in me now and I hope I will not be his ruin if we meet again. I hoist my sail, intending to play no more bloody games with the endlessly feuding Greeks. I am sick to death of war's lingering miseries and have only one hope left. But with all my lost loves adding wound upon wound, I accept the truth with reluctance.

War, whether on the field or in another's loving arms, is what I am best at.

THE ONI AND THE FISHERMAN

George Squares

"See how it swells?" said Shōgun Katsumi. The stern white fox, calm in his decorum, pointed to the base of the maple, his onion-colored claw protruding from his gauntlet. "We must rip it from the earth, like a traitor from her child."

To my eyes, Shōgun Katsumi was an evil man. He had indeed ripped many traitors from their children. Often, when a loved one died, before they were burned to ashes, water of the last moment would be placed upon their lips to bless them in the name of Buddha. Katsumi often said that the rice paddies were wet enough. But my master Daiichi told me, as he often did, that if I sat upon his shoulders, I would be tall enough to understand the reasons of higher classes. I did not feel short when comparing myself to other stoats, but to a fox, a tall stoat was still small, if not in stature, than in importance.

But I was clean, and I could listen, and I could keep my paws inside my pockets when the lord let me eat off of silver. My name is Gorou, the traditional name of a family's fifth son. I was sold to a noble house for rice paddies. This transaction was not enough to keep my family from starving.

***

When Daiichi carried me that morning, my feet dangled from his shoulders, and the thought passed my mind that the tall are fewer in number than the small, and there would only ever be so many shoulders.

"You are afraid, Gorou," said Daiichi, whose tone was boyish but deep. My legs shook against his neck, which, despite being red and warm like a kindling flame, could not cast light upon the temple on the horizon. It was the spire of the Daimyō. The shining husks of black centipedes dragging their white bellies crawled into my mind when light reflected from the pagoda roofs until Daiichi's voice burned them away. "The winter's made you white, like death."

"There's still a patch of summer left in my fur," I said, my voice trailing off. "You just haven't seen it."

"There's always summer in my fur, if you have trouble remembering," he said, squeezing my ankle. "You cannot flinch in front of Katsumi. The Daimyō can see us too, and will report what he notices. The emperor will know, too." At that point it was still a mystery why the boy emperor had come to our district. Although the capital believed he was a god, Shogun Katsumi was Buddhist like the peasants. He held the true power over this land, and he had little love for the boy-god. Visiting was a risk, and would happen only in urgent circumstances.

"I understand. I am not afraid of the emperor," I said, staring at the tracks Daiichi's paws left in the snow.

"That's wise," said Daiichi, crossing his arms and twitching his fiery ears. "Surely you know, little banner-bearer. Do not be afraid of anything but negligence. We are all only strong as our frailest in this society. That is why all we can do is strive to make each other stronger. Otherwise, we perish." He put me down, and the snow crunched beneath my feet as his russet tail swayed neatly, attentively, in pace to the war beat of the taiko; the massive drums sat upon lacquered posts and reverberated to the beat of the soldiers who struck them in blows.

Neither I nor Daiichi had been in the garden of Daimyō before today. Although Daiichi was a noble, his family held less power than Katsumi's, and they were not often summoned to the tower. Here, the maples and cherries were barren. The bronze statues of Buddha on marble huddled back-to-back, as if watching the path for one another, afraid.

There was but one maple in the garden that had all of its leaves. Its crust-laden body coiled, serpentine, in and out of the ground with arcs that turned like the napes of dragons, thick and twisting hungrily skyward so that its shade burnt the soil black.

When Katsumi pulled his katana from its sheath, the plates of his emerald great armor shifted, and the white fox bared his teeth.

186

"There is no place for filth in my subject's garden!" He snarled, gauging his enemy, before pacing forward, moving faster as he broke into a run. Although Katsumi was large in his emerald great armor, compared to the maple, he was but a beetle with a soft belly in an over-sized shell. There was something impressive to me, watching that insect in his jewelled carapace assail the gnarled welts and the roots that looped into the soil like earth-eels, fattening themselves on clay—but that was before we saw the branches start to move.

Some of us screamed. Some of us wailed. But that would not change what we had seen—that the tree had taken our Shōgun, and in his absence had it acquired a new piece, silhouetted as a man in eternal pain before slinking into an amorphous tuber.

Such was the end of one of the most powerful men in Japan. Katsumi had died in his hubris and I could not even smile. Without his orders, we would have little tactical direction. The Daimyō shrieked out distraught orders of advance. The quickened pace of the taiko blows beckoned the Samurai forward. I could not tell Daiichi not to fly at the tree. I could not even show it on my face, although I knew my mind and my heart were not one and the same. Betraying the orders of the Daimyō meant betraying him too. He would see it no other way.

He would have an honored death, be remembered by me, all his underlings, and his proud family, who would drink to the boy who fed the blood tree in the name of the emperor. Surely, I would be the first to finish my saké.

A command was issued from the tower behind us, higher than I could see, bellowing to halt the attack. "The emperor sees no gain in this assault," said a hoarse woman I could not see. "He will not have them feeding it anymore. This is not working."

The eyes of the men trailed to the Daimyō, who wore a blank expression. Normally, his will was second to that of only Katsumi, but the Shogun was dead. Without the leadership and military power of the Katsumi, the assassination and instillation of a new emperor was not a threat in this district any longer. He bowed sharply, saying nothing more. The emperor's servant spoke again.

"Your emperor has come to this district only to see proof of a rumor so monstrous. With his curiosity sated, there will be national action taken. Katsumi's men has our emperor's sympathies. All men henceforth are dismissed from his presence."

***

Inside the Temple, I stripped Daiichi's armor away, which had made his shoulders appear wider than they really were. Some of the men had soiled themselves, but I was relieved to see my lord had not. I boiled water, and washed him with rags in the quiet of muffled voices that bounced off the walls of the barracks.

"Sometimes I am frightened by your loyalty, Gorou," he lilted, resting his arms behind his back, shoving his chest forward in a gentle stretch of the spine.

I scrubbed between his knees, where the red fur met white, and the pink of him often sagged. When he was clean there, I bent to scrub at his shins, wrinkling my brow.

"Disloyalty is perhaps a wiser thing to fear," I said, relieving an itch on my outer ear, accidentally dampening myself there.

"You would have tried to stop me out there, would you not?" said Daiichi, slouching, studying me as if I were a piece of stale bread.

"No," I said. "I would not have." This was the truth, although it seemed he did not know it.

"Your intentions... were transparent. A servant putting his lord above the will of the emperor would be a shameful display, indeed. It would make me look bad... and it would not end so kindly for you, especially."

I squeezed out his rag, moving to the space behind his ears. "Sentiment is not the same as action, my lord. Trust me. I know that impertinent people do not eat."

His ears splayed. "We are not children anymore, Gorou, but I am afraid that is something we both struggle to forget when we are around one another."

"Might I relay the tale of the two fishermen?"

He opened his mouth to speak, but his mouth was left agape, before it slanted into a crooked smile, and with his clawed foot, he sloshed a bit of the water on my nose. "You would tell it to me anyway if I said no, wouldn't you?"

I growled, rubbing myself dry on the hem of his sleeve before blowing out breath, attempting to concentrate. I pinched the bridge of my nose, and let the old story come back to me. "There were two men in a fishing village. One noble, one poor. They grew up together in their youth. The noble man was very good at cooking the fish, and the poor man was very good at catching the fish."

I rose, dropped the rag into the bucket, where it made a soft sloosh, and began to pace.

"One day, it just so happened that the two men were searching for a new trade route along the western pass, when a snowstorm forced them into a cave in the mountainside. They were ill-equipped for a long stay, and knew that if they left the cave, they would freeze. They also knew that if they stayed in the cave, they would starve. Do you know what the men said to one another?"

"Surely the poor man offered his meat to the noble man?"

"Yes, so he did." I closed my eyes, and put my paws behind my back. "But the noble man did not accept. Do you know why?"

"Of course! Because the idea was revolting."

"Yes, it would have been grim... but no, that is not why. The noble man realized that if he ate his partner, he would have no future, for he was hopeless at catching fish, even if he did, by chance, survive. Despite being of noble blood, his family no longer had any money to their name. His riches would wane, and he would die in disgrace. His end would be the same both inside of the cavern and outside of the cavern."

"So if his fate was the same, why did he still refuse the meat?"

"Because he wouldn't have to die alone," I said as I dried him and reached for his wool. "I know what choice you will make if given a foolish order. That is how I know mine, too."

His lip curled into a snarl as he looked down at me, flushing with anger before he choked. "There is nothing foolish in dying for a noble cause."

"I am sorry," I said. "I have been cruel." Perhaps it was ironic for me to fear for Katsumi, worth fields of livestock, when I was but a mere rice paddy.

"You have been ruthless," he scolded. "But not cruel. No. At the very least, I know that I can trust you."

⁂

In the following weeks, the maple tree amassed in girth, and height, and soon any trace of the initial garden was gone. The tower of the Daimyō had collapsed, and the shadow it had cast over the village was replaced by the overbearing maple, stagnating the free flow of wind.

The emperor sent for his best scholars, priests, and counsellors while the festering wood of the maple overtook the temple. Thick trunks snaked into the forest, blotting out the light of other trees and laying waste to the undergrowth. After it had conquered the wild, it came for us, past the countryside and into the village. The spread of the wood turned the rivers black, killing the fish with a tarry, sap-like residue that stank of iron.

All we knew of the maple was that ire fuelled its growth, and those who charged it were consumed by the branches. Sinewy vines furrowed through stone, plaster and silk, enveloping the village in a weedy parameter. Layers of the gnarled, wriggling wood criss-crossed and overlapped until it trapped us in a wooden maze. Those who tried to escape perished into the skin of the branches. I dared not watch when a villager went too close to the forest. Often, nothing was left but their clothes, which were folded into the wedges of the wood.

It was weeks before we heard from the emperor, who had managed to break in from the outside.

My lord's presence was requested, as usual, with one servant at his side. More samurai had formed at the opening, underneath a clearing of the wood where we could gaze at the sky and remember what the stars looked like. There was fresh water here. The sickly sweet smells of bloated fish and sap were overcome with the purifying aroma of nothing: melting ice and windward snow from the mountainside.

There was a congregation of guards. The emperor sat in a palanquin held by six white foxes, his face hidden by the curtains. One of the foxes called out: "A horror has been unleashed upon us all, facilitating a necessary act of courage and skill. We do not know if any of you will live. But we do have a stratagem, designed by counsellor Sumia. She will now speak."

"Thank you," said a crone of a cat in black robes. She had waddled out from behind the palanquin, her robes billowing as if the smoke of the forge became her. Puffs of her opium swirled from her nostrils and dispersed into the air. "It must be strange, to approach you, offering an escape from the stories of your childhood. I did not believe it. The emperor did not believe it. But this weed of the world, which stretches to the sky, as if to nip at the heel of the gods, is real. A karma eater has manifested itself as this tree."

Whispers hissed about the camp. I dared not speak up to my superiors, but I had been raised on the stories of the karma eaters. The hate begetters. The stories said they might appear as a sick villager, or a bloated fish, but never a tree. The only effect the tales and the tree agreed upon was that frustration made it fat. The old cat continued.

"Like a nasty rumor, karma eaters cannot be slain with swords." She opened a fan, tore it with the twist of her digits, and threw it to the ground in a clackering whirl. "Weapons are futile. Fire is smothered and stymied with the stink of brimstone. But, on the contrary, a karma eater is highly responsive to emotion. Hatred feeds it. Trust destroys it. It recoils, and shrivels. That much is certain."

"And emotion is to be our weapons?" spoke a Shiba holding an uneasy stance. "Emotion as a weapon to be wielded by those who have mastered the blade?"

"Emotion is always a weapon—especially when concealed and directed with the finesse of a handled dagger," said the cat. She shot the dog a glare. "Many can master the blade if they have a name and a coin purse." The shiba inu's posture straightened, and she continued. "And that is why we must ask the trial of trust from the warriors who have not yet failed us. Each servant must kneel before his bushi, undress them, and please them as the act of ultimate loyalty. You must know one another's body, or you will fail this mission."

A paw lifted the curtain of the palanquin, and I saw the emperor, watching from his chair. Surprise and horror twisted his face. So he really was just a boy. Did he think this would even work?

There were murmurs of discomfort and displeasure. The shiba spoke first.

"Pardon my impertinence, but what is asked does not seem possible. I do not desire my servant."

A hare chimed in. "I agree. I do not think my loyalty could be measured in pleasure. What is asked by the hag is shocking."

I looked immediately to Daiichi. He was guarding his expression. I knew he would not speak his mind, for that was not his way. More interruptions of discontent filled the air when a tiger paw drew the palanquin's curtain. The emperor stared at them all, eyes burning bright yellow. "I speak to you all directly as your emperor. Sumia has never erred me. You will do what Sumia asks, or you will be banished. It is a grave thing that I am speaking to you all, now."

The emperor tugged the curtain again, and he was visible no more. A small army of servants brought forth lanterns, stools, and many silk dividers. Oil lamps were burned to illuminate the insides of the screens so strong shadows could be cast. There were no more questions.

I heard rustling, and falling cloth as the bushi around me were stripped naked, their bare forms shivering in the snow, tails twitching nervously. Masters and servants entered their screens, separate from one another. Daiichi looked down at me, his eyes cold. I did not want to disappoint him, but he knew I was afraid. My paws pulled the top-knot of his kimono loose, and I did as the others did. I had dressed him before. We entered the enclosed silk structure together, and I had to adjust my eyes to the intensity of the light. The shadow of my body mimicked my form in detail on the side of the wall facing the emperor and Sumia. My paw brushed against the piece of him that was beneath the inner layer and he closed his eyes.

I pulled the wool shirt from his skin, and lowered myself, hinged upon my knees to see him. His was like mine, but slightly different in basic shape. Broader. Longer, with a tapered tip. His legs did not shake. He was brave, and I could be too. I touched him, and didn't flinch. His length smelled like firewood and his bed sheets. I kept his soft skin warm with a kiss, all the while my breath fogged on him. Some kind of ache in me panged as I watched him thicken. His length was often in this way when the morning came to greet him, but his bed sheets were to be touched only after he left them. A globule, like dew, formed on his tip before I lapped at it, holding his balls to shield them from the cold.

"I know my choice," I said. A gush of breath emptied out of him when he heard me, while white fog billowed from his maw. Something shifted in him below, and my eyes widened as a bulge formed around his base. Curious, I cupped my hand around it, and he growled pleasantly. Then he barked, and I could feel his piece twitch in my mouth, splattering something into my muzzle, tasting like murk and salt. My arms held his soft waist in place as I drank my fill, bound to him, eager to save him, and to save myself.

When I had finished, I brushed the traces of Daiichi's sex from my mouth. I stood awkwardly, a tent pushing my clothing away from my groin. Around us, the wood retreated, twisting away where it could not be seen. There was a light burning bright inside me after it occurred what I had done. I had never wanted a wife, or a child, although I knew it was expected of me. I knew I would be pitied by the village had I not fulfilled my duty. But was there no other way to do that? Was there another way to be useful I had never seen?

But still, Daiichi was bothered. He could lop off heads for his nation, and let himself be strangled, but he had never been asked to mate. Could he do it again, if he was asked? Of the two of us, I had always believed myself the weaker. How strange that now, here, I did not want that to be true. There was fear in Daiichi... and ahead of us was only forest.

Each samurai and servant exited the screens and walked into the wood. I recognized the shiba, who looked as if he were wounded. The hare, however, seemed to have a skip in his step. We were followed by the words of advisor Sumia: "In the forest, you will find the garden, and the center of this devil. Show your trust, and purge this evil."

***

We pushed on for hours into the forest. When the wood is eerily silent, and there are no birds or insects, there is a feeling in your gut that a predator lurks close by, quick to lunge and suckle from marrow. But when the wood slivers and shifts without the force of the wind, and the world is maddened by your presence, it is all too easy to infect the spirit. It had been apparent that not all of the samurai and not all of the servants approved of the ritual of trust. Their curses echoed ahead, before they were silenced forever by the wringing of the bark-scaled fingers of the wood, and naught but their clothing remained.

We took a break by a stream, found crabs to boil, and sat back to back, ensuring that no root or branch could sneak up on us.

"Perhaps sex was not the best way to form trust," I said, stripping the cloth from a servant's shirt to use as gauze.

"We often believe those we mate with are closer to us forever," said Daiichi. "But isn't that often the contrary? For how many of us is sex meaningless? That is why we buy our whores with currency, not trust."

The forest rattled us on. Somehow or another, I felt that it wanted us to argue. I wanted to speak, needed to speak, but I knew that an argument would end in anger, and silence would end in sadness, or frustration. This trap was sophisticated. Even the spiders don't force the moths to wrap themselves.

"Perhaps trust had to be there in the beginning for the sex to work."

"I don't think that's the case. I trusted you before... you did that to me."

"I see no reason to be worried," I whispered, feeling the fur on his back bristle. The wood seemed to be taking notice, which forced a twitch in my ears, and my involuntary scamper backwards.

"Will things be quite the same?" He panicked.

"Certainly not," I said as Daiichi's eyes widened in horror, and I could feel his heart palpitate. He saw the forest slithering toward us from every angle. "But we will die soon if you fall into despair." I could not afford to panic too, or else we would be immediately consumed.

He opened his mouth to speak, but I stopped him with my tongue. I pushed him to the ground and kissed him, feeling him, smelling the scent of a warrior who must not succumb to the poison of the forest. His paw reached up to me, gingerly, like a child as I petted his face.

I lowered my head for him, whimpering, snuffling the soil trapped in his fur as he pet my ears and whispered to me, "I must know your body, too." His paw pushed me down into the grass, tearing at my trousers and exposing the long, thin leaking length that clung to my belly, oozing my want for him. His long tongue lapped up the mess I had been making, and I saw him wince before a sharp grin curled up his cheeks, a fox smile broader than any I had known without fearing. He pointed to the side of my belly, where a lone patch of brown still clung to me.

"I see summer, there."

He sniffed deeply as he took me into his mouth, sucking and bobbing. I cringed when his vice-grip tugged on my tail, and his spit slathered my groin like thickened honey. He grunted as I fit tightly into his long, slender muzzle. A muscle in my inner thigh twitched involuntarily and my leg kicked. That's when he swallowed as much of me as he could.

I squeaked.

I had never been sucked before, by a man or by a woman. He was hungry for me, and there was more in his eyes for me than just duty. I had spent more time with this fox than any other. I forgot what a family was. My importance as a piece of a mechanism didn't seem to matter anymore, so long as Daiichi was here, looking at me in the way he always had, but with a new and gentle fear in the gaze. I closed my eyes and heard the creeping of the branches, surrounding us, snapping, recoiling, wilting while the doubt in my lord struggled to stamp itself out. I whispered his name, and stroked his cheek as the warmth of his mouth rekindled me, making me squeak for him.

For summer.

"Will not leave me," I gasped. A spasm deep inside of me quivered, as my balls retracted, and a giddiness drowned all sense of restraint I once had. Sticky white fluid pumped from my member, pungent and plentiful, clotting his smooth fur into a matted tousle. My smell covered Daiichi, as he sat there, happy, dazed in my stink before he licked himself clean.

We held each other in the clearing until the wood snapped. The leaves withered and all that was left in front of us was the marble slab, cusping the two statues of Buddha, their eyes now cracked, and with woody tendrils spiralling from the sockets.

Passing the statues, we approached the trunk of the maple, whose sides had eaten into the temple. It seemed we were the only ones to make it, or to try to make it. With haste, we scampered over twigs and rushes caked with ice to approach the tree at its face.

When a child clumps clay into a doll, there is some semblance of a person. A semblance too misshapen to be convincing, but irreconcilable in its doomed familiarity. Such was the face of Jubokko. A giant's face, simian, shifting, as if it did not know what an expression could look like, and could not make up its mind. Three eyes, sloppily placed on the form focused on the two of us. Its sideway mouth struggled to open, more like an expanding orifice than a hinge. The wail of a woman eked its way out of wood all around us, and the false mouth warped into a puppet-like expression.

"Who comes, with fire and sword, and the stink of the mind that wanders, that wanders."

Frightened, I said, "We are here. Two men."

"Men with fur. Men with bark for skin, like me, gone. Where have you been for long, so long, so long. Long."

Daiichi growled. "It is you who have recently arrived. It is you who have taken the Tower of the Daimyō. We have always been here. What do you mean?"

"Here is food," said the monster as one of its eyes spun in place, squelching as it revolved. "You are not food. You are source. You have left me. You have ruined me. You made me grow. Your food. Your food. My food."

"I don't understand," said Daiichi, holding me back, his burly arm outstretched. "They never told us a karma eater could speak?"

"I speak… if you speak. I am Jubokko. Everything I have has been given to me. I was planted when the lives of ten thousand men soaked into the soil. The men who bleed without having to bleed have made me full, for so long. Then the blood stopped. Then the blood stopped. The blood turned to blood thoughts, so I drank. I have longed for the blood to rain once more, to parch my thirst. Why do you not want me anymore? Animals fight. They fight."

"We don't only fight," I piped up to the wood woman, repulsed by her countenance. "We sculpt, and we garden, and we make each other shoes. We dream in images. Fear and anger keep us alive, but we don't need them so much."

"So says you," boomed the forest. "You who give me so little space. Who give me so much food in blood thought. You who deny me nutrition, who give me my meals in poison. A weed is a weed is a weed. You can pluck me but your claws are green. You can cut me but I always grow stronger. You must answer, not ignore. You must not burn me down, burn me down. I am you but you are not me. You must not forget me." The tree rambled through her howls and hisses, and her angry intonations whistled from the skin of the bark.

"Enough of this!" Daiichi yowled. "I must ask you want you want, Jubokko! What do you want from the people? What will make you stop taking life? Augh!" He covered his snout with his paw, and I shrank back too when I saw the fetid water rise from the murk in Jubokko's roots, welling up as the veins in her third eye blushed purple.

"I want… a war. The war to end all wars. The war that will give me what I lost so long ago. The war that will feed me all blood and will undo us both forever."

Daiichi's fur bristled, and he waved his paw at the tree. "What you ask for is impossible," he said. "I refuse to end!"

"Every beginning has an end. One cannot be, without the other. As I am, I will be unhappy forever, until the end."

I stood there with Daiichi, trying to calm him, trying to keep the hatred away as the second of Jubokko's eyes rolled in its socket, maddened. I mustered my courage to speak, once more.

"If you grant us safe passage, we will tell the emperor your wish."

The eyes stopped rolling, ending cross-eyed before they fell into place, all three upon me. "Then that is your promise. I will wait, as I have waited. Waited. Waited. You will tell your emperor. If you fly, as men without wings have always tried, I will grow, and I will find you."

* * *

Outside of the forest by the river, we heard the windmill turning in the distance, grinding wheat for bread that tongues would never taste. The sun shifted from behind a mountain in the horizon before we remembered that we had not slept for days during our journey. I crouched on the ground, and so did Daiichi, where I laid my head on his tail, pulling it over me as my eyelids drooped.

"You mean to tell the emperor Jubokko's whim?" said Daiichi, cleaning moss from my whiskers.

"I owe no oath to the demon tree," I said. "Death is a hollow threat when it is every option she has to offer." I had been in this field of barren cherry trees before. I remembered gathering bamboo to make baskets for the fruit with Daiichi, before he was a samurai and before I was a servant, back when we said we'd never need wives, and we picked our teeth with leftover switches. "I don't know the answer to the best decision. There is no story to guide me in this."

"You're frightened to take a chance without reason to guide you. Isn't that so, Gorou?"

I shuddered and squeezed his paw. Winter crickets chirped in the distance, and the bubbling of the stream marked signs of an early spring. The world was neutral, here, like a mattress.

"So I am the one who must takes risks. That is because you will not... Very well."

I kissed his thigh, and his voice faltered.

"I don't think you should tell the emperor. He'd do it."

"That answer sounds... unlike you." I rounded on him, lowered my head, and sifted my paws through the fur on his crimson shoulders, pressing my forehead to his white throat. Daiichi sighed.

"Our lord is no monster. But there is a monster. A monster with demands. Our country may survive longer if we agree. I think many would choose that option to stave off their own doom. Either way, a lot of people will die. And if I were emperor, and that weight were on my shoulders... compliance would be the only choice."

I choked back a sob and dragged him to the ground with me, where his soft tail wrapped around me, and he shushed me quiet.

"Do you know why I chose you to be my serving man, Gorou?"

"No."

"I chose you for this, out of all my servants, because your heart is platinum, and that is something that I lack. You can recover from a lot of pain and disappointment. Most people cannot do that."

"There is some fire in your heart, too," I said, staring at my lord. "Take from my lantern, if your oil burns low."

We slept in each other's arms that night, and I buried myself in his warmth, smelling his chest.

***

I woke to the gentle crackle of flame and a whistling kettle. Daiichi crouched, handing me a cup full of nettles, pouring the hot water over them.

"I had a lot of time to think when you were asleep."

"I'm not sure I would like to think, for a while," I said.

"Here's a worthwhile ponder, though. There is another way to solve our problem. Trees are grown from seeds, aren't they?"

My cup swirled, and viridian splotches clouded the water. "Most of them, yes. Jubokko told us that she was grown from a seed, I remember."

"So it's not as if her spirit demands as much space as she claimed. She merely hungers. She expands to satiate that hunger. But that's what trees must do to survive."

"But she doesn't want to survive."

"Not as a tree, no. But I do not think she was always a tree. There is the maple, and there is Jubokko. Their spirits conflict."

Slouching, I grumbled, warming my paws on the mug, wincing from the bitter nettles. "What else was she but a tree?"

"Certainly something as small as a seed."

"But that would only make her angry. If she made herself small again, that would prolong her judgement. She'd never agree."

"But what if she wasn't a seed. What if she were a boat, or a piece of parchment? Something that could move without struggle?"

"I can't imagine why you would want to help her move."

"Because we cannot deny that Jubokko has a point. Men will always hate. Men will always murder. Those feelings are a part of us, and will not be repressed. If she is free to move, she will not have to drink from the soil. She will have her fill, without forcing tragedy. She is an evil we cannot eliminate... but we can keep her from taking us all. I think her confusion would clear if she weren't bound to the earth, or tucked into a seed. I think a mask might work. But it's very risky. The moment she is free, she'll ravage to the closest source of fear or hatred. We will be the first to cross her path. We'll have to keep her away. With trust."

I squeezed his paw, feeling the warmth of it. "I was scared you would no longer want to do that, after we don't have to."

Daiichi didn't say anything, and looked forward into the wood. He had often looked forward where the rest of the world and I could not see him. Wind blew through his fur, and it was time to busy myself with other things.

***

That night, we returned to Jubokko's core. One of her eyeballs had left her cheek, and had replaced itself on her forehead. Her mouth had formed jaws, with a splintered maw, and her nostrils became more pronounced, flaring like a lizard's.

Although I was exhausted, my concentration on Daiichi helped me to forget fear and anger for a short while. Daiichi showed no symptoms of fatigue, his spry steps leading to the center of the forest, and his arms akimbo as he faced Jubokko.

"My message," he orated, putting on his most official decorum, "was given to the emperor, and was accepted. But there is a better option than that. If you are to drink the blood of the people, why must you be confined to your roots, your woods, your body? Were you not born from the smallest of seeds, no bigger than the padding of my paw?"

Her nose compressed, exuding ichor as she thought. "Yes... there was once a time where I was no larger than a dove's egg, lighter, lighter. Long before the promise was made, and the heaviness of betrayal seeped into my very nature."

Daiichi's eyes lit up, and the fire I had seen there days before was back. "If you make yourself very small, I can carve you from your tree, and your roots will not entrap you in this place. You can wander freely to where the blood is spilt. No more waiting for battles. No more roots that seep into the dry cracks of the world. You may take the blood that is yours, and leave the burden of your promise behind."

The tree's mouth cracked and splintered as it morphed into a grisly rictus.

"The promise will shift. I consent."

Our work was slow as I stood on Daiichi's shoulders once more, carving into the tree with a whittling knife. Slow, careful traces of the blade left white marks in the tree. Her bark was unnaturally hot, and a staccato beating sound quickened when bubbling sap oozed from the first stab into the tree, blackening my gloves.

Once I had placed my incisions, Daiichi helped me saw the face from the tree. The smell of fetid coagulation lingered as we removed more of her. She made no sounds and exhibited no pain while we worked her face, almost as large as a shield, away from her trunk. The cursed spirit was expunged from its body and roots, channelled into the center of the mask, where small flames erupted from the eye sockets, the mouth and the nose. Leaves fell from above me as I listened to the forest rustle and die as we had to drop her giant hollow face that grew too hot to hold.

Her corners crunched like parted firewood, splitting and molting. Thick appendages sprouted from her jagged edges. Legs with clawed feet that seemed to be a grotesque caricature of Daiichi's paws stemmed from her back, inverted. Then came segmented arms that ended in the claws much like a bear's.

There was a crunch, and a thick neck jutted upward; from its base blossomed a head. From her head sprung crimson grass that writhed and twisted without the wind blowing through it. Pike-like horns sprouted from her crown. She bent over and crawled, crablike, scuttling along the forest floor.

Daiichi bumped into me and flinched as the demon disappeared into the decaying remnants of her old forest body. Trembling, I spoke: "She was an oni. She had been tied to the soil for so long that I am surprised she remembered her original form."

Daiichi's tail hair prickled as a bush in front of us was set aflame. "All her existence had been bitterness and pure wrath. We must run. We have to get away before she can sprint!"

"No. No running," I said. I kissed Daiichi, tasting the velvet of his tongue in my mouth, reminding him of his promise. He blinked, splaying his ears. His golden eyes listed from my chest to my groin. "She will catch us when we run."

He stared at me, his brow scrunching into sadness. "Even if we die together, I don't want to die yet." He kissed me again, holding my back tighter, using the full extent of his muscles and nearly putting me out of breath.

"I have had my fill of evil things, Daiichi," I said. He groped my groin.

"Then take your fill of me," he murmured, putting his paw into my pants, plucking at me, playing me better than any stringed instrument. I stripped off my shirt as his neck stretched, tasting me again with his tongue, tickling me with his prickly whiskers, making me squeak.

"I want to lie with you, like I should a woman."

"You may," I said, as his finger brushed between my balls and my waist. "But I am still your man."

"And I am still your lord," he said, shifting his back and swishing his tail as his belly touched mine, and he lay on top of me. The wail of a devil howled in the wood. The close sounds of claws slashed tree trunks, toppled soil and shattered rock.

The freezing floor was nothing compared to the blaze that burned through Daiichi's member as he dragged it across my balls, leaving his mark on me while my white tail thrashed against the soil, my black tip trembling.

Daiichi's breath was heavy, and his low bay blew warmth into the fur of my neck. He drooled on me, as if taken by heat, and nudged his tip against me. I squirmed underneath, struggling to put myself into the right position. I knew that some lords took their servants, but it had never been asked of me before. I blushed in my inexperience, but finally lifted myself high enough to feel his warm, wet tip brush against my bottom.

Daiichi panted, but his breath wasn't all I heard. I could feel the beast watching. We were defenceless there. But I knew if she could have devoured us, she would have done so already. I pressed against Daiichi, clouding my mind from any other thought than his pleasure, and the scent of sweat, and the smells of home.

"When I put myself inside you, you'll be bound to me for a while. We won't be able to run."

"We aren't running. I'm bound to you already."

His eyes were slit as he stared at me, and he pushed himself deep. I felt the pinch when he entered and the taper of his length widened within me, hurting slightly, while his round, rigid bump forced itself against my bum.

I panted for him, louder than the noise of the beast above us who covered us in its shadow.

His piece pulsed as it throbbed inside me. He thrust his hips, moving in me, forcing his bulge against my sore muscle. His throaty growls echoed through the forest. "Take me Gorou. This is what will hold us together."

"I'm... trying... I... Ahhh. You're touching something!" I squeaked.

"T-touching what?" he said as a speckled of spit dripped from his mouth.

"Something wonderful inside me. Something— S-something that takes me out of my own control... I... I..." A small popping noise sounded, and my end burned. Daiichi bit my neck and whined, stuck in place while his warmth flooded into me, sealing us in happiness.

I held him, lying still as the snow fell on us. The shadow had gone, and took with it the life of all green things around us.

Years passed, and the world believed me dead. With the forest barren, the nearby village collapsed into ruin. The temple was abandoned, said to be the site of a great schism, and the lands subsequently salted. I never told the emperor, or the Daimyō, or anybody what we had done. Jubokko disappeared from our lives forever, living only as a rumor; an ogre running through the countryside, plaguing the footsteps of warriors and conquerors, where blood vines and war banners draped over the bodies of the fallen.

I walk as an older man now outside my cottage in a village south of Kyoto. My pelt is brown at the height of spring, when the azaleas peak up from behind mounds of earth and sweeten the air. When we ford a bridge and walk from one part of our lives into another, we are often encouraged to burn the bridge behind us, as a conqueror would. I was never one for flames, or for violence, but looking away forever was a skill I had picked up a long time ago.

There are no lords with me now. The emperor still lives, but I do not see his eyes nor hear his commands from his faraway castle.

There are no slicing blades here, nor are there tests of guile or leadership. My gardens are to be tended. My geta clack against stone as I observe the yams and the cabbage.

There are no buds such as Jubokko in my garden. It is hard for me to understand how she appeared in any garden, or why taking and destroying are exalted over giving and creating.

All of destruction owes its existence to creation. There must be wood before there can be bonfires. There must be stone before it can be hurled. There must be food before it can be consumed. Her voice echoed inside of my head: Your food. Your food. My food. Still, I did not weep, even as I sat there alone. I kneeled and brushed some earth from the cabbage.

A paw took me under the arm and brought me to my feet.

"You've been out here a little long, haven't you?" said Daiichi, the confidence still in his voice. He dresses in the common clothes of a fisherman, now. "Dinner's ready."

"I feel old. But I felt old even when I was young." I leaned on him, warmed by his sides. Much of the color had faded from his fur, but the warmth did not. He picked me up and sat me on his broad shoulders as we walked to the house.

He sat me down to a plate of tuna and vegetables. I took small bites. "I was thinking about her again."

Daiichi regarded me with sympathy, and poured me some water from a ceramic pitcher. "We have kept her away from our beds for years. We can do it again tonight."

I squeezed his paw. "Or today. Or in the morning. Any time, as you do."

He pet my face and gave me a kiss. The house of two fisherman are best filled with food and laughter.

PERYTON MOD

Ross Whitlock

"The revolution's finally started, Lalit!"

I raised an eyebrow at my friend Io. Her virtual Cubbyhole was still forming around me, baroque textures popping into focus, and she'd given me no time to get my bearings. Her arms were folded tight in impatience and her ears flicked madly.

"And good morning to you," I said. "May I have a little context?"

"I tin-canned you, like, three hours ago."

"My real body needs to eat, y'know," I replied. "And my real fridge was empty. Now, again…?"

She sighed dramatically and waved a paw across her feed, which she currently had skinned to resemble a magic mirror. Opening two fingers, she brought a headline to the fore:

FUR FLIES OVER ANATOMICALLY-CORRECT DUNGEON ULTRA BEASTIES

"Sounds fascinating," I said, grinning.

"It's brilliant, is what it is. Some prudes went apeshit 'cause of a newly modded ice dragon with a cloaca. Apparently the local Sheriff didn't notice, it being internal and all."

I laughed. "So who was looking closely at a dragon crotch?"

"Someone who doth protest too much, obviously. Anyway, this is it! The good fight! A whole bunch of modders have come forward to demand full freedom of expression."

"In regards to monster junk. Wait…" I looked hard at her. Io was pretty easy to read, even as an avatar. She and I agreed that your virtual self should reflect your real self, maybe with better ab muscles, but you know how it is. I was simply me—a male pine marten—and apart from some gold filigree decorating her face and limbs, the online Io resembled the petite black fox she was for real. And she wore her emotions on her poofy purple sleeve.

"This is about your peryton, isn't it."

She nodded. "What else? Lalit, you have to see it. I've added so much modding; it's beautiful. And now I can actually patch it into DU, if the forces of freedom prevail."

"You know it's up to the Game Gods."

"The Game Gods aren't stupid. Seriously, my peryton is a masterpiece. The fur texturing alone … and the muscles, and the A.I., and the fluid dynamics." She was babbling. Her Sunlands accent had grown more pronounced. I had to grab her shoulders.

"Okay, calm down. Is there a reason I'm here, or is this just a big eff-why-eye?"

"I told you! I want to show you the peryton!"

"So it's done?" Io had been working on her monster for what seemed like a lifetime. It'd been pretty crude the last time I looked at it, and I'd secretly doubted she'd ever finish it to her lofty satisfaction. Io takes modding very seriously.

"I think so! Apart from some tweaks. I want you to be the first to look it over and give feedback. I mean, I trust your opinion most."

"Aww, thanks." I really was flattered. Io and I had been close friends since we met in one of DungeonUltra's main quests. We'd never met in the flesh, but does that even matter these days? I supported everything she did, even a crazy mod project.

I quickly pulled up my Backpack and linked to DungeonUltra. Io's hands moved in a quick flurry as she did the same. A bouncy little fox icon flashed, letting me know she'd invited me into a private cell: a nether space, within the game but free of its Terms of Service, where modders could test-run their work. I rubbed the fox's head, and I was in. The Cubbyhole phased out, baroque ornamentation giving way to bare stone walls and torches. The cell was as generic as you could get; not even a door. I barely registered it.

I was staring at the peryton.

Hang on. I guess I'm being cruel to the uninitiated. Well, you've certainly heard of DungeonUltra (DU for short) even if you know nothing about gaming. It's the hugest Massive Multiplayer Online World, or MMOW, of them all, and the seventh-biggest name in the virtual economy. Millions of players every day. Its genre is typical high fantasy—swords, spells, dragons—with an emphasis on questing and exploration. Like the best MMOWs, it relies heavily on player mods, expanding through input from its own community. Just about any type of gameplay is available. Want to reduce an army of kobolds to red oatmeal using just your fists? You can! Prefer a more peaceful, intellectual experience? Try one of the countless puzzle dungeons. Depending on how much time you spend in the virtual world, you can have your own business, take on and train apprentice players, even get married. The moderators, or Sheriffs, are chosen from the best, and do a good job of keeping order and penalizing unruly players.

Back before all this happened, sex was considered unruly.

And that was the big thing, right there. DU was originally conceived to be kid-friendly, and there's plenty of child-appropriate content to this day, but the gamemakers soon bowed to the inevitable and allowed in the blood and guts and curses. However, they'd always kept sex out of the game, claiming it had no place, even if your characters lived in wedded bliss. That rule extended to the bestiary. Dragons, gnolls, werebeasts, ghouls, and all the rest—they may have been stark naked, but they were also as smooth between the legs as a storefront dummy. They had to be.

Io was part of a movement that believed this was wrong, not necessarily because they wanted to fuck monsters (though I can guarantee some of them did), but because they felt it distracted from the game's otherwise unparalleled realism. The group largely consisted of modders who made monsters, and they resented having to compromise their vision in the name of prudence. I was more or less on their side, though I didn't mod myself.

Truth to tell, I found a lot of the DU creatures sexy. I hid that information from most people. Io knew, though. Probably the real reason she wanted me to look at her peryton.

Because it was damn good-looking.

The creature stood with its back against the stone wall. Heavy manacles held its arms above its head—a cute touch from the gamemakers, who felt that an exhibited monster should always be restrained. Io had the peryton in peaceable mode. It watched me calmly, breathing in and out, shifting its legs slightly as I looked it over. Looked him over.

It was most definitely a him.

"Vishnu's balls," I swore.

"You like?" Io's voice echoed from nowhere.

"Um, wow. You've done a lot since last time."

The peryton was almost eight feet tall and thickly muscled, with a large chest and heavy haunches. For the most part, he resembled a deer: cervine face, spreading rack of jet-black antlers, short brown fur. His lower legs erupted in dark feathers, ending in a pair of cruel-looking black eagle talons. Feathery black wings framed his form. And, yes, he was "accurate." I looked over the thick sheath and low-hanging balls, and felt the distant twinge of my real-world body becoming aroused. When you're online, you can still sense your physical self, a ghostly echo behind your virtual experience. Especially if you're in pain, or have to go to the bathroom … or if you have an erection.

This monster looked utterly alive. I couldn't believe how well she'd rendered him. Monsters in DU can look a bit choppy if the modders lack funds, but Io's peryton could have stepped in from real life. I could see every strand of hair, make out the complex bunching of heavy muscles as he moved in his bonds, trace the tendons and veins with my eyes. He yawned, displaying a black tongue and razor-sharp fangs. I saw my reflection in his crimson eyes. He was terrifying but also beautiful in a feral kind of way.

"Did you spend all your money on making this, Io?"

She dodged the question. "No worries. I got a ton of help from GnollBros. They provided the basic body model and a lot of the patches."

"GnollBros?" I repeated, alarmed. GnollBros was a small online business that provided material to modders, but they weren't known for their scruples. They had to operate outside DU, ever since they got permabanned for stealing armor designs.

"I hear your tone," Io said. "But they gave me some amazing deals. They're totally onboard with the anatomic accuracy movement."

I sighed. Io's judgment skills weren't always the best. But I found it hard to argue with the results.

"Go ahead and touch him!" she chirped.

I stepped forward and placed my paw on the monster's chest. I wore the skin of my rogue character—my normal pine marten avatar, basically my real self with rustic garb added—and I felt incredibly vulnerable. The peryton kept looking at me. I felt his broad pectoral muscles tense. I ran my paw across them, taking a moment to tweak a large black nipple between my fingers. Damned if I didn't feel it stiffen slightly.

"Utter realism, yeah?" Io's voice enthused. I kind of wished she wasn't watching me right now. My game character was just as smooth in the crotch as the monsters, but my real-world body had grown very hot and bothered. I have a kink for large, imposing guys with big muscles, which describes a lot of fantasy monsters, doesn't it.

To distract myself while idly tracing the monster's flawless abs, I said, "Remind me what a peryton even is."

"Predatory flying creature, supposedly originating in Atlantis," Io intoned. "Actually created by some fantasy writer ages ago."

"Is there one in DU already?"

She scoffed. "Technically. Low-level creature in the Yphenean Wastes. Looks like a chicken with antlers. Believe me, my boy here's gonna overwrite their peryton in a flash."

"Assuming they actually allow anatomically correct monsters."

"They'll bow to the inevitable. We just need to show that ... Lalit, what are you doing?"

My paw had been exploring the broad furry curves of something. I realized I was groping Io's monster. Worse, the peryton had begun to make a low rumble in his throat. An unmistakable sound of enjoyment.

I jerked my paw away. "Sorry! I, uh, wasn't—"

"You were." She sighed. "You are such a pervert. I knew you'd do this."

"Then why'd you invite me to ogle your naked stud here?" I snapped.

"Because you're a pervert." She giggled. "I mean, I have to test all his reactions. And I've worked accurate responses into every facet of his brain. That includes sexual arousal. Now, who do I know who likes them male and studly?"

"Why don't you fondle him yourself?" I asked. I couldn't take my eyes off the peryton's sheath. It swelled at my touch, the delicate opening at the peak drawing slightly apart to reveal a dark, gleaming interior. I could see the very tip of his penis. It rose, pushing the sheath wider, hungry for fresh air. The peryton stared at me, lips parted, each breath whooshing against my face. His pecs heaved slightly and his eagle talons pawed the floor. I'd gotten him quite aroused.

"I'm biased," Io replied, sounding devilish. "I need someone who doesn't know every line of code in the peryton's being. Someone who can pretend he's real."

"You win," I grumbled. "But you'd better keep him in peaceable mode. Okay, big guy, show me the goods."

He did. His cock continued to emerge—ten, eleven, twelve inches. An ebony pillar, shaft decorated with veins, head flared out before narrowing to a slightly hooked tip. I drew my fingers lightly over the flesh and felt it twitch. The peryton rolled his thick hipbones. His lips vibrated, blowing my virtual fur back with a loud exhalation. He groaned, eyes half-shut. Gods, he was hot. Every move he made, every ripple and twitch of his hide. I noticed drops of sweat beading on his fur, gliding into the grooves between his muscles. I stopped thinking, let my urges control my actions. I leaned forward and licked a bit of sweat off his chest, my tongue circling a nipple. He shuddered and his cock leaped against my fingers. I wrapped my full paw around the shaft and began slowly stroking him off.

Io had outdone herself. It felt utterly real; even the salt taste of his sweat on my tongue. I could smell him: musky, masculine. Most virtual creatures have no smell—why bother?—but Io hadn't overlooked it. How many patches, how much code, to make her glorious beast come to life? I gazed up at his face, feeling almost shy. His features were kind of handsome, despite the low, glowering brow, heavy jaw, and lethal teeth. I realized that there had to have been a live model involved. It's near-impossible to get so much detail if you don't mo-cap and scan an actual person. That should have set off warning bells in my brain—where'd GnollBros get the model?—but I was kind of thinking with my cock at the moment. It felt so sexy, having him at my mercy: bound while I was free, naked while my avatar wore clothes. Mine to play with, for these moments.

I toyed with him, letting his need grow, keeping things slow as I worked his shaft. My other paw fondled his heavy nuts, bouncing them gently, feeling the shift of weight that let me know they were brimming. He groaned and huffed, trying to rut against me. I grinned and kissed his chest, nibbled along his breastbone. His whole body gleamed with sweat, and the manacles clanked as he strained. For a moment, I thought he sought to get away, but then he humped at me, seeking more pleasure. I showed mercy and jerked him off faster, looking down to see clear pre oozing from his slit. Io stayed silent, probably feeling a bit wet in real life too. Me, I'd have to paw off as soon as

I logged out.

"C'mon, stud," I murmured, my teeth teasing a nipple. He gasped and arched his spine, haunches rolling forward. Beneath my palm, the veins popped out. His balls contracted. Almost there. I stroked as hard as I could, wanting to see him cum, to feel it. Both of us panted, me from exertion, he from sheer animal lust. His eyelids drooped, he bared his fangs, and ... released.

The cum wasn't quite right. I've heard that semen's one of those things that's damned hard to render. Io had done an admirable job. Still, it looked a little too white and felt a bit too much like warm water as it splashed across my torso. Believe me, it didn't diminish the hotness of the moment. The peryton remained poised in orgasm for several seconds, muscles taut, eyes shut, mouth open in a soundless cry. His seed marked us both, dripping down our chests and bellies. I tasted some: slightly salty, like his sweat. Again, not quite realistic. But, gods, the beauty of that monster.

He sagged, panting, opening his eyes to look dazedly at me. His fierce muzzle couldn't smile, but I imagined he would have.

"That went well," Io's voice said perkily.

"Io, you..." I caught my breath. "You're crazy and brilliant and I love you."

"Love you back, pervert. So, I know the cum wasn't quite right, but I doubt there's gonna be a lot of peryton sex in the game."

"And yet you built him so he could." I chuckled. "Realism."

"If you leave anything out, you're compromising your principles," she said firmly. "I'm willing to put in the effort. I mean, this is my one shot."

Something about her tone gave me pause, but I was too horny to think much about it. I flicked out a quick command with my fingers, and my cum-covered clothes instantly cleaned themselves. I glanced at the peryton. He'd gone back to standing up straight in his chains. His cock had retreated into its sheath and his hide was clean, as if nothing had happened.

"Io," I said. "I'm gonna chat more with you later. But right now—"

"Tend to yourself," she said. I heard the laughter in her voice.

"Yeah. And...yeah. Your peryton is fucking amazing."

"Thank you! I knew you'd like him!"

I phased out, awakening in my Pod with a raging boner. I quickly gave the open command, then sat up in the SmartGel, pulling my breathing mask off. As I stood, the gel slithered off me, leaving my fur dry. I'm one of those people who goes online in the nude. I stepped out of the tank, staggered over to my armchair, flopped, and started jerking off hard.

It didn't take long. Less than a minute, and the whole time I pictured the godly muscles and frozen O-face of the peryton. I raised my voice in a deep moan of bliss and came all over myself. Best orgasm I'd had in a while. Afterwards, I lazed for a moment, admiring the pattern of jizz across the umber fur of my belly. Like most pine martens, I'm slim and trim, and I keep myself that way—too many net addicts turn into blobs. My online time was followed by a bit of stretching and working out. Which I also do naked.

As my mind fit itself back together, I remembered what Io had said. It was her one shot. I could grasp the connotations. No way could she have modded such a flawless creature without spending way more money than she had. She was banking on the Game Gods of DungeonUltra allowing monsters with dangly bits. And on making a mint in royalties when the peryton became a popular in-game adversary. If those things didn't happen, my friend was up shit creek. Especially if she'd fallen in with creeps like GnollBros. If she owed them favors.

I swallowed and tried to tell myself she'd be fine. She was resourceful; I'd known her for years and she'd always muddled through despite her reckless tendencies. This, though, was her magnum opus. If it failed, she'd have nothing.

I lifted weights and tried to think of ways to help her. But that got me thinking again about my tryst with the peryton. And when my workout was done, I had to paw off a second time.

***

The peryton remained in my thoughts for the next couple days. You can imagine how I felt when he turned up on my doorstep.

It was Friday and I'd gotten my work done early. I do accounting for several successful little online companies; nice clients, but you can see why my leisure time is so exhilarating. I hadn't had another chance to talk to Io, but I planned on sending her a tin-can over the weekend. For now, I just wanted to kick back and relax utterly. I was about to dip into some leftover Cajun shrimp when the door chimed.

I groaned, got up, and checked the ID pad. The holofeed just showed a blanket of fuzz, a concealed identity. Religious nuts, most likely. I quickly rehearsed the angry fake-Hindu rant I have prepared for such an occasion, and opened the door. And then all words and cohesive thought fell out of my skull, because Io's peryton was in front of me, looking stern.

I stood there like an idiot.

"Lalit Chowdhury?" the peryton asked. His deep voice had a tinge of Quevenoc Union accent.

"Um," I said, or something like that.

I must have nodded, because he replied, "I'm Fletcher Ansible. May I come in?"

He had the kind of voice that you obey. I stepped back. He came in, looking around my modest but well-furnished apartment without much interest. My brain began to work again. Of course this wasn't Io's peryton but a real person, a tall deer with a handsomely muscled body and wide antlers. He wore a fine-looking LeatherOid jacket and perfectly tailored slacks. His eyes were hazel, not crimson, and his face, while strong-jawed, lacked the savage expression of the monster. He had the build of a person, not a beast. But the resemblance so close. Too close.

"Can I get you anything?" My voice came out a bit squeaky.

"Information, Mr. Chowdhury. Answers. Or so I'd hope." Ansible flipped open what was definitely a state-of-the-art wristie. As his fingers flicked over its surface, I saw tiny motes, like grains of diamond, glint on his paw and around his right eye. Nanites. Only the wealthy had them. I felt more than a little terrified.

"Uh, Mr. Ansible, what's this about?"

My voice trailed off as a holo of a transparent chamber appeared over his palm, miniaturized but crystal-clear. Inside the little box, a pine marten dressed in rogue's gear was standing before a large, shackled monster. The marten touched the beast's chest.

"Oh," I said quietly.

Ansible's voice darkened. "Please don't lie to me. Tell me about this."

I was a giant idiot. During my encounter with Io's peryton, I'd been officially in-game, in a space the gamemakers allowed for test-driving mods before their formal submission. When in-game, I always logged everything—and kept the log public, because what did I have to hide? Well, this. Me molesting a monster. I hadn't even thought of it at the time.

"Would you like to sit down?" I squeaked.

"I'd like you to talk."

"Okay. Um … look, sir, I don't know much about this. The monster, it's something my friend modded. She's been working on it for awhile." Was I selling out Io? Wait, this wasn't her fault! "She's been working with this company, GnollBros. They're very unscrupulous; you should look into them."

Ansible's fingers darted over his wristie. "I will. But tell me more about this friend of yours."

"She's just a modder on the side, sir! A hobbyist!" I felt desperate. "Sir, she…we didn't know you'd been modeled without your permission. I swear we didn't."

He looked closely at me. His eyes were piercing, but after a moment, they softened just a little. "I suppose I have barged in on you unexpectedly. I thought to call the authorities, but due to the personal nature of the infringement, I wanted to do my own investigation first. I'm a lawyer."

Of course he was. I fought to calm myself. "Well, sir, I'd like to help you. If I may, how exactly did a model of you get stolen?"

"Two years ago, I had a full-body mo-cap done of myself. I was updating my avatar with new tech and I wanted something as real as possible. The company who did the modeling was trustworthy, but not too long after, they were hacked. They let me know, said there was a chance my body model had been pirated. Said they'd keep an eye out. I haven't given it much thought lately. But yesterday, an in-game friend contacted me and said he'd seen something very interesting while he was browsing public logs for rogue skill techniques. And he showed me this." His eyebrows rose high. "Sexual content isn't allowed in DU."

A gamer. This rich, handsome lawyer was a gamer like me. I didn't know whether to be relieved or more worried. He was probably on a first-name basis with half the Sheriffs. "My friend believes in … anatomical accuracy. There's a movement to get it accepted. She wanted her peryton—"

"Her what?"

"The monster. It's called a peryton. She wanted it to look and be-have exactly as a real creature would."

"Even in ways that would never come up in the game itself?"

"Yeah." It sounded stupid, from this angle.

'Well, I admire her attention to detail," Ansible muttered. "And you're just an innocent bystander, is that it?"

"Sir, you can't blame my friend for this. She's ... she doesn't always make the best choices. But she would never willingly steal modding material. She can tell you that herself."

"Believe me, I plan to ask her," Ansible said. "Mr. Chowdhury, I would very much hate to involve you and your friend in the kind of lawsuit that destroys lives, not to mention the E-Gov's penalties for stealing real-life body models. However, I don't trust you yet."

"How can I earn your trust, then?" I asked. To my shame, it came out a bit fawningly. Hey, the guy was ridiculously hot, and though he was no monster, he shared some of the ferocity of his peryton counter-part. The sort of thing that turns me on. I felt naked in my tank top and silk shorts. Compared to Ansible, everything about my body seemed inadequate. And I liked that. Because I am happily enslaved by my fetishes, thank you very much.

"Am I interrupting anything?" he asked. "Because if not, you can come with me right now."

"To where?"

"To my place. I want to log in, talk to your friend, and see her little creation for myself."

"Why do I need to physically be at your place, sir?"

"As I said, I don't trust you. But if you're to be trusted, I'd like to win your trust in return. I'm not going to approach the authorities without sufficient proof of theft; online law is a tangled can of worms. More importantly, from my place, I can plug you into my private server. Full security requires your physical body. We can do things we couldn't do otherwise."

"Like what?"

He gave me an utterly enigmatic look. "We'll see, Mr. Chowdhury. Will you come?"

I didn't see as I had much choice. I stuck the shrimp back in the fridge, put on going-out clothes, and we went.

He led the way down the hall, giving me a chance to admire his muscular ass, mostly unhidden by his pert little deer-tail. We rode down the airshaft in silence. In the vehicle pool, Ansible did something with his wristie and his car glided up in less than a minute. A sexy little number from Rimea, dark blue in color with one-way windows. Inside, the passenger seat molded itself to me and a pleasant female voice offered me whiskey. I declined. Ansible slipped on a pair of sunglasses and we drove.

It'd been awhile since I'd left my district. He took the high road, coasting on a magnetic cushion above the gleaming sprawl, weaving in and out of dreamy spires. A city can be a beautiful thing—if you live in the right part of it, at least. Funny, how the magical castles and kingdoms of a fantasy realm like DungeonUltra have been replicated in the real world as skyscrapers, biodomes, space elevators, megahabitats, you name it. You'd think one day we'd catch up to our imaginations, but maybe what's truly beautiful is that we never will.

We still didn't talk. I got the sense that Fletcher Ansible wasn't one for chit-chat. Okay by me; what would I say? That this all vaguely turned me on? Instead I watched through the window as we entered one of the wealthier districts, a layer-cake of green terraces and bridges, dotted with private homes like glittery seashells. The type of place you dream of owning. Maybe I was dreaming right now.

Ansible lived in a home like a swooping half-moon, a big portion of which was glass. "Stylish, sir," I commented as we descended down the magnetic strip and parked on the cobbles outside. Ansible rewarded me with a small chuckle. A clear force-bubble encased the car as we disembarked. We walked up a ramp, through a force-door, and into his domain. All the furniture looked streamlined and avant-garde, and all the tech was as high-end as his wristie.

"Are you married, sir?" I asked. Something about the place said *bachelor*.

"No. Single, at the moment. Can I get you anything?"

"Glass of water, maybe." I felt torn between wanting to get this business over with and wanting to linger in the land where the rich people play.

He literally summoned a glass of water for me; it flew over on a small magnetic cushion and I drank deeply. Ansible himself had a tablespoon of something bright purple in a shotglass. Whatever it was, it made him gasp.

"Did you just drink what I make in a month?" I asked.

He chuckled, more openly this time. "I wouldn't go that far. Apologies if you're overwhelmed. You should see my neighbors. Their bedroom is inside a waterfall made of powdered DiamondOid."

I nodded. "Your place seems pretty spartan by contrast, sir. Which means you spend a lot of time online. Gaming?"

"Gaming, working, socializing. I'd say you and I are fairly similar, Mr. Chowdhury."

I begged to differ. Instead, I said, "Can we do this, then? I'm sure Io would like to know that someone gave her a stolen model."

He nodded briskly. "Right. I'll show you to my Pod."

His Pod. As he led me up a ramp to the second floor, I didn't consider the implications. Needless to say, his Pod had its own room, albeit a small room. I nerdgasmed a bit upon seeing it. You picture a Pod as looking like a big seed or kidney; maybe clear, maybe opaque, depending on the brand and model. Most are horizontal, because it's easier on the body to lie down for a long time. Ansible's Pod was a marvel; it looked like the world's most beautiful hot tub. A pearly basin, ringed by sphincter-nozzles where the SmartGel would be pumped in, and cradled in intricate nanotube structures. I guessed the latter were for generating an impermeable force bubble. It was the sort of Pod you saw on a big marble pedestal at an expo: the Future.

"These are on the market?" I asked.

"Not yet," Ansible replied. "I have a client who did me a favor." He tossed his jacket on the carpet, revealing a professional white shirt and tie.

"Your life is a fairy tale, sir," I commented, taking off my coat without really thinking. Then my brain caught up. "Wait. There's only one Pod."

"Not a problem. It can accommodate more than one body." He began to unbutton his shirt, exposing his wide pectorals. Then he paused. "Ah, yes. I should mention that this type of Pod works best if you're nude. Would that bother you?"

I gulped. "Well, I don't know, sir."

"It's not strictly necessary."

"It's fine, I guess," said my mouth, with zero input from my brain.

"Good." Off came the shirt. His torso was about as gorgeous as I'd imagined. I kept mentally layering the peryton's form over his, comparing the two. Similar wide chest and deeply grooved abs. Creamy fur down his front. His nipples were pink, not black, and one had a small silver horseshoe piercing it. It looked really good on him.

He noticed me staring and said, "I work out a lot."

"Me too," I replied quickly, yanking off my shirt. A pleasant shiver went through me as his eyes flicked over my lean torso and its coat of dark umber fur, a banana-yellow patch on my throat and chest. He smiled a little.

"You look good," he said. "Good build."

Then he took his pants off, exposing simple black briefs. I made a stealthy little sidestep to view him in profile. He had toned thighs, but not huge like the haunches of the peryton. His ass was a fine half-moon. Strong, bulging calves swooped into graceful ankles and cervine hooves that looked weird, because I kept picturing the peryton's eagle talons. Ansible stretched, popping his back, then casually slipped off the undies and stepped naked into the basin of the Pod. My host turned, waist curving beautifully, and asked, "Coming?"

It took a mental effort to undress completely, but I did it. Then, hugging my long fluffy tail, I joined him. He gave me another once-over, taking in my trim waist and slender legs. As he faced me, I tried really hard not to look at his package. The glimpse I got told me his sheath and balls were not quite as big as those of his monstrous twin, but still impressive.

"So, uh, how does your Pod work?" I asked.

"It's keyed to my nanites." His hand moved over his wristie. The nanotubes rustled around us like restless coral, their tips glowing. Looking closely, I saw the air shimmer. We were in a bubble.

"Stand closer to me," he said quietly. "My tech will pick up your body signature and brainwave. Then I can allow you into my higher security levels."

I stepped closer. He put a hand on my shoulder and drew me in even more, till our chests almost touched. I swallowed. This close I could feel the heat of his body, smell his natural scent. My body responded.

"Sir," I said. "I have to say this. I'm gay, and this is really homoerotic."

"Are you?" he asked. "Well, I don't mean to make you uncomfortable. I suppose I'm used to my circle of friends; we're very casual about this sort of thing. I apologize."

"No need," I said giddily. "Just warning you that I might be getting an erection right now."

He chuckled. "Well, if you're all right with it, you can touch me. It helps the nanites get a reading of you, since they're biotech."

Could this be a tease? The whole time, I'd told myself he wasn't flirting, that my romantic imagination had assigned motives that weren't really there. But come *on*. He'd just invited me to press my naked body against his. I felt a bit confused, like a hummingbird who's not sure if the large, vibrant, sweet-smelling flower before him is carnivorous. But I'd already dipped my beak in to drink.

I put my paws on his chest, resting them against the muscle. I could feel his heart. My own was going off like a deranged butterfly. He put an arm around me loosely, resting his paw on my lower back. My sheath, my cock, brushed his. I looked up at him shyly. He looked back, face composed. Then he kissed me.

It wasn't a sexual kiss. I could tell from the way he did it that he was just establishing a closer link. His nanites would work from the traces of saliva I left on his lips. Still, it was a nice kiss. His lips pressed to mine for several seconds, warm and slightly parted. In those seconds, I really felt like this man, Fletcher Ansible, came from another world. A world where resources weren't a problem and boundaries didn't matter as much. A world where adults could play like children and not worry about prudence or social restrictions. A world where you'd think nothing of kissing another male to swap DNA.

I imagined kissing the peryton, feeling those sharp teeth clack against mine. Ansible was the peryton after all: a creature alien to me, and all the more desirable for it. I pressed my body closer against his, knowing that he didn't mind, that in his world, it was just what people did. He too had an erection; I could feel its warmth between our bellies.

He broke the kiss and nodded, as if we'd simply exchanged business cards. "That should do it."

The nozzles whirred faintly. I looked down to see pinkish SmartGel pooling around our ankles. It rose rapidly.

"Don't we need breathing masks?" I asked.

"This gel is breathable. Have you ever experienced it before?" I shook my head. "The trick is not to panic. Ignore what your body tells you. I'll help you."

I took deep breaths, calming myself, as the gel rose up our legs, then our midsections. It felt nice, warm and slightly tingly. Being held by Ansible comforted me a great deal, like I had my own warrior to guard me. The gel rose up my chest and I instinctively tilted my chin up and took a deep breath. I closed my eyes and felt it engulf my head. When I opened them again, Ansible was looking down at my face curiously. The gel rose over his antlers and filled the invisible bubble completely. My footpaws left the floor of the Pod and we bobbed.

I felt Ansible's chest rise and fall as he breathed the gel. I was afraid to. My body felt the stirrings of panic. It thought I was underwater, in danger of drowning. My cheeks puffed. Ansible leaned down and kissed me again. Gently, carefully, he exhaled SmartGel into me. Before my body could reject the gift, I inhaled. I had a moment of nausea and discomfort as it flooded my windpipe and entered my lungs. But it didn't hurt, just tingled. He pulled away. I exhaled and took a deep breath of gel. A few more, and I was fine. It felt really weird, but not unpleasant. I gave Ansible a thumbs-up.

He nodded, then closed his eyes. I did the same. He embraced me with the other arm so he could work his wristie. A familiar shimmering behind my eyelids, and all real-life sensations, the feel of his body against mine, his cock touching mine, faded into the background. We were online.

***

Ansible's Cubbyhole surprised me. I'd expected something really awesome-looking, but instead I found my avatar standing in a blank white room with nothing but a black LeatherOid couch against one wall. Ansible's avatar resembled him perfectly, except that his antlers were gold. He wore a white T-shirt and jeans. I felt silly; my own avatar was dressed like an Hindi wedding guest.

"This is minimalist," I commented.

"I don't need anything fancy," he replied. "Most of my online time is spent in DungeonUltra, or private spaces my friends and I have set up. Anyway, I'd like you to invite me to your Cubbyhole instead."

"Why?"

"So I can paint a better picture of you, Mr. Chowdhury."

"Okay, first of all, you can call me Lalit. Secondly, are you asking for access to all my personal crap?"

He shrugged. "In a lawyerly way, yes. You're a nice kid, Lalit. I want to trust you, but I need to see you're not trying to cover anything up."

I sighed. "Okay. You can look at my logs, my personal files, whatever. But I reserve the right to tell you if something is off-limits. Deal?"

After a moment of silence, he nodded. "Deal."

I brought up my Backpack and phased us both to my Cubbyhole. I'm totally obsessed with my own heritage, so I had my Cubbyhole done up to resemble a mandir—a Hindu temple. I had a really nice statue of Ganesh that I asked for advice, semi-ironically. A lot of candles and red paint, too. Ansible looked around with interest, then accessed his wristie. It took on its virtual form: a serpentine silver dragon, thin as a chopstick but three feet long, that uncoiled from nowhere and wrapped itself around his wrist.

"Good afternoon, Master," it said in a lilting voice.

"Hello, Xing," Ansible replied. "Will you please access Lalit's personal database? Anything with a high privacy rating, let me know and I'll ask him about it."

"At once, Master."

The process was kind of boring. Ansible just stood there, eyes closed, looking through everything that made me who I was online. Every now and then, he asked me about a file or log. He was very courteous. I didn't mind him looking at most of it. I held back one or two intensely private things, but, obviously, none of it related to the illegal use of Ansible's body model.

"You're clean," he said when he was done. "Good. I can let you go."

"Let me...?" I stared at him. "Did you have me locked online?"

"I did, and I'm sorry. I had to be sure."

I felt my virtual fur bristle slightly, reacting to my discomfort. If someone's under any sort of net-related investigation, you can lock them online so their real-world body can't make a run for it. I wasn't happy that he'd done it to me—but at the same time, it was kind of thrilling, being under his control. If I concentrated, I could dimly feel our physical bodies pressed close, his strong arms around me. I was his. It made me shiver.

"Now," he said. "Your friend."

"She's probably working," I said. Io did graphical work for an e-card company, mostly rendering pretty flowers. She didn't like it much, but it paid her bills. In theory.

"What company? I'll tin-can her employers and tell them she has to phase out early. They'll listen to me. You send her a private poke."

I tin-canned Io, hoping she'd forgive me for this. Her icon popped up in my Backpack. "Lalit? I'm working; what's up?"

"Hey, Io. Uh, you need to stop work and phase to my Cubbyhole. This is really important and it has to do with your peryton."

"Oh! But I'll get in trouble…"

"You won't. We've fixed it."

"Who's fixed it?"

"Just come, okay?"

She must have picked up the serious note in my voice, because her avatar popped up in seconds, looking exasperated. "Okay. I'm here. So—" She caught sight of Ansible. "Oh. Hi." It took a second, but then her eyes bulged and her mouth fell open as she recognized him. His body, that is.

He just looked at her.

I sighed. "Io, this is Fletcher Ansible. Mr. Ansible, this is Io Hattori. She made the peryton."

"Who gave you the physical body model that you used as a basis for your creature mod?" Ansible asked her, back in stern lawyer mode.

Io could tell she was in trouble. "My contacts at GnollBros. They're—"

"I know who they are. Did you have any notion that you have been given an illegally obtained model?"

"They … they said it was legit."

"And you believed them? You didn't do any of your own checking?"

Io looked at the floor. "I … they've been good to me," she mumbled. I felt awful for her.

"Ms. Hattori, are you really telling me that you mod without questioning where your materials are coming from? That sort of thing can get you in tremendous trouble. For all we know, my body isn't the only illegal patch in your creature. How on earth can you justify this?"

Io's eyes snapped up and she glared at Ansible. "Okay. I don't care who you are. But do not talk to me like I'm a naughty schoolgirl. I have spent *years* modding; it is my absolute passion. Have you ever been passionate about anything in your white-collar life, *Mister* Ansible?"

"I have," he said stiffly.

"Then you know what it feels like, to throw your whole being into something, someone, whatever. Fine, I admit it. I didn't think too hard about where all the material came from. Hell, I know GnollBros are scumbags. But they gave me what I needed, and what I needed was to make this thing that's been in my head for so long, and make it perfect. So perfect that anyone who looks at it knows it was a labor of love. So no matter what happens to me next, I get to live inside my monster."

A damn good speech, though I couldn't tell if Ansible was at all moved.

"You've been foolish," he told Io quietly. "But I suppose I understand where you're coming from. Still."

Her bravado vanished. She looked terrified. "Oh, God. You're going to make me delete the model, aren't you."

"Well, I—"

"I'm going to have to start from scratch," She looked at her hands. Her voice wavered on the edge of a sob. "All I did with it. My w-work."

I hugged her. "Io, calm down. Let Mr. Ansible talk. He's not here to ruin your life." I gave Ansible a hard look, daring him to say otherwise.

"I try to avoid ruining lives," he said. "But I am a lawyer. That said, I'm afraid I haven't been entirely honest with Lalit here. I have an ulterior motive."

I glared. "Seriously, sir? You dragged me from my home, made Io leave her work, did a really good job of *scaring* us both, and you've been lying?"

"I haven't been *lying*, I've—" He bit back his words and took a deep breath. To my amazement, he looked slightly abashed. "Ms. Hattori. I'd like to see your peryton up close, and interact with it."

Io stared at him, suddenly hopeful. "You would? Wait … so you can verify that it's illegal?"

"More than that. Lalit has probably figured this out by now, but I am very deeply involved in DU. My friends and I play it religiously. When I saw your peryton, I was angry at the illegal use of my body model, but I was also impressed by the quality of the mod. And, I confess, it's a wee bit flattering to see myself made into a fine-looking monster."

"Damn right it's fine-looking," Io said defiantly. Then she flushed. "Wait. You didn't see Lalit's log?"

"I did," Ansible said. "The sexual nature of the encounter intrigued me as well. It was very realistic for something that's forbidden in the game."

"It won't be forbidden forever," Io blazed. "Not if the forces of free speech have their say!"

"Ahhh." Ansible smiled faintly. "You're with that movement I keep hearing about, aren't you. Anatomical accuracy, is that it?"

"Sir, don't you believe that a game as immersive as DU should be without boundaries?"

"I do. Although I can't condone some of your people's tactics."

"Oh, right, we're a bunch of cyber-terrorists just because we value our true vision. If the Game Gods weren't scared of pissing off a tiny group of obsolete prudes—"

I cut in before she could really get going. "Io. We agree with you. It's okay. And, sir, you could have told me what you were really after."

"I hadn't decided how to deal with the use of my body model. And I still haven't. But before I make a decision, I want to encounter your peryton as if it were a monster in the game. Perhaps, when all's said and done, we can work out some arrangement."

"You mean, you might actually not want to sue me or arrest me?" Io asked.

"The people who need suing or arresting are the good folk at GnollBros. Lalit has won my trust, and he vouches for you. I'll want to look over your personal information, but first ... I want to meet the monster you made from me."

Ansible smiled. And it was a smile of deep anticipation. It made him look like a different person.

Io looked at him for a moment. Then she, too, smiled. "I'd be honored, sir."

Ansible phased us into the game.

We appeared on a grassy hillside under a bluish crescent moon. Pretty typical DU environment. At the summit of the hill stood a great meadhall, Viking-style, with huge blazing torches all around. I was in my rogue outfit, while Io wore the billowy robes of an air mage. And Ansible—damn. His "armor" consisted of spiky shoulder-plates, golden gauntlets, a thick belt, and a red silk thong. Nothing else. I was awed. Armor that skimpy could only mean one thing: a very, very high-level character.

As if he'd guessed my thoughts, he said, "Level 83 paladin. I'm guessing you two still have a ways to go."

"Yeah," Io squeaked. "Wow, your avatar is something else."

He dipped his head in acknowledgment, then led us up a stone path to the meadhall. We both stared at his ass. I leaned in close to Io and murmured, "I'm sharing a Pod with him right now."

"You son of a bitch," she replied, grinning.

The meadhall door was carved oak with no knob, handle, or knocker—just a hideous gargoyle face in the center. The face demanded something in a made-up language I couldn't identify. Ansible responded in the same tongue. They had a brief dialogue, and then the door swung inwards. Light and heat spilled over us, and we went in.

Thick tree-trunk pillars formed two rows down the length of the hall. Curtains of golden moss hung from the sharply peaked ceiling. Long tables lined the walls, but most of the marbled floor was empty. A few other avatars moved about the place. Judging from their armor, weapons, and glamours, they were all at least level 70. One or two people waved at Ansible. I felt like any second, someone was going to kick me and Io out for not having enough XP.

"Xing," Ansible told his dragon, "activate true-mod."

His form rippled and phased. The change was subtle, for the most part. His hide took on a better texture and his muscles became more realistically defined. He now bore a faint gleam, as though his fur was oiled. The biggest difference was the large bulge that appeared between his legs, sheath and balls defined by the tight thong. Before, it had been smooth, sexless, like any other avatar. Now he looked *real*, package and all.

Io gaped. "How did you do that? It's not allowed!"

"Ah." Ansible smiled. "Smoke and mirrors, m'lady. At this moment, we aren't actually in DU. We were up until we entered the hall. But this is a privately-owned pocket space, connected to the game but not officially part of its code. The Game Gods allow it, because we're high-level players who have lined their coffers. A lot of us are investors as well. This is our play area."

I could see Io grasp the implications. "Does that mean that I can phase my peryton in here and it won't violate the game's TOS?"

"Indeed. I hope you don't mind, but I put out an open invitation. A lot of my peers are going to want to see this."

Sure enough, more high-level players were trickling in the door. Some wore stylized versions of their real-world selves, as we did, while others took far more fantastical forms: dragonoids, direwolves, orcs, gryphons, and even some unique custom mods. One player had the guise of a flaming horse skeleton, while another was some type of insect, iridescent and cloaked in its own shimmering wings. Beautiful, all of them, sporting the best avatars money and XP could buy. I felt so plain.

"What exactly do you want, sir?" Io asked Ansible.

"I want to fight your peryton. I assume it's capable."

She gulped. "Well, yeah. But, sir, it's intended as a high-level encounter. It doesn't fuck around. Pardon my unladyness."

Ansible smiled in amusement. "Do I look like a beginner, Ms. Hattori? If it defeats me, I won't lose a thing because this isn't a real gamespace. If I defeat it, we'll know it can be defeated. Either way, I'm going to enjoy this."

He made his shoulder plates and gauntlets vanish, leaving only the belt and thong. I guessed they'd have given him augments he didn't want in this case. The other players formed a ring at the room's edges. Io looked terrified but determined. She said, "If I didn't know better, sir, I'd wonder if this was really about legality."

"Oh, it is. But it's also about having the opportunity to battle myself. In a way." Ansible stretched, flexing his gleaming torso. "I truly hope your peryton is as realistic as you claim."

Io's hackles rose. "Just you wait, friend-o," she said, grabbing my arm and yanking me back to join the audience. She opened her Backpack and her fingers flashed, summoning the creature. Bringing it into being.

"Don't hold back," Ansible said. "Put it in aggressive mode."

"He's gonna be gunning for you and you only," Io said sweetly. "Here he comes!"

And the peryton was there.

The beast's appearance drew forth several gasps from the onlookers. He stood there in all his frightening glory, heavy muscles twitching, veins popping out. Then he turned slowly and pawed the floor with his cruel talons, spreading his wings. Black lips drew back to reveal his massive fangs. An even blacker tongue ran across them, dripping saliva. His eyes were demented. Having only seen him in peaceable mode, I was scared. But it didn't diminish his beauty, not to me.

"Hello, monster," Ansible said quietly.

The peryton whirled to face him, balls swinging from side to side.

They took in each other. It was bizarre, seeing those two forms mirrored—one monstrous, the other almost angelic, but both cut from the same clay. Ansible crouched, readying himself. The peryton blew hot breath from his nostrils. His eyes opened wider, pupils shrinking to points.

Talons screeched on stone as the peryton flung himself at Ansible. The deer met him, their bodies crashing together. Muscles strained as they grappled. I saw Ansible's spine bend back as the peryton used his weight to try and overpower him. Ansible grimaced, holding his face back from those snapping fangs. His hooves slid backwards several inches. Then he found purchase and kicked, a hoof connecting with the peryton's knee. The beast snarled and stumbled, and Ansible was on him. Both hit the floor with a great thud.

In the chaos of scrabbling limbs, Ansible got the peryton in a headlock, squeezing down on his thick neck. The peryton flailed, kicking about with his heavy lower limbs, trying to lever himself upwards with his wings. We all had a good view of his body, and I was confused and thrilled to see that his ebony cock was out, slapping against his belly.

"Why is my monster aroused?" Io demanded.

"Master has activated true-mod," said Xing's polite voice beside us. The little dragon hung coiled in the air. "True-mod includes the option to trigger a virtual pheromone that affects specified targets. Useful for private fantasy orgies."

"Are you telling me that Ansible's making the peryton hot for him?" I asked.

"Indeed, venerable sir!"

"This meadhall must get pretty wild on the weekends," Io said.

We watched the fight, riveted by how those two powerful forms came together in combat. The peryton managed to lever himself up enough to break the headlock. He spun and bore down on Ansible, pinning him to the floor. Ansible thrashed and snarled. The peryton's muzzle lowered, jaws clamping around Ansible's throat. Several watchers groaned, anticipating the end, but the peryton didn't bite hard. His haunches rolled downwards, pushing firmly against Ansible's pelvis. Ansible moaned and arched his back. Another heavy thrust from the beast, sweat-slick muscles slapping together. I caught a glimpse of Ansible's thong. It was tented, his virtual cock straining within the fabric, just as aroused as the peryton. He wiggled to be free, but kept moaning.

"Why isn't the peryton killing him?" I asked Io.

She shook her head in annoyed wonderment. "His true-mod thing. The peryton's acting like it would with a comely female peryton. Trying to subdue and mate with her. Him."

Which was, I could tell, exactly what Ansible wanted.

He was grinning as he tried to free himself from the clutches of the amorous monster. Sharp claws dug into his wrists, keeping his arms pinned. The peryton frotted against him, smearing pre across his crotch and thighs. Drool from the beast's lips ran down Ansible's chest. He strained harder. The peryton shifted, and Ansible managed to ram a knee against his opponent's inner thigh, producing a grunt. A second knee, this one connecting with those mighty balls. The peryton tensed up in pain and let go of Ansible's neck to snarl in protest. Ansible head-butted the beast in the jaw, rolled his entire body, and gained his freedom.

Both fighters faced each other again. The peryton's cock drooped from its own weight, hard as iron. Ansible flicked his hand and his thong vanished. His rigid shaft sprang into view, smaller than that of his adversary but pretty damn impressive. His balls dropped, hanging low in their cream-colored pouch. The sight of the exposed deer made the peryton even randier. He flung himself at Ansible again, and again their bodies collided. This time, Ansible ducked, shouting the words of a spell. Golden light blossomed from his hands as he drove them into the peryton's abdomen. Both of them hit the marbled stone, rolling back and forth. I saw a spray of blood as the peryton's claws raked Ansible's chest. His gold-lit fists moved like a whirlwind, pummeling the monster. Their cocks smacked together, drawing groans from both.

The whole time, I could feel Ansible's real-world body pressed to mine, his cock throbbing between us, my own member nestled next to his. I shivered at the distant sensation. Ansible's pleasure was fueling mine. My body tingled in desire.

Dripping with sweat, huffing and groaning, twin fought twin. Ansible used the monster's lust against him, sneaking in tugs to his nipples, hard smacks to his rump and cock. He was bleeding from several shallow slashes, and his expression mirrored the peryton's: fury, lust, determination to win, to dominate.

"Io," I muttered, "what happens if the peryton loses, but isn't killed?

Did you program that outcome?"

"I guess, based on his behavior fractals, he would go into submissive mode. He does have one. I figured male perytons might have dominance battles."

Bit by bit, minute by minute Ansible wore the peryton down. Io had made him realistic, and with realism came finite endurance. Muddled by lust, by an enemy that just wouldn't give, the monster flagged. Ansible pinned him and he struggled and snarled, but his movements were slower, more halfhearted. He panted heavily, tried to rise and failed. Ansible ground his hips against the peryton's crotch, drawing forth a deep, rumbling moan. Then he slid upwards, pressing his knees down on the peryton's forelimbs, his ass pushing at that wide, heaving chest. He wrapped both hands around the peryton's muzzle, forcing the jaw shut and the head back. Antlers scraped stone as the monster made one last effort to pull away. His legs kicked a few times, but he was done. He shuddered, flexed gently, and went limp. The soft rumble that emanated from his nose wasn't angry. It was a sound of surrender.

Ansible looked up at Io and said, "He's mine."

Io scowled. "Yeah."

The hall erupted in cheers. I let out a whoop of my own, though it turned into a choked gasp as I felt Ansible's real-world body grind against mine. He looked down at his defeated foe and I knew what was coming next.

Ansible roughly rolled the peryton over. The monster rumbled again, face slack, as Ansible ran a hand down his spine and gave him a light smack on the rump. He took one of the peryton's wrists and pinned it on his back like a cop making an arrest. The peryton had no tail to cover his meaty backside. Ansible's eyes blazed with lust as he got into position, crouching like a feral animal over the peryton. I saw his cock descend and force its way between the muscular cheeks, finding the hidden pucker. The peryton's body jerked and he groaned weakly, blowing breath out his nostrils. He raised his ass slightly as Ansible took him. The deer let out a loud moan of need and buried his shaft deep.

"I didn't program the peryton to act like this," Io said, startled. "Must be a natural evolution of his A.I. I should look at the fractals more closely."

I barely heard her words, because Ansible had begun to thrust, rocking his hips and slamming his cock into the peryton's rear, again and again. Their balls slapped together, drawing more groans from both. Ansible ground his hips hard against the peryton's buttocks, leaning over the beast, head drooping to nip his neck. My knees wobbled. Ansible's real-world self was still grinding against mine. When you're online, your body is basically dormant, but it can unconsciously mimic the actions of your avatar. I could feel his naked form rubbing me, his cock frotting with my cock. I trembled, paralyzed with pleasure. A soft moan escaped my lips, thankfully swallowed by the cheers from around me as Ansible's rich friends egged him on. Io looked pouty, but I could tell she was trying to hide her fascination.

Ansible fucked the peryton like a goddamn porn star, letting out moans and cries of bliss as he pounded his twin's hole. The peryton responded with deep rumbles of need that almost made the floor vibrate. His wings flapped slowly, surrounding Ansible in a cradle of feathers. The two cervines almost looked like one conjoined creature. Each powerful flexing thrust of Ansible's hips reverberated in my own body, and I could feel myself thrusting back. I didn't dare move for fear of revealing how crippled I was by bliss. My eyes stayed locked on the erotic scene before me. At one point, Ansible's eyes met mine, and I knew that he knew. And he approved. I shuddered. He was dominating me too, making me a part of this sexual claim, just because he could. I belonged to him in those moments. I can't describe how lustful that made me. I didn't ever want it to end.

Gradually, Ansible built to climax, thrusting harder and deeper with each second. The peryton's eyes rolled. From beneath his sweat-slick body came the soft splat of pre dripping on stone. Ansible grabbed the peryton's antlers and jerked his head back, and the beast roared. Ansible roared with him, body tensing for a second, all muscles rippling as he came. We could hear the squelch of cum, trapped between the thrusting cock and the peryton's anal walls. Soon enough, it was dripping down both their legs. Ansible's real-world body came at the same time. I felt the tense, the hard grind against me, the sudden warmth. My avatar fell to its knees, hunched over, gasping. My real-world self arched against Ansible and fired off, adding a second cloud of jizz to the SmartGel. I almost passed out from bliss.

"Lalit?" Io asked. "What's wrong?"

All I could do was wave a hand vaguely in her direction. My eyes stayed on the two mating forms before me. Ansible went partially limp, laying across the peryton as he sank into an afterglow. I saw a spreading pool of peryton cum underneath them. The peryton closed his eyes and licked his lips, huffing through his nose. For the second time, I thought he would have smiled if his fierce face had allowed it.

After a moment, Ansible hoisted himself off his opponent, cock pulling free with a another squelch. He patted the peryton's back, almost fondly, then stood and stretched, virtual joints popping. Xing flowed through the air to him and coiled back around his wrist. Ansible's form flickered, and all signs of lust and sex fled. He was back in his armor and thong, not a hair out of place. He came over to us and helped me stand, giving me a deadpan look that left plenty unsaid.

"Uh. You like?" Io asked.

"Very impressive," he nodded. "You've worked realism into most every line of code. Even in places you didn't expect." A small smirk traced his lips. "I'd like to make a deal."

"So, I don't have to delete the body model?"

"You can keep your peryton exactly how it is. I'll even offer you some patches to improve him. However, I want free access to him. I want a personal copy that I can call up whenever I wish, for whatever purpose I may wish."

Io laughed. "I guess you've earned that. I didn't see any of this coming, but he does make a good bottom, doesn't he. If you can beat him."

Ansible turned and looked at the peryton, who now lay on his back, relaxed and lazy. "Actually, I may commission you to build more behavior mods into my copy of the peryton, so fighting him won't be the same experience over and over. I like a challenge. I like being surprised."

Io's grin blazed. "I can try to make it so you can't beat him?"

"You can try with all your might. Who knows, I might be on the receiving end of his lust sometimes. It'll just encourage me to better my skills." Ansible grew serious. "Also, you need to credit me in the copyright code, and I still want to look at your personal info to be absolutely sure you didn't knowingly steal from me."

"Right, right." Io turned to me, flushed with excitement. "Lalit, he could totally help the cause! Mr. Ansible, if we had someone like you onboard with anatomical accuracy— "

He held up a hand. "I'd be glad to discuss it with you some other time. Now I have work to do. This has been fun, but I have a legal case to build against GnollBros. I'm sure I'm not the only person they've wronged; it'll bear a good deal of investigating. However…if you'd like to stay here in our hall, m'lady, feel free. Don't be afraid to chat. I'm sure all my friends have many questions and compliments regarding your peryton."

Io looked around, shy and happy, at the high-level adventurers. "I'd be delighted. How about it, Lalit?"

Ansible cleared his throat. "I'm afraid that Lalit will be logged out along with me, since he's directly connected to my personal network."

"That's okay!" I blurted quickly. "I should, y'know, get home and such."

"Aww, okay." Io gave my arm a squeeze, then headed over to examine her reclining peryton. I looked at Ansible, who nodded and put a hand on my shoulder. Xing coiled his body around us both, quick as flowing water. We phased out together.

I was back in my real body, pressed close to him in that deep embrace. The product of our lust had dissipated in the gel, leaving only the memory. Ansible held me as the gel drained from the Pod. And for a minute or two, he kept holding me. My hands rested on his chest, right over the languid beat of his heart. The heat of his sex bathed mine; I could feel his emptied balls twitching gently. We regarded each other's faces in silence, serious, yet filled with an inner delight.

It wasn't romance, but it was something. The unspoken knowledge of what we'd shared in those moments. Us and the peryton. He and I had been connected to the virtual world in a way that wasn't quite supposed to be possible. It was like a glimpse of potentiality. Of something evolving in the code.

Maybe it wasn't just Io and her personal hobby. Maybe we were all making monsters.

Ansible gave me a kiss, as if to seal what we had hidden between us. Then we left the Pod and dressed. We had a snack and a drink, and he drove me home. We didn't talk much. No need. We knew, without a doubt, that we'd see each other again.

If nothing else, we both wanted more time with that peryton.

***

The rest is history, kind of. When the great DungeonUltra hack occurred, it made headlines everywhere. No one had quite realized what GnollBros was up to. Hell, it turned out that "GnollBros" was just a smokescreen, a dummy company for some very powerful online lurkers looking to raise hell. They'd specifically courted people like Io, modders who supported the cause of anatomical accuracy. Those devious bastards had a million spiderweb strands reaching to countless places; their hacks were invisible, the work of socially dysfunctional masterminds crouching in dark spaces, cocoons of high-end tech and labyrinthine networks. Hollywood's making a movie about it, that's how ridiculous it all was.

I was playing DU when it happened. It began as a ripple of news and gossip: something major had changed. Something the Game Gods definitely had not authorized. All the Sheriffs were suddenly poker-faced and tense, waiting to learn what had gone wrong. But us normal players, well … we went in search of trouble. It's in our gamer blood. What we found was that the entire MMOW had been flooded with new monster mods. And these mods had cocks, balls, breasts, vaginas, anuses, and all the things monsters aren't allowed to have. Not only that, but some very unusual patches were turning up in treasure chests and NPC shops. Collect one, and your own smooth-bodied avatar could have naughty parts as well—crude, but functional. Suddenly, sex was an option.

Torn between outrage and delight, I searched for Fletcher Ansible. I found him on a clifftop, watching as a troupe of well-endowed bugbears engaged a party of mid-level adventurers in something that was part battle, part orgy. The poor players didn't stand a chance; their newly-acquired orifices were getting a mighty workout.

"Fletcher," I said. "What in all the fucks is going on?"

He looked at me and grinned the grin that made him look more than a little peryton-ish. "Hello, Lalit. I suspect we don't have much time before the gamemakers win back control and shut down the network. My legal allies and I are going to roast GnollBros alive for this, but in the meantime, we're just feckless players and can't be held responsible for our actions. Would you like to go on a quest with me?"

"I thought you'd never ask, sir!"

We got forty-five minutes before every single player was booted from the MMOW. You can do a lot in that time. Fletcher and I chose a likely-looking cave, and wouldn't you know it, we found a trio of very familiar perytons guarding the riches therein. I got captured and well-ravaged before Fletcher came charging in to combat the perytons with blasts of holy fire. Who knows what delightful hijinks might have ensued if we'd had more time. Ah, well.

Io was livid. She missed the whole thing. But she saw plenty of footage on the newsfeeds, and was directly involved in the subsequent revolution. The people hiding behind GnollBros intended to sabotage the game and make a bundle in the process, using the anatomical accuracy movement as a stooge, but their stunt turned out to be what pushed the debate all the way over. Many players condemned the hack, whined, promised to ragequit forever, but a lot more asked why exactly DU, the pinnacle of realistic gaming, had no sex in it. People who'd been on the fence found that they preferred the dangly bits as an option. And the gamemakers had to listen.

The end result was a compromise. An "adult mode." Anatomically correct creature mods were allowed for submission, but only if they included an alternate, sex-free patch. That way, players could choose to play with or without sexual content. Io wasn't entirely happy—she told me that erasing the peryton's sheath and balls felt like an "act of Satan"—but she still got her monster into the game, junk intact, and he already had the stamp of approval from a number of high-level players. Funnily enough, a good chunk of the original in-game bestiary started turning up with private parts too. Guess the good folk at DU were less prudish than they themselves had thought.

I do a lot more gaming now, though I still make sure my real life isn't neglected. I've reached level 55. One day, I hope to be one of those gorgeous, frightening, high-level gods who get to romp and play in their own private spaces. I could be invited back to that meadhall if I asked, but I'd rather earn it the honest way.

Besides, there's plenty of other benefits to be had when you're friends with someone who, by now, is a level 96 paladin, a few steps away from being one of the most powerful individuals in the entire MMOW. Fletcher spends his days in gleeful courtroom combat, right in the thick of the ongoing, endless attempts to hunt down and prosecute the GnollBros ghouls in their hidden basements. But he leaves himself time to go online and quest, and I'm often by his side. Io comes too, when she feels raunchy. She's weirded out by the thought of fucking her own peryton, but there's plenty of other monster flesh out there. And, thanks to Fletcher, both Io and I now have "true-mods" of our own.

I have no idea if Fletcher is secretly one of the very people he's trying to catch. And I'm far too polite to ask.

What's best, though, is what Fletcher and I have together. When he invites me over and we get into that Pod of his, body to body, kissing not to share DNA, but just because it feels good. Our adventures are so much sweeter when we can feel each other's heat and desire radiating in from the real world. And you can bet we seek out monsters.

Somewhere, in some dark dungeon or feral wood, the peryton is always waiting. Fangs bared, wings spread, in all his savage glory. To take us, or be taken by us. To continue the private game we play. Sometimes I lose track of which one is my friend Fletcher and which one is the monster.

In the heat of the moment, it doesn't really matter.

THE DESERT RUN

Tym Greene

Odard made a face, spitting more sand from his mouth. No matter how much he tried to get rid of it, he could still feel the grating grind between his flat teeth. One grain of sand, one little speck of grit. That was all it took to upset the delicate balance of turbines and coils and gears, to jam between teeth or stick in some joint. The spluttering cough as his jetpack's turbine had given up the ghost still fluttered in his ears.

The camel grunted, trying—and failing—to shift the weight of his jetpack into a more comfortable position. The thing was heavy enough in flight, let alone dead on the ground. The straps crisscrossing his body made for comfortable flying but awkward carrying. *The Queen only knows why I carry the thrice-damned thing,* he thought as his footing faltered among the dunes. Behind him, left where they'd fallen, lay punctured water-skins and sand-spoiled rations; his crash had not been as easy on his provisions as it had been on him.

In his descent, however, he had seen some low outcroppings, dark against the dun sand. He lifted a hand to shade his eyes and block the biting wind. *If I can get to them, if they offer any sort of shelter from the wind, and if I still have the right tools, maybe I can fix my jetpack.* And *if* he could do that, he might be able to make it home. *That's a lot of ifs.* But he knew he couldn't lose hope, not just yet.

Something glinted, maybe half a furlong ahead of him. He shifted his course slightly and kept on trudging. He wasn't even supposed to be out in the wilds of the South Desert. *And to think, I could have been sailing over tundra right now.* He thought of the soft heather-filled mattress and fresh orc-ham stew that would have awaited him at his first waypoint, in little Edessa. *But no, I had to play the hero. Just my luck.*

The camel had been scheduled for a simple mail run up from

Queenton all the way to the northern hub station in Altbury, the same route he'd had for the past month now. Then Wilmott hadn't returned from his own run—down to Merce—the southern hub city. Indeed, the bull was over a day late when the decision was made to go in search of him. For one of the Queen's fliers, that much of a delay was almost unheard-of.

That was when Squadron Commander Janice Ros—a pretty-enough kangaroo with perfectly-coiffed hair and a bulldog's demeanor—had called on Odard Flynn. "The north run can wait," she had told him. "Take water and supplies and go find Wilmott. Damn bull probably stuck his pack with his horns," she added in a stage whisper.

Flynn had remained at silent attention, glad not for the first time that camels had neither horns to trim nor long tail to bob nor ears that—without docking—could get sucked into a jetpack's turbine.

"And bring a toolkit: see if you can't *both* make it back here alive. We can't afford to lose more fliers, not with the Queen's jubilee coming up."

He may not have been given much choice in the matter, but he'd still felt a measure of pride for having been selected—at the time. Now, however, he just felt tired and foolish. *Still,* he thought, blinking blown sand away, *of all the Queen's fliers, I'm probably the only one who could survive this forsaken hell.* Small comfort indeed.

The glint had turned out to be polished bronze: the winged-cog badge affixed to every flier's orc-leather helmet. It was probably Wilmott's helmet, with the horn holes cut into the leather at the top like that. Flynn hoped it was his helmet—they hadn't lost *two* fliers down here, not that he knew of anyways. He snorted, realizing that, if he didn't return, they *would* have lost two fliers.

Maybe, if they lose enough of us down here, they'll cancel the southern run entirely. Won't that be nice. Not that he'd be able to enjoy it. Far better to survive, rescue the bull, and get both of them back to Queenton.

Bits of canvas harness lay scattered around the helmet—most looking like they'd been ripped off—as well as what seemed to be dried blood, partially soaked into the sand, partially covered-over. There was also, he noted with a snort, an animal scent to the crash site, as though some beast had come and rutted on the sands. Still, it was not entirely unpleasant. Flynn snorted again, clearing his mind so he could further investigate.

There were no bones, no scraps of flesh, and certainly no pack. Thankfully, there was also nothing to indicate that Deon Wilmott had died and been eaten after crashing. A tiny lizard sidled up to the blood-stained sand, clutching an even tinier spear (little more than a sharpened stick) in its foreclaw as it sniffed at the patch, then skittered away. Flynn watched as its mud-painted back disappeared into the dunes. If that was all the native life in this desolate place, then where was Wilmott?

He looked up. There was really only one answer: the rocks. The light breeze that had half-buried the helmet and harness scraps continued to blow, shifting the sand's surface, eradicating any tracks. Still, where else would a crashed and injured flier go?

He judged nothing worth saving from the litter of strapping, but the camel did tuck Wilmott's helmet under the belt of his own harness: if the bull was alive, and they could fix their jetpacks, he would need the helmet. At least it still had the goggles attached.

As he made his way towards the outcropping, he chuckled cynically. Even flying low, he would probably have missed the helmet entirely, and Wilmott would be just another traveler swallowed up in the wastes. "Figures. It just figures." Such was the sole comfort of being seldom wrong.

The sun was low by the time he reached the long shadows of the rocks. He had to squint, but he thought he saw an opening—a regular, almost symmetrical opening. The desert had its legends and kept its secrets, but he knew of nothing in *this* region. As he drew closer, he could see that it had just been a trick of the light, making a natural cave mouth appear as though it had been hewn from the stone.

He looked around, but didn't see any other openings. There might have been some on the other side of the rocks, but why would Wilmott have dragged himself from his crash all the way here, only to walk around searching for other places to shelter? No, it had to be this cave.

Flynn edged up to it, trying to keep his harness from rattling, thankful for the soft pads of his feet, once again thinking that few of the other fliers could have done so well. He paused just to one side of the entrance, listening. The wind must be whipping against some unseen opening, making the whole cave sound like a giant's flute. It seemed deserted...then he noticed the dark, clumped sand just within the entrance: more blood. *So he* did *come this way.* Flynn breathed a sigh of relief that his hunch had paid off, and crept into the cave.

A few paces in, however, and he had to stop. This far from the cave's entrance, he couldn't see a thing. *Hadn't there been something in the toolkit?* He padded back closer to the entrance, and unclipped the small pouch from his strapping.

Like everything issued to the Queen's Fliers, the toolkit was neat, orderly, and compact. A flier's back had no room for excess; they kept themselves fit and trim, the messages they carried were written on the thinnest paper, and as a result still the fastest way to get word from one side of the Empire to another, if not the cheapest. A small loop within the toolkit held a brass tube with a cut quartz crystal at one end.

The pen-shaped light was intended more for close-in work—illuminating the innards of a pack, for example—but was all he had, short of making some sort of torch. It would do, if the chemicals inside were fresh enough. Brandishing it before him, he worked his way through the cave.

Not forty paces from where he'd first stopped, the cave seemed to end. He drew closer, and saw that it was a brick wall composed of circular, filled-in arches. Each brick was a long, weathered, hand-sized rectangle, with the mortar half-eroded in spots. Sure enough, in the far corner, the mortar was weak enough for the bricks to have been pushed through.

He squatted and crab-walked through the rough opening and into a stairwell. *So it* is *a ruin,* he thought, looking around. He had come out on a landing, the crumbling brick wall he'd gone through still mostly plastered on this side. The stairs curved away from him, going both up and down. He pointed the pen light upwards, but saw only the ragged boulders of an old cave-in. *Not that way.*

As he descended, the plaster on the walls seemed to get thicker, cleaner, as though whoever had built this—whatever it was—hadn't put as much effort into maintaining the upper portion. Eventually he started seeing little niches built into the wall at regular intervals too, each one spouting a frozen waterfall of something dark and shiny. His light glinted off a few tiny hexagons, trapped within the substance: *beeswax?*

He was suddenly aware of a vast open space, somewhere further along the staircase below, and realized that he must have stumbled on something far bigger than an abandoned hermitage. He knew that sands shifted, rose and fell like slow dry tides. Could there have been some kind of city here? Were there dwellings, temples, storehouses buried, swallowed up by encroaching desert? They'd had bees, and bricks, and plaster…who had lived here, and how long ago?

At the foot of the stairs yawned an archway, with black nothingness on the other side. He could hear…something. *Was that a moan?* He realized just how obvious he was: his light would show more of him than it could of any space he went into. *Or anyone—any*thing*—I might find waiting.*

The camel swallowed hard. He had no real weapons—apart from a finger-length dagger stuffed into his boot—no means of escape, and no idea what waited for him. If he died here, or if he couldn't fix his pack, then it wouldn't matter if he found Wilmott or not. He tried not to think about it.

Odard Flynn stepped through the archway.

He found himself in a jewelbox. The light from his pen-lamp glinted back at him from nearly every surface, as though the whole space were encrusted with diamonds. *No, not diamonds…glass.* The wall behind him, the colonnade stretching to the left and the right before him, even the walkway's ceiling a scant handsbreadth above his head, were covered with glittering mosaics.

He forgot his mission while he examined them. Clearly the work of master craftsmen, or generations of master craftsmen, the mosaics seemed to have mostly survived their abandonment unscathed. The flat-sided columns carried spiraling leaves and sheaves of wheat. The wall behind him, however, was far more interesting.

As far as he could tell, it was a single story, like a pictorial scroll unfurled and mounted on the wall. He padded along, trying to understand it. The main figure seemed to be a matronly woman, full-figured and with a queenly bearing. An oryx, white from head to tail, with straight black horns and a black triangle across her strong-looking muzzle. *She must have been important.*

The camel's nostrils flared as he stared at the voluptuous mosaic. There was something, some flavor to the air here that made his pulse quicken…it was almost like the scent on the sand, but much stronger. He had never really been attracted to women, but found himself imagining the oryx without her lapis and gold robe, those breasts pert and heaving, her smile at seeing him approach and undress. He was so distracted that he almost missed the moaning voice that echoed up from the vast empty space beyond the columns: "...help..."

It came again, and this time he heeded it, spinning around to the short railing that spanned the colonnade. Somewhere, maybe a story below him, there was firelight. And in the flickering reddish glow, propped against a massive chunk of masonry, was a figure. He might have imagined it, but the figure seemed to have two gleaming horns, cut short.

"Wilmott?" he called, then louder: "Deon Wilmott?"

"Aye..." came the weak reply. That was his voice, sure enough.

"Hold there, I'm coming!" Flynn cast around, the unbidden fantasy forgotten, searching for a way down that didn't involve leaping over the railing and breaking both his legs on the pavement below. He found it in another archway set into the story-wall, with stairs that led down to the main floor.

Nearly falling twice on broken shards of mosaic that littered the steps, he made it to the bottom. A quick glance upwards nearly toppled him: the space—how could it have been anything other than a temple?—soared above him, with arches leapfrogging up into the darkness that neither his penlight nor the fire's glow could reach. Another groan from Wilmott drew him back.

He dashed up to the fire, and dropped to his knees beside the bull. "Damn it, Wilmott, what happened?"

"Odard, is that you? I..." the bull looked chagrined, despite his obvious pain. "I got bored, figured I'd drop down, fly low, get a closer look at things. Sometimes I'd do that...but the wind blew sand in my pack."

Flynn's ears tucked back, and he looked at the fire. "Mine too."

"Yours—?" Wilmott tried to push himself up, forgetting his injury in his agitation. He was reminded soon enough. "Odard...look at my leg," he said through gritted teeth.

Odard tried to make sense of the lumpy, shadowed mass. Basic medical training was part of every flier's mental toolkit, just as were survival skills, and maintenance. There was a lot of unsettled land between the various hub cities. Perhaps that would change in a few generations, now that the wars were over, but perhaps it might not. But the camel was no healer. "Does it hurt?"

"What," came the reply, halfway between grimace and ironic grin, "do you think?" Deon tried to shift his leg into a better position, but could not.

Flynn bent forward, holding up his penlight. He hadn't been able to see much, in the shadow from the bull's other leg, and the way the fireglow danced didn't help either. The cold white light coming from the small quartz crystal, however, showed him exactly what was wrong with Wilmott's leg.

Dried blood had stained his regulation trousers, making the light cotton fabric stiff around an odd bulge, halfway down his shin. The lower part of the bull's shin and hoof were angled in one direction, and the rest of the limb in another. "Wilmott, I'm going to have to cut your leg off."

"My wh—?!"

"Your pantsleg, your pantsleg." The camel was getting tired—the last time he'd seen the sun, it had been only a few degrees over the horizon. *Who knows what time it is by now.* And with fatigue, came mistakes. If things were as he suspected, he would have to hurry. He couldn't afford any errors. Neither could Wilmott, for that matter.

He slipped the small dagger from his boot holster, then withdrew the orc-leather sheath as well. "Here, bite down on this, just in case. I don't want you losing your tongue." The bull did as he was told, and Flynn had to look away to keep from giggling. Despite the determined expression in his eyes, at that moment Wilmott looked every inch a hayseed farmer with a bit in his mouth.

Between Flynn's fingers, the blade twirled, light like everything else fliers carried. He slipped the tip between two cotton threads, just above Wilmott's knee. The knife was sharp, and severed the weft strands one by one, allowing the camel to make his way around the leg. He went as far as he could without moving things, then started from the other side. Every snag, every shift, every time he accidentally brushed against that unnatural bulge, made Wilmott whimper. Drool was starting to drip from the sheath's tip, dampening the dust below them. Flynn could smell the bull's sweat, mixed with something else. Licking his lips, he tried to focus.

A quick slash of the cord that held the hem closed around the bull's ankle, and he was able to slide the pantsleg down. Every inch seemed a torment to the other man, *but what else can I do?* The ragged upper edge was about to clear the bulge. Flynn dug the fingers of his left hand into the hem, reaching up with his right to lift the raw edge away from the bull's leg. It wouldn't do to let it get snagged. With a slow, gliding, easy motion, he pulled the fabric down.

What he saw, when he picked up the penlight and again aimed it at the injury, was exactly what he'd expected. Still, it turned his stomach. Sticking out of the blood-matted nut-brown hide—indeed, shredding it—was a point of bone. In all, it was only about the size of a horse's front tooth, and much whiter. He coughed to keep from retching.

Wilmott moaned low, the damp sheath dropping from his open mouth. He sounded more like a man in the throes of ecstasy than one about to black out from pain. "How...?" he managed.

How in all the hells should I know? The camel was a flier, a messenger, not a medic. He hadn't even thought—*or been told*—to bring any medical supplies. Who would have guessed that he would need to fix the pilot as well as the pack? So he let the flickering firelight mask the uncertainty on his face, and lied. "It looks...fine. Just fine. Besides, you don't need your legs to fly, do you? They weigh the same whether you can use them or not."

His weak laugh did nothing to ease the bull's pain. "Well, fix it then."

I hope this works, he now thought, recalling a medic's trick he had once seen performed on an unlucky porter. "Now, if your bones are ever going to, um..." he fished for the word, "sew, we're going to have to see to this wound. It won't take but a minute." He was trying to inject a light-hearted smile into his voice, just as the medic had.

"Odard...you're lying. I can...see your ears. They wiggle like that... when you bluff at cards."

By the Queen's teeth, he blasphemed, *so that's how they win.* He was not great friends with any of the other fliers, but they all played cards together. There wasn't much else to do, to pass the between-flights boredom atop the Aerie—the fliers' tower in Queenton. One either read, and books were costly as well as heavy, or one played cards, which were neither.

"No, I mean it. Now, hold fast to that rubble," he flashed the penlight at the broken lump of brick and mortar that must have fallen from the ceiling above them. The bricks would make good handholds for Wilmott, even in his current condition. He leaned forward, dusted off the little scabbard, and placed it back in the bull's mouth.

He watched as the bull dug his thick nails into the mortar, then moved back down by the distorted leg. "Deon, I'm going to pull your— Relax! Relax…I'm not going to do it yet, not until you're good and ready. Now," he gingerly wrapped his fingers around the ankle, the bull's hoof and flesh felt equally cold. *That can't be good.* Once he was sure he had a good grip, he continued. "I'm going to count three, and then I'll pull your leg, nice and slow. Good? Make sure you've got a good grip."

The bull nodded, jaw set, nostrils flared, fingers digging further into the masonry.

"One, t—"

The bull's bellow echoed through the vast temple to the oryx goddess, thankfully loud enough to cover the sounds of bone and flesh grating in unnatural ways. Once Wilmott's eyes had focused again, and he had pulled his fingers from the holes they'd dug in the ancient brickwork, he turned to Flynn.

"Where…was…three?" he panted after spitting out the knife's sheath, nearly bitten in two.

The camel, trying hard not to be sick, was heartened to notice the leg was now in its proper position. He also saw that the blood had started flowing again. "I saw a doctor do that, once," he said as he cast about for a…*a what? What did that medic use to…*his eyes caught sight of the discarded pantsleg. It would have to do. He hacked off a few fingers-width of material, and tied it around the leg. He managed not to move it too much. "That should stop the bleeding."

But he was still missing something. He tried to remember what the medic had done. First, there was the trick with the counting and the swift sharp jerk, and then a stick. "A splint. I need a splint." He leapt up, his feet narrowly missing the bull's leg as he strode over to the pile of firewood. Something long and straight was sticking out just enough to catch the light. Pulling it from the pile, he held it up. It looked like a table leg, elegantly turned, and likely as ancient as the arches above them. It was quite dry, but seemed strong. The remainder of the trouser leg he cut into strips, and tied the makeshift splint onto Deon's leg as tightly as he dared.

"How does that feel?" Flynn asked, rocking back onto his heels and looking down at his patient.

It took the bull several panting minutes to answer, and when he did it was to mutter, "Great," with as much sarcasm as he could muster. "You're...a heartless...bastard, Odard."

"I'm not sorry, Deon. You're the one who caused all this, you know. If you hadn't crashed and broken your leg...where's your pack?" He hadn't seen it—nor had he been looking—but that much polished copper and brass should stand out even in the constant gloaming within the ruined temple.

"He took it, hid it somewhere," the other flier replied sulkily. He tried to push himself up into a better sitting position, and winced at the pain. Even with his leg set and splinted, it would take a while for the bone to actually heal.

"He? Who?" Flynn's head swiveled from side to side, his ears twitching as he tried to listen. He had on other occasions envied certain men the attributes granted to other breeds; right now, a pair of wolf's ears would have been useful. His nostrils flared and caught another whiff of that scent, like cinnamon, and old soup, and wet orcleather. It made everything seem a bit fuzzy, like the world was a soft boudoir, just waiting for a lover's appearance.

"How do you think I got here? I...that's him." Sure enough, there was a dull tramping, off in the distance and the dark. It sounded slow, and far away, but there was no way Flynn could tell for sure. "He must have heard me scream...sorry about that."

"What *is* that, Deon?" Nervously, the camel yanked a length of wood from the pile: another table leg, this one with a bit of table still attached. He brandished his makeshift club at the shadows all around him; his knife was too short to be of use in any sort of a fight.

"He's an orc. I think his name's Mazhug, or something."

"Oh, an orc?" Flynn relaxed somewhat. He was no country bumpkin, but he'd seen the vast orc ranches in his flights north. He knew where the soft supple green leather came from, as well as the rich-marbled meat. Sure, there were wild orcs, but they were rare nowadays: the species had mostly been domesticated. They were fat, lazy, and stupid. Most of them had just enough brains to keep from drowning in their own filth. And he'd heard tales of orcs so dumb they would stare up at a rainstorm, with their mouths wide open. "I'm sure we can just..." Then he actually listened to the mental echo of what Wilmott had said. Domesticated orcs didn't have names.

Off in the distance a bellow rang out, echoing back from arches and columns. The sturdy table leg he clasped in both hands suddenly seemed more like a toothpick than a warrior's club. He looked down at Wilmott: "We need to leave. Maybe my pack will be able to carry us both…hells." He remembered why he had headed for the cave mouth in the first place: his jetpack was no more fixed than it was when he'd sought shelter from the sand-laden wind. "Look, maybe we can hide…"

Deon clearly could hear the uncertainty in the camel's voice. "You might. I'm going nowhere, not for a while." Just as clearly, the bull was set on being the hero himself. That was fine by Flynn: *better to lose one flier than two, right?*

That thought lasted almost a full second, before it was quashed by two unpleasant facts. First, he would hate himself if he turned out to be the sort of person who would leave a fallen comrade in the clutches of a bloodthirsty brute. And then there was the issue of his jetpack. He could run away, sure, but to where? He wouldn't be flying unless he were able to fix his pack, and he couldn't do that if he was always looking over his shoulder, waiting for a giant hand like a green paving stone to clamp down upon it. No, he would stay, he would fight, and he would probably die.

"I'm staying right here."

"Then you are a fool. He'll—" Flynn never found out what Wilmott thought the orc would do, because there was another roar. This one was definitely closer. So too were the thundering, lumbering footsteps. Running footsteps, punctuated occasionally by a slapping thud, as though the beast were uncertain if it should run on two legs or all fours.

Taking up a stance with the fire and the bull both behind him, Flynn stepped forward and braced himself. He bellowed his own wordless challenge at the on-coming orc. *I sound like a strangled goose,* he thought with some part of his mind that was still rational, despite the burly creature lumbering closer with each second.

So intense was his focus on the impending clash, that he nearly fell forward when the orc stopped short, perhaps an arm's length beyond the club's wavering tip. It rose from all fours to stand, nearly a head shorter than Flynn's own lanky frame. But in terms of sheer physical presence…

The orc's bare arms flexed. His whole body was furless, with thick muscles, and looking for all the world like someone had compressed a burly draft horse into a too-small green skin. Sweat gleamed on his body, and traced rivers of firelight through the dust that coated his flesh. His only clothes were a loincloth and a few bands of rough brown leather. Flynn tried not to think about where that leather had come from. *Certainly not from a domesticated orc, the way* proper *leather does.*

The orc raised both fists and roared at Flynn, sending streamers of spittle flying between them, and leaving a few strands glistening from his battered tusks. Flynn stood his ground, even when the orc leapt up and slammed down. The camel's tongue darted out—as though of its own volition—and licked up some of the orc spit that was clinging to his own upper lip.

They are *animals,* he thought with a growing confidence. A brutish show of dominance, that's all this was. He allowed a cocky leer to tweak his muzzle. Taking advantage of a confused lull in the orc's display, he stood tall, threw his head back, and *hawwwnk*ed at the ceiling. He was loud enough—or at the proper pitch—to cause several bits of brick to rain down. "Ha! Beat that, beastie."

Flynn only realized he had spoken aloud when the orc replied: "Mazhug no beast, beast." His use of the Queen's Tongue was halting, rough, bastardized; who knew where the orc had learned it.

"You *are* a beast, Majook," he deliberately mispronounced the name, "or else you would not have treated my friend so badly."

The orc followed his gesture and, now looking at the helpless Deon, licked his lips. "He mine. Mazhug find, Mazhug take."

"How *dare* you!" the camel brayed, lunging forward with the table leg as though it were a fencing épée. Swordplay was, after all, a gentleman's art, and a gentleman would not stand idly by and allow a sweating, hulking, cinnamon-scented brute to claim ownership of his comrade. He caught the orc by surprise, and managed to prick his chest with the broken end of the leg.

At least, he thought he had…but the tough, thick skin repelled the splintery wood. Flynn knew his own hide wouldn't be nearly so durable. Mazhug looked down, eyes wide, jaw slack, then back at the camel. His brow furrowed. "You want fight? You fight Mazhug?" When he smacked his chest with balled fists, Flynn half expected to hear a bass boom, as though the orc were the big drum in the Queenton band.

There was, however, only the wet smack of flesh on flesh, followed by a rough shuffle: the creature was dancing. Side to side he swayed, arms raised then lowered, body flexed then slack. To Flynn, it was primitive and it was pointless, nothing more than a further display of strength. He gripped the table leg harder and resumed his stance.

"Well, come on then, *Majook,* come meet your fate." He had read that phrase in one of the few books that had been carried to the top of the Aerie and were now handed around the fliers' quarters, borrowed and lent so often no one could remember who had owned them in the first place. It had been a swashbuckling tale from maybe two decades before, where the hero swung from ropes and trounced the villains and stood about making grandiose speeches. With his tall, lank form, Flynn couldn't help but see himself in that role, even if the "damsel" he was defending were a man. Not that he would have preferred it otherwise.

Mazhug seemed to have gone through the requisite steps of his dance, and now stood, hulking down, fists balled at the level of his knees, legs spread wide. He answered the camel's challenge with another bellow, adding "Mazhug take, Mazhug fuck, Mazhug eat!"

That got Odard Flynn's attention. The orc's short loincloth had flipped to one side; indeed, it had practically been pushed aside by the malachite-green tube nosing out from under it. He had noticed the cocks of the domesticated orcs he had seen, and had wondered at their unusual shape. But they may as well have been withered sticks compared to what he could see of this wild beast's. It flopped—half-hard— from thigh to thigh, sometimes behind the loincloth, sometimes peeking out; perhaps it was simply the friction and motion of the dance, or perhaps it was in anticipation of the fight (and the victory) to come.

He tried not to think of that, tried to focus on the thick chest, or maybe the jugular vein visibly pulsing in the corded neck. *A good target, that.* He was still thinking when the orc lunged forward and swatted the table leg aside, sending it skittering over towards where Deon lay.

Flynn's fingers stung where the old wood had rasped through them, and his wrist ached from the blow. He could smell the animal stink of the creature, could taste the sweaty musk, even as he was barreled into. There was a metallic crunch and a disconcerting sproiing sound when the camel landed on his back, as the jetpack still strapped to his body took most of the force of the blow. Thick green fingers shredded the canvas strapping, just as they must have with Wilmott's pack, out on the desert sands. Deon's helmet was tossed aside, to slide and skitter into the darkness along with the shreds of strap.

Drool dropped onto Flynn's face and into his mouth as the orc panted above him. He tried to push the massive creature off, only to have both hands grasped in one meaty palm. They were now nose to nose. He could taste the stench of never-washed teeth now, and behind the flavor of old meat, there was that same musk, the same scent he'd first noticed on the sands above. His head felt strange as he tried to focus on his opponent. Searching the square-jawed muzzleless face for any hint of weakness, any clue, Odard noticed an old scar running across the orc's countenance. He followed that scar to where it ended, just below the left eye.

That eye. He stared at the eye, knowing then how an ant feels when looking up at a boot. Or how a trout feels with a hook in its mouth. Or how...

The emerald iris was flecked with gold, spiraling him around and around the pupil, coming so close to going down that bottomless drain. The skin around the eye creased, as though its owner were smiling; Flynn wanted to smile too.

He was smiling, and his legs were cold. His mouth was full of the taste of cinnamon and meat. He blinked. The eye was gone, replaced with dull marble paving stones. Little bits of rock were cast into sharp relief by the fire on his right. A hand—thick and heavy—had hold of his tail. It felt good; the debris pressing into his chest through the front of his shirt felt good; the cold on his legs and rump felt good. The hot breath under his up-raised tail felt better. He started to drool when a tongue like a slab of fresh meat pressed up between his flanks, pushed against his tailhole, and found easy entry. There was a surprised snort behind him, as though the tongue's owner hadn't expected so eager a welcome.

Flynn moaned, trying to remember where he was. He could still see the eye, twirling in the shadows behind the rubble scattered on the floor around him. Who was that behind him? He had never had a boyfriend, but neither had he been celibate. There were too many exotic men in the different cities he flew to, and too many who would agree to do anything with a man in a flier's uniform. A rhino, perhaps. He had known a rhino once: his tongue was big like that, but he'd preferred to be ridden to doing the riding. And this whoever-he-was, having thoroughly soaked the camel's backside, now proved very intent on doing the riding.

A pressure, a sliding, a heat, and a weight on his back. Tiny stones prickled against his thighs and sheath, but he was so befuddled that even those small pains felt good. There was not the familiar sensation of fur against fur, however, and this confused the camel. *Maybe it is the rhino,* he thought; that had been the only hairless man he had ever bedded.

"You Mazhug toy." The voice was harsh, raspy, and sounded as though it were spoken around a mouthful of marbles. Or tusks: two thick tusks. Sudden realization flooded through him. Flynn tried to buck off a man who was easily more than double his own weight.

"Deon!" he cried, as the orc pushed him down easily with a single hand. The orc continued fucking him, pumping him, using him. And damn him but he liked it, even though he knew what was happening, he liked it. The rough ground beneath him hurt, the position was awkward at best, but the orc knew what he was doing…and he kept doing it for longer than Flynn would have thought possible. It was as though he could feel every ridge and vein of that shaft, and any effort on his part to push, to squeeze it out, only served to spur the orc to higher passion.

After a while, his mind started to slip back again, the sensation of that odd, mushroom-shaped head popping in and out made him think of the eye, the flecks of gold in the emerald iris, and the deep deep pupil. *Toy,* the word kept circling around his head, weaving a pattern with the scent and taste of the orc, the heat and mass of the beast above him. He wanted to fall in to that spiraling pattern, to feel this forever. "Maz…hug…" he whimpered, practically begging.

"Good," came the guttural reply, which sent shivers coursing through the camel's body. He wanted this, needed this. "Mazhug master." It was neither question nor order, but a statement of simple fact; Flynn's addled brain thrilled with those two words. Was there the crackling of some sort of power behind the orc's dominance over him? Stories—fairy tales, really—about the wild orcs, told of their power to enthrall.

"Mazhug…" He was begging now. Flynn's own cock was out, pressed against the floor, dripping a puddle that smeared around as he was rutted, matting the short fur on his belly and thighs. The orc bent forward, hands on Flynn's shoulders, digging into muscle. Hot wet beautiful breath tickled his ear and flowed through his wide-open nostrils.

"Good toy," The gruff praise sent shivers through the camel. This beast, this handsome, sweating, slick-bodied brute was giving him more pleasure than any other man he'd ever bedded. That thought alone was nearly enough to make him climax.

Then the orc pounded deeper even than he had been, plunging in all the way to the root. The head of the orc's cock flared wide, thick as any horse's, stretching him inside as the hands again gripped his shoulders, fingers digging into the joints. Pelvis crashed against pelvis once, twice, then ground together as the orc lowed. Deon had made that sound, late one night in the bunk room of the Aerie when he must have thought everyone else asleep. Flynn had been taking care of his own need—albeit in relative silence—and had heard the bull climax noisily. Not so loud as the orc, though: Deon Wilmott didn't shake dust down from the ceiling.

In the panting silence that followed, the soft sound of orc's cock slipping out of him was practically obscene. The camel lay on the floor, motionless, feeling the muscles within him stutter and jerk closed, trapping orc cum inside. He felt drained, relaxed, and yet on edge too. He couldn't think why, couldn't think at all. Then he heard a shaking voice whisper, "Odard?"

The orc had gone again, leaving his two prizes alone by the fire. Flynn didn't know how long it had been since Mazhug had so thoroughly rutted him; a few minutes? An hour? He pushed himself up on bruised elbows, groaning as his spine popped and cracked. "Deon... I'm ok...." But was he? Half expecting to hear his innards sloshing, he staggered towards the bull.

He couldn't keep his thoughts in order, had to keep shaking his head, trying to jog them into place. Why had he allowed himself to be overpowered so easily—why had Deon for that matter? The bull answered his question as though he could see into the camel's mind: "The eyes. You've got to not look at them. It's hard. I know he'll probably end up eating me...and," the bull swallowed hard, "I'm not averse to that. I keep thinking of being *part* of him, of powering those eyes..." The bull's hand drifted down, catching on the tented fabric of his trousers.

"You fool..." it sounded weak, even to Flynn. "We have to escape."

But I don't want to. He found himself hungry for the orc. Not just for his body, but his smell, his voice. Especially his voice. In an irrational flash, he pictured himself, sitting naked at the orc's feet, handing up a shank of meat (was that a bull's hoof at the end of it?), and listening to the bass rumble as the orc told campfire tales between belches and bites of half-raw food, stories passed down from wild orc father to wild orc son, legends of the past glory of such an awesome race. Then Flynn's eyes fluttered, and he was once more in the oryx goddess's ruined temple, with a sore rump and bare legs.

He spied his pants draped across the rubble a few paces away, and stiffly made his way over to them.

A few hours later, Mazhug waved a stick over the flames. It had been speared through half a dozen of the same little lizards Flynn had seen out in the desert. The flames licking up their tiny bodies changed colors, stained by the mineral bodypaint. "Good slave eat, bad slave eaten," Mazhug explained matter-of-factly, withdrawing the makeshift spit momentarily so he could prod them with a thick finger. He grinned fiercely at the camel when he thrust the stick back into the blaze. "You good meat, better be better slave."

"Aye, sir," was easier for Flynn to say than "master" ever would, and it seemed to please the orc, who turned further around to better tend to the cooking meat. His hand inched back behind him. Earlier he'd felt something pressing against his now-exposed back from the rubble pile he and Deon rested against. Trying not to think about the damp slickness now seeping into his undershorts, he grabbed and slowly withdrew what turned out to be his club. Now that he knew what he was facing, it felt more substantial.

He glanced at the bull. Deon was staring at the fire, one hand still pressing idly against the crotch of his uniform trousers. As though he felt the weight of the camel's gaze upon him, he dropped his hand and looked up. He clearly saw the club and read Flynn's intent: Mazhug's back was turned. "No!" Deon mouthed silently, raising a hand to gesture. Mazhug started to move, his gaze sweeping towards the recumbent bull.

Odard Flynn somehow managed to combine his lunge forward and the swing of his ersatz club, and aim the whole force at the back of the orc's skull. There was the sound as of a fist knocking on an empty pot, and a sudden silence, followed by the soft thud of the thick green body dropping to earth.

"You idiot! What have you done? He'll kill you—maybe both of us!"

Flynn wasn't listening; all he could see was the thick black-red blood that clung to the splintered end of the table leg, the tang of hot wet metal filling his nose and mouth, the taste of unfiltered orc. He couldn't believe what he'd done to his master. Flynn tried to remind himself of what that "master" was, what he wanted to do, but even still, waves of guilt washed over him. The wood dropped from his fingers to clatter on the flagstones. Then he saw that the orc was still breathing. *He will kill us...if he catches us.* He shook himself and snorted, as much to ward off the thoughts of the orc's green eyes and scent as to stir himself into further action. "Come on, we need to leave. We need to leave now."

Throwing one of the bull's arms over his shoulder, he half-dragged the injured flier across the marble floor to the stairs he had descended...*how long had it been? Five hours, six?* It didn't matter. He could still taste the orc, could still smell the scent of the cum and sweat and drool that saturated his body, could feel the fuzzed edges of reality threatening to overpower his momentary strength. They ascended the glittering, tile-littered steps. On the landing, they passed the oryx goddess in all her depicted iterations. "Protect us, whoever you are," Flynn whispered, trying not to think of sex.

He had just pulled Wilmott through the hole in the brick wall at the top of the white-washed staircase when they heard a low moan echoing up behind them. Flynn had not bought them as much time as he had hoped: the orc was quick to come to his senses. That, or his skull was thicker even than the stories would lead one to believe. "Hurry," he prompted needlessly.

They emerged into the still, cold air of a starlit desert. A little fire some yards away was ringed by more of the lizards. *Perhaps they're dancing to send their comrades on to the next life,* the camel thought, picturing the spitted carcasses and trying to keep his stomach from growling. He hadn't eaten since...not since his last waypoint on the flight down from Queenton. And a tail stuffed with orc meat didn't quite count. Still, being out in the open felt better, as though he might leap into the windless air and soar all the way back to the Aerie.

Then he remembered: both jetpacks were down there, back on the floor of the oryx goddess' temple, and a very angry orc was likely closing the distance between them. Flynn looked around, unintentionally jerking the bull who clung to him from side to side as well. *There has to be* something, *anything.*

But there was nothing. Bare rock—black in the starlight—and barren sands. Then Wilmott spoke. "There…was a ravine," he said through pain-gritted teeth. "That way," he gestured in the direction Flynn had been flying; the bull must have flown over it himself before he had crashed.

"You think we can hide there?" He was already heading that way.

"It's worth…a try. Though, I'd give anything for a bed…do you think Mazhug would like that? They have good beds…down south. Hammocks, made of netting. Let the cool air flow…around you. They sleep in the middle of the day too, when it's too hot—"

"Shut it! He'll hear you." As they limped along, Flynn realized that it probably wouldn't matter if the orc could hear them or not. They were leaving a trail as readily as if they had been pouring bright white paint on the dunes. In the sand behind them their tracks stretched out in an irregular ribbon. He couldn't leave Deon to stand on his own while he ran back and tried to obliterate them with hands and feet— what little good it would probably do.

No, all he could do was keep running, and hope that they would come to rocky ground, or maybe a river; something they could use to mask their trail, somewhere they could hide, and rest, and plan. It was with a growing weariness that he glanced back, and saw the hulking form. Its sweaty bald head gleamed in the starlight as it looked around. *At least I can't see his face…at least I can't smell him.*

Making a conscious effort to not think of the orc, Flynn didn't look back any more. He just kept struggling forward, dragging Wilmott at his side.

Dragon Therapy

Whyte Yoté

Calvert lay back against a cushion of moss and let the loose leaves swirl around his chest. Though the ram could not recall how he'd found this serene pool and the waterfall that fed it, he found himself unconcerned by the fact. What he knew—what seemingly mattered more than memory—was that he had peace and quiet and thoughts unfettered by obligation. Perhaps it was the idyllic beauty of the place…perhaps the serene calm shrouding it, and him, from the unforgiving sun and the outside world.

With effort, he opened his heavy-lidded eyes and idly took in the experience of the place. Most certainly fed by mountain snow, the water nonetheless flowed tepidly through his pelt, perhaps warmed by an upstream glade. The woods bore no resemblance to the forest around his father's farm, so that particular worry had no purchase in his thoughts.

Closing his eyes, the ram let his horns grind on the rock and vibrate his head. A cool mist settled over his face, chilling him slightly. Calvert breathed in the humid air, clearing the farm dust from his lungs to make room for the smog of the upcoming city. Somehow he knew he was on his way to the smithy in Teiru, representing his father on business, but he felt neither the pressure of a timetable nor the impetus to find out whether or not they were still on schedule.

So he settled back and let his thoughts wander just as the water wandered away from the pool to the faraway sea.

A light whoosh of air and soft click-clops brought him out of a shallow doze. First he saw that the light had changed to late afternoon bordering on early evening. Shafts of red-orange sun penetrated between the trunks beyond the pool, but for the most part it was becoming oppressively dark.

Calvert looked up to see a little blue hippogriff staring down at him from where he perched on the rocks. "What are you doing here, Azifer? Shouldn't you be with the others?" Never mind that, to the ram's knowledge, the others could be anywhere, or nowhere at all.

Azifer folded his wings and bleated softly. "I decided to come see what you were doing all in private. Nobody needed me." Calvert found that hard to believe; in addition to being a pet of sorts, Azifer was his father's best aerial scout when it came to spotting bandits or planning routes mid-trip. Unless his party were camped nearby…

"I found this pool," Calvert half-lied, "and wanted to relax. You can join me if you want."

Azifer flapped over his head and hovered above, smiling down in that goofy way the ram liked. "That would be nice," said the hippogriff, folding his wings so he dropped right into the water, splashing the parts of Calvert that weren't already wet. Normally Azifer was touchy around water, since he couldn't fly when wet. The ram had been joking, really, but now Azifer had ahold of his knees with his front claws while he treaded as best he could with his rear hooves. "I wanted to spend some private time with you anyway."

Calvert gulped. "Is that so?" The way the creature stared at him with those deep blue eyes above that compact little beak was unsettling. It was almost as if Azifer knew something. It was almost as if he'd found something out.

"I found out." With his smile still in place, the griff kicked and crawled his way up Calvert's legs until he could sit astraddle his thighs, half-floating. With one set of clawed digits he gripped the ram's chest to steady himself, while the other disappeared into the water and between his legs, finding his already-hard length. This should have surprised him, but it felt like he was supposed to be erect, so he let it be.

"How?" The proper reaction should have been to push the little guy away and excoriate him for his lack of propriety and breach of morals. But instead he just asked a stupid question.

"That's no matter." Azifer stroked him gently along the entire shaft, the sensation much softer than he thought scales would be. "What matters is that we're alone." The kiss was not as awkward as Calvert had thought it would be, either; his muzzle and the griff's beak seemed to fit together perfectly. Like they were made for one another. It was too good to be true.

The stream faded into the background of the ram's mind, the water's babbling replaced by his racing pulse in his ears. Azifer's forefeet held his face now, keeping him close and their tongues busy. He became aware of a pressure on his cockhead, a comfortable moist warmth. With eyes closed, he ran his fingers down the griff's soft side to his tail, confirming what he suspected. His other hand ventured under the belly and gripped Azifer's erection, which jutted out stiffly.

"Take me, Calvert. Please, master." Azifer asked no permission, but instead bore down, popping the ram inside so suddenly that he... started licking his face. "Please?"

Calvert woke with such a shock that he almost rolled right over the hippogriff, who skittered out of the way to a corner of the tent just in time. Wide-eyed and out of breath, the ram quickly gathered his senses so as not to appear crazy in front of his pet and confidant. The tent. The bedroll. Azifer not kissing him. Azifer not aroused. Calvert *very* aroused.

"Sorry, sorry," he stumbled, gathering his sheets about his waist. "I hope I didn't disturb you."

"No," giggled the griff. "I've been awake since before sunup. You were making funny noises, though. All moaning and stuff." He didn't seem to notice the musk-filled air one bit, and Azifer wasn't dense by any means. Enchanted, yes, and the size of a feral dog, but not dense. "Baro says you need to get your lazy tail out of bed and go get water, or he's telling your father when we get back home." He smiled as he said it, though.

"Did he, now? Well, you go and tell him I'm on my way, and apologize for my tardiness. Don't tell him I was moaning in my sleep."

"I won't. Yet!" Azifer was through the flaps before the ram could think about swatting him on his horsey rump. He was, however, eternally thankful the griff hadn't thought it prescient to ask questions. Azifer asked a *lot* of questions.

The ram went to fold his sheet, saw the puddle in the middle of it, and just threw the wad into the corner.

***

The Grand Aqueducts flowed out from the center of Teiru to its satellites in the countryside, some of them more than a month's journey away. The water flowed much faster than a man could walk, and the great hills upon which the metropolis sat never ceased to be a plentiful source of rain and snowmelt. With the exception of troublesome terrain, the Grand Roads followed each Grand Aqueduct, the polished and trampled cobbles describing the path of least resistance.

Baro had stopped their little group on the leeward side of a small hill, further protected by a copse of trees, a little ways off the path. Calvert's hooves threatened to sink into the soft earth as he dipped each of two buckets into the cistern and hooked them to his yoke. It wasn't that heavy, really, but he grunted all the same. Somehow the noise made it easier.

He took his time on the way back to the camp to think about his dream. He'd been mortified by it—by the thought of Azifer coming on to him like that—but not without reason.

Gods love him, the ram couldn't deny it. The more he denied it, the more it invaded his life . And now he'd had an infernal nocturnal emission over it, something he'd not done since he'd come of age some seven years ago.

Something had to be done. But nothing could be done without an explanation, and with Calvert's father that meant the truth and nothing but. What would he say? *Father, we need to get rid of Azifer. Why? Because I feel an unnatural lust toward him.* Yes, that would go over well. He couldn't bear false witness against the hippogriff; that would most likely end in the creature's death, and that was unequivocally unacceptable.

One of the buckets shifted and the ram stumbled to keep them level. Why had he decided to leave his wraps back at the tent? Oh, yes, he'd been distracted keeping his dick from the innocent eyes of his pet.

Pet. The word rang hollow nowadays; no one in Calvert's family really saw Azifer as a pet anymore, and the duties he performed went above and beyond any of the draystock on Chaucon Griot's farm. And, unlike the draystock and F'rith, their resident dragoness, Azifer wasn't a slave. Had never been, ever since Chaucon had rescued him from an orc-pillaged town a few years back.

Enchanted with two spells—reduction and speech, both effective but neither much of a curse—Azifer could tell his story but could never utter the name of the warlock who had cast the spells (long before said pillage), lest the man return and silence him forever. It didn't make sense, really, but magic didn't necessarily have to make sense.

As the griff had accustomed himself to life on the farm, he'd taken a liking to Calvert. And the ram, among the rest, had done the same as they discovered Azifer possessed a high level of intelligence. First helping with chores that put his wings to use, then more complicated tasks, he proved his worth time and again, even once warning Chaucon of incoming bandits in the middle of the night. Now, every time a trip was to be made to Teiru, or to any other city, Azifer came along to guide and protect.

But oh, how difficult it had gotten for Calvert lately.

Setting down the yoke, he sat next to it to massage his aching ankles. He might as well be walking on a sandy beach. It was bad enough that he got a perfect view of the griff's anatomy every time he took off, but this dream—this unbidden image—wouldn't leave his head. He'd never seen Azifer fully aroused, but he'd glimpsed that the sheathed flesh was black. He knew neither its length nor its girth, whether it had spikes or a knot, but in the dream it had had both.

Calvert was hard again, uncomfortable in his tight traveling breeches. He squeezed himself and cursed whatever god was responsible for unclean thoughts. It didn't make the squeeze any less pleasurable.

***

Though beaten down by centuries of paws, hooves, and various other appendages, the Grand Road was not kind to carts and coaches with rudimentary axles. F'rith had magic—her purpose as a slave dragon was exactly that—but miracles were not part of her skill set. Nor would Chaucon approve of such shortcuts; he was a man of means and of personal responsibility.

Thus Calvert had to take the long way everywhere, but the ram wasn't soft enough to want to complain about a sore rump from a two-day journey, including a night at the Dragon's Hoard Inn, one of the more luxurious places in Teiru. He, for one, couldn't wait for a nice hot bath, followed by a grooming and powdering, compliments of the house. Not soft, indeed.

Azifer landed atop the carriage with a *click-clop*, out of breath from his latest reconnaissance flight. "The road's clear for at least five miles, Baro."

"Good work, Azifer," the red fox commended. "Help yourself to the icebox if you're hungry."

"No, thanks," replied the griff. "I found a snack along the way. The River Teiru is full of salmon!" Calvert got a whiff of it, not as sickening to him as red meat used to be. Baro looked over at him, grinned a carnivore's grin, and returned his gaze down the path. Azifer crawled down to the seat and squeezed into the middle, pushing both males out of his way. He radiated musk in a way that turned the ram's stomach, among other reactions. "Hey, Calvert!"

"Hey, you." The griff put a forefoot over his shoulder and nuzzled up close, the latest of hundreds of times he'd done the exact same thing over the years. Why was it so different this time? Why did it make him nervous? "See anything worth reporting?"

"Same horizon, same path. No bandits."

"That's good."

"Very good! I can't wait until we get to Teiru. Can you?" The claws flexed on his exposed arm. Black as his beak.

"Nope. Pampering and a good going-over never hurt anyone." The ram dared to put his arm over Azifer's back, running his fingers through the short soft feathers of his side. He was so warm underneath. Azifer started to make a content chirping sound, and he would have continued if F'rith hadn't spoken up.

"Master Calvert," she said. "Beg you for a rest break? I need to fill up and empty out, to put it indelicately." A ripple of tension gripped the ram, like it always did when she spoke. It never failed to remind him of her power, albeit neutered by her enchanted collar. As much as he wanted to keep the innocent-but-not contact, he allowed they all needed water and a good bit of rest from the bumpy road.

"Good idea. Baro, pull off anywhere you see fit, since we have both the aqueduct and the river for our use." A few hundred yards up, the fox told F'rith to pull into a grassy side clearing, and unhitched the dragoness. Azifer flew up to the aqueduct to grab his own drink, and Calvert walked around checking the equipment for wear and damage. If their trailer cart couldn't make it to Teiru unladen, it certainly wouldn't make it back to the farm with a big new iron plow.

Though not unbearably warm, the day was sunny, and all his kneeling and fiddling about put a sheen of sweat on the ram's forehead. Taking a bit of cloth from his pocket, he trotted to the riverbank, where F'rith was just finishing her business behind a thicket of berry brambles. The flora failed to conceal her dark red scales,

"Master Calvert," she acknowledged, sounding unusually patient for a slave of several hundred years.

Calvert bent, soaked the cloth in a clear part of the river, and tied it behind his head and under his horns. "How're you holding up, F'rith? Same as always?" He ran his hand along her side and felt no such thrill as he would have from soft blue feathers.

F'rith settled on the bank, arching her neck out into the river and taking long, massive gulps. Her scales seemed to shimmer in the sun, soaking up the energy she needed to make it to Teiru. As she always had, she took her time in answering, as if the world ran on her schedule. Which, since she was the dray for this trip, it did. "I am fine, young master. It is you about whom I am worried. You reek of anxiety. Would you like to share why?"

"Oh, gods." The dragoness wasn't asking the question because she wanted to know the answer. It was rhetorical with her. She knew, and probably had known for some time. Since the day she'd been captured by Calvert's ancestors, her telepathy had both come in handy and been a bane to the Griot family. Used for both therapy and blackmail, it was a wonder she wasn't yet running the place.

"The gods cannot help you with your problem," said F'rith. "In fact, they might frown upon it." She gasped theatrically. "What would your father think?"

"You can't!" Calvert's desperation surprised even himself. "That's instant exile. Unless I throw myself on his mercy, but even then…I'll never inherit the farm."

"We cannot have you losing the farm, can we?" As lizardlike as she sounded, there was a twinge of care to the words, as if she would actually regret such a thing. But it made a certain kind of sense.

Sitting down, the ram put his head in his hands. Beads of water dripped onto his hooves. "If I lose the farm, you'll lose me. You'll go to the highest bidder."

"I will. So no, Calvert, I will not be talking to Chaucon about this. To tell you the truth, I do not see much problem with it. But I am of a unique mind. I have seen plenty in my life, and many times, tenets are made where they are not necessarily needed."

Calvert looked up. He looked into F'rith's green eyes, and was mesmerized by them like all who did the same. She could read his thoughts, but as far as he knew she couldn't control his mind. "I don't know how it happened."

"What a silly question. Of course you do. It is no different than if you had seen a handsome gentleman in the street and found him attractive. Or gone to a pub and struck up an intimate conversation with another." The dragoness seemed unaffected by the ram's slack jaw.

"I give up. What's the point of keeping it secret?"

"You have good reason." F'rith put a claw to her forehead and tapped. "You are expected to raise a family and bear offspring. Which you will."

Calvert sighed. "Why can't I be myself?"

"You can. Many females will let their husbands do anything they want, as long as they are there for their family. In these times, it is more common than you think."

"Do you feel it when we go to town, or to Teiru?"

A nod. "Everywhere." F'rith brought her tail around to scratch the back of her neck, laying it back down with a *whump*. "But you have a unique problem, I think."

The ram nodded back. It wasn't that he didn't want to talk about it. It wasn't even that he was embarrassed, which he knew he shouldn't be. But after the dream, not much else remained but to face it, and either let it go or engage it. Both scared him near to death.

"I guess it just happened over time," Calvert admitted, diving right in. "When he stopped being just 'the pet' and started being part of the family, it changed."

"But you did not suddenly start staining your sheets dreaming of him," said the dragoness.

"Is nothing sacred?"

"Not to me."

But she was right. He couldn't hide from her; none of them could. A thought struck him.

"Does he feel the same way?"

Smiling an easy, ancient smile, F'rith said evenly: "I cannot tell. That does not mean I do not know."

"You worthless reptile."

"Words about as sharp as your horns." Which Calvert kept dull for safety's sake. "I do not take offense, because I know you mean no harm. Love is difficult."

"You think I love him?"

"You lust for him. Love comes after time. You love him in one way, but not the other. Not yet. But you want to try."

Calvert stood up. He had to do something, so he paced. "I don't know what I want." Except he did. He wanted the dream.

"You want your feelings validated and returned. It is simple. Not so simple to act, though. Unless…" She licked her lips, glancing off into the middle distance. She was playing him, waiting for him to ask how she could help him.

So he did, not liking one bit the need in his voice.

"Regret is sometimes as painful as heartbreak. Some wish for a second chance. Some would give anything for it, you might say. I can give you a second chance, of sorts."

"I can't free you," the ram blurted.

"I know, Calvert. It is not freedom I want anyway. But if I offer you this, you must honor your word to repay me."

"What do you want?"

"Not yet," the dragoness said, shaking her head to re-seat her collar. "What I can do, young master, is change my form to suit your needs. Not forever, but for now."

The ram put the words together in his head, finding it immensely difficult to picture F'rith in Azifer's body. "I didn't know you could shapeshift."

Chuckling, the dragoness replied, "No one asked it of me until now. " It made a certain kind of sense.

"So…you'll change to look like him…and, sort of, *practice* with me?" F'rith nodded. "How far?"

"As far as you want to go," she said sagely. "I know Azifer as well as you, but I also know his mind. I cannot be perfect, but I can try. If you can try."

Calvert could try. He could definitely try. And if he failed, he could ask questions. And maybe, just maybe, he might not sully it up. This new depth to dragon magic both scared and humbled him.

"It will be easiest before we return to your father's farm."

"When will we have time? Azifer's rooming with me tonight."

F'rith appeared to think on this. The ram couldn't tell whether or not she was just acting. "Near bedtime I will ask him to guard the equipment while I speak to you about something. He will not question it. I will transform before coming in, and you will act accordingly.

When we are done, I will return and send him in. Then, you are free to do what you wish. Though I do hope, if it goes well, you will be able to perform a third time."

"Quit grinning like that." Calvert couldn't fathom that he was agreeing to, using his father's slave dragon as a sexual proxy for seducing his own pet. It sounded evil, but it didn't feel that way at all. "Wait…a third time?"

"Which brings me to my fee." Now the ram could feel it, in his brain, down his spine and between his legs. She was doing something to him with her mind, and it felt good.

"I didn't know you could do that."

"No one ever asked." Maybe Calvert should ask her questions more often. "I am sure you are aware of your own needs from time to time. I think it relevant that you are aware of mine as well."

Calvert's vision doubled. He stumbled to one side and caught himself. And caught a whiff of pheromones so strong he felt drunk from them. His cock surged against his will. "How come I've never smelled you before?"

"It would be a distraction," said F'rith. "Do you not agree?" She stood long enough to walk to a nearby tree and lean back against it, wings outspread. Calvert found himself walking over to her, her scent all but visible. He knew he shouldn't be aroused, but it was no longer under his control. "My needs are as strong as yours," she murmured when he reached her tail, gazing at the neat slit between her belly scales. "All I ask is that you give me your pleasure, as Chaucon once did. It has been too long."

Barely registering the words about his father's exploits and lack of potency, the ram placed his hand on the flesh. Spread it open, releasing another cloud of musk. Let it close with an oozing of slick fluid. He wanted to sink his muzzle into it, but knew that wasn't what the dragoness wanted, or needed. His breeches were at his ankles without him remembering he'd untied them.

"They'll come looking for us."

"I have put them to sleep."

"We'll get caught."

F'rith's wings folded and surrounded them in a blood-red cocoon. Aside from a small space near the ground, they were hidden. "We will not."

"Gods help me," Calvert prayed as his legs carried him up onto the thick tail, knelt him between her powerful haunches, and laid him down onto her. She took him in up to the sheath with no resistance.

The rest was a feverish tumult of hormones and heady lust, F'rith driven by need and Calvert driven by F'rith. Several times he came close, and several times she backed off so he wouldn't go over. He barely reached halfway up her belly, but he seemed to be hitting all the right places in the tunnel that was her sex. She would utter directions and he would comply, dimly aware as he went along that she was slowly giving him back his mind.

By the time the ram grabbed handfuls of her scales and slammed himself to climax, he was in full control. And he was liking it.

He liked it so much he napped all the way to Teiru.

***

Calvert was in a pool, but this time he remembered just how he'd gotten there. His day's work was done and now he was relaxing, trying not to be nervous thinking about what the rest of the evening had in store.

Retrieving the new plow from the smithy had been practically boring compared to what was on his mind. After wending their way through Teiru's many alleys, the ram had jawed with Jaun the big bull-terrier blacksmith. They had downed a pint together at the pub next door before the inspection and acceptance of the implement. Coin had changed from hand to paw, F'rith had helped load it onto the cart, and off they'd gone to the Dragon's Hoard Inn.

While the dragoness guarded their equipment and Baro went off to have a pint himself, Calvert and Azifer had retired to the spa section of the inn, where they split off into different areas based on their pelts. Now, the ram soaked in a scented tub of water loaded with minerals to enhance his coat and encourage new growth, while the hippogriff bathed in a different solution, in a separate room, to help keep his feathers clean and aerodynamic.

A diminutive otter entered the space, two towels over one arm. He wore a simple undergarment of servitude and nothing more. "If Sir is ready for the powder?"

"I believe so," Calvert said, putting a bit of Teiruan accent into his speech, feeling richer than he really was because he was traveling on his father's purse. After he dried off the otter tied the other towel around him (the poor guy only came up to his waist) and led him through a doorway into the heavily-scented powder room.

Two dry tubs occupied the central space, coated with years of stray powders. A belt-driven fan spun on the ceiling, operated by another otter in a corner to keep down floating particles. Little drifts had collected in the corners of the room, and everything smelled great, if not generic. Calvert stepped into the near tub and handed his towel to his attendant. As he turned back-to the wall, he saw Azifer being led by his own otter into the next tub.

His hands got halfway to his groin before he stopped himself. What kind of self-respecting male still stooped to such pubescent ridiculousness? Certainly not Calvert.

Azifer seemed not to care about the ram's nudity. Why would one, when one has never worn a scrap of clothing? "I hope you feel as good as I do," he said, sitting on his haunches. A little cloud of powder settled around his rear hooves. "I've never gotten a massage specifically tailored to quadrupeds before. Did you know that's a whole separate level of study?"

"I didn't. That's very curious."

"What scent, sir?" asked his otter, showing the ram a wooden board with a list. The griff's otter did the same, and Calvert marveled (not for the first time) about his pet's ability to read. He actually swooned a little when the little guy spoke.

"Lavender sounds pretty." He looked to the ram for approval, though he didn't need it.

Calvert nodded.

"Cedar for me, thanks."

The powdering had to be a quiet process, unless one wanted a lungful of scent and a night of fitful coughing. Calvert and Azifer stayed relatively still while no fewer than four otters covered them from head to toe in a thin layer of fresh scent, sometimes standing on one another's shoulders to reach the top of the ram's head despite his offer to kneel. The whole time, the griff made his pleased churring noise, sending Calvert's heart aflutter thinking about how he would get things rolling in a few scant minutes with F'rith's version of the griff.

No sooner had the ram tipped the otters (one gold each, they were that good) than Azifer came up to him with a quizzical expression.

"F'rith wants to see me outside before we go to bed. She was talking inside my head. Felt weird."

Stomach roiling, Calvert said, "Go on, then. It must be important. I'll see you in our room soon enough. You remember the number?"

"Twenty-two, second floor," Azifer smiled on his way out, the tight muscles of his rump all but begging.

Ten minutes later, Calvert had finally talked himself out of pacing the length of their room and sat on the bed, the spa towel still around his waist. He checked the clock on the nightstand for the millionth time as its hands slipped past minute eleven, feeling foolish for being so scared of what amounted to a training session.

He still jumped when the doorknob clicked and the hippogriff who wasn't Azifer stepped in, closing the door with a rear hoof. Lavender flowed in with him. F'rith had even replicated the scent of the powder, so exacting was her attention to detail.

"That was odd," the creature muttered. "F'rith just wanted me to fly up to the rooftop to see if there were clouds building in the west. Which there aren't. But she'd never asked me to do it at night before." So, it was a true immersive experience the dragoness offered. Calvert had wanted to at least pose some questions beforehand, but he understood now. This was the best way.

"Odd, but not unreasonable. We don't want rain to rust the plow before it even gets to turn any soil."

Azifer groomed a few errant feathers. "Good idea. I wish I'd thought that far ahead."

"Sometimes you do."

"Yeah?"

The ram nodded, trying not to reveal that his mind was spinning out of control with things to say and ways to steer the conversation. There he was, sitting there with that adorable grin on his beak, waiting for the ram to make the next move. "Nobody's perfect, not even me."

"Now, *that's* the truth." Azifer click-clopped over to the pile of straw the attendants had set out for him before they'd arrived, and was just about to lie down and settle in when he paused. He looked over to Calvert with his down mattress and abundant pillows and blankets. And though his face didn't look it one bit, Calvert knew the body language.

It had been years since they'd cuddled. Not since they were about the same size. Why had they stopped? Calvert couldn't remember. Maybe that would be a good place to start. So he patted the empty space next to him and managed a convincing smile.

The thing that looked like Azifer paused mid-step and tilted his head. "Really?"

"Kind of chilly in here." The words rolled more easily now. "Bed's big enough." Azifer's brightened face was all the ram needed to know he'd done right. He hoped F'rith's approximation of the griff's personality turned out to be accurate.

Azifer hopped up, bringing his cloud of lavender with him. Calvert had to scoot to make room, which afforded him plenty of time to take in the view between the creature's rear legs. He averted his eyes before it got to the leering stage and mercifully, the griff rolled onto his side against Calvert's belly. He only came about two-thirds up to the ram's head, but the combination of feathers and short hair teased Calvert's chest and quickened his breathing. How long had it been since he'd given a petting?

The aquilid neck flexed, bringing deep blue eyes around to stare at him with what was surely feigned interest. But it was convincing. "I remember when we used to do this when you were growing up," he said, and giggled. "I was bigger then."

"Now it's my turn to be the big spoon." As he spoke, he ran his fingers under one wing and through the space between Azifer's foreleg and chest, into the soft undercoat. The curve of his chest fit the blue wings perfectly, even better than all those years ago when their positions had been reversed. But he heard the churring anyway and knew they were both enjoying it.

He still wondered how the real thing would go. He might have to replicate every move, and adjust based on reactions. But at least he would be confident, in that case.

Azifer admitted what they were both thinking after just a few minutes of the ram's idle strokes. "I missed this. And I didn't know how much."

"Me too."

"Why'd you stop?" Suddenly it didn't feel like F'rith anymore. Maybe that was what the dragoness was trying to do, in the end. Take down his guard so he'd act more naturally. If he tried to make up some stupid excuse it would be awkward now, but even more so later. To hell with his father, who had no moral ground after F'rith's admission, and to hell with what was supposed to be moral. He wanted a lover in the griff—had wanted it for a long time—and it was time he came clean.

"Turn around." Azifer started, and the ram helped him the rest of the way over, careful of his wings. Calvert snorted back his runny nose. A soft squawk. "Why are you crying?"

Calvert touched his cheek and felt wetness. "Oh, hell." This was all too real. Maybe too real for him to handle. He considered calling the whole thing off, asking F'rith to turn back (though she'd have to do it outside) and taking care of his feelings with his hand and a furtive eye. Forever.

It would be torture. But if he bared his soul and was rebuffed, at least he'd know. And he could move on, in time.

Azifer still looked concerned. He wasn't stupid, and if F'rith knew that much about him, the griff would be picking up on his emotions and changes in his scent. And yes, his brow furrowed, the sides of his beak turning down slightly. He looked sad, sadder than Calvert felt. The ram couldn't be so bad off with a friend like that. With Azifer there was no context, no second-guessing. The four-legger bested the two-leggers in that category.

"I'm sorry," he said, leaning in to bury his muzzle in the deep feathers of the griff's neck, wetting a few in the process. "I don't mean to upset you. I just care about you an awful lot and don't want that to change."

Talons softly stroked along the ram's back. "Why would that ever change, Callie?"

The use of his lambhood nickname pushed him over. F'rith or not, it meant something. It meant closeness and comfort. It meant innocence and easy happiness. It meant that Azifer remembered, because the dragoness couldn't recall memories that weren't there to recall. So, not thinking about a trial run and not caring whether or not it ended up working out, Calvert did the thing he'd been wanting to do for years and hadn't allowed himself to consider until this moment.

It was awkward, pressing his muzzle against the oddly-rubbery enchanted beak, but once they fit together they stayed. He held Azifer by his neck feathers, his fist bunching them up like a thick collar halfway to his shoulders. At first the griff jerked and squirmed, talons digging into the ram's back but not pushing away.

Calvert just held them together like that, pressed up tight, daring to go no further. One step at a time. Patiently he counted the racing pulse in his ears until the griff fell still, then released. And he opened his eyes.

Azifer wore a mask of stunned silence, infuriatingly unreadable. His beak worked but mostly did nothing, his black tongue twitching for words. Again, Calvert became aware of his misty eyes, but this time he let the tears fall free, their muted plop practically the only sound in the room.

"Please tell me I didn't make a mistake," the ram said thickly. He felt so vulnerable now. He hadn't expected to feel vulnerable.

"I..." He smacked his beak, tasting it. Snorting. "You smell different." Azifer took in a long, slow draught through his nostrils. "Do it again."

"Kiss you?"

"Yeah."

"You liked it?" What he really wanted to say was *You like me?*

"It felt good." Azifer pulled the ram back in and the contact was much better this time. After a few moments Calvert dared to stick his tongue out, and found it received with gusto. His brain shut off, mercifully, and he let himself swim in the emotions. Relief gave way to a delicious naughtiness in which he reveled, not least because no one knew what they were up to, and if they did, he didn't care.

All those conversations he'd had with himself—in case Azifer said this, in case Azifer did that, in case Azifer just left—melted away into a big pot of *None of that matters anymore because he kissed back.* Calvert wondered if this was the first time the griff had actually kissed; gryphons and their ilk usually nuzzled when expressing affection or preparing to mate. No doubt, watching Calvert's parents or just being exposed to greater society would have at least shown him it was a similar thing. But the way Azifer took his tongue and suckled, reciprocating by birdlike mimicry, seemed to indicate he was a fast learner.

Or, F'rith was doing her best to play into the "innocence turned lust" angle. In any case, Calvert couldn't be sure, so he kept it in mind. For now, his towel had become a nuisance, so he whipped it off and threw it to the floor. His cock twitched against Azifer's flank, the short hair lighting up his nerves like wildfire. Emboldened, he scooted closer, lifted the griff's top leg and pressed their groins together.

Azifer squawked into the ram's mouth, clutching painfully with his talons. Calvert engulfed the proffered tongue, thinking that he could suck on that thing all night long. But he felt the griff swelling against him and had other things on his mind.

"I've never smelled you like this before," said Azifer when they parted. "It's making me dizzy. Should we be doing this?"

Of course they shouldn't. Not according to most. "What does it matter?"

"What if your father finds out?"

"He's got enough to worry about." If F'rith acknowledged the comment, she didn't let on. "Azzie…"

The griff giggled, little bits of spittle making him look less feral. "You remembered."

"So did you." Before the griff could speak, he continued. "Azzie, I've wanted to do that for so long. I don't know what's wrong with me, but—"

"What's wrong? I never thought anything was wrong with you," said Azifer. "I like you. And as far as I know, you've always liked me." His logic was disarmingly simple. If only Calvert could think like that. He suddenly realized that he might not be able to explain the depth of his love. He could try, in terms the griff would understand, but…but that might complicate things further.

Smiling, the ram said, "I have. I kind of love you, too. Otherwise I wouldn't be doing this."

"Otherwise you wouldn't be aroused?" Azifer flexed his sheath against Calvert's already-exposed member. Calvert didn't dare look down yet.

"Not exactly. It's complicated."

"No. You just like to make it that way." Now, *that* sounded like F'rith talking, reminding him of his overthinking.

"I love you, Azzie."

Azifer squawk-growled in response, watching with beak ajar as the ram pushed them apart so they could see the other's maleness. Calvert was already fully unsheathed, pressed up against the emerging black length of the griff's cock. To his surprise and utter pleasure, he found out that the dream had also been a premonition. A prominent swelling filled out the blue-haired sheath, while little nubs adorned the tapered head.

Without waiting for approval, Calvert slid down the bed to bury his nose in the musk-filled bits. Azifer growled more deeply, the sound neither aquilid nor equid, not even canid. It was just Azifer. He took hold of the shaft and just pushed his lips down as far as he could go, loving the way the griff's body tightened and hunched, the way his balls drew up into their sac.

"I love love," the griff whispered. His legs splayed apart, rolling him more or less onto his back, spread and on display. With plenty of room to maneuver, Calvert brought the length vertical and skinned back the sheath with his other hand. The thing glistened from his attentions; it smelled of wilderness. He doubted it was the griff's first time (only F'rith knew that yet) but it didn't matter. It was a first, and the ram intended it to be memorable.

He went back down, allowing the girth to spread his jaw wide, keeping his flat teeth away from the flesh like he knew he should. He'd done this a few times before, in secret, and even with one of his father's hands. That wolf, sadly, had moved on to another city.

Nose filled with lavender and musk, Calvert serviced his pet as he thought his pet would like being serviced, his ears canted forward listening for the smallest grunt or hiss to direct him. However, once Azifer grasped his horns with his forefeet and held him down, not much needed to be said besides a throaty, "Oh, oh, oh," from time to time.

Eventually the base swelled so much that he could no longer hilt it, but the shaft was just as tasty. Azifer liked it slow, when the ram would drag his tongue along with his lips, over the slight swelling mid-shaft and up to tease the nubs around the head. Calvert fell into a rhythm, and the rhythm fell into a trance that was mouth-on-cock, cock-in-mouth.

"Has anyone ever done this to you?" he asked, licking teasingly.

"Of course not!" The incredulously shy face was adorable. The ram had made the right decision. "This isn't part of mating."

"For us, it is."

"I like…your version better." Calvert slid the griff's length down his throat and Azifer let out a moan that made the ram's cock twitch. Would he be amenable to intercourse? Would he let himself be entered?

Only one way to find out.

Maintaining a steady pace, the ram used his free hand to clutch the large blue balls, rolling them around, squeezing slightly, tugging on the underside of his sac, which acted like a trigger for a shot of thick presemen almost without fail. Keeping a couple fingers there, he spread his middle finger down and glanced over the flesh of the tailhole, gaining a gasp that was not a rejection. He knew he was venturing into unexplored territory.

"Gods, that's…interesting. Do it more!" Calvert smiled around his mouthful of cock and pressed the blunt tip in a bit, making tiny circles to loosen up the muscle. That farmhand wolf had taught him that trick, and the ram had been a quick study.

With hooves pawing at the air around his head, Calvert kept nursing while working in one knuckle at a time. When he met resistance he took a mouthful of spit and pre and let the mixture drop, working it into the hot flesh. Once the ring gave way, Azifer gasped and let out an almost catlike yowl.

"Did I hurt you?"

"Gods, no! I didn't know that could feel good! I guess, if females can like it…"

Calvert laughed. "It's not quite the same."

"Right. No babies." No fault there.

"Doesn't mean we can't try," Calvert said, tugging behind the griff's knot. The ram's finger slid home and a stream of fluid decorated Azifer's belly, up to the point where his short hair turned to feathers. He looked decidedly undecided, his face contorting every time Calvert made a move. The ram wouldn't force it, not even knowing that it wasn't really Azifer in there. F'rith could make up anything she wanted, but he hoped she empathized enough to stop him if she thought the griff really would stop him.

"Try…yeah…I can try. If you can try." Their eyes met—Calvert made sure of it—and the ram gave a solid nod.

He honestly hadn't thought it would come to this. He'd thought, perhaps foolishly, that they'd end up with the hippogriff fucking his brains out to a deep breeding. Not that it couldn't or wouldn't happen down the line, but he hadn't thought Azifer would let himself be mounted just like that. But now that he was lubed up, flushed and willing…

Calvert went down on him again and gathered another load of slick stuff, applying it to his own member and the rest to the griff's hole, trembling as he went and hoping Azifer couldn't tell how nervous he was. F'rith probably smelled it plenty, but relied on naïveté to guide them next time. Giving the black cock one last lick, he positioned himself with one horse leg on each side, placed himself at the entrance, and pushed.

Watching Azifer's face overshadowed the pleasure of taking the hippogriff's virginity. Calvert had no idea a beak could show so much expression, but it did. He recognized it all from his own experiences, both as top and bottom: the strain, the relief, the dull pain and the satisfaction of being filled. Though not gifted, the ram was sizable, and more than enough for a smaller partner. He looked down in wonder as the flesh spread upon entry and tugged gently as he withdrew.

Azifer drew his forefeet up to his chest, his talons curled up, his head thrashing back and forth. The sensations he must be feeling.

"Are you okay?"

"Uh huh," the griff nodded with a slight grimace. "It takes some getting used to."

"It does. It can be your turn next, if you want. Would you like that?"

"You'd let me?"

"Of course. I wouldn't dream otherwise."

Azifer panted. "You're so good to me, Callie."

"I love being good to you." Calvert pressed in another couple inches. Azifer started drooling onto the sheets.

"Keep being good to me. I like being good. Oh!" The griff's inner wall gave way and the ram shoved home, sheath meeting hole. Suddenly there was a puddle near Azifer's navel.

Calvert lay atop his pet, nuzzling up into the feathers of his chest to feel the runaway heartbeat while he pumped himself through the thick white heat. It clenched, it loosened, it reacted to whatever he did with just the right amount of force. And soon, it was the ram fucking the griff's brains out, no less fun than the opposite he'd expected.

His world contracted into scent and sensation. Beneath the powder he could smell the downy undercoat, the places closer to the griff's skin where F'rith had taken pains to replicate the natural aroma, though Calvert had no clue how that was even possible. Magic didn't have to make sense. Eventually, all he knew was his building climax, their labored breathing, and Azifer's feet holding onto his horns for dear life.

He hardly noticed when the creature went stiff and splattered his chest, the mess soaked up by them both as the ram plowed him into the bedding. He *did* notice the bellowing cry when Azifer's trapped wings tried to unfurl themselves and ultimately failed.

It wasn't Azifer's guttural grunts that finished it for him, though they went a long way toward helping him get to the edge. It was when the griff started babbling, "I love this," that kept his hips thrusting and put thoughts of hurting his pet out of his mind. When they turned to, "I love you," the ram fell right off the edge and into a fit of frenzied bleating as his whole body seemed to divest itself of seed. He lost count of the shots when his hips started shaking and he collapsed.

He couldn't believe there was a dragon somewhere in that little blue-black body.

They would have fallen asleep if not for the griff's need to breathe, so Calvert rolled off, further mussing up the bedclothes. He doubted the otters would mind, as they likely dealt with this on a daily basis.

Calvert did end up dozing off, and when he woke he found Azifer snuggled up close, his head nestled in the crook of the ram's arm. He wondered why F'rith hadn't changed back, and then laughed at himself when he thought of the dragoness trying to fit in the small room. It wouldn't be pretty. So then he wondered if the real Azifer was getting tired, or bored, or suspicious outside the inn. As much as he wanted to lie in the bed and just watch the sleeping form, he knew he should probably make the switch.

Disengaging from the not-griff, the ram pulled on a pair of breeches and left himself shirtless. Worries about Azifer smelling sex in the room would just have to remain worries.

The cool night air ruffled his chest a bit and set his tail atwich. An almost-full moon lit his way in addition to torches set at intervals along the walls and stairwells. At the foot of the stairs he stepped carefully over the cobbles and turned the alleyway corner to find F'rith lying next to the carriage and cart, smiling a dragony smile.

He nearly screamed. He'd had the picture of the little hippogriff, either sitting or hovering, in his head so clearly that seeing F'rith had jarred him nearly out of his skin. Clutching at his chest, he sagged against the nearest wall.

"You almost killed me!" he whispered as loudly as he dared. "Yes, I'm sure no one ever asked about your teleportation powers either, right?"

Little tendrils of smoke drifted like twin ghosts from F'rith's nostrils. "What powers?" she purred. After a full minute of the ram's silence, she continued. "I do not have teleportation powers."

Calvert sagged further down the wall until he was sitting on the stones, his horns drawing shallow furrows on its surface. He didn't care about his horns. He kept wanting F'rith to laugh and say she was lying, it was a joke, couldn't he take a little humor. But she said nothing. She just smiled, and he saw in her eyes there was nothing to say that he didn't already know.

The lavender scent. The raw reactions. And, oh Gods, her collar, the collar that kept her a slave and that no one but her true owner could take off. And Chaucon was far, far away. The Azifer in that room had no collar.

"I would say this is one of the more clever things I have done in my lifetime. Would you not agree?"

"You tricked me."

"Into pleasuring me, or into thinking your pet was me in disguise?"

"Both."

"No," the dragoness rumbled. Her scales shifted, red waves luminescing in the flickering light. "The former, yes. I will admit to that. As for the latter, you could have easily told the difference. If you had wanted to."

Calvert stared down at the street and tried to think up a response. Something accusatory, anything to put blame on F'rith. But then he remembered the sleeping griff up in his bed, the bed stained with two types of cum, and scented with mutual consent. And the more he thought about it, the less righteous his anger became.

"You did it," said the dragoness. "Do you realize it? Perhaps with my help, but not as much as you thought."

"I suppose so."

"You have more strength than that for which you give yourself credit." She was right, of course. In matters such as these, she was always right.

Picking himself up and dusting off his breeches, the ram crossed the space and put his arms around the dragoness, though he couldn't come close to reaching the other side of her neck. "Thank you."

A rumble. "You may thank me by pleasing me again, from time to time. I believe my estrus is upon me."

Calvert didn't mind, actually. It had been fun, in a mind-control sort of way. "Can you give me some time? We're both awfully tired."

"Oh, not tonight. I understand. But soon. You have a very satisfactory technique. Better than your father." Was the ram blushing? Maybe a little.

Halfway to the stairwell, Calvert paused and turned. "Did you ever find out if we have clouds coming in from the west?"

"Clear skies as far as the hippogriff could see," F'rith said. "We shall have blue skies until we reach the farm." They shared a wry smile.

"Good," he said, and mounted the stairs. It was a two-day journey back home. One long night without fear of being caught. Baro wasn't immune to dragon magic, either.

Calvert went up to bed, now unconcerned about keeping warm.

ABOUT THE
AUTHORS

Tarl "Voice" Hoch is primarily a horror and erotica writer based out of Alberta, Canada. When not trying to horrify or titillate his readers, he can be found trying his pen at other genres such as steampunk, fantasy and science fiction. When not writing, Tarl is one of the four hosts of the writing podcast *Fangs And Fonts*, as well as a servant to his feline overlords. His work has been published in *Trick or Treat 1 & 2* by Rabbit Valley, *Taboo* and *Will of the Alpha* by FurPlanet, and he was also the head editor of FurPlanet's horror anthology, *Abandoned Places*.
https://www.goodreads.com/author/show/5759304.Tarl_Voice_Hoch

Sarina Dorie is the author of award-winning, YA paranormal romance novel, *Silent Moon*. Her Puritan and alien love story, *Dawn of the Morning Star*, is due to come this year with Wolfsinger Publications. She has sold over 80 short stories to markets like *Daily Science Fiction*, *Magazine of Fantasy and Science Fiction*, *Orson Scott Card's IGMS*, *Cosmos*, and *Sword and Laser*. By day, Sarina is a public school art teacher, artist, belly dance performer and instructor, copy editor, fashion designer, event organizer and probably a few other things. By night, she writes. As you might imagine, this leaves little time for sleep.
http://www.sarinadorie.com/

Marderschaden is a terribly British tree weasel living in the south of England. He thinks he reads too much, and writes too little, and would like to address that imbalance. He's also very, very fond of weasels, because they're so cute and adorable and have so many of those pointy teeth things, and eldritch horrors from between the stars, though they can only claim the teeth as a common factor.
http://www.furaffinity.net/user/marderschaden/

Kandrel is a little fox with big dreams. Monsters march across his mind—dragons and kobolds and gnolls in a row. He decided that his only chance to get those beasts out of his head was to force his favorite friends to write about them and splash it all over the pages here in *Dungeon Grind*! The fox is also rather simple, and prefers to publish in works that can be expressed in a single syllable. You can find the majority of his work in *Heat*, *FANG*, *ROAR*, and even in his first book, *Pile*.
http://kandrel.sofurry.com/

The mad scientist known as **Rechan** has been hard at work, helping mix the right bit of editing alchemy to make *Dungeon Grind* pop. He awaits with claws steepled to hear the results unleashing this book's sexy monsters into your hands. You can find other wicked creations he has unveiled in *Will of the Alpha*, *Taboo* and *Heat*.
http://furaffinity.net/user/rechan

Slip Wolf has sought fortune far from his home shores for more than three harvests, crying Nike to the *ROAR* VI and *FANG* VI gods in FurPlanet's acropolis, burning offerings in the temples of Sofawolf's *Heat* XI and XII, and battling terror and seduction in the distant lands of Rabbit Valley's *Trick or Treat II: Historical Halloween* (the further lands give their monsters peculiar names, don't they).
http://www.furaffinity.net/user/slip-wolf/

George Squares is an author who writes for both adult and general audiences. He is interested in the implicit questions stories can ask, and how endemic features contribute to the personalities of lives and locations. His favorite genres are historical fiction, science fiction and mythpunk. He has experience in studio art, storyboarding and digital design and has a bachelors of science degree in biology. He currently lives in Charlottesville, Virginia in the United States with his husband.
https://georgesquares.wordpress.com/

Ross Whitlock has been writing fantasy, science fiction, and anthropomorphic fiction for many years. *Peryton Mod* is his first story to be accepted for publication, and he hopes to continue the trend. He lives in Colorado.
https://www.furaffinity.net/user/hengeworlds

Tym Greene is a writer and artist, particularly of anthro things, and aspires to work in concept art. In the meantime he fulfills his world-building desires with fiction. Apart from a few entry-level college courses, he's mostly self-taught with regard to writing, and has to thank the pantheon of authors (both classic and otherwise), his editors, and his boyfriend for helping him to be the writer he is today.
http://www.furaffinity.net/user/tym/

Whyte Yoté has been writing erotic furry fiction since 1995 when he was probably too young to be doing so, and he has been seriously pursuing his craft since 2000. He claims works published in multiple volumes of *FANG*, *ROAR* and *Heat* magazine, as well as the anthologies *X*, *The Fortune Teller's Poem*, *Holidays*, *Will of the Alpha 1 & 2*, *Taboo*, *Plowed* and *Trick or Treat 1 & 2*. When he's not writing, he... wait, never mind. He juggles personal work with publication submissions as well as paid commissions. He lives with his forever boyfriend Tym in Sacramento, California.
http://www.furaffinity.net/user/whyteyote/